Phoenicia Rogerson is altogether mortal with a rather less chequered past than Hercules. After a decade of not being able to find his complete story on bookshelves, she decided to pull her socks up and write it herself. She's had two short stories published in the UCL Publisher's Prize. She lives and works in London. *Herc* is her first novel.

H
E
R
C

PHOENICIA ROGERSON

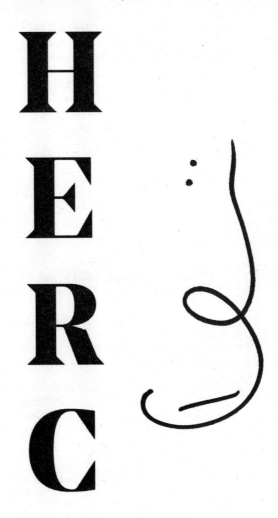

ONE PLACE. MANY STORIES

HQ
An imprint of HarperCollins*Publishers* Ltd
1 London Bridge Street
London SE1 9GF

www.harpercollins.co.uk

HarperCollins*Publishers*
Macken House, 39/40 Mayor Street Upper,
Dublin 1, D01 C9W8, Ireland

This edition 2023

1

First published in Great Britain by
HQ, an imprint of HarperCollins*Publishers* Ltd 2023

Hardback: 9780008589820
Trade paperback: 9780008589837
Special Edition: 9780008658977

MIX
Paper | Supporting
responsible forestry
FSC
www.fsc.org
FSC™ C007454

This book is produced from independently certified FSC™ paper to ensure responsible forest management.

For more information visit: www.harpercollins.co.uk/green

This book is set in Caslon by Type-it AS, Norway

Printed and Bound in the UK using 100% Renewable Electricity at CPI Group (UK) Ltd, Croydon, CR0 4YY

For Hope

Amphitryon I

We wanted a girl. Alcmene, my wife, and I were born of heroes, which sounds dramatic but mostly meant we had a family history of fire, glory, and dying young. So it came up one night, our legs tangled around each other. *I'd like a girl, for our first,* whispered, like it was something to be ashamed of. But being born of heroes means nothing runs smooth and we had twin boys.

The conception took place over three nights, and one.

Alcmene was an incredible woman. Smarter than I am, by half. She could hold a thousand thoughts in her head at once and always know exactly which one she needed. She was beautiful too. She stood tall and straight, with muscles in her arms and with eyes that took in everything around her, and she loved me. I defy any man not to find that beautiful.

Maybe, then, it shouldn't have come as a surprise when she attracted the attention of a god – Zeus, the king himself – but it did, because when he appeared to her, he was wearing my face.

There was a prophecy. It said a descendant of Zeus born

around a certain time would rule all those around him. I don't know why this particular prophecy was so important to Zeus – his progeny tended to grow up to be kings anyway – but it's best not to question the gods. He decided this son should have a particularly impressive bloodline, so he turned to my wife, born of heroes.

I'm older than I was. I've had time to come to terms with it. I've tried very hard not to be angry with her. I know, logically, there's nothing to be done when the king of the gods appears looking like your husband, but I have to wonder. Did he have my mannerisms too? My thoughts and my words and my movements?

The night Zeus appeared to my wife – did he knock on our door? – the world went dark.

I was away, trying to mint myself as a military leader before our family grew. I wanted to be a father to be proud of.

Three days, it stayed dark. What should have been the first morning, we brushed it off. We laughed that Apollo, who drives the sun, was being lazy, distracted by some nymph, maybe. By afternoon we'd stopped laughing – something about the utter blackness choked it off – and quietly speculated that this was the end for man. We supposed the Titans had risen from their prison in Tartarus and deposed their children, the gods, dragged them someplace even darker than the world we inhabited.

By what should have been the evening, I was riding home. Screw war. Screw honour. If this was the end, I wanted to spend it with my wife. By the end of the ride, my steed, a warhorse from as long and splendid a lineage as my own, was fit for nothing but pasture, but it didn't matter. As our house crept into sight, so did the sun, rising behind it. I didn't stop to speak to Alcmene, save fervent whispers of relief, as I scooped her up and carried her to bed.

Even in that state, I noticed the smell. The sheets were well worn, if we're being polite. I thought nothing of it; my wife was probably lonely while I was at war. I told myself she didn't want to wash my smell from the pillows in case it was the last she ever saw of me, but it wasn't. I came home.

We enjoyed each other's bodies and, for all the fear that preceded it, it was the last time my life was truly simple. When she woke, Alcmene stretched. I've always loved the way she stretches, her arms reaching behind her as though she'll be able to catch the world within them, but this time she winced.

'Not that I didn't have fun,' she said. 'But that last round may have been one too many for me.' She grinned. A woman may have said she was glowing. My soldiers would have offered a coarser adjective.

'What last round?' I mumbled sleepily, enjoying the feeling of my own bed as much as I was the woman beside me. It was good to be home.

'The last one,' she said slowly, like I was some kind of idiot. I often am when I'm half asleep. Less often when I'm fully awake, but it happens.

'There was only one.'

'If that's your definition of one round then I'm worried for my back, dear. Just because it was one night—'

'It was morning,' I said, frowning now.

'Yes, the *last round* was in the morning. The rest of it was—' She trailed off, the shape of a *no* forming on our lips as we realised we'd been opposite punchlines in a terrible joke. 'We should go to the priest.'

'Let's,' I said, wrapping an arm around her shoulder so she'd know, for all my shortness of words, I was with her.

The priest confirmed everything I've just told you, though by the end of it he couldn't look Alcmene in the eye. Rather uptight creature, that priest. He added something, too, much scarier than any army or monster I've ever faced – *twins*. One for each father, he said. At least one is yours, he meant, which was wrong. They were both mine.

Well, they were both Alcmene's and I was also there. The point is, I never thought of Iph as more mine than his brother. I worked hard not to.

The pregnancy felt unusually fast and unusually hard, but maybe that's the fear speaking. Alcmene's aunts certainly thought so, laughing it off as the paranoia of any new parent, but I couldn't shake the feeling that something was off.

'I like Alcaeus. Alcaeus and Iphicles,' my wife said when we talked about their names. 'What do you think?' Personally I thought Alcmene, Amphitryon, Alcaeus, and Iphicles sounded like we were singling Iph out from the start, but they were *inside* her. She could have wanted to call them both Zeus and I'd agree.

'Sounds wonderful, dear.'

'It would be nice if they shared a room, I think. They should be friends, as well as brothers.'

'Sounds wonderful, dear.'

And on and on it went, Alcmene trying to choose which way to go, as if we'd get a say.

The birth was another horrible three-day saga. After months spent praying to, and blessing, and offering dedications to the goddess of childbirth, she took the day off. No matter how hard Alcmene breathed and pushed and cursed, nothing happened. Not until the middle of the night ticked by and Artemis moved her moon beyond our seeing; then it all happened at once.

I'm told that was because of the prophecy too, that Hera didn't want Zeus' preferred offspring to rule, so she delayed his birth until after my brother's son, Eurystheus, was born. That stung. It wasn't the child's fault, but one day he would rule the city that was meant to be mine – it would have been mine, bar an accident in my adolescence. But I couldn't complain about that. My wife had been in labour for *three days*.

Our eldest was born, the son of Zeus himself. He was big, for a baby, but that was good. It meant he was healthy. As did the bellow he immediately emitted, scaring off every bird for miles. We handed him to his mother. She must have been shattered, the gods know I was shattered, but the smile on her face when she took him was breathtaking, like everything was suddenly right in this world.

After that, I almost missed Iph being born. He was smaller, but still healthy, still crying with a fine set of lungs. We – and by that I mean she – had done it. We were parents, juggling the boys to and fro as we tried to get them cleaned up.

Alcmene insisted on putting them to bed.

'The first time at least.' She smiled.

'Sounds wonderful, dear.'

Only it wasn't. No sooner had we sunk to sleep – honestly more of a plummet – than we were woken by a bloodcurdling cry.

'Iphicles,' Alcmene whispered. A laxer parent, I couldn't tell the difference between the cries of our newborns. 'There's trouble.'

'Babies cry, love. We shouldn't pander to them,' I mumbled, but she'd already left.

She was right, of course. Our eldest son had disappeared.

'Where's he gone?' she said, almost too fast for me to follow. 'How can he – the servants? No. Hera?'

Hera was, for lack of a better word, our eldest's stepmother. She's Zeus' wife, and the goddess of marriage – a combination that must have been equal parts infuriating and embarrassing given Zeus' general inability to remain faithful to her. She was never a huge fan of his illegitimate offspring, but I couldn't imagine she'd stoop to killing an infant.

'He probably just rolled out. We'll find him,' I tried to reassure her, but I was panicking too, and the panic made me stupid. We woke the servants and got to searching. We checked every inch of our home and grounds, but nothing showed, not until morning came. We were half mad by then, jumping at every little noise. It's a wonder my heart didn't stop altogether when we heard one of the maids scream.

'Ma'am?' She sounded afraid as she approached Alcmene. My heart plummeted in my chest. No no no no no. 'I got him. He's okay.'

He was more than okay. He was beaming where he lay, two feet deep in a muddy hole that fit his shape as if it'd been dug around him.

The story they tell is that one of the gods stole him from his crib, then gave him to Hera to nurse. If she had, it would've granted him more strength, something he really didn't need. As it was, she realised who he was – salt rubbed into the still-open wound of Zeus' infidelity – and flung him back to earth, the milk from her breast spreading across the sky, staining it with stars.

Stories. New stars were always appearing, marking the death or birth of someone or other. It would be vain to claim so many for my son.

Whatever the reason, we got him cleaned up and back to bed, none the worse for his little adventure. If anything his face said: *please, Dad, can I go again?*

The next night I put them to bed, just in case. We were woken by a scream, again. Iphicles, again. We went running, again, but they were both fine. Iph was crying, our eldest gurgling happily.

We looked more closely. Our eldest held the mashed remains of a snake in either hand, curled possessively towards his chest. Alcmene scooped him up.

'Shh, Mummy's here, you're going to be safe. We've got you.'

I felt only seconds away from being called over to tell our newborn that yes, I was here too, and he was safe. I moved over to Iphicles instead. He was still screaming. I held him so he'd know he wasn't alone. I didn't promise him anything.

We called the priest, the same one as before, who seemed particularly grumpy to be making early morning house calls but there you go. He ummed and ahhed while he avoided touching the snake-mash that seemed to be getting everywhere.

'Maybe it was a coincidence?'

'No,' Alcmene said, her tone implying the priest possessed some mental deficiency. 'I don't think an incredibly rare venomous snake *coincidentally* slithered into my newborn's fists.'

I thought it was a bluff, about the snake being venomous, but she shook her head when I asked.

'I asked an expert. With the pregnancy, it seemed prudent.'

Over the years I'd find hundreds of things my wife had learned because *it seemed prudent*. Emergency medical care. The smell and colour of any easily available poisons, and many of the more difficult ones too. How to pacify wild animals, and wilder men. She kept knives in her sandals, and I found them hidden on high shelves more than once.

'That's two in two nights,' I said quietly to the priest. 'What do we do?'

'Appease whoever's trying to kill him,' he said flippantly, before realising who he was talking to and flinching. 'I am sorry, my lord. It's early – I forget myself.'

'Don't be,' Alcmene said. 'You're right.'

How does one appease a goddess? We couldn't make offerings that would have any meaning to her – what does a mortal, even a general, have that a god wants?

'She wants our son,' Alcmene said finally.

'You don't mean—' I was horrified.

'No. No, gods, no. We name him after her, so she can claim a share in his glory too. It might help.'

So we didn't call our son Alcaeus. We named him after a woman who'd already tried to kill him. Twice. We called him Heracles – the glory of Hera.

She stopped *directly* trying to kill him after that.

We put the boys to sleep in different rooms. We had to. Iph's first word was *snake*.

That was the first word from either of them. Anything physical, Herc got: he could roll over and then walk and run before his brother – but words and numbers were Iph's domain. They spent their childhood tying each other up in knots in the different contests they'd invented, weighted so they'd win.

The depth of Herc's strength became obvious when he was five, and he started breaking more than just the gifts his father's wife sent us. (Alcmene and I joked about opening a menagerie with them. The strangest was the swarms of cicadas that descended upon the house. We spent years debating how exactly Hera planned on killing him with *cicadas*. Still, Herc scared them off with one of the bellows that characterised his childhood. Even into his teens, a stubbed toe could scare off every herbivore within the city walls.)

It started with his toys. Sturdier than average already, grips were bent, twisted and crushed. Then chairs, until we swallowed the expense of replacing all our furniture with solid marble. Uncomfortable, yes, but safer.

He tripped, one day – his feet grew out faster than the rest of him, so he went through randomly clumsy phases – and put out a hand to steady himself. He left a dent in the wall, a perfect handprint. The boys thought it was funny, would measure themselves against it as they grew. *Look how big I'm getting, look!*

We tried our best to let them be kids, to let them *stay* kids when the world was pushing them to grow up too fast. We even consulted with seers, the best we could find, like knowing the future would give us some power to avoid it. It didn't work. They all promised the same things, and all of them were true.

Herc's going to be a hero. He's going to kill monsters. His life is going to hurt.

Iphicles I

He's my twin – my slightly older twin, if you want to get technical about it, which he did. I've never known life without him, so I can't tell you how he's different from other brothers, but I can tell you how he's different from *me*.

He looks shorter, for one, though our mother insists we're the same height. It's his shoulders – they're so broad they dwarf the rest of him, especially when we were teenagers. He kept his hair shorter than I did, called it a nuisance, and he hated water, pouting every time Mum made him take a bath. He pouted like no one else.

He wasn't smart, really, no matter what Mum insisted. He had no time for words, deriding oration and metaphor as *confusing bullshit*.

Language and rhetoric were my best subjects, in retaliation. It's not that I loved them, especially not to begin with – who doesn't look at the declensions and wonder why anyone would possibly *care* – but I liked to win nearly as much as Herc did and I could beat him every time. I found a talent, or made one, and that was that. We got separate tutors, since he was so much better at the fighting and I at the words.

Our parents had some famous teacher come look at him. They kept emphasising that, hoping Herc would suddenly become passionate about his lessons, Mum telling us about the kings and heroes he'd guided, forgetting that absolutely the coolest thing about Chiron was he was half *horse*. But it didn't really matter because he came for the day and told Mum he didn't want to teach Herc because he wasn't focused on the right things, and Chiron didn't want the weight of teaching him the wrong things on his conscience. Mum took great offence to that and we weren't really allowed to talk about him after.

Herc was kind of upset about it, after all the amazing stories. He worried he couldn't be a hero if Chiron didn't teach him. So I whispered in his ear.

'He's an idiot.'

'How can you tell?'

'He's got shit on his shoes.' There was a trail of grubby hoof-prints leading out of the house. It was probably dirt, not shit, but that wasn't the point.

He laughed and agreed he didn't want to learn from Old Shit Hooves anyway. Only I wasn't very good at whispering – I was ten – and our parents heard. Dad nodded approvingly but Mum pursed her lips and threatened to box my ears because being a hero is all well and good but we were too young for such language.

Herc's lessons were mostly in sharp objects and hitting things, until we turned eleven and, for complicated reasons, he knocked half a forest down with a flying sheep. After that, Mum and Dad decided he needed to learn to be *delicate* and *gentle* and whatnot and he should learn some music.

Three broken harps later, his music teacher stormed out, insisting my brother's fingers never touch an instrument again.

'Do you think he has shit on his feet as well?' I mused, this time out of Mum's earshot. I'd been learning too.

'Maybe that's why he kept clenching: 'fraid it would come out.' Herc grinned. The teacher's shoulders had been so tense they almost rose past his ears. But my parents paid well, so he was happy to keep teaching me. I kept a close eye on him, waiting for the day I could gleefully report to my brother that he did, in fact, have shit on his shoes.

Mum asked around for a sturdier musician for Herc, and thus came Linus. Lovely alliterative Linus who played the lyre and liked, presumably, lions, litotes, and lightning.

He was a fiddly kind of man, always tapping or readjusting something. He was skinny too, and out of proportion. His whole body was stacked heavier on the left, making you squint when you looked at him.

'Too much of the lyre,' Mum told me when I asked why, a phase of mine that lasted many years and was as formidable as it was annoying. 'You see the same on swordsmen. That's why you two have to learn a bit of everything, keep you balanced.'

'I've never seen someone lopsided from talking too much,' I said hopefully.

'You still have to go to wrestling.'

'But Mu-um,' I started.

'Iphicles.'

'Fine.'

I liked Linus. He wasn't my tutor so it didn't really matter, but he had a famous brother too – Orpheus something? – so he went out of his way to be kind to me. Herc though: from the moment Linus passed him his lyre without fear, my brother loved him. Linus knew what he could do, of course. Mum led with it when she offered him the job, in the spirit of fairness. (She's a big believer in the *spirit* of fairness.) But he handed it over anyway, and Herc looked back at him, shy, or as close an approximation of it as he had.

'Haven't you heard what I do to nice things?' Like I said, an approximation of shy. It came out more like a threat. Adolescent boys aren't so great at the wide-eyed and innocent thing.

'Tell me,' Linus said, pretending Mum hadn't sat him down and explained exactly what my brother did to nice things.

'I break them.' We'd just started puberty, and it wasn't treating my brother well. His voice cracked unattractively mid-sentence. I, of course, was perfect.

'What do you think you'd break, on the lyre?'

'The strings?'

'So what?' Linus smiled.

'What do you mean? Then the strings will be broken and I'll have ruined your instrument like I ruin everything and—' I'd have laughed at that, if he didn't sound so upset. Plus it'd get me caught eavesdropping.

'Calm down,' Linus said gently. 'Strings break all the time. Two did last week. I'll teach you to replace them when they do.'

It was the first time anyone told him he could fix things too.

'The neck?' he tried, again.

'It's not so easy, but it can be mended.'

'I don't understand. Wouldn't you be mad?'

'Music doesn't belong in a museum. It's meant to be shared and played and carried between people. That means sometimes instruments get broken. It's okay.'

21

I don't claim to understand my brother, so I don't know why that conversation meant as much to him as it did. I thought it sounded flowery, lame.

Linus started Herc off on the double flute. It looked less fragile than the golden curve of the lyre. They practised breathing exercises, to coax the notes out.

'They can be nervous, like animals, but if you're gentle they'll come out and say hello.' It was a nice story, and a good one for his other students, probably, but saying *hello* to the fluffy woodland creatures was never my brother's style.

'Like this?' Herc asked, blowing. It was not the sound of small woodland creatures. It was the sound of a stampede, or Dad snoring.

'Not quite,' Linus said. 'Imagine gently releasing a thread, or the breeze that cools you in a swordfight.' Herc fought with such intensity that nothing short of a hurricane would cool him.

'I get it,' Herc exclaimed.

He did not get it. His next blow was, if anything, harder. It failed to elicit any sound from the double flute, save splintering as it split into thousands of pieces.

'Oops?' Hercules offered, still holding a shard of flute optimistically. Linus handed him the lyre unflinchingly. 'Really?'

'Really.' Linus swallowed. 'It may suit you better, and it's easier to demonstrate fingering than breath patterns.' It says a great deal about the respect Herc had for him that he didn't laugh at the word *fingering*.

Linus demonstrated until his fingers were blue. He ran his hands along Herc's arms so he could feel the pressure. He had my brother do the same, and Linus came back with purple fingerprints enrobing his wrists.

The first time Herc ran his fingers over the lyre, not aiming for any particular note, just to recognise their touch, he snapped every string on it. He looked like he was going to cry.

'It's okay,' Linus exclaimed. 'Remember what I told you? Strings we can replace. Strings are fine.'

'They are?'

'They are.'

They spent the rest of the lesson working on finger exercises, normally for children to strengthen their hands, not to weaken them. Linus found bird's eggs and told him to practise rolling them between his fingers without smashing them.

Brother would never tell Linus this, but he went through twenty-nine in the week between their lessons. The house smelled of egg for months.

Their next session, Linus brought not only spare strings, but a spare lyre too. He held Herc's hand in his and together they got notes out of the instrument. They weren't good notes, and they certainly didn't belong together, but they were, technically, *music*.

A few months later, Linus' cousin got married and he took us to the wedding. There were beautiful songs performed by Linus' other students as well as the man himself. I even sang a tune, though Herc didn't. Outside of that, we tried not to get too bored when the bride and groom were doing their offerings to the gods because it would be disrespectful. But it took *forever*. Herc grinned and stood a bit straighter when they said Hera's name and Linus' eyebrow went all the way up.

'He's proud because it's his name too,' I whispered. I was getting better at that.

'Doesn't she—' Linus trailed off.

'Try to kill him? Yeah, all the time. But he always beats whatever she sends so it's all right.' Linus looked unconvinced, but we couldn't get into it any further before he had to go and be helpful, so me and Herc were left to our own devices.

We snuck a few drinks and we bickered. Nothing new, we're twins.

I can't remember which of us made it a fight, who threw the first actually harsh words. Probably me. Brother never worked out the art of a good insult.

I called him stupid. He called me weak and pushed me into a ditch for good measure. It was a gentle shove, from him. I was used to them – it made me a great sailor when I was older – but I was drunk, so I fell awkwardly. When I stood back up, I was covered in dust, which meant a bath and a lecture from Mum. Worse, I looked like a fool in front of the girls.

(We didn't have a chance with the girls, we were twelve – nearly thirteen! – but it stung.)

'So how come Linus didn't ask *you* to play?' I called after him gently. Condescendingly. It was cruel. I knew exactly why. His songs were a discordant mess and he broke a string roughly once every two minutes.

When he was older, there'd be people begging to write his songs for him, but there weren't yet. He hadn't *done* anything. So he pushed me back into the ditch. I pulled him down with me, and by the time we were home we were laughing, brothers again, united against the horrors of baths.

He might have forgiven me easily, but my brother can hold a grudge for decades, and I wasn't the one who'd truly snubbed him.

I can't remember why I was eavesdropping, the day it happened. I was probably bored. I miss that.

Linus was grumpy when they got to their lesson. Maybe his family had been harping on – literally, I imagine, with harps – about finding someone to settle down with. Or maybe the wedding reminded him what music should sound like, out of the hands of an exceptionally untalented child. Maybe he was just a good teacher and he knew eventually he'd have to coax Herc into playing something approaching a song.

Herc was used to Linus lauding him for just picking up an instrument without immediately breaking it. Shocking, then, when Linus held up his hand in the middle of the lyre's torture and said *no*.

'You need to move your fingers a little, so they lie flatter,' he said gently.

'Like this?' Herc asked. He didn't wait for an answer, returning to his strumming before his tutor stopped him again.

'No, you're not trying to kill it. Cradle it. Feel the music in your soul.'

The only change, as far as I could tell, was that Herc strummed louder. A string snapped, and then Linus did.

'It's *music*,' he shouted. 'It shouldn't be this hard. Do you not *have* a soul, Heracles?'

I imagine both of them felt a lot of things in that moment. I imagine it was a blur when my brother lifted that lyre above his head.

And I imagine it was an all-too-sickening return to reality when it landed and he didn't know if the crack came from the lyre or from Linus.

(It was both.)

Herc collapsed on the floor nearly as fast as Linus did. He sat there a moment, cradling a head that didn't look so very much like a head anymore. I didn't move an inch.

When Mum came running in – she knew not to trust crashing noises in her house – she found him like that, tears running down his face.

'I'm so sorry. I'm so so sorry! I didn't mean to.'

The Linus Letters

Dear Linus,

How is your new charge treating you? Is his temperament as you feared, or have you been granted some small reprieve in that matter?

It's selfish, but I must say I'm glad you've kept Father's lyre from him. I've been working on my latest piece, and I can scarce imagine it played on anything else. It will be good enough to raise the dead, when it's ready.

I had been hoping this new job would distract Mother from her nagging, but it seems not. I'm blessed by Apollo himself – so they claim; personally I think I would've noticed such a thing – but there's no honour to that, she says. Not unless I do it bearing a sword. Alas. Why did she invest so much in music lessons if she wanted soldiers?

But she had been distracted at least, for I have met a woman! She's as beautiful as if Aphrodite painted her, and she sings sweeter than any bird I've ever heard. Sweeter than me, even.

Your ever-loving brother,
Orpheus

Dear Orpheus,
Like so many young men, his temperament changes by the minute. He's funny, when he breaks out of his adolescent blasts of temper. He tells a wonderful joke about a fisherman and— Well, it doesn't work on paper. Remind me when next I see you.

But at other times, his soul is sluggish, and his fingers refuse to channel the music. We may move on to singing instead, though the breaking of his voice and a lack of natural rhythm make him sound altogether Stymphalian. Maybe appropriately, given his parentage, he doesn't truly sing, he thunders. It is probably for the good that he is reminded he's not the best at everything. His father has started entering him in local contests of wrestling and the like; some days I can scant see his head below the laurels.

The other son seems a nice boy. He and his tutor carry easy tunes together while we labour repairing the strings. For our sins!

Of course you've met a woman. You've always met a woman, all of them too lovely even for your music – and I must say, you may have become even vainer, which I didn't think you could manage. What does she think of you, layabout? Loveliness is well and good, but

28

just lovely has not so entranced you before. And your masterpiece, does it raise the dead yet?

All my love,
Linus

PS: Yes. Mother is very proud of me. She says if neither of us can join the army at least I work in the service of a war hero. I'm not convinced this is an improvement.

My dear, sceptical brother,
No luck on raising the dead yet, but I did make a young lady faint in pure paroxysms of delight, so I move closer.

The woman – Eurydice is her name. Beautiful, no? – is no average girl, no passing fling or whimsy. I'm hurt to hear you accuse me of such rakishness! As if I would ever carry on with a woman just because I found her beautiful.

(Even if I had, I trust your employment isn't so lucrative you could afford enough ink to detail all such indiscretions, nor your heart so cruel as to do so.)

She's the first woman I've met who doesn't love me only for my music. She hadn't heard it when we first met, if you can believe. Both of us were taking a walk in the local gardens, her chaperoned and singing lightly to herself. When her brother asked what she thought of me, she said I make her laugh. A fine reason to love a woman, is it not?

I do love her, and that's the truth. I can only hope she feels the same for me, for I believe I should like to marry her. I haven't asked her yet.

Should she take me, I'd be most honoured if you could play at our wedding.

Your delighted brother,
Orpheus

Brother!
That's wonderful, Orpheus, good luck. No, the best of luck. All the luck!

I'd be thrilled to play, of course. Anything I can do to help, I'm there. Does this mean you'll be providing me with my obscenely talented nieces and nephews?

I jest, of course. I assume you have enough of it from Mother.

With greatest congratulations,
Linus

Brother,
The wedding is in six weeks. Come home and join the celebrations! It's a perfect excuse to leave your petulant charge. Besides, we miss you.

Love,
Orpheus

Dearest brother,
I received the news only moments ago, and I'm devastated. I cannot say I understand how this fate could have befallen you, or why I'm writing to you at all. From

what the messenger said, you'll not be reading any more letters, but you're my brother. I need to talk to you about this.

I'll be making my way to you imminently.

Forever your brother,
Orpheus

Dearest Linus,
Eight months now, it's been since you passed. Every day, I miss you. Every letter I receive, I hope to find some lost missive penned in your hand.

I recovered Father's lyre from your things – I do hope that's okay. Eurydice and I use it to play lullabies to our son.

That's right, we have a son. We call him Musaeus. Not after you – you know how Mother derides that as tacky. But he is Musaeus, for both of us, and for our family. He's only days old and already he takes after his mother. It's good that Mother approves of the name. We've been forced to rely on her to look after him.

My wife – I never did tell you enough of her – is sick. It has taken her voice, though she sang more beautifully than you can imagine, outstripping even me in talent. Though I was recently heralded at a party as the greatest musician Greece has ever seen. You were right, unchecked by you, my ego has been allowed to swell dangerously.

She smiles easily, and her eyes shine when she's in the sun. I joke that her talent is blessed by Apollo because she follows his other aspect so closely. She says she's blessed by Apollo simply for her charming personality. I could believe it.

I hardly know what I'll do, should the worst happen. Since you've been gone, she's the only thing tethering me to this green Earth.

Do look after her in Hades, won't you? If I cannot save her. I think she'd like that, having a friend in the land of the dead. She's much nicer than I, with a smaller ego. The two of you will get on brilliantly.

I miss you.
Your dedicated brother,
Orpheus

Trial Summary of
Thrace vs Heracles

The accusation is thus: Heracles, with malice of will, struck his music teacher – Linus of Thrace – with a lyre with such force it killed him. The claimants argued this was done without adequate extenuating circumstances.

In his defence, Heracles explained haltingly, that he was provoked. When using the instrument, a perfectly reasonable action for a student of over a year – the teacher snatched it from his hands, and began to shout at him. Heracles claimed that when the shouting failed to cow him, his teacher struck him with rods. Quoting Rhadamanthus – a well-educated boy! – he said that for defending himself against a wrongful aggressor, he should go free.

The accuser, Orpheus, brother of the deceased, took his turn. He sang the tale, and it struck the hearts of all who heard it.

As he sang, a tremendous storm picked up, threatening to rip up the very building in which we stood. The song was cut short and, after brief deliberation, Heracles was acquitted of the act.

Amphitryon II

Sending our son away never meant we hated him. We did it to punish him, and we did *that* because we loved him.

Like my eldest, I grew up rich and strong. Like my eldest I once did something stupid and impulsive and killed someone in the process, and I was punished for it. I believe my son didn't want to kill his music teacher when he struck him with that lyre. I'm not convinced that qualifies it as an accident.

I'm sure my son wanted to hurt Linus.

(It's either that or there's some problem with his hearing. Neither Alcmene nor I missed an opportunity to tell him: with his strength, hitting someone would always hurt them. Always.)

My wife, having been a wiser youth, and a nicer person than I in general, didn't get it. She sat with our son after the whole Linus business. She insisted it wasn't his fault to anyone who would listen. It was an accident. He couldn't be held responsible.

So Alcmene searched for legal loopholes and drafted Iphicles to prepare his brother's speech, and I considered what we'd do when the result inevitably came back in his favour.

I have the utmost respect for our legal system, but there are people in the world, like my son, for whom certain rules cannot apply. Admittedly, I wasn't expecting his divine father to send a storm to speak for him, but it certainly made the point.

He was released, and I took to arguing with my wife over what to do.

Our conversations came to form a steady routine, with me suggesting options to make him reconsider his behaviour, and Alcmene refusing them on the grounds of cruelty, embarrassment, and pain.

'I'm not trying to hurt our son,' I snapped, finally. How could she not see I was worried *for* him? 'I want him to grow up whole.'

'You want him broken,' she said.

'Just—' I waved my hands in frustration '—tamed.'

'What's the difference?' she said, her voice tired now, crashing like a wave. 'His life will be complicated enough already. Why are you pushing this?'

'Hera—' I said, the last sword in my arsenal.

'Don't talk to me about that woman. She did this,' Alcmene snapped.

Hera wanted to see him suffer. Maybe if we punished him ourselves, she'd be sated and she wouldn't take matters into her own hands. It would surely be better for Herc to face the consequences laid down by his parents than a god. But I wasn't as good as Iph; I didn't have the words to explain.

Iph came to me a few times during this wonderful stage in our lives. Alcmene was always so dedicated to whichever of our children needed her most. Sometimes there wasn't space for anyone else.

'What's up?' I asked him.

'I heard you fighting,' he said, sounding smaller than he was. 'I'm scared.'

'Don't be scared. If we're fierce enough to take each other on, the monsters have no chance.' I grinned, but he didn't look convinced. Rightly so. I'd rejigged an old platitude from when he suffered from the very legitimate fear of Hera making monsters appear in his bedroom. The boys did look alike, when they were young.

'But do you have to be so fierce with each other?'

When people say my wife and I are born of heroes, or anything in that nebulous semi demi hemi-divine region, it's some meaningless title. They don't think about what it actually means. It means the urge to fight is *always* there; the only question is how deep it's buried. I was never going to tell our kids, but for us, fighting was a way of showing we loved each other, that we respected our heritage.

'It's okay, son, I promise,' I said. It sounded weak. 'Why don't we go for a walk? Just the two of us?'

When we got home, Alcmene was comforting Herc, an altogether too common sight in our house. I have nothing against showing boys kindness but, at a certain point, you coddle them. I wondered if you couldn't see Herc chafe at it a little.

My wife and I exchanged a look.

Hers said: *see, he's distraught about what happened. He's already punishing himself more thoroughly than we could.*

Mine said: *this isn't helping anyone. He should do some official retribution; then he can forgive himself. Otherwise he'll be like this forever.*

What can I say, it was a long look.

In the end, it wasn't any of my arguments that did it. It was the arrival of our daughter. With everything else that was going on, we'd been less careful than usual, and Alcmene got pregnant.

By the time Laonome was born, I was tempted to call the argument moot. It'd been well over a year since the Linus Incident. Herc hadn't had a new teacher of music, nor the arts. We left him to the swordsmen and the athletes, whom he liked well enough, but otherwise he spoke to scarce few people outside Alcmene and Iph.

Laonome seemed to appear in minutes, though Alcmene informs me differently. She was perfect. All the fingers, all the toes. Alcmene's lovely ears, my shoulders. Beautiful, already.

As my wife held her, she resolved our war.

'We'll have to send him away,' she said. I could hear the breaking of her heart.

'I insist upon it,' I said, casting my voice like stone. 'No matter how hard you protest.' My heart was forfeit. Hers didn't have to be too.

'What do we do with him?'

'He can go up to the mountains and tend my goats. Just for a year. It's traditional.' I'd never be a king, thanks to my own youthful indiscretion, but between our families and my time in the military we had more land and money than many true royals. Our world was an endless series of cities, all claiming to be a kingdom in their own right. You could barely turn around without bumping into another one.

'And then?'

'She'll be bigger, and he'll be calmer.' I hoped. Sending him to the mountains was a stalling tactic, waiting for a life that was surely going to come. Truth is, we didn't know what to do with our son even before he killed his music teacher. It never seemed like he had much choice in the outcome.

'We'll tell him together.' Alcmene smiled weakly. She always was braver than me.

Our son, predictably, shouted the house down over it.

'That's not fair. The courts found me innocent,' he tried, the latter being a more effective argument than simply whining *it's not fair* had been.

'I'm not having this argument with you, Heracles. That's my decision and it's final.' I turned and left the room, left him to shout himself out.

Iph immediately rounded on me.

'It's because of Lao, isn't it,' he said. 'You're afraid he'd hurt her?' he asked, relentless, his voice escalating. 'That's stupid. He would never, you know. He loves her. He told me.'

'We're not worried about anything he'd do on purpose,' I said gently, hoping my wife wouldn't hear and castrate me for taking one of our children into confidence about the other. 'Come on, let's go wave him off together, like a family.'

It wasn't enough. I'd fucked it. Herc kissed his mother on the cheek, whispered something to his brother that made him snort, but he refused to look at me. There wasn't even a lazy hand thrown up in my direction as he stomped off into the hills.

I turned to my wife.

'He's so angry,' I said, feeling more helpless than I had since I was a kid, and in the same situation as my son was now.

'It'll be okay.' She wrapped an arm around my shoulders. 'It's only a year.'

It might have been for her, but my eldest never spoke to me again.

Hylas I

My father wasn't a nice man and I wasn't a good son. Maybe that means we deserved each other, but I didn't think so. I was going to run away.

Our mighty kingdom was located in a scrubland atop the least fertile mountains in Greece. It was populated mostly by goats with a sideline in the unlucky souls who tended them. Soft-handed and softer-brained, I thought I could waltz out of the palace and survive on my own.

My first try at leaving, I went back after a day, cold and hungry, unsure whether anyone had really noticed I'd gone. I resolved to do better next time, to practise this living rough thing.

I met H six months after I started work on The Plan. I'd taken to sneaking out and meeting the farmers at their preferred taverna. If anyone were in the habit of asking, I'd insist it was to better equip me for my escape. Truth is, I was lonely.

The first few months going there didn't help that. Everyone was old and big and loud. I wasn't small exactly, only months away from outgrowing Dad, but I've always had the kind of personality that fades into the background. They paid me less attention than their goats. Then H arrived, and everything was different.

He was shorter than me, and maybe twice my width across. He jutted his jaw out, like it'd stop people seeing how shit-scared he was. I knew because I did the same. In years to come, when people looked at him in awe, I had to fight to stop myself doing it again.

(Sometimes H would notice and slap me. He may not have been in the habit of noticing these things, but trust me, one slap from him and you remember.)

He didn't like his name, even then.

I never much rated my parents but at least they didn't make me answer to the name of a woman who wanted me dead. Worse than dead, *ingloriously* dead. So I called him H and he thought that was funny because I have an H name too and it was this whole stupid teenage thing.

In a different world, that time on the mountain would've rubbed off all his rough edges and he'd have grown into a different man. In that world he would've taken real penance from the experience, and the change might've inspired his enemies to lay off a little.

Unfortunately, H was a teenage boy, from money, with the dullest job in Greece – he dossed about as much as he could possibly get away with. In later years, he'd be given other jobs, other punishments, but they played to his strengths and he attacked them with vigour. He liked fighting things. He didn't like goats.

Things changed that year. His beard grew in and his shoulders grew out. His voice broke. He met me. I'd really like to believe that's an important part of his story. More often than not, by the end of it, people saw him, and they saw a man.

He spent the first three weeks of his punishment sulking. He sat on the mountaintop – and really, I lived there: mountain is an exaggeration, but the great Heracles cannot be sent to a mere hill to carry out his penance, so a mountain it must be – and scowled. He found a stout stick and wrote rude letters to his brother in the dirt. He glared at the adjacent flocks, resented the shepherds who were perfectly happy to be just that.

Three weeks of glaring before one of them got close enough to him to bellow and drag him to the taverna with promises of wine. H wasn't left with a choice in the matter, but that's a good thing. He would have said no when he needed to say yes.

His new friend brought him to a taverna whose most notable feature was its smell: half man, half goat. The place burst into cheers as they walked in. H grinned, though they weren't for him. Mester, the guy who'd dragged him, was the life of the party, and he was sometimes good for a round, which was better than we could say for anyone else. Mester held up his hand for silence and rattled off our names with such speed H had no hope of remembering them.

So we met.

'An' that's Hylas,' Mester finished. 'He's not a real shepherd, o' course. His father's some fancy king over the hills, but he's a good boy. Comes over here to get away from all the pomp and circumstance, ain't that right, Hylas?'

I nodded, feeling like my throat might be trying to choke me. We'd never had anyone my age and, like, my *class* in the taverna before.

H slid in next to me. The unsureness on his face fell away as someone passed him his first cup of wine and told him to get it down his neck.

The shepherds taught him to drink, the same way they'd been failing to teach me for months, and they taught him songs to keep him company while he did it. For years, those songs were the only music he could stand.

'You finishing that?' he asked me roughly, well into his sixth cup of wine. I was on my second, already suffering.

'Feel free,' I said. I was, I fear, rather lacking in personality that first meeting.

'Do you not drink wine?' H, instant convert to the religion of alcohol, asked.

'I do,' I said sharply. 'Who doesn't? It's different from the wine at my father's, is all.'

'Is it far from here?'

'A few hours due north. It's nice to get away sometimes, you—' I was cut off as more wine and more songs swept up H's attention.

H was famous for his strength from the day he was born. He was already getting there with his ability to eat. But his drinking he learned with those shepherds, and it was the most dangerous thing he ever did.

'Here, I'll help you walk home,' I said, well into the night, too late for respectable boys from respectable families to be out.

'Mm still drinking,' H slurred.

'The wine's gone. Wait any longer and Mester'll take you. Are you ready for more of his singing?' I asked. Mester sang like sirens looked. But that's not the reason I was offering, and we both knew it.

'Save me,' H said, sweeping a hand across his brow, and letting me drag him out. We walked home together and, the next day, I wrote him a letter. He wrote one back, and it was this whole stupid teenage thing.

42

Heracles,

I enjoyed meeting you last night. Your fortitude and strength are very impressive, and traits I hope to emulate. Mother's on at me to improve my writing. You seem more agreeable to correspond with than who she suggested. That's my primary reason for writing this letter.

Would you like to write? If not, I look forward to seeing you at the taverna soon.

Best,
Hylas

H,

You're not a goat. Your company, even written, is better than any I spend my days with.

My mum complains about my writing too. I don't know why she thinks a year in the company of goats will help. It'd be a nice surprise, though, if I get better. She won't like my skills with the animals.

I'll be at the taverna on the next market day. My allowance doesn't stretch to more, and people no longer make wagers of strength against me. How is your life?

H

H,

I'm glad I rank higher than a goat, though to hear my mother speak of it, my handwriting is no better than one. I mostly spend my days being forced to dress up and suck up to various nobles – a bane upon my life. Not that I wish for your fate, either. Animals do not like me. My mother's cat tried to kill me while I slept. Little eejit crawled onto my face and stuck its tail down my throat. Then I'm the bad guy for throwing it off me.

I'll see you at market day. I normally restrict my visit to such, also, though for opposite reasons. My allowance is enough that there's some competition to see who can fleece me of most of it. It may be fortuitous then, for me to challenge you to a test of strength. I hear an arm wrestle is the least likely to cause permanent damage?

H

H,

Forgive me the state of the letter. I tested to see if the goats wrote better. I think we can agree that they do.

Your mother's cat sounds like an arsehole. The goats might be stupid, but they haven't tried to kill me yet. My father's wife doesn't much like me and often sends murderous animals while I sleep. My brother complains that we can't have pets, but am I to be blamed for a violent reaction when someone sent snakes into my crib when I was days old? Urgh.

Does the cat live? If so, try blowing in its ears. They hate that.

I'll teach you how to cheat at dice. Don't get all noble about it. Everyone does it. I just know a better way. And maybe destroy this letter.

See you in a couple of days,

H

H,

Thank you for the tips with the dice, and the cat. It no longer looks so smug when it looks at me. Progress. Now, I just need to get out of dressing up and life will be perfect. Though then my father would find some other fundamental flaw to beat me for.

I don't want to wait for the next market day to see you. Would it be sage for me to come walking in the area? I have a better relationship with my mother than my father, and she's more passionate about furniture arrangement than any human should be. I may be able to make your current accommodations more comfortable.

H

H,

It was a good day for me also. You're stronger than you look! With some tutelage, I imagine you'd be formidable. If you want, I could teach you? A more noble art than cheating at dice! You did that well too, though. I can scarcely imagine anything you're not talented at.

As long as you continue to not be a goat, I'd be glad to receive you. Just look for the fire. I keep it running most of the time now, with winter coming. Could you bring more paper too? Supplies are hard to get out here.

H

H,
I'll bring paper. And blankets. You know how I feel the cold.
    That sounds fun. I'll try not to be too useless.

See you soon,
H

H,
You did well, honest! I'd offer to tutor you formally, but all of our parents would pitch a fit. Zeus' wife might like it, though. She thinks my being a servant is funny.
    I've taken to wearing the blanket as a cape, otherwise the goats will sleep on it. You wouldn't like the smell of goat. I look like some barbarian king. I'm thinking of growing my beard long. Thoughts?
    You should return soon. The goats miss you.

H

*

We wrote our letters and we went out with the shepherds. H drank more and I drank less. We walked home together, laughing and swaying through the hills.

If H was ever young, it was during those walks. It was during conversations about our families, talk of shared lessons and shared tutors.

'Oh I had him,' I exclaimed. 'With the—' I gestured atop his head.

'What did he put in there, to make his hair so high? Mother insisted Father must have struck him for it to stick up so.'

'Amphitryon struck your tutors?' I asked, confused. It took me a good long time to remember who he was truly the son of. He didn't speak of it often; he called Amphitryon *Dad*. At least he did when he forgot how mad he was that Amphitryon had cast him out.

'Zeus.'

'Ah, yeah. The tutors never did say great things about my memory.'

'I wish I could forget, too, sometimes, about my father,' he said. On another night, another drunk walk, H had opened his mouth and let his voice crack as he whispered, '*I killed a man.*' Even then, his voice didn't reek of pain like now.

I didn't know what to do with pain. How would I? So we walked more, maybe ten minutes, in companionable silence, until I broke it.

'What did you think of Old Pointy Hair? He hated me.'

'Why would he possibly hate you?' H asked.

'I never was much good at fighting.' I shrugged.

'I could teach you?' So that too became tradition, when we

were ensconced in the hills with nothing but sheep to see us. My tutors marvelled at the quality of my progress.

The first time we kissed, he was showing me a wrestling move – a pin.

He kissed me with such force my head slammed into the ground – only good chance saved me from the rocks beneath me.

'Mgah,' I cursed. H leaped up faster than I'd ever seen him move.

'I thought—' he said, but he didn't finish. He turned around, as if to run away, and I did the bravest thing I've ever done. I sprinted and caught him in a tackle, pushing him into a facsimile of the pin he'd been trying to show me.

'I liked it, H,' I said, with more angry force than I meant, but it was a lot, you know? The fighting and the kissing and the liking all coming from different bits of my head and tangling together. 'Just gentler, yeah?'

'What do you mean?'

'Do you like this?' I said, flicking his ear.

'No.' He scowled. I didn't want that, so I kissed him again to show I wasn't mad. My lips were bruised the next morning, but I didn't feel it then.

'Well imagine my hand was a *rock*.' Another kiss, for punctuation. And a laugh, because I'd never done this before and it was fun and exciting and he was my friend and not some woman and—

And H laughed too. He rolled over the top of me, only this time he had a hand behind my head. There was no less force to it – there couldn't be, with him – but he was there to take the excess, and that worked for us.

48

It wasn't all plain sailing from there – I learned a whole lot about fashion so I could hide the bruises that popped up on weird parts of me – but it got better. The unplanned marks got fewer and the planned ones ended up in better places.

When it did go wrong, I could show him how it hurt, and why. We experimented, found how to have the fire without the burns.

I chipped his tooth once. He gave me a split lip two weeks later. We were running to meet each other over the mountain. His brow hit my mouth and boom: blood everywhere.

'Oh fuck. Shit, H, I'm so sorry, it was—'

'It's fine,' I winced, leaning forwards so the blood didn't drip on my new fashionable cloak, with the high neck. I'm not known for my stoicism, but H made me want to change that. 'Told you I was taller than you.'

'Are not.'

'Am too.'

That night he kissed the corners of my mouth. He kissed my neck and my ears. He ran his hands through my hair, and the next day, there were no marks. I brought him a basket of honey cakes to celebrate.

(The morning after *that*, there were marks on both of us.)

There wasn't a name for what we were, but *Hylas and Heracles* started to trip naturally across people's tongues. H taught me to hold my drink, how to hold my head without looking afraid. I taught him to speak so people would listen, and how to arrange your plate so people didn't notice you were eating more than your share.

Months went by. And more. We talked about what he'd do when the year was up. At least, he did.

'I'm not going back there,' he said vehemently.

'Where?'

'Dad's— I mean Amphitryon's. I'm not going back. If he doesn't want me then so be it. I'll go be a hero, make my own way.'

Don't heroes still need a place to sleep? I thought, but I didn't mention it. I was too busy stumbling over the question I really wanted to ask.

'Will you come back here?' *To me.*

'I'm going to every corner of Greece,' he said simply. The cadence of him saying that had changed through the year, taken on a seriousness you couldn't doubt. 'I'll be back.'

'Will—'

'Even if I weren't going to every corner of Greece, I'd come back.'

'Really?'

'Once a shepherd, always a shepherd – got to check on my flock.' Such dedication, though when he was drunk he still got fuzzy on the difference between a goat and a sheep.

'You remember where your flock might have wandered to?'

'A couple of hours due north of here. I remember, H. I'll find those sheep if it kills me.'

'Goats.' I smiled. 'That calls for another drink, I think.'

The night he left, the shepherds came together to float him home. It was only proper. In future years, when his myths came back to them, and their children said: *no, that's impossible*, they'd say: *now, I don't know about killing those beasts, but that Heracles boy sure could drink.*

I walked him home. You couldn't call it tender. Lots of back slapping and the bluster of boys who don't know how to be men.

'You keep a good eye on those sheep, you hear me,' H said.

'I'll take care of them. You make sure to see every corner of Greece. Got that?'

'Every corner. Especially the ones a couple of hours due north of here.'

He slung his bag over his shoulder and, with that, we were done.

Megara I

We met in a rush and we married faster. The meeting was my father's choice – I didn't have a face to be covered in front of eligible suitors, nor was I worth launching ships over – but the marriage, that was all you.

You swept into our halls like a cyclone, the power of you raging against the pillars, and I feared what you'd do confined by walls. You were no real beauty either. Your skin was dark, but not from birth. It bore the lines and patches of something beaten by the sun. Your hands were huge. When I looked closer – I had time to inspect you, since I had no place in the discussion of my nuptials – I saw your clothes. They were fine, but dusty. I heard your voice. That was fine but dusty too.

You knelt respectfully in front of my father. That surprised me. To this day, that surprises me. You never bowed to conventions. Once you dragged silk – *silk, Husband* – through a pigsty. But you did kneel, and you gave your respect to the host and the host respected you back. I liked that. I wouldn't have been glad to see my father killed if he hadn't.

Formalities over, you knuckled down to business.

'I heard of your offer,' you said, haughtier than you had any right to be. You were still a supplicant in our house.

'And which offer was that?' Father replied. He wasn't normally like this. He was kind, and his voice ran with praise like honey over olive wood. Unlike so many men, when he stood next to you, Husband, he never looked small.

'Help with the Minyans, in exchange for your daughter.' Father knew precisely which offer you were talking about. He didn't have so many daughters he could afford to throw them away. But the mere mention of the Minyans aged him, pallor drawing at his eyes and the corners of his mouth.

'You sound confident,' he said. You weren't the first to come calling. I was sick of endless respectable generals who followed the same script, asking for my hand like I was some interchangeable thing.

But you? You smirked at the idea.

'I am confident. I'll take the agreement if you will.'

So you agreed, and that was that. I wasn't afraid of marriage. When I saw women with their children my heart longed for the same. Dreaming of being a mother, I offered my prayers to Hera. When you, named as her glory, *Hera*cles, arrived asking for my hand, it seemed the work of the Fates. That night, I thanked her.

The Minyans, as far as I suppose you care, were a tribe of barbarians trying to claim our lands as their own. They alternated between attacking us and demanding enormous tribute. The whole thing was patently ridiculous. We were no two-donkey kingdom in the countryside. We were *Thebes*.

When people mention me, do they say that I was the princess of Thebes? Or am I relegated to being only your wife, and not even your only wife?

Your confidence was well founded. You returned, successful, in days. I didn't know you could even ride to the Minyans' camp that fast. In slaying them, you saved us a hundred cattle in tribute a year – a story Father is not keen to propagate – but, like everything, it came with a cost.

You cut off their hands, their noses, their ears; you brought them back in a bag whose material was preposterously fine for the purpose. It was woven by your mother – Alcmene always was clever with a loom – and it featured scenes of growing trees, before the blood soaked through and stained it beyond recognition.

You held the bag loosely from the bottom and sent them tumbling across the floor where you'd so recently knelt and smirked like a boy. You weren't to know this, but Mother took me down that evening to scrub away the stains. She said I ought to know this about the man I was to marry.

I felt the bile, blacker than sin, rising through my throat, but I swallowed it down. Enough fabric had been ruined by the humours that day.

That's when we first spoke. You held my hand in your paw, still slippery from the blood, but gently. You always held me gently.

'My lady, it's an honour.' Did it sound stilted, even then? Or is it only looking back that I know you weren't the man you pretended to be?

'Is that so?' I asked, a weak attempt at being coy. I gave that up quickly. Honesty came more easily to me, and coyness has no place in a bloody chamber. 'I believe the honour is mine.'

We spoke maybe three times over the course of the engagement, but then we were married within the month.

My own mother dressed me for the wedding. She layered me in cloth and jewellery and painted my face. When I saw

54

my face reflected in the vases I dragged a deep breath. Maybe I was beautiful enough to launch ships, after all.

But when I looked down I saw blisters on my hands from scrubbing blood from the floor. That was the wife I had to be. I thought I could be happy with that.

We said our prayers and made our sacrifices. Drinking and revelry abounded. To be honest, I don't remember much of it. My sister flirting with your brother, though he was already married, was a particular high point.

Father reminded me to take care of myself, and Mother reminded me I was a princess of Thebes. Together, one hand on each of my shoulders, they reminded me I was their daughter.

I met your brother – largely distracted by his own son, who was just about big enough to walk and talk and generally get himself into trouble – and your sister – already wrapping the men of court around her finger. Laonome came to stay with us a few times, when we were married. To give us practice being parents at first, then to give your mother a break from the same thing.

I loved Alcmene. It was silly, but when I first met the woman, I followed her like a hound, asking a thousand questions about the man who was to become the centre of my life.

'Oh, you should never say that,' she said when I voiced that thought to her. Her hands looked like mine, soft and pale. 'You're strong enough to stand alone. You must believe that, especially around my son.'

'I should hope I never have to.'

She hummed at that, but said nothing. I left the interaction feeling much too young to be getting married at all.

I never met Alcmene's husband, the man you took so much

care not to call your father. You forbade him from visiting. I asked you about him, to understand your anger, to understand *you*.

'He does what he thinks is right. He always thinks he's right.'

This seemed to be a shared trait. I didn't mention it.

But guests don't stay forever, and soon enough we were left alone. 'To be married,' my sister said with the raise of an eyebrow.

We didn't rush to our marriage bed. When we did get there, it was gentle. You were gentle, as long as you'd been able to burn out that part of you too strong for mortal bodies to hold. In the early days of our marriage, I'd send you to chop wood, which would take the edge off it, but Mother said it wasn't appropriate for a man of your station. Days later, I found you bristling and swearing in the halls. I tried to embrace you, pull you into our bed, in case that would help, but you pushed me away. So the hunting trips were born.

Find me the biggest bear there is. Bring me the swiftest birds, so they can sing for me. Capture a deer so large it can feed the entire palace.

My sister said I must be the most demanding bride in all of Greece, but you understood. With your shyness with words, and my shyness with anything at all, it was difficult for us to communicate. Those were the only times the message passed clear as day. We didn't whisper sweet nothings in our bed, or pass notes and coy glances across banquet tables. I eked each and every secret out of you by listening more than you knew how.

You brought me my bear, my deer, even a mountain lion once, but never the birds. At first, I thought it was because I hadn't given you anything to kill, but I looked and I listened, *because I was a great wife*, and I worked out the real reason.

It had nothing to do with the birds.

You couldn't bear singing. You didn't listen to the epic songs brought by the bards, and you twitched when anyone mentioned the harp. You didn't listen to music, because it reminded you of what you'd done. You were a good man, I told myself more fervently than I'd ever said my prayers.

I told myself that was why you drank too. One day, we discovered a corner of the wine cellar was spoiling, and you offered to clear it. My wonderful, helpful husband, who did things around the house! Without being asked! With your strength, it'd take an hour or two at most.

We didn't expect you to clear it by drinking it. But you were a good man, Husband. You had to be.

I held that within me that night. I had to. With no wood cutting and no fights to distract you, you weren't gentle. You didn't caress my arms and marvel at the softness of me, the curves that contrasted with your angles.

You held my wrists, not down, but not freely either. If I'd fought you in bed, if I'd given you something to quench the fire that threatened to burn you, would we have lain together more often? Would you have loved me?

I didn't generally worry about this business of love – that's not what marriage is about – but, on days like that, I wondered. The next morning I vowed to find something for you to kill and, nine months later, I gave birth to our daughter.

I wanted to call her Heracleia. You hated it, walked out of the room the moment I suggested it, knowing I was too sore to follow and too tired to argue. I held her in my arms. She was so gentle. Even if she was the biggest newborn I'd ever seen, it was hard to believe she'd come from you. All I saw when I looked at her was *mine*.

I named her Pyrrha, nominally after my sister and your

grandmother, but really, it was after you, the fire you wrought upon this world. I hoped she'd always be able to protect herself. I guess your namesake being your undoing is something you two had in common.

You were a good father, really. When you took Pyrrha into your arms, you trembled, holding the strength back from her. When we found out how to make her laugh, copying the animals from the gardens, you mooed like a cow for hours.

I bore you a son in time, but it took *time*, a concept you seemed woefully unfamiliar with. I questioned how you passed that year alone with the goats, when every pregnancy failed to go fast enough for you.

I did the unforgivable first, had another daughter. I didn't suggest Heracleia for this one. I didn't ask for your thoughts at all. You were busy enough with your own name. So I called her Deiphile, lover of the gods, and I make no pretence that I hoped it was prophetic. I hoped she'd have luck and love and happiness.

Were you so angry with me, after, that you spread the rumours about her? Even with everything, I can only pray you didn't, that it wasn't your lips whispering she wasn't your daughter at all, but your *nephew's*. He was *five* when she was born.

Besides, anyone who'd so much as laid eyes on her knew she could only be yours. She had your shine, and the curls of your hair, though both suited her better than they did you. When it became clear she was beautiful, I cried – did you know that? I spoke with your sister, who knew what it was to be in the background, and I never wanted our Pyrrha to feel that way. It shouldn't have mattered. Where Deia had beauty, Pyrrha had strength. She could chop wood faster and better than boys twice her age. True or not, she said that mattered more to her.

You finally got your son next. Therimachus was the mirror image of your brother, oddly enough, though he had your smile and a habit for mischief neither of us would own up to. Another pathetic attempt at coyness on my part, Husband, I was never one to break the rules.

I do question whether Therimachus was your first son, if I was too slow delivering the goods you so desperately wanted. I can imagine you now, staring with those woeful eyes you thought could control me. You'd look so lost and, if we were still together, I'd be forced to drop the subject. But I won't, Husband, not this time.

The first time you lay with another woman, you didn't hide it at all. You came home smelling of her perfume – a flower I personally find abhorrent, to add insult to injury – with streaks of paint from her face in places they couldn't have possibly found themselves by accident. I don't know what made you better at hiding it, whether I stiffened at your touch – not altogether regular, unless you were pursuing another son – or whether one of your women sat down with you and explained it's best not to anger your wife unduly.

I didn't sit on our bed and breathe in the fabric of your infidelity. I didn't cry for promises you didn't keep. I simply moved your tunic into the pile of washing that required further attention. I was *your* wife, Heracles, not some common nobleman's. I was married to the greatest hero in Greece (whether or not people were officially calling you such yet). Who could I possibly cry to when I wasn't enough to entertain you? My sister would have listened, but she'd moved away, and she wasn't responding to our letters.

So I thanked the gods when you got better at hiding it, but you could never quite mask it. You didn't wear perfume, viewed soap as some personal affront. Your shirts and tunics and layers smelled so aggressively of *man* that any touch of a woman was bound to linger.

I'm only postponing the inevitable, I think.

The next four were all boys, as if you'd found your stride. People don't speak of your daughters: did you have more, after those I bore you?

Creontiades was our fourth, named after my father. Clever, and he learned mischief from his brother. He had a way with words that left him running rings around us from infancy. His hair grew straight, like my family's, though that was the end of any resemblance he bore to my father. Neither of them cared, and the two were closer than anyone. While you were hunting and fishing and generally making yourself a menace to the animals, my father was taking Creontiades to court.

He was betrothed. I don't suppose you knew that. Since he was so young, he was a favourite with one of the noble ladies. It was jokingly suggested he should ask her father for her hand – you may remember her, Myrina, who made those honey cakes you were such a fan of? Creontiades did ask, I suspect in pursuit of honey cakes, and the unofficial betrothal was born. He took it rather seriously, picking her flowers when he knew he was to see her and saving sweets in his pockets should they chance upon each other in the street.

Deioneus and Deicoon were built the most like you. As babes they had the shoulders of oxen. Deicoon spoke softly, and he peered at any tablets he passed like he could make sense of the words. Deioneus would promptly grab said tablet and smack him round the head with it, and Deicoon would slap it out of his hands, the both of them giggling.

I have little to say of Ophitus, as you know, but I'll try. He's the only one of our children whose eyes stayed blue, and the labour was so painful I swore he would be our last. You smirked at that. He didn't cry, but he was needier than our others. He wouldn't suffer to be held by men, not my father and certainly not you.

'A heartbreaker, this one,' you said, handing him back to me. I couldn't tell whether that hurt you.

Pyrrha, Deiphile, Therimachus, Creontiades, Deioneus, Deicoon, and Ophitus. Our children. Remember them.

Here I should like to reach for a story of the nine of us together, all happy and laughing, but I'm unable to bring one to mind. The closest I have is from shortly before Ophitus was born. You carried me – you did know how to make a woman swoon – to the riverbanks, kids in tow, so we could enjoy the last of the autumn sun.

You helped Pyrrha and Deia plait flowers into my hair, even allowed them to thread one behind your ear. You found sticks for Therimachus and Creontiades and even the twins and you played around – you teaching them to swordfight.

You set up Theri and Creontiades in a little duel, fairer than you realised. While Theri had both height and weight on his brother, he was loath to let anything hurt him, perhaps not so much out of filial affection as fear of my father's wrath.

(You remember, I hope, when the two of them went exploring, Creontiades fell down those rocks and broke his arm. We didn't think the kink in it was ever going to come out. Yet, after my father Had Words, it was Therimachus who yelped each time he walked past the area. For the record, Creontiades had no ill effects from their little misadventure, once his arm had healed. If anything, he grew fatter on honey cakes and sympathy.)

They had a good stab at it, but the ground was uneven and Theri missed his footing and fell. He tried hard to be a man for you, blinking tears out of his eyes as his brother bumped his shoulder and compared him to the old cow Father never had the heart to slaughter, which distracted Theri well enough.

You didn't see any of this. Some young man – how young was he? I never could tell; they were all children when they stood next to you – came sprinting over.

'Heracles, sir.' He panted, breathless, and you preened. Because he called you sir. 'There's an emergency. You have to come quick.'

It wasn't an emergency. You didn't have to come quick. A distinctly unmonstrous lion had wandered too close to someone-or-other's farm, and your presence in Thebes had taught us helplessness. Why fight yourself when the mighty Heracles can do it?

You didn't tell the boy that. You didn't tell him you were spending the day with your family. You picked up your club and set off to save the day. I patched up Theri's knee and the seven of us walked back home together.

You brought the lion's skin back with you that night. Tried to wear it as a cloak, though you'd not skinned or cured it properly. Even in the weaker autumn sun it reeked, attracted flies. I ordered it off you, said we'd leave it as an offering to the gods so you wouldn't sneak off and retrieve it the next day. I can't remember which god we dedicated it to. Maybe Poseidon, since I just wanted to throw the darned thing into the sea, but more likely Zeus. I always encouraged you to send your offerings to him, to see if you did have some connection.

I suppose it doesn't matter. What happened, happened, and you will have to live with that for the rest of your days.

It was some kind of nothing dinner. It must have been some festival to have you there, sitting with all of us, and to have my parents and your mother there too, all the kids, dressed up in clothes too big and too nice for them. Even Ophitus was wearing jewels, and he could barely support his own neck.

There was a lot of food, but that was hardly a surprise. There was always a lot of food. Once, in the early days of our marriage, I set the meat for you to carve and, when I came back with the rest of our dinner, you'd eaten it in its entirety. I thought Pyrrha was going to cry, the little carnivore. After that, we had the family plate and Daddy's Plate.

For whatever reason, that day, your plate wasn't enough for you. Your eyes grazed over to ours. I hurried to scrape enough out for each of the kids. When I got to her, Pyrrha shook her head slightly and winked. It was piled high already. We had smart girls.

You took the rest, and called for more wine.

I agreed, more wine would be lovely. Nine times out of ten, wine calmed you, made you sleepy and content. I asked for it to be watered so the children could have some, but you refused, demanded it pure. You were thirsty, you said. I don't know why watered wine couldn't have slaked that thirst just as well.

I didn't like the taste of drink that strong, and Father found it didn't agree with him in his age. Even our mothers nursed their drinks, but not you.

As you drank, you got bigger, your arms and your shoulders going out and your voice booming as you told story upon story of your exploits. You forgot I was married to you. Not only did I know these stories, I also knew when you inflated them.

The kitchens ran out of wine, the servers explained uncomfortably, standing by the door ready to escape. You demanded more.

The servers said nothing. Mother and Father shared a Look and went to find more. They'd been married a long time, and I can't pretend to be fluent in the language of their looks, but I'm fairly sure that was an evaluation of how poor the wine could be before you'd notice and take offence.

I took the distraction to escape your diatribes. I knew fully well you hadn't charmed a monster into bowing to you and offering you its treasure. The monster was probably more charming than you.

Ophitus had rolled over by himself for the first time that day. I was excited. Your mother was excited. We spoke briefly about you and your brother and how like you your sons were. Your mother remarked that our boys were developing even faster. It was flattery, Husband, any mother knows how to win the favour of another.

If you wanted us to say you were the greatest infant the world had ever known, we would have. We would have said anything.

You dropped down in front of Ophitus. You could barely get your haunches close enough to the floor to do so, but you got eye to eye with him. The air grew sweet for a moment, like fruit ready to decay.

'What's so great about him, huh?'

I wasn't scared. I'd spent years convincing myself you were a good man. You took our son by the foot, his left, which I used to blow on after I washed him because it made his face crinkle with happiness. You held on to it and swung our son in a perfect parabolic arc into the stone of the wall.

With more time to think, I would have vomited at the sound of bone splintering. Like the second time we met, it wouldn't have been appropriate. Back then, I had to be your wife. Now I had to be a mother.

'Doesn't seem so strong,' you said.

I stabbed you. They always leave that out. I took the knife you'd been using for the meat and ran it into your thigh, just where your muscles formed a crevice. I yelled *run*.

I saw Deia grab her sister. That was the last thing.

I will not describe how it felt when you threw me into the fire, Husband, or the peculiar sensation of burning alive, for the simple reason it will not bring me or Ophitus back.

You got Theri next. He tried to stop you. He went into the wall as well. Then the servers, who went through the table. Father treated his servants well. They both stepped in front of you, as if anyone so wholly mortal could save my children. I kissed their feet in the underworld.

Their bodies blocked the exit for the girls. You didn't even stop to kill them, just trampled them below your feet, in the effort to eradicate your sons.

I don't know who you killed first of Deicoon and Deioneus. They went out of this world together, as they came into it. You held their throats until no spirit could pass through them. You held them tight enough to pierce their skin. You knocked over the end of the wine – unacceptably watered down – and it mixed with their blood on the floor.

The last of our children living was Creontiades. You didn't take his life until my parents came back into the doorway. My father was there to see you rip his namesake in two.

They call it madness, what you were struck with that night, but I'm not sure. I don't think madness has such good timing.

With no one left to save, my parents didn't fight you. They watched you stampeding like an angry bull until your mother could herd you out of the room and into isolation, where you waited until someone was summoned to bring you back to sanity. They say you sobbed, when you came to, cried that the gods had forsaken you.

They say you were struck with madness. They say you deserve sympathy for what was done to you. If you were mad, Husband, then it was my patron goddess who struck you with it. Do not talk to me about being forsaken.

For obvious reasons, you never returned to Thebes.

Doctor's Notes

The patient was brought to me late in the night, babbling and covered in blood. It dripped from his hair and his eyes didn't focus. They darted across the room, seeking windows as though he would run. He did not. An arm held him in place. His mother — she introduced herself as such.

Alcmene, and this is my son, Hercules, she said. She emphasised that, as though she weren't sure what her son's name was, though he was well past his twentieth year. I asked about the lack of clarity, assured them I would not tell if they were choosing a fake name, to avoid the law or some such, but I should know. Context is so important in these complicated cases. Alcmene said no. They weren't hiding from the law — her tone implied it was something else they hid from — and Hercules just fancied a change.

She had the trappings of an elegant woman, sans blood and obvious distress. Were it not for the state of her companion, I may have mistaken her for a patient herself.

I digress. The patient was of average height and significantly above average breadth. Despite his presentation, he had no significant physical maladies. Talking to him did not elucidate the nature of his madness. The sole treatment available was to wash him off and send him to the oracle. Some plagues belong to the gods.

Eurystheus I

The man was clearly insane. Sure, they'd found some barely competent backwater healer with a two-bit shrine to Asclepius, and just about stemmed the flow of gibberish emitting from his mouth, but I don't find silence any more convincing a sign of sanity than I do whining that it's other people's fault when you brutally murdered your entire family.

Needless to say, I wasn't delighted by the gods' decision that he should serve his penance with *me*, Eurystheus, fabled King of Tiryns.

My cousin, for the madman now known as 'Hercules' was he, was led into my halls by his mother. When people spin tales of his brave deeds, they don't mention this cowed and broken man-child. Yet he struck terror into the hearts of my men; the soldiers on the gates fled from him. After reports of their cowardice reached me, I had them permanently removed from their posts and replaced with sturdier sorts. Even they flinched at the monster before us.

'Cousin,' he boomed. 'You're no longer so weedy.' We'd encountered each other often as children, when my stature was less impressive: a result of being born several months early. Hera and I were both keen for me to make my mark on this world. Having seen most premature babes wither and squall themselves into nothing, I've always felt I owed her my life.

'I hardly think you're in a position to be casting insults.'

'It was a compliment,' he said densely.

'Any compliment from you is an insult for normal people,' I said. He didn't understand. He struggled with such things. 'Leave my presence until I find something for you to do.'

He left. In the absence of simple instructions made of short words, he paced, and he didn't cease for eleven days and nights. He dragged riverbeds through marble floors in his rooms. When the maids began to trip on his gouges, I moved him to the stables. Apparently that makes *me* the monster.

His mother left shortly after his arrival. She held him as though he were a chickling fallen from the sky, but there was no trace of sentiment to be found in his hardened features.

I fear you've scarcely been reading these words since I said we were cousins. It's true. We're both descended from the hero Perseus – Amphitryon and my father are brothers. As a child, Amphitryon was in line to inherit my throne, but he carelessly miscast a stone in practice, killing my eldest uncle. Amphitryon was banished and my father became the king. Murder carries down family lines.

Of course, Amphitryon went and scraped together something he called a home, though the title of *king* would always be out of his reach. That goat-filled Asphodel served as a permanent punishment for his actions and the perfect place for the oaf to grow up as the barbarian he was always meant to be.

When the prophecy was spoken, the one that appeared to

apply to Hercules – a descendant of Zeus, bound to rule all those around him – the lovely Hera twisted things so it would describe me instead. Only one of us was worthy of such.

Hercules made himself comfortable in my palace. Enough manners had been crammed into his underdeveloped head he at least didn't claim my place at the top of the table, but he insisted on being by my side. Mindless of his former errors, he called endlessly for wine, flirting with the maids all the while.

Ordinarily, on acquiring such a poorly broken beast, I'd send a missive to the former owners, but it seemed unwise to bother Thebes. My wife and I lost a daughter to sickness when she was young. I cannot imagine losing one to the actions of such a brute as this.

The oaf came with minimal rules. For the ten years he'd been sentenced – one for each life he took that night, as if that were even close to fair – he wasn't to accept help from others, and he wasn't to take payment. *Obviously*. Work in exchange for wages isn't penance, it's a *job*.

At first, I set him small and useful tasks around Tiryns. My dislike of the man could be minimised if he'd serve usefully, but it wasn't to be. He was boorish in my palace, and he knew no subtlety. You'd ask him to build a wall around a single field and he'd hollow out a mountain to make it, blocking the sun from the crops. *That* debacle took months to fix.

There was nothing for it, I sent for the priests.

Antimache, my wife, and I followed Zeus and Hera primarily, though of course we'd give respect to others when appropriate.

The priests came back with news typical of marriage: conflicted in reasoning, but united in outcome. The priest for Zeus said Hercules was a great hero and he should be treated as such. Luxurious rooms were well and good, but he should go out, perform heroics. Hera's advice was less cloying. Hercules had performed horrific acts. He shouldn't be allowed to lounge in Egyptian cotton and goose feathers, he should *suffer*. I understood this better. If it'd been a man, not a plague, that took my Philopatho, I'd have cut off his hands, feet, and nose, and left him to bleed in the street.

Give him ten tasks, they said. One for every person he killed, they said, so he might clean his soul up enough to deserve anything approaching freedom. As though it's easy to find a life-threatening and unpleasant task suitable for a son of Zeus. I was trying to get the man killed but I didn't want retribution delivered unto me in the process.

When that lion started attacking the outer reaches of Greece, I sacrificed a hundred cattle to Hera in thanks.

They don't exaggerate when they speak of the enormity of the creature – the lion, not the oaf, though they didn't exaggerate that either. I had all too much opportunity to become acquainted with the lion's pelt since my darling cousin took to touting it like a headscarf. It would have stood with its belly brushing against the top of my head, and I'm no short man, I just seemed more so next to the lumbering fool who invaded my house. The remains of buildings bear witness to the size of its jaw, and its undiscerning appetite for flesh or stone.

The peasants got it in their heads that this was a curse from the gods, not the blessing I knew it to be. What do scared peasants do? Do they talk to kings or priests? Do they worry their little heads at all? No. They panic and get to sacrificing their virgin daughters to the beast.

Even without the oaf at my disposal, I would've sent men. When too many peasants send their daughters into the eagerly waiting mouths of beasts, I have to send girls from the city to balance the population, an arrangement unacceptable to all parties.

But I had the oaf, so I didn't have to risk good men.

'I have a task for you,' I said formally, so the almighty Zeus couldn't take offence. The idiot was eating the leg of a goat. Where had he got a goat?

'Mhmfgh?' the oaf grunted around his food. Gristle rolled around his overdeveloped jaw. He swallowed. It was like watching a snake devour its prey. 'More butchering?'

I'd taken to making him skin and prepare meat. He had a natural talent for it and, once it was explained in short words, it didn't offer special opportunity to destroy my kingdom.

'Of a sort. There is a lion—'

'In Nemea,' he grunted, mouth occupied again.

'How do you know of the lion?' I'd only just received word from the fastest messengers at Hermes' disposal.

'Servants talk.'

'But how did the ser— Never mind. I command you to slay it. You leave tonight. Don't return until you have proof the beast is dead.' Demanding proof was just part of the ritual. I didn't believe he'd drag the entire bloody carcass from Nemea to Tiryns.

'Supplies?'

'Given your history, I don't trust you with weaponry within the city limits. And you remember your rules?' I said.

'Uh-huh.'

I didn't tell him that the beast's skin was impervious to swords and arrows alike. He left the palace, and the city, and I sighed in freedom, however fleeting.

It was very fleeting indeed.

When the messenger arrived, out of breath, I let myself believe the oaf was dead.

'King Eurystheus, sir, I bring glad tidings of your cousin Hercules,' he said. 'He has defeated the lion. We're free!'

A man can dream.

'How?' I said, my voice cold and hard as marble.

The long and the short of it was that he, Hercules, had killed the thing with his bare hands. He tried stabbing it, several times, resulting in several broken swords and many whiny demands from peasants that I pay them back for the damages the oaf caused to their land and weapons, like whatever my stupid cousin did should be my problem. When stabbing didn't work he punched it in the eye.

I've studied war. I know blinding your opponent to be a good tactic, but I'm told it was largely unsuccessful in this case, for the lion followed its sense of smell. This was touted to me as a near mythical ability of this particular lion but I suspect it was more a result of the oaf's failure to wash. He kept punching the softer bits of the lion's face until eventually it fell. He took one of the broken swords and stabbed it through the inside of its mouth, to ensure it was dead.

That's what the bards claim. I'm not convinced I trust them. He could just as easily have annoyed the thing into submission, but I didn't care enough to go hunting for more details.

Miraculously, I *still* didn't see the oaf for nigh on a year. I suspect he took a detour into the beds of formerly virginal peasant girls who'd been lined up to go into the jaws of the beast.

When eventually he did return, he sauntered in. *Sauntered.* If I thought the man conceited before, it was nothing compared to him showing off a fresh kill, like a particularly satisfied cat. In some ways, he was. He'd skinned it to wear as a cloak.

'I have completed your task.' The most words I'd ever heard him successfully string together.

'I can see that.' He kept billowing out the cloak, already all too aware of his own image.

'So, what's next, cousin?' he asked impetuously, as if my sole purpose in life was running around finding banal tasks needing only strength to accomplish. Which, thanks to the instructions from those above us, it may well have been.

Shortly after his return, his blasted nephew showed up, as if this were some family bonding activity. The boy, for it was a boy, lacked much of his uncle's strength, but at least held himself in a manner that indicated he'd seen humans before.

He rode up in a chariot. Not to the gates of the city, nor even to the outside of my palace, but to my very throne, half destroying my steps in the process.

'I am Iolaus,' he announced. I fear my countenance gave away how little I cared. I was, at that point, supremely irritated. His uncle had eaten the food set aside for my mid-afternoon tea. Running a kingdom becomes irksome without adequate snacks. 'Son of Iphicles.'

Again, I didn't care, so he continued to speak.

'Nephew to Hercules, grandson of Perseus, and, sir, your cousin.' The *sir* may have gained him some points had I not written him off due to both his uncle and his rather interesting claim that Perseus was his grandfather. He was in fact his great-great grandfather.

Counting to three can be so difficult for some people.

'What purpose do you have in Tiryns?' I asked. He looked at his feet. 'You don't have a purpose in Tiryns.'

'I've been sent to seek an audience with my uncle.' Blast the youth and their uneroding self-confidence.

'It's my business to know any business you have with my *slave*.' Gods above, it was like pulling teeth, but I managed to eke some garbled semblance of an explanation out of him. He wanted to be a hero, so his father had sent him to try it out. Brave man, given the oaf's track record with children.

'How old are you, child?'

'I have seen sixteen summers.' A bare-faced lie if I've ever met one. I have the misfortune of sharing a day of birth with the oaf. Presumably, his twin brother also had that dubious honour. For him to be sixteen, his father would have been eleven at his conception.

'You may travel with him, but not take up permanent lodging in the palace.' I didn't mention he was forbidden from helping the oaf with his tasks. I thought he'd understand that. 'And Iolaus?'

'Yeah?' he said gormlessly.

'If you ever ride a chariot in my palace again, I will have your feet cut off. Do you un-der-stand?' I slowed down on that last word. It seemed he had the oaf's proclivity for idiocy.

He swallowed, only emphasising a throat that couldn't yet grow a beard, and relieved me of his presence.

As luck would have it, I'd recently heard of another beast that needed slaying. The Hydra. Apparently when one head was cut off, it grew two more. Or three, seven, or twelve, depending which bard was speaking. I wasn't naive enough to believe the bastard would die, but I hoped for some light maiming.

They were back in a matter of weeks, bearing only one additional head and matching idiotic grins. Had no one told the oaf he wasn't supposed to *enjoy* these labours?

I suppose it didn't matter either way. I wasn't going to count the jaunt towards his penance. After all, his little nephew had done as much of the work as he had and, presumably, the child hadn't any murders to atone for. I decided not to tell the oaf right away, though, since he was having such a wonderful time.

I thought long and hard over his next task. How to make the brute miserable without disrespecting him? In the end the answer was simple. Forbid him to kill.

I had him capture the Ceryneian Hind. My sources – Hera – said it was not in Greece.

'Capture it, like, dead?' the oaf asked. He wasn't eating, a miracle in itself, but his eyes roved over my newest guard as if he could take a bite from him instead.

'No. Capture it, as in, alive. It is sacred to Artemis.' Should he kill it, it'd irritate Artemis to such an enormous degree she may turn him into some wild animal and hunt him down herself. I used the thought to amuse myself in particularly dull meetings.

Alas, he did capture it. He tied a rope around an arrow – dexterity I thought beyond his clumsy mitts – and shot it so it tangled around the hind's legs. It was to become part of my menagerie, had he not untied it before letting it down upon my floor whereby it promptly ran away.

I raised my eyebrows. 'Well?'

'What?' he asked. It sounded as though he had food in his mouth. There was no logical way he could have food in his mouth.

'Fetch it.'

'Can't.'

I sighed. 'Why not? The task was to deliver me the Ceryneian Hind. I don't consider it delivered.'

'It was in your palace, you just weren't fast enough, Cuz.' *Cuz.* Perish the thought.

'Fetch, slave,' I snapped.

'Can't.'

'Why. Not?' I did not make him clean, or tend animals, or attend the feet of the ladies at court, all of which would be considered below his mighty station. This was his sole purpose.

'Promised Artemis, didn't I?' he said, turning his back to me and wandering off, presumably in an effort to find more food.

I turned to the sprat, who still couldn't pass for sixteen. Maybe he'd be susceptible to my imperious glances. Alas, the oaf had rubbed off on him. He shrugged.

'He did promise Artemis. Sorry.' He didn't seem sorry. He seemed smug. Maybe I should have had his feet cut off, after all. I'd done it before, and it guaranteed a certain level of respect.

I took a certain pleasure in ridding my palace of Oaf Junior. 'Your father desires your return with the greatest of haste. You must leave now – the guards will ensure you do not get lost.'

I sent Oaf Senior to Arcadia, to bring back the boar there, alive. Bigger than a house they said, more murderous than fire, they said.

It was midwinter when he returned. I remember because Antimache had gifted me a rather resplendent standing vase to celebrate the season. I was inspecting it as the oaf made his entrance.

I did not hide in the jar.

I was merely examining the beautiful engraving contained inside when I was startled by the *fee fie foe fum* of his giant feet clattering across the floor. It wasn't dignified that I fell in, but it was *not* motivated by fear.

'Got the boar, Cuz, gotta run,' he said, dropped it, and left. He'd acquired some new young man behind him. This one at least demonstrated the ability to grow a beard.

From then, he took what can only be described as a two-year sabbatical from his penance.

Iolaus I

Dad said yes but Mum said no. They fought about it for ages. Stupid 'cause we all knew I was going. I'd have permission or I wouldn't but I wasn't a kid anymore. They couldn't stop me.

It started when my Uncle Herc came round for dinner. Mum and Dad didn't talk about him much anymore because Mum said he was a bad man and Dad said he was his brother and Mum said that didn't stop him being a bad man and the whole thing went round and round and round, like when I pushed my cousin down that hill.

My uncle was wearing a lion. Like, a whole one. It was really cool. But he hadn't cleaned it yet – he'd only just come from Nemea – so it dripped blood everywhere. I remember 'cause Mum and Dad agreed on that, that my Uncle – Uncle Her-q-lees, Dad said – shouldn't be allowed to wear it for dinner because it would stain things, so he shrugged and hung it on the door, to scare intruders he said. I thought that was great. My stupid parents didn't agree.

'Can I wear a lion?' I asked while Uncle Herc went out to drop some things off in the sea. I didn't know what that meant either but Mum wrinkled her nose and told him to wash his hands after.

'I think you're a little small for that, son,' Mum said. 'You'd have to fight a nasty old lion, and you don't want to do that, do you?'

'*I can fight a lion?*' I squealed so loud the gods themselves could hear me. My sister told me so. Mum just said I was annoying the neighbours.

'Maybe when you're older,' she added firmly. We all know what that means.

'Your uncle killed a lion when he was about your age,' Dad said. Mum made that face like when you try and eat seven handfuls of olives all at the same time and you don't know how to keep them in your mouth but you can't spit them out because then you'd look like a loser who can only eat six handfuls of olives, which anyone can do.

'I *have* to do that. Can I, please, Dad, please?' I said. He suddenly got all panicky, like this pissing-off-Mum idea wasn't so smart after all. I could have told him that. Mum's scary when she wants to be. Which is a lot, 'cause none of us know how to behave, she says.

'Why don't you ask your uncle what he'd advise?' Dad said. Mean. He was just passing on the problem, like when I pay the peasants to do my chores and my parents say that's cheating though I know it's just being smart.

But I wasn't going to let Dad's stupid cheaty tactics or Mum's stupid frowny face stop me. I was going to be a big famous hero and wear a lion and eat *eight* handfuls of olives and no one would ever laugh at me again. I could imagine my name, written across the stars. *Iolaus: Best Mortal Ever.* Maybe they'd paint it on vases. Maybe they'd paint my *face* on vases.

I waited 'til dinner when Dad had a mouthful of meat and Mum had a mouthful of wine to spring the question.

'Hey, Uncle Herc—' I began, but he looked across and that look was so scary it cut me off right there.

'Uncle Herc?' he said, voice totally flat, like the top of his nose. 'Do you know the things I've done? And you presume to call me *Uncle Herc*?'

'Well, Uncle Her-q-lees was kinda long, and it's what you've done I was getting to, see,' I said, fast, so he couldn't interrupt me again. Mum says it's rude to interrupt. 'I heard you killed a lion when you were, like, my age, and you killed another one now and it's your cloak and I want to kill my own lion and be a big hero, so I can have a cool cloak too.'

'I like you,' Uncle Herc said. Weird.

'Well yeah, you're my uncle. So? What do I do to kill lions and be super great and stuff?'

'Well,' he said slowly, his face still doing that stupid grinning thing. He better not be laughing at me or I'd break his face. He might think he's some great hero but I'm sneaky. 'I'm doing some missions at the moment; maybe you could come with me on one of them?' he said, not looking at me but at Mum and Dad like it was their decision. Me and Mum erupted at the same time.

Mum said no. I said yes. Dad looked like a sheep who needed to do a poo.

Uncle Herc looked at Dad with a shrug, making it his choice, which was funny because Dad dumped the whole thing on Uncle Herc in the first place. Good revenge.

'Do you promise to keep him safe?'

'With my life,' Uncle Herc said, and for all the goofy grin he had on, he looked proper serious and I was about to fall off my seat because I was so excited but Mum got involved and there was a whole lot of shouting about *the appropriate behavioural parameters for an excitable child,* whatever that means.

The shouting lasted *days.* Uncle Herc didn't stick around; he said he had some things to sort out first and I should meet him in some place called Tiryns when I was ready.

While Mum and Dad were shouting, I practised my fighting with some of the local boys – I'd done the basics with Dad, but we were both sick of how each other fought. Seemed like every time I practised I'd catch one of my parents staring at us, all thinky and weird. It must have been good though, because I came in from one lesson and found Mum packing my things.

'This one trip, okay?' she said, like it was no big deal, but we both knew it was. I squeaked and wrapped my arms around her.

'I love you, I love you, I love you,' I said over and over. I got to go away with Uncle Herc and slay monsters and have a cloak and be the coolest. Everything was coming up Iolaus. Especially when Dad told me I could borrow one of our chariots and *ride* to Tiryns.

I liked riding horses 'cause when I sat on one, I could pretend I was some great commander telling everyone where to go. But I liked chariots even better. On chariots you could go *fast.*

Mum said I was a bit young for that and I should learn to look after the creatures first – which I did, just fine. My girl cousins squealed and complained about picking up poo when they visited, but it wasn't so bad, not like human poo or anything. But sometimes when Mum was busy, Dad would take me out on a chariot with him and push it as fast as it would go and the wind would catch in both our hair and we wouldn't have to say anything because we were feeling the same thing.

You're not meant to say stuff like this in case they get annoyed, but I reckoned riding a chariot was pretty close to how it felt to be a god. The horses did what you told them, and people got out of your way, and you moved faster than people can, more like a bird diving and swooping.

I got to Tiryns really fast. Only when I got there I realised I didn't know what to do with a chariot when you're not charioting. Dad dealt with all that before and Mum only made me look after the horses, not the mechanics. So I just kind of . . . kept riding it. And no one stopped me, not until I was all the way in the palace – I had to do a trick shot to get myself up the stairs, where I stopped the horse really fast and then threw myself up so I'd get some air and then jumped forward to cover the distance – and even then, they didn't stop me.

So I kept going. People opened doors for me. Until I got to the guy I figured was in charge. He was sitting on a throne and he was fat and grumpy and bored-looking, which tends to be a king thing. Everyone else gets excited when they get to sit on thrones.

I pulled the reins to slow down but I guess the horses were as excited as I was 'cause they didn't want to stop. I had to yank all of us sideways until we almost hit the wall and then they reared up and neighed, kind of pissed off, but the angles came out pretty well and my face ended up right next to the king's.

I introduced myself and he was prickly but he didn't stop me so I went to find Uncle Herc. He was sleeping in the stables, which was awesome 'cause it was kind of like camping but properly dry and I don't know where I would have put the horses if we were inside. Mum said they weren't allowed in the house, at home, so it was probably the same for palaces. I stayed with him for the night and then the next morning it was time to go.

'I didn't know if your parents would let you come,' he said.

'Me neither. But Dad said he had a message for you. He said—' I paused while I thought about it because Dad said it was important for me to get the words exactly right. 'He said someone had to stop you from getting shit on your shoes.'

And Uncle Herc smiled, actually smiled, because of something I said.

'That sounds like your dad.'

'Yeah?' I asked, because I guess I'd never really thought about my dad like that, having emotions and stuff. 'What else?'

'He's very smart,' my uncle said slowly. Boring, but I guess he could see that, because he hurried it up. 'But he wanted to use his lessons in everything. I remember once Amphitryon – that's your grandfather—'

'I know who Grampa is! We go there every summer. Us and Auntie Lao, but not – not *you*.' Gran always said it all sad, like. *Nearly* the whole family was there together, then she'd glare at Grampa.

'Amphitryon made it clear I wasn't wanted,' he said, like I should know what he meant, but I didn't really. I knew he'd been sent away for something or other but the way Dad talked about it, he chose not to come back. '*Anyway*, Amphitryon wouldn't let your father go riding because the weather was so bad. So your dad prepared this great long speech with all the different bits of rhetoric in it to convince him, only by the time he thought it was ready the weather had cleared up.'

I laughed, and asked him to tell more stories about both of them. Uncle Herc hadn't wanted to take the chariot with us so we had to walk all the way to the Hydra. It was a lot of walking. Weeks. I asked Uncle Herc why he didn't ask Zeus – his dad! – to zap us there but he said it didn't work like that. I said *my* dad said he'd move mountains for me and *his* dad actually *could* but then he looked all sad and said they were different kinds of dads, so I didn't ask about that anymore. I wasn't really used to spending time with grown-ups, apart from Mum and Dad, so I kept asking all the wrong questions and making Uncle Herc sad.

He was never sad when he was talking about his adventures, so I stuck to those, building myself up so I could finally ask him.

'How did you kill the lion?' I'd been thinking about it every night. Did he grab the jaw and pull the two halves apart? Did he summon Zeus to strike it with lightning? I had to know.

Uncle Herc smirked. 'Which one?'

He was so cool.

'The biggest one?'

'Okay.' His voice dropped to a whisper. 'It went like this. I asked the people in town where they saw it last and tracked its pawprints from there. They were huge, bigger than my whole face, so it wasn't too hard, even in the dark.'

'You fought it in the dark?'

'Lions can't see in the dark,' he said simply.

'But people can't see in the dark either,' I said. Apart from if they eat their vegetables, Mum said, but I didn't really believe her. Uncle Herc winked at me.

'Not all people. I thought I could creep up on it while it was sleeping, but it heard my footsteps – its ears were so big I could have crawled in them and slept there – and it woke up. It roared so loud I thought I'd never hear again, and it slobbered so much it was like taking a bath, but while it was distracted I took my club—' he patted it where it was belted to his side '—and brought it straight down on its nose, so hard that it fell.'

I burst out laughing. Uncle Herc looked confused.

'Why are you laughing? It's a good story.'

'Bad kitty,' I ground out through my laughter, miming hitting something on the nose. 'Kitty, no!' Mum would have been mad at me, for embarrassing a guest, but Herc started laughing too.

'It was a bad kitty,' he said, failing to keep a straight face.

'The worst,' I agreed. Next time I heard him tell that story, he hit the lion in the eye instead.

We found the Hydra in the same kind of way. It didn't have paws, obviously, but it had claws that it dug into the earth beneath it and created grooves that'd last forever. We could already see loads of snakes hiding in the old holes.

'It keeps them cool,' Uncle Herc said. 'Good for nesting.'

'Right,' I said, but I kind of didn't believe him. It seemed more like they'd sprung from the Hydra itself.

The monster was as big as a house. Not, like, my house, but a peasant house. It was all scaly, like a dragon. It already had three heads when we got there, the same kind of colour as the sea, but a bit darker, a bit dirtier. All the heads were hissing and spitting. It didn't look like fire coming out, but it had the same sort of effect, burning everything it touched.

I stepped sideways behind my uncle. He didn't notice for a bit because he was already drawing his sword and preparing to run in, but he caught me just before he did.

'Are you okay, Iolaus?'

I swallowed and nodded. I could hardly tell him I was scared, could I? Not that I was, obviously, but the Hydra was *huge*.

'I have a special job for you. They say when you cut off one head, three more grow back—'

I shrunk even further behind him.

'But we're not going to let that happen, are we?' I shook my head. He continued. 'So we're going to build a fire and you'll be in charge of keeping it going, yeah? When I cut off a head, you pass me a torch so we can burn the stump and it won't grow back.'

I nodded, a bit stronger this time. I didn't really get why we had to cut heads off at all if this was a risk – he didn't cut the lion's head off – but he sounded sure.

We built the fire. Uncle Herc ran in.

He was amazing. He moved so fast, faster than me on a chariot even, and it was like he just knew what the Hydra was thinking. Whenever it swiped at him he was already out the way. He only really got hit once and it didn't move him *at all*. A kick straight in the chest from the Hydra and he kept standing. And that was only because some little crab thing had crawled out of one of the holes and kept biting at his feet and distracting him. It had kind of cool markings, blue and green like a peacock, but I didn't really get a good look before I set it on fire.

After that I wasn't afraid. Uncle Herc was too good to die in a fight. The whole thing was over in maybe five minutes. The thing flumped to the ground, not scary anymore. All its heads were gone.

Uncle Herc kept two of them. He had me pick them up 'cause they'd rolled quite a long way. He wrapped one up to give to that king guy, Eurystheus, who he said asked him to do it as a favour, but I'm not sure I believed him. His voice went weird when he said it.

He pulled some arrows out his bag, too, and dipped them in the blood. I never saw him shoot with a bow, but he said there was something special about the snakes. Their blood would come in handy one day; he could feel it.

He gave me the other one, a prize for my bravery, he said. I don't know, a Hydra head is cool but they were kind of creepy. He made me sit with them when he did his next task – he had to catch some deer and talk to the goddess Artemis and he said he didn't want her to turn me into a dog or something – and their eyes kind of followed me.

I hid my one under my bed when I got home. I don't know what Eurystheus did with his.

Hylas II

Oddly enough, it was my awful father who brought H back into my life.

Mother had decided Father and I should bond, so we were taking breakfast *as a family*, though neither of my sisters were present.

Father remarked that old Creon was having trouble with those damned Minyans again. He said this with no small amount of glee, despite reliable sources telling me Creon was a summer *younger* than Father, who had his own perfectly unfixable issues with bandits stealing the cattle on the mountain – we rarely made it through a meal without him cursing that damned Autolycus. It was making him lose his hair at a rate that frankly terrified me for my future.

'Is that so?' I said instead. *Is that so* was a nice, safe thing to say to Father when he was ranting about richer men than he.

'Offered his daughter in marriage for it,' he said, with a not subtle cough in my direction.

'You remember Megara,' Mother said brightly, appearing in the room with an almost painfully orchestrated bowl of fruit. She'd probably been waiting at the door for this.

'Unfortunately, I'm not yet in a position to slay an army of

Minyans,' I said blandly. 'I must help Father with the bandits on our doorstep. Shall we not clean our house before tending to the dirty garments of others?' I was quite proud of that argument. Of course, I had no intention of helping Father with the bandits either, but it did save me from fighting a war alone.

H had no such compunctions. He slayed the Minyans and married Megara, though I didn't know the full extent of what he did to either of them for a long time. I can only be glad for that. Back then, I would have swallowed the knowledge and pretended to forgive him.

I've seen the Minyans, without noses or ears and with maybe three fingers per four men. It carves holes in parts of my stomach I never knew existed. What he did to Megara I can place more easily. It was fast and it was brutal, but he didn't mean to do it. He couldn't have. He's not the first man to tear his family apart, even if he was the most literal about it.

Regardless, H single-handedly destroyed the bandits and demanded twice payment for everything they'd taken from Creon. Creon kept his word, and H and Megara were married.

I knew Megara, vaguely. We met a few times as children, being around the same age and rank. When the wedding invitation arrived, it was from her. I didn't read it, Father did, but he'd already planned some trip to some other noble over the date so he threw it to Mother to reject more kindly than he could be bothered to, and I never saw the name of her betrothed.

Their first child was born nine months to the day after the wedding. Gossip travels. People questioned whether Creon's girl and that peasant – as Father affectionately called the happy couple – had waited to consummate their marriage, if H was the father at all. Until the infant came along, a daughter the size of a small buffalo.

No one talks about H's daughters. It seems so inconceivable that the manliest man to ever be a man could have begat a *girl*.

I'm no better than the rest of them, because I couldn't tell you what her name was for anything in the world. Not her name, nor her sister's.

H and Meg had a boy after that. Then another. Then twins, I think. Then one final boy.

I don't feel it's my place to comment on H and Meg's relationship, given who I am, but I bear no ill will towards Megara. I don't remember her being particularly slight, but the way they described her next to him, she must have been. By the sounds of it, her head barely grazed the top of his ribs, her waist dwarfed by H's arms. I don't know. I remember a little girl who loved birds, who trailed her arms behind her to copy their wings.

She was quiet, like she couldn't quite believe the world of responsibility she was born into. She was handed this big, shiny beast of a man like a prize, and she had no idea what to do with him. This man who was loved and hated by the gods in equal measure, who could defeat any monster you cared to throw at him, but couldn't sing for shit.

We only crossed paths once while he was married to Megara, at a wedding for some couple neither of us cared about at the time, let alone now. He was alone. Meg had been left at home, having whelped another one – I'm sorry, she's a nice girl, but the way H went around with women, I can't imagine anything but animals.

I'd say our eyes crossed in the darkness as revelry went on around us, but H has never been within spitting distance of anything so romantic. And anyway, his presence is almost oppressive. You'd choke on it if you weren't so busy breathing it in. I noticed him, but I didn't approach.

It was petty of me, and young, but I *was* young. I desperately wanted him to notice me like I noticed him, but he didn't, not until I'd circled him closer and closer and we were sitting side by side in the darkness.

'Oh,' he said, flat. Always what you want a former lover to say to you. *Oh.*

'Oh?'

'By Zeus, H, I'd almost forgotten.' He saved it. The nickname. The reminder of who we were together. 'How are you?'

I didn't answer. He hugged me. You see the Styx when H hugs you. It's ferocious.

'How are you?' I said awkwardly.

'Good.' *Sigh.* 'Good. I hate these things.'

'Weddings?'

'Parties.' *Sigh.* 'Never enough food.' He grinned, though his heart wasn't in it, and it was hard to believe when he had an entire leg of boar in his hand. Were they even serving boar? I don't remember anyone else eating boar.

'You can finish mine if you want,' I offered. 'It's just fish, but . . .'

'You need that to grow big and strong.' He smirked. I was the third tallest man there. 'In fact, you need more. Fetch us more wine!' he bellowed at the closest serving girl. The glance he took at her backside as she walked away was almost unpalatably overdramatic.

I hummed the tune to the old drinking song from the mountain. H heard and laughed, the real one that feels like the power straight from the Earthshaker and repeated the first line at me. But when curious glances followed over to us, he shied away. Old friends from his time as a goatherd didn't fit the story of Hercules.

I thought he'd leave then, crushed under the weight of his own shoulders, but he didn't.

'Drink up, or I'll summon ole Mester to lambast you.'

'Steal it from my hands more like,' I snorted. I never saw Mester pay for his own drink, though he'd buy them for others happily enough.

'Like this?' H said, snatching it with a preternatural grace that contradicted how much wine he'd had.

'More like this,' I retaliated. Soon enough, the wine was on the floor and we were bickering over who was the stronger and the smarter. (I won stronger, he smarter, since I was holding the cup when we were forced to cede under the weight of too many shaming glances.)

'Well played, sir, well played,' he conceded, and for a second I thought he was going to rest his hand over mine, but he was called away to meet someone or other. 'Talk later?'

'Later.'

It was years before we spoke again.

He had more children in that time, then, a night later, he had none. He began his penance, and he travelled so far from where we'd both grown up that when he came back he didn't realise where he was. He got hungry and pissed off the landowner, who challenged him to a duel. The landowner lost, and died.

So I met H again. I wore black and he wore blood.

'I . . . am sorry,' he said, head bowed.

'No, you're not.'

'He did challenge me first,' he said, as if that improved matters.

'You killed my father.'

'Duel.'

'Why?' I didn't shout. Shouting is unbecoming. 'Don't tell me he didn't like your face.'

H's mouth scrunched up, as if he wanted to smirk but couldn't, on account of having recently killed my father. 'I was on his land.'

'You've been on his land before,' I pointed out.

'He didn't know then.'

'How did he know now?' I was glad for my experience with him, then. If I hadn't known him, I'd have mistaken his short answers for arrogance and challenged him to a duel myself.

'I slew his cattle.'

'Zeus, H, you know the problems he has with thieves and those cattle.'

He did smirk then. Maybe citing his father's name against him amused him. 'Not anymore?'

'Sit down,' I said. 'We'll talk properly.'

I had the servants bring wine. This was going to be a long conversation. Honour is a funny thing. Because my father challenged H, and H won, he was technically an honoured guest. By the rules of good hosting – a much bigger deal than the name implies, I assure you – I was bound to treat him well, to honour him for his victory, and to grant him any boon he wished.

That's not why I treated him well. I hated my father. The world felt a better place without him in it.

'What do you want?' I asked, more bluntly than I would have with anyone else. 'As your prize for victory. He has nice horses. They keep going like none I've ever seen, even if they don't look flashy. Please don't take my sisters. They're Mother's pride and joy.' The loss of my father she'd cope with just fine, but losing the girls would kill her.

'You.'

'Me?'

'You.'

'But I'm no good at anything.' This wasn't self-pity. My talents lay not in fighting but in neat tallies of numbers and placating angry ambassadors.

'Train. I'll come back when I need you.'

That was so delightfully vague I half-expected not to see him until my deathbed, grandchildren tugging at his armour, his face still impossibly young. I know, truly, he aged like everyone else, but he was never meant to be an old man.

I should have clarified when he'd come back to me, but chasing him for numbers would never work. I reached a hand out.

'Eat with me.' Things escalated. We woke up in bed. Spend a week with my father before you judge me. 'I heard you got married,' I said, twining my toes around his, marvelling at the smoothness of them.

'She died.'

'Raising the kids alone?'

'They died too.' H was a silent man, but it deepened, sucking into him from any corner of the room. I let him take three deep breaths.

'Why is there a fuck-off lion skin on my floor?'

That he was happy to talk about, his adventures – or just the one adventure, back then, fresh from his first labour – and his awful cousin Eurystheus. It didn't take a genius to work out why he was doing what he was doing, or to realise I shouldn't mention it.

He stayed a week. I kept him from Mother and my sisters, none of whom were quite so forgiving as me, though Mother did pass me a ring of hers to give him. As thanks, she said.

I trained for him, bow and arrow, mostly. I remembered it being his worst weapon. I thought, optimistically, maybe one day

I'd save his life. I attended to the rites of my father, mourned him properly, and searched for a part of me that was sorry he was gone.

Two years later, H came back to me. He looked the same, covered in dust and blood and a million and one other things that would never come out of his clothes. I didn't bother with hello.

'Is that a fuck-off boar in my vestibule?' I asked.

He grinned. I could see the tooth I'd chipped. 'Pack your things.'

Over the course of our friendship, that's the phrase he said most often: *pack your things, we have places to be; pack your things, we have monsters to catch; pack your things, her husband walked in.*

My mother threw a banquet. Since Father died, she was always looking for an excuse for a banquet. On this occasion, she wanted to pretend I was a hero too, not just beholden to one. She rested a hand on my shoulder.

'I'm proud of you, son, going out there, making a name for yourself.'

'That's not how—'

'Really proud of you.' She might not have let me contradict her about the nature of my work or the motives of my sponsor, but she didn't mention Dad either. I was glad for that, glad for not being compared to him, or to the son he thought I should have been.

'We should away,' H said, saving us further awkwardness. 'The boar—' He didn't need to finish his sentence. He scarcely did, with me. The boar was still alive, wrapped in some net. It flailed mostly, but occasionally loudly took a shit. It stunk to high heavens. I joked that, through the clouds, you could see almighty Zeus recoiling from the smell.

'He does not recoil,' H said stiffly. 'It would not be his way.' We didn't speak of our fathers again.

I said my goodbyes to Mother and my sisters, told them I'd come home soon, and that was that. We were off. I was a hero.

This hero business involved an awful lot of walking. We walked out of the city and up the mountain and over the mountain and down the mountain again. It didn't matter that these first roads were familiar to me, because we were heroes. It made every road longer, stretching them into infinity.

I thought it'd be like when we were younger and we'd pitch camp in the wilderness, travelling only as ourselves. Instead we stayed in other people's houses, a different one every night. H bowed and flattered and flirted, all of it awkward, though that proved irrelevant. The glamour of who he was burned through any of his true personality. I hadn't realised penance for murder involved so much politics.

I'm not a fool, and I'm not blind. I saw the food prepared for him, the smiles and the thanks, even uncomfortable offers to feed the boar. I saw the sidelong looks as he ordered for another jug of wine, as they ushered him into their beds. I saw children hastily swept out of rooms and out of view. I never told him, though. What would be the point of hurting him?

I missed home more than I can say.

'Why do you cry?' H asked. I was taken by some small thing, the sounds of birds chirping in a garden that looked so much like my mother's, but sounded different. How dare they sound different!

'I miss home.'

'Why?' he asked. He stared so intensely his eyes seemed a different colour. They were greener, somehow, like the clouds behind them were gone. As I stalled, he spoke again. 'There's a whole world out there. Your home will be waiting at the end of it, H.

Enjoy the rest of the world with me, before home claims you.'
If I blushed at that, it's none of your business. He wasn't prone
to great romantic gestures, but it was restful to be beside him.

'You think?'

H sighed. 'How do you feel about being a sailor?'

'Why?'

'There's a whole world, H.' He smiled, though there was more
to it than that. He made no secret that Amphitryon didn't care
to have him in the house, even less of one that he'd never again
be welcome in Thebes.

I came to know the latter particularly well, as we walked past
on our journey. He took a tremendously uncomfortable loop
around the city, while I went in to buy supplies.

I went to Megara's mausoleum, a testament to what I stole
from her.

I didn't go to honour the dead. I sat on the steps and pressed
my face to the cold marble and I apologised. I said sorry to this
dead woman, to this woman I would've unthinkingly called my
friend, because I still loved him. Hera influenced him, but it was
still H who killed her, *and I loved him anyway.*

I traced her name with my finger on the stone. I didn't feel
a reassuring warmth around me, or her voice in my head. I'd done
what I could and it had to be enough.

'But I am sorry,' I said finally. I hefted my bag across my
shoulder and walked away.

Jason I

I didn't exactly interview for my Argonauts – the people who'd sail with me on my quest for the Golden Fleece, so I could reclaim my throne – but that doesn't mean I wasn't selective. Every man – and woman, I should say, lest Atalanta hit me – on that ship had some talent that outstripped the rest of the world. There was Argus, of course, who built and gave his name to the finest ship ever known. His talents were in engineering and he exuded an air of confidence that was frankly calming to be around.

Atalanta sprinted faster than a tiger, a fact I can confirm thanks to one night featuring too much wine and a footrace. She was quietly competent when she wasn't busy slapping me. When I was married, my wife would lie in bed and stroke the wrinkles around my eyes, laughingly call them my Atalanta lines.

Attie was funny, in a caustic way, though I once heard one of the men refer to her glances as testicle-withering, so I'm not sure why men were lining up to marry her when she returned home. She openly demonstrated her disgust at the concept of wifehood – my patron, Hera, wasn't a fan of Attie – but I do pity the man who won her hand, especially since he used trickery to do so.

Look, my crew was fifty strong and were I to give all of them appraisal we'd be here a long time. Most of them were asked specifically to come along, either through my own acquaintances or by Hera. I know for a fact neither of us invited Hercules.

I knew of him before he showed up and his troubles with Hera. Unlike him, I didn't have an immortal parent to fall back on. The closest of the immortals in my family tree was Hermes: four generations back, and via a thief. I was fortunate to have Hera's support.

After my uncle stole my throne, I was raised in the wilderness, where one day I came across an old woman struggling to cross a river. I volunteered to carry her across – I was raised in the wilderness, not by wolves – and I lost one of my shoes in the process. She revealed herself as Hera, and so she became my patron.

I'm not really sure why she chose to test me like that, but I do know a single shoe for Hera's patronage is the best trade I ever made.

Her help – aside from gifting me the finest sandals I'd ever seen – was subtle. She didn't imbue me with incredible strength, or the ability to fly, or to walk on water – all tricks various members of my crew had been given by their parents – but she was always there. The winds supporting us were fair, our receptions warm. She brought birds and fish near the ship for easy hunting, and she kept the men from fighting too much, that little sense of family doing wonders to hold us together.

More than that, she was there for *me*. When it was all

too much and everyone was shouting different ideas about where we should go and what we should do, I could close my eyes and feel her around me, the closest I've ever come to unconditional love.

When people started calling me *'Amechanos'* – helpless – she reminded me: *Jason, stand tall. You are my king.* There were days when only that reminder kept me going – Attie making a joke of it and calling me Amy could go either way.

I know exactly how much she helped me. My life ended shortly after I crossed Hera.

So when Hercules, her sworn enemy, boarded the ship without so much as a by-the-by, I couldn't help but think the journey was cursed. I think that still, though I won't blame Hera for my wife's actions.

If I could only have one of them, I would've chosen his companion, Hylas. He was a beautiful young man, which is always useful. More than that, he was competent with a bow and had an easy-going manner. In retrospect, were I to build another large group of men to share a small boat – not to disrespect Argus' wonderful work, lest *he* slap me – I'd select them based on that, not the tales told of their exploits.

Hercules' very presence was a boost in morale, though. He could row the boat alone. As a sailor, he was fine. He didn't stumble on deck unless the waves were particularly large, and he wasn't prone to sickness, unlike a number of the men who swore to me they were seasoned seamen. Looking at you, Eribotes.

(Though I'll concede he suffered additionally for being the only half-useful physician on the ship and unable to attend to himself.)

As a subordinate crewmate, I'd count Hercules as just about adequate. He could do the work of four dozen men, when he felt so inclined, but he ate that much too. He didn't entirely understand the trip wasn't about him. But I knew that before we set sail.

A letter was delivered to me in an irritated hand.

I hear the oaf has run off to join your 'adventure'. He is a slave, bound to me, for crimes against his wife and children alike. I've never met an excuse for a human so insolent and pointless. The last I saw him, he released a live boar in my palace. You're welcome to him. If you should encounter danger, throw him bodily in its path. Nothing I've tried thus far has stuck.

Eurystheus, King of Tiryns

However I felt about him, that guaranteed Hercules his place, and his presence did ensure a warm welcome wherever we touched down, whether through gratitude or fear from his prior deeds. We scarcely had to land for servants to be running to us with pitchers of wine.

Our first stops were uneventful. This seemed to irritate him. On the third stop he even asked the local king if anything needed doing.

'The roof's falling down round the back, but I don't suppose that interests you lads,' the king offered with a shrug. Forgive me, but I've forgotten his name; the trip illustrated the sheer quantity of kings in Greece. It was a wonder we had any peasants at all.

'Is it under attack by wild animals? Endlessly ravaged by missives from angry gods?' Hercules asked.

'Nah. It's just the wind on these long nights, isn't it? I'd ask my son but he's off courting some woman who won't give him the time of day.' Atalanta, as it turned out. He was still waiting for her when she returned. She described him as a backwater moron with an accent so pompous you'd have to rip out his teeth to understand him.

Hercules lost the glint in his eye and went back to his eating. Calais snuck out after dinner and did a dedication to his father – god of the north wind – which did the trick.

Our next stop, Hercules took one look around and grinned like a pig in shit. Hylas, on the other hand, grew miserable. The island was called Lemnos and there were no men on it, not even a baby. Not even a priest.

There were no men, because their wives had killed them.

When we landed, I got off first, to investigate. There was a woman already waiting on the beach – we were many things as a travelling group, but quiet was not among them – her name was Hypsipyle. She was beautiful and formidable and she assured me she was too young to have had anything to do with the husband-killing.

'The women were cursed by Aphrodite to smell atrocious,' she said plainly. 'It was some combination of rotting fish and perfume, though I think the latter was probably an effort to cover the former.'

'Did it work?' I asked. Call it research. You never know what situations the gods will throw you in. They all smelled fine to me, certainly better than the boat.

'Of course not. You got a headache just walking past.' Hypsipyle grimaced. 'So all the men found new lovers.'

'Whose stench didn't induce the desire to vomit?' I joked. She raised an eyebrow smoothly at me. What it must be to be so sure of yourself.

'Their presence did induce the desire to murder, though. Would you like to see the pit where they burned the shrouds?'

It was a big pit. The women had, unfairly, I feel, murdered not only their husbands but also their fathers and children.

'Could Aphrodite not be appeased?' I asked, as gently as possible.

'You know nothing of women.' I don't deny it, but it wasn't an answer. I stayed quiet as we walked back to the ship.

'Where have my men gone?' I asked. I expected them to be partying, enjoying solid ground beneath their feet, but all was quiet. The wind billowed gently against downed sails.

'There weren't any men on the island,' Hypsipyle said slowly, as though I were an idiot. 'I imagine they're in bedrooms changing that.'

'I see.' I heard a noise, the scuffing of a foot against sand, maybe. 'Hello?'

Hylas appeared from behind the bow, looking vaguely smug.

'Jason,' he said formally. Even when everyone was drinking and laughing, he was formal. 'H and I stayed to guard the ship.'

'Where's Atalanta?' She'd told me in no uncertain terms that if I called her Attie in front of people she'd rip my testicles from my body and feed them to the listener.

'Gone for a run.'

'And Hercules?' They were normally inseparable.

'Getting something off the boat.' Eating all the food on the boat, more likely, but the women were more than happy to stock us up afterwards. An exchange for services rendered, they said.

'Keep it up, then,' I said and, since no one was around to judge me, I followed my guide to her waiting bed. I expected something small, ramshackle without someone to hold the home together. What I found was the largest room in the palace.

I looked at her.

'Didn't I mention? I'm the queen here.'

We spent four days and nights there, being fed and entertained to our hearts' content. It would've been easy to start a life there too, but no one becomes a hero for *easy*.

On the fourth day, Hercules entered the city. Starting at the outer reaches he burst into bedrooms and ordered the crew back to the ship. If they didn't leave immediately, he grabbed them by their ears and dragged them back, much to the amusement of the women of Lemnos and Attie, who sat on deck and laughed at their shamefaced expressions. He came for me last. The queen and I were lying in bed. I was feeding her honey.

'It's leaving time,' Hercules boomed with neither shame nor volume control.

'I'm rather in the middle of something.'

'It's leaving time,' he said again. A small movement rippled through his body, starting with his shoulders and ending with a big old vein on his forehead popping out. I shivered. It was leaving time.

I knelt in front of Hypsipyle and kissed the largest ring on her hand. 'Thank you for your hospitality, my queen. Neither I nor my men will forget it.'

'The sons you've given us will serve as wonderful recompense.' She grinned. 'Fair winds, my sailor.'

Those were my first children, conceived as the sun set on our first day in Lemnos. She called them Euneus and Deipylus. With the best of both of us, I thought, they'd run the world. These days, Euneus is the King of Lemnos, which will do for now.

Our next stop was known as Bear Island, due to its shape and not, as the crew was hoping, a particular proclivity for the ursine. They wanted adventure, and slaying an island full of bears would have delivered that. A king who pleasantly welcomed us – once we assured him we didn't want to remove him from his throne – didn't.

All things considered, we had remarkably few problems with kings thinking we were after their thrones. We were, after all, a troop of the greatest fighters and thinkers in Greece. Amazingly, when kings *did* take offence to our presence, they thought they could take us down in the blink of an eye.

Regardless, King Cyzicus – which, trust me, isn't an easy name to keep straight at the best of times, let alone when you're straight off the boat and you've had a couple of drinks – welcomed us in. Invited us to dinner. He had another *esteemed guest* we should meet.

Her name was Laonome. She introduced herself with a delicate hand and eyelashes that batted themselves. Had we not so recently been in Lemnos, most of my Argonauts would have swooned. As it was, a mere dozen of them caught her eyes and refused to let them go.

It wasn't that she was particularly beautiful. She radiated calm and awe in equal parts. She knew how to be around heroes.

When Hercules entered the room there was a flash of jewellery and linen as she sped into his arms. He lifted her clear above his head. *Of course she favours him.*

'Brother.'

'Sister.'

His muscles tensed as they embraced, but his face shone.

'What are you doing here?' they said at the same time. I never had siblings: is that what it's like?

'Mother. Nagging,' Laonome said flatly, her eyes losing the sparkle she had when talking to the rest of my men. 'We needed a break from each other. You?'

'You know,' he said, waving his hands in the general direction of themselves, an uncomfortable movement in itself. I'm unsure why he tried to hide. His penance for killing his family was known not only among my Argonauts, but throughout Greece as well. He still got more warm welcomes than cold. Say what you will about what he did, he saved more lives than he ended, which is true of few people, and seems the only proper way to repent. He shrugged and waved me over. 'This is Jason, our captain.'

The sparkle returned. If you avoided her gaze you'd notice a flat nose, eyes set a little too far apart. I made sure to focus on those. I didn't want a repeat of Lemnos.

'I've heard of you.' She smiled at me, almost too demurely, now. 'May I see your ship? I've always wanted to see the greatest ship in Greece.'

Her eyes are far apart, I told myself. Her nose is flat. Her eyes are far apart. Her nose is flat.

'Well, that's really Argus' work. Why don't I introduce you to him?'

Hercules snorted, so I led him to King Cyzicus, who must have been feeling neglected by all this attention going to his guest. They got on well. When Hercules left to relieve himself, the king leaned over to me. 'He's not what I expected.'

'Oh?' I asked.

'His advice about the goats is second to none. I'll have to pass it on.' With so many of us on the ship, we had epithets, to keep the names straight. Despite Hercules being the only person on board – other than myself and Argus – who didn't need one, Hylas had drunkenly called him *the goat whisperer* one night and it stuck. Neither of them would tell us why, so it remained the subject of long debate and conspiracy.

'I see.'

'Oh, by the way, Jason? I should mention—'

'I have brought more wine,' Hercules rumbled. I kept an eye on how much he drank, an honour not solely reserved for him. On one of the earlier islands, Talaus had imbibed too much, got lost, and pissed directly onto a sleeping shepherd. I'm sure you can imagine his epithet. 'Did I tell you about the Minyans' wine? Vile stuff, stewed from—'

To hear Hercules tell it, it was stewed from the blood of their enemies and bore a scent worse than the women of Lemnos. Regardless, I didn't hear what the king was going to tell me.

We left the next morning, well fed and hungover. Maybe that's why the wind caught us wrong. Barely a mile from the island, we spun out and it took us right back. Honestly, what's the point of having several children of the wind on your ship if it can still blindside you?

The small benefit of this was that it allowed me to catch, and remove, Laonome. She'd become infatuated with one of my men, she claimed. Even she couldn't keep straight which of them it was – either Euphemus or Polyphemus. I don't believe in stowaways and, if it was Euphemus, the bastard could walk on water, so he could carry her wherever they wanted.

When we were spun back by the wind, the guards thought

we were attackers and defended themselves. He was a good host, King Cyzicus, and I wouldn't have chosen to harm him. Under those conditions, though, there was nothing for us to do but fight back. They didn't stand a chance.

Eventually, Attie made it through to the king and he called off the attack, though not before three dozen of his people were dead.

We helped perform the funeral rites before we left, and we cut our hair in penance.

Well, most of us did. Euphemus, who Laonome had decided was her beloved, chose to stay on the island and marry her – I was sorry to lose him, but better that than a stowaway or, worse, a child on my ship. By rebuilding what was destroyed, he saved his hair.

The other, bizarrely, was Hylas, who I hadn't marked down as particularly besieged by vanity, but so it goes. Hercules claimed Hylas' powers lay in his hair. The less charitable men on the *Argo* questioned *what powers*? But the hair stayed.

The men were irritated. I didn't let them show it, we couldn't be seen bickering like children. So they expressed their displeasure in more subtle ways, giving Hylas the worst shifts of watch – they all knew how to rig a draw – and making him run inglorious errands. It was unsurprising when we reached the island of Pegae and they sent him to fetch the water.

He didn't come back.

For hours we tried to calm an angry Hercules. He paced the ship trying to hit things; Attie and I ran interference so he couldn't. I feared he'd snap the mast in half.

'I must retrieve him,' he snapped.

'He hasn't been long gone,' I pointed out, using my reasonable voice. On a boat with forty-nine angry men, I used my reasonable voice often. 'He may return still.'

You develop a certain sense about these things when you go on as many adventures as Hercules and I did. My men nodded along as I said it was fine, of course he'd come back, he was only fetching water. But I knew, as Hercules did, something was wrong. You feel the spite in the air, prickling against your skin.

'I must go,' he said.

I dropped my voice to a whisper. 'Consider yourself, Hercules. If you go running after him when he is capable, what will the men think? What of his pride?'

'He'd rather his life than his pride.' Hercules spoke with certainty. Hylas was probably alone of the Argonauts for thinking such a thing.

'Give him more time.'

'No.'

That was the last word Hercules spoke on the *Argo*. I sent men to look for them. They told me they'd seen Hercules frantically shouting Hylas' name, again and again. When they walked up to him, they said, his eyes scarcely showed recognition. All he said was: 'I'm not leaving without him.'

We pulled anchor the next day without either of them. I never saw them again.

What? You want me to invent some fantastic reason Hercules left my ship? Shine him up or dust him down? To me he was only a comrade, and a frustrating one at that. He drank too much and ate more than his share. He farted in his sleep so potently we prayed for winds to cleanse us. It remained a joke to shove people's faces into the sails near where he slept.

He rowed better and with more heart than anyone else. He was willing to die for any one of us. He didn't choose the ship for glory, he surely had enough of that already, and he didn't cheat at cards, a recommendation I can only afford to him, though he did at dice, so he was no paragon. When I speak of Hercules, I don't speak of the hero or of the slayer of beasts. I speak of a man who served on a ship to get out of the rest of the trouble he was in and that, my friend, is a tradition older than time itself.

Laonome I

I didn't run away from home to spite my mother, no matter what she tells you.

No one was allowed to have fun at home, not ever. Drinking was banned and I couldn't talk to boys at all because *you know what can happen*, which was a stupid thing to say. The boy most famous for hurting the girls who talked to him was my brother, *the* Hercules, whom I had to have in my life either way and is completely unmarriageable for a whole plethora of reasons.

(Another, smaller reason I ran away was to get away from my friends. I love them, but they wouldn't stop telling me what a dish Herc is. Like, he's not hideous or anything but he's pretty squat and he's got a chipped tooth *and he's my brother.*)

But whatever, it's not all about him. Do you hear me, Mum? It's not always about him. I'm the youngest of three children. Three! So why did I spend the first sixteen years of my life being called, almost exclusively, Herc's sister?

Then when my darling mother did call me by my own name, she'd stretch it right out into four syllables, Lay-oh-no-mi, with a kind of whine to it, like I'd done something wrong.

She was old when I was born. Not super old, not gossip-worthy or anything. But my brothers are like fourteen years older than me. I imagine that's how long it took her to forget having a *three-day* labour with the first two. In contrast, I'm a freaking dream. Her being older meant I was always going to get away with less – not surprising considering the shit Herc did.

Herc had his accident with his music teacher, I was born, and Dad sent him away. Then Herc was all upset and Iph got married because *he* was allowed to talk to people and I kind of got lost in the shuffle.

So I ran away. It makes more sense when I say it like that, doesn't it? Rather than when Mum harps on about my easy life and forgets I was barely allowed outside.

Obviously other stuff happened between the being born and the running away, most of it not very exciting. I went to Meg's funeral, the only one in our family who did. She liked me.

I liked Thebes. No one remembered who I was there. Otherwise I would've been chased right out again.

It took me a long time to forgive Herc, which is stupid. He can't have meant to do it. Not my brother who used to swing me so high above his head it felt like I could see Zeus himself. Not my brother who said so solemnly and seriously that if anyone dared to hurt me he'd hoist them by their arse and cart them to Hades the long way. Not my brother.

There should have been nothing to forgive, but in the end it felt like there was.

Meg was dead and we were barred from Thebes so I picked myself up and planned my escape. I told Iph, because I needed to tell someone, the secret burning a hole through my chest. He disapproved, but he was so busy dealing with his son he didn't have time for me either. The time came, and I did something I'm not proud of.

I bribed my nephew.

'Hey, Iolaus,' I said. He squinted at me, suspicious. Got those eyebrows from our side of the family, I'll tell you. Automedusa has lovely eyebrows, slender hands too. He got those off her, which was nice. The rest of us look like we'd be best off wrestling boars.

'What?'

'You send letters to Herc, right?'

'Sometimes,' he said, still suspicious, or just confused why I'd ask him anything. He was, after all, thirteen. I'm only a year older, but that always felt like the world.

'Where's a happening place right now?'

'There's some people getting a boat together,' he said. He even had a swagger when he said it, like he was already some mighty hero when all he'd done was stand at the back and hold the torches.

He was talking about the Argonauts, though he wouldn't tell me more. But, whatever, I'm the sister to heroes after all and no shrinking flower myself, so I got out a map and listened to the rumours and made the executive decision not to go to Colchis. Colchis was a stupid place to go. Full of war and sheep, my two least favourite things in the world. (Though my brother made a real go of convincing me goats are the true enemy.)

I packed a bag and left a letter for Mum. I sailed somewhere they'd undoubtedly have to stop for supplies and ingratiated myself with the local court until they invited me to stay. When my brother walked in I genuinely thought he was going to piss himself, he was so worried I'd embarrass him. Stupid worry, that – I've been trained in courtly manners since forever.

Though I couldn't wait to see his face when he found me on the boat.

Hylas III

My encounter with Eurystheus was brief and unpleasant. He called me boy and smelled both bizarrely and unpleasantly of untreated clay. We dropped off the boar, turned around, and left. At least we freed ourselves of the smell; the final few days, we'd walked in a cloud of flies.

I don't know how H found out about Jason's mission. I can only assume he heard whispers outside Thebes while I cried over his wife. When we arrived at the right port, he walked directly to the captain, and I thanked the gods that a boat meant less walking.

'I am Hercules, and this is my companion, Hylas,' he said, despite the fact Jason was deeply in conversation with the builder.

'Oh I know who you are,' Jason said, not taking his eyes off the ship. I'd never seen anyone so unruffled at meeting H. But then, Jason was a hero too. He was a head taller than H and more stately somehow, like he'd been born to be a king. Technically he had, but someone else was holding his throne at ransom, hence the adventure. The impostor-king promised to trade his throne for the Golden Fleece, which seemed unlikely to end well.

'We'll be serving aboard your ship,' H said, bowing. H was always awkward when he bowed, but with Jason, when you could feel the competition pumping between them, he looked ridiculous.

'Is that so?' Jason said, and, bizarrely, it was me he cast an appraising look. 'Do you promise to keep him under control?'

'I'll do my best?' I said.

'I'm holding you personally responsible for any shenanigans.'

'And damage to the ship!' the builder added vehemently. I was lucky to be loved fiercely, by friends and by family, and by H, but no one will ever love me with the force Argus loved that ship. I saw him scold people for putting their feet up on the benches, and they listened. Big, burly sailors listened because Argus carried a hammer and, given the majesty of our vessel, clearly knew how to use it.

'And damage to the ship,' Jason said sternly, though it might have been a joke. There were people – Atalanta, Argus – who could always tell, who could read the flatness of his eyes and wind him up the right way and make him laugh, but I couldn't, so he stayed stern and I stayed cowed.

We rounded the crew up to fifty. H rowed. He rowed and he rowed and he rowed.

We slept on deck, both of us crammed under the lion's skin and, for the first time, it felt like an adventure. We landed on Lemnos.

I didn't let H go. It was partly jealousy, mostly thinking of Jason's threat. An island full of murderous women seemed like the perfect set-up for my beautiful idiot to cause havoc. So the two of us sat on the sand as the rest of the men had the time of their lives. We may have indulged in some of that also, but mostly we talked.

'How are you finding it?' H asked after a while.

'Feel bad for stealing me away from my easy life?' I joked. I always joked when he asked these things. The journey was going smoothly, but every time the boat approached a storm I was afraid. I didn't want to die.

'Would you choose that?' he asked, more abruptly this time. 'An easy life over a glorious one?'

'Of course I would,' I said, and that was stupid, to say it with so much force, because H didn't ask out of whimsy. He asked because he had to make these choices every day. Did you know a sea nymph appeared to him one night on the boat and promised her daughter in marriage if he could help her find something? Or that she threatened him when he said no?

'I didn't.'

'That's a choice too, that's *yours*,' I said gently, trying to repair my earlier duff-up.

'It was stupid.'

'You love being a hero,' I tried again.

'But imagine, we could have stayed at your palace, we could have—' He cut himself off. 'Is that Jason?' It was. He was with the Queen of Lemnos. She had the same stately bearings he did, a perfect matched pair.

We literally had to wrestle him off her and back to the boat. None of the men wanted to leave the warm embraces they'd found themselves in, but H wasn't going to abandon his mission. They came back. You don't argue with H.

We sailed. We kept sailing and sailing. There was a misunderstanding and we fought and people died. The other men cut their hair to atone, but H wouldn't let me. He liked twirling my curls in his fingers, liked touching something soft that he wasn't going to break. He looked so young when he did it, I let him throw that foolish lie at Jason. *His power comes from his hair, honest.*

I bore the angry looks I got from the rest of the men for escaping that penance, and I was proud to do so. I so rarely managed to make him happy, but that did.

That's why they sent me to get water, when we next landed. They never sent me to do anything. I was too soft and weak and royal. But I kind of deserved it so I didn't complain as I hefted the bucket and went on my way.

I'd finally got the knack of getting off the ship smoothly. What? I grew up on a mountain; this whole seafaring life was new to me. But I swung myself off with a gentle splash.

'You can do better than that,' H shouted from the deck.

'The water barely moved,' I said with mock-affront.

'Not like that,' he said, miming how he'd hit the water like a rock and the tidal wave that would ensue. I laughed.

'I—' I started. I could genuinely feel the weight of the other men's glares on me from the deck. There were fifty people on that boat; privacy wasn't really an option. 'I'll be back soon. With lots of water,' I added, like that would help with the others.

'What, you got another bucket hiding in that pretty hair of yours?' Talaus mocked. I ignored it and went on my way. Nothing good would come of it.

H thought differently. A splash erupted behind me. I turned, managing to get hit full in the face by the resulting wave. He'd pushed Talaus off the boat.

'That's what we're looking for,' H called down to me cheerfully.

Talaus glared at him but Herc didn't have to give a shit. He knew his worth.

'I'll try harder next time.'

So I stepped onto the island. From the moment my foot touched the ground, the proper ground, I heard singing. It was a gentle lilting thing at first, tickling at the corner of my hearing, asking if I wanted to follow it. It sounded like Mother, like my sisters, like the birds from *our* garden.

Of course I wanted to follow it.

A few more steps and I couldn't even *think* because I was sprinting so fast for it. It got louder, through a whisper and a hymn all the way to a crescendo, a battle march. Enchanting and intoxicating voices were weaving around me, promising I was safe.

I could have been on the most beautiful island in the world, but all I ever saw was the water. Sight and touch and taste were left on the shore, because I didn't need them anymore. All I needed was this. And I needed it now.

When I reached the pool the voices grabbed me, pulled me into them. I dove straight in. Fully clothed, sandals on. I couldn't see them – whoever these beautiful singers were – I didn't need to. I was exactly where I was supposed to be. Surrounded by their voices, I was home.

It was H who shattered the bubble. It was always going to be. He was shouting for me, screaming at the people who tried to drag him away. *I'm not leaving without him*, over and over again. *I'm not leaving without him.*

But I was already gone.

Iphicles II

My wife was understandably pissed.

'You slept with another woman.' There was no denying that fact. My other son had just shown up at our doorstep and announced it. Not in those words, but his very existence was proof enough. I tried to collect myself, but it wasn't exactly how I'd been expecting my Tuesday to go, so I didn't do a great job at it. 'More than one,' Automedusa concluded.

I really did not do a great job at it.

'Only two,' I said.

'Only,' she shouted. It was loud enough and high enough it felt like the foundation of the house would crack around it. A good enough metaphor for what was going on, really.

I didn't say everyone else was doing it. I didn't say I was drunk. I *definitely* didn't tell her it happened when I'd gone to visit my brother, when he was married and, obviously, so was I, or that I'd never known a child came out of it – please, gods, let it be only one child that came out of it. It was easy and fun, and for the first time since we were *twelve* I could talk to my brother again.

It was hard, when mentioning my father made Herc's eyebrows crumple in on themselves, but I missed him.

Pyrrha, *the woman*, had been spending the night with friends. She was smiling and relaxed and she didn't have a small Iolaus waiting to spit on her at the first opportunity. (I love our son, but why always with the spitting?) She moved away from Thebes not long after that night.

I didn't tell my wife any of that, either, not even her name. Megara's sister had kept our secret long enough – I wasn't going to out her now.

I said, 'I have to do right by him.'

By the look on Automedusa's face, that wasn't better than any of the other options.

'Him?' The screeching remained very present in her voice. He was at that moment sitting in the next room, eating bread and, if he was anything like the rest of the family, eavesdropping for all he was worth. 'What about us?'

'His mother died, dear.'

'You've been keeping up with her, then?'

'No, it was a one-time thing,' I protested. It wasn't hard to avoid conversation about Pyrrha. Herc tends to forget people when they're not in his eyeline. 'It didn't mean anything.'

'So we're worth less than nothing to you? We can be thrown away for some night with a woman who meant nothing to you?'

I had no defence. I still have no defence. I'm an adult with full faculties and I made a decision – two decisions – that were undeniably wrong and I had to take ownership of that. But my wife wasn't the only person who was hurting and for all that I loved her – I loved her so much – she was an adult and Pyrrhus was only twelve. He needed me more.

'I won't keep him here,' I told her.

'So you're abandoning us?'

'Please, gods, no. I'll sort something out. Honey, please tell me I can come back.'

'I don't know.'

'What?' I said. So much for all those rhetoric lessons.

'It's not fair of you to put all this on me right now. How am I meant to know what I want?'

That's kind of how I felt the night I slept with Pyrrha, but saying that didn't seem like it would help.

'Okay. I'll take him, give you some time, and then we can talk?'

'What are you going to do?'

'Herc—'

'Your brother,' she said with a disdain she reserved for nothing else in this world.

'—Is still my brother. And he's missing. We'll go find him.'

'Maybe he's dead,' she said. It was not one of our finer days.

'We'd know.' That was a fact, as undeniable as Pyrrhus' existence. 'I'll talk to Iolaus.' *Our* son, who was sitting in a different room from *my* son, drinking wine he thought we didn't know about and, I was sure, eavesdropping for all he was worth.

When I went to his door, though, I found it was more than that. He had a bag beside him, fully packed, along with a sword I genuinely hadn't known about. Good timing on his part. Normally we'd have to have a talk about that kind of thing but I didn't really have a leg to stand on at that point.

'When do we head out?'

'Pyrrhus and I will go this evening, but you're staying with your mother.'

'What? No I'm not. I can help. I helped with the Hydra, didn't

I?' That fucking Hydra. I never would've let him go if I'd known he'd keep bringing it up. 'And I want to help find Uncle Herc. We're friends.' There was a whole separate conversation we needed to have about how maybe your adult uncle shouldn't be your best friend.

'Iolaus, listen to me,' I said stupidly. There was no faster recipe for him to tune out. 'You need to stay here with your mother. I'll find Herc. This will be a very boring trip, and if I find you've followed us, I'll personally take the wheels off your chariot and make you learn poetry instead.'

He made an evaluating face, like maybe it would still be worth it.

'Not war poetry. Poetry about flowers.'

'What's he got that I haven't?' Iolaus said. 'You've never taken me on a trip.' That's because I didn't go on any trips. I stayed home and ran for local government.

'We'll go on one when I'm back, yeah? Something fun. Maybe we can find some chariot races to enter.' That was a pretty big concession. He'd been begging for years and we'd said no on account of not wanting him to die in the giant ball of flames he'd somehow create.

'I don't want to go on your stupid pity trip. I have better things to do. You have fun with your new son,' he spat. I don't mean that metaphorically. For all our efforts at respectability, we'd raised a floor-spitter.

'I love you,' I said.

'Whatever.' He kicked the door open. If nothing else, I've learned to give up on the fights I'm not going to win, so I went and got Pyrrhus, who was also waiting with a packed bag, but that made more sense, since he'd arrived with a packed bag and it'd been pretty clear from the outset that he wasn't staying here.

'You're not mad at me, are you?' I asked, maybe the third sentence I'd ever addressed to him. *Who are you? Why are you at my door?* He'd answered honestly, and in front of my wife, so I'd stopped asking questions.

'I'm a bit mad at you.'

'What did I do to *you?*'

'You slept with my mother.'

'Right. Do you mind waiting outside a moment?'

'Whatever.'

I went to where my wife sat by the hearth without anything planned to say to her. This wasn't a situation words can get you out of. But I had to say something, because you never know what might happen.

'I'm still pissed,' she said. And then she wrapped her arms around me, making me feel safe and warm like no one else could. 'But you never know. You stay safe so I can beat the shit out of you.' And my brother thought she was uptight. Though I guess everyone is uptight in comparison to Herc.

'I love you.'

She didn't say it back, but I didn't expect her to. I headed out and started getting to know my other son. He was twelve, and he liked reading better than he liked fighting, though he was good enough at both.

'And look, I can do this.' He stuck his tongue out at me, all rolled up like a tube. 'Mum couldn't, and apparently it runs in families. Can you do it?'

'I can't say I ever tried.'

'Well, try now.'

I did and I could and it ended up being kind of our thing. When he was bored or trying to distract me he'd look over and roll up his tongue and I'd have to do it back to him. I wondered if Iolaus could do it too, and if I should be asking kids about that and not which of their lessons they liked the most.

But that was dangerous territory, so I tried to avoid thinking about it. There was a lot of dangerous territory.

'Is he okay?' Pyrrhus asked. 'Your brother?'

'That's what we're going to find out.'

'No, I mean, he was married to Mum's sister, right? Mum didn't talk about her family, but people said things . . .'

I turned him round to face me, crouching just enough that we'd be eye to eye. 'Herc has never hurt anyone on purpose, you understand? You're safe with him.'

He nodded, like that explained everything. 'How are we going to find him? Are we going to ask the gods? Or is it a twin thing where you just know where he is all the time? You guys are twins, right?'

'We are,' I said. 'But for how we're going to find him, well, I have to have some secrets.' It wasn't a secret, it was just boring, and it had been a really long time since I'd had a son look at me like I was cool. I knew where the Argonauts had been going, which islands they were most likely to stop at, and once we got there I followed the very Herculean smell of meat and misery.

My brother lay across the rocks, like some beached sea creature rotting in the sun. His beard was long and bizarrely grey, given we were only just past thirty. His skin was so puckered and pitted I might have missed him in the sand, and he was thin. In all the years, in all the bullshit my brother ended up in, he'd never been *thin* before. If you'd told me he had ribs I'm not sure I would have believed you, but you could count them through his back.

'That's him?' Pyrrhus said, distinctly unimpressed in the way only children can be.

'Be nice, that's my brother,' I whispered. 'Herc?' He didn't move, not even to roll or snore or mutter, and I worried for a moment that I was wrong and he had died and we really hadn't known.

A fly landed on his chest. He moved no hand to bat it away, but a breath came, gulping and frantic, enough to dislodge it. Okay then. We had a job to do.

'Oi, shit for brains,' I shouted. He didn't even turn his head. 'That's a piss-poor way to greet your brother, isn't it?'

Again, he said nothing, so I leaned to my son. 'You said you were strong, right?'

'Strong enough.'

'Grab his legs. We're going swimming.' And for a second I was glad Herc was so emaciated; otherwise there's no way we could have lifted him. He barely stirred as we hoisted him to the ocean, only beginning to growl as we dunked him in the water. If there's anything reliable in this world, it's my brother's aversion to baths.

'Fuck me, Iph, what's that in aid of?'

'You're dying, you little shit.'

'Who you calling little?'

'Have you seen yourself?' I exclaimed.

It seemed he hadn't. He looked down and grimaced. 'Well, you got any food?'

'Bath first.'

'Thanks, Mum,' he complained. My son looked on in abject horror. I don't know which of us he was more startled by, but I imagine this isn't what he was expecting when his dying mother sent him to find his father. 'Who's that?'

'Herc, this is my son Pyrrhus.'

'Your son's called Iolaus, isn't he?' I prayed that the unsureness was a result of how ill he was and not him holding Iolaus in such small regard. It would have broken his heart.

'This is my other son.'

'You don't have another son. Automedusa said pregnancy made her all—'

'He's not hers,' I said, my teeth so tightly clenched together even the four winds wouldn't make it through. How in the name of Hades did he remember all this and not the basics of eating and tending to himself? 'What happened to you?'

'Hylas—' And then he began to choke, whether on his own grief or on the salt water, I don't know, but it was enough to put those pieces together.

'Well, being on this island's not helping any of us. Let's get you fed and head off. Somewhere with beds.'

'I like camping,' Herc said petulantly. It takes a lot to look petulant when your skin is so dried up you'd make a good pair of shoes, but he managed.

'No one asked you,' Pyrrhus said. I grinned. I shouldn't have worried. Of course I loved my kid.

We found a stream, laid some traps for food, and got everyone washed up and fed and moved off the island as soon as I could manage. Once he was walking around again, Herc started talking about some spring and Hylas and how we should go back there.

'Brother, it's been months,' I said as gently as I could. 'We have to go.'

He was unconvinced, but he was still weak from the nearly dying, so we hustled him onto the ship and took turns distracting him.

I got him drunk, in case it would help him talk about it, but it didn't. He just got bigger and louder and told stupider stories to my son, his willing audience. He found more wine and poured it out for all of us, until we collapsed in a pile. Herc and I woke up feeling gentle, Pyrrhus bouncing around, in the pure mockery of youth.

'Uncle Hercules, can you do this with your tongue?' Pyrrhus asked, demonstrating. I worried it would get stuck that way.

'What? No. Can do this, though.' He cracked his neck from side to side, clicking it loud enough to echo. Not a new trick to me, but one that's always sent shivers down my spine. Pyrrhus was fascinated, though, and I was immediately demoted from being the cool one. My brother's disturbing body horror carried the two of them through to the next island.

That's where everything went to shit.

Even for Greece, the town was properly on the coast, with the ocean racing to hit against the city walls. It was a shame. The beach would have been beautiful without them blocking the light. Things would have ended differently.

The two of them went into the town to get food. Probably so Herc could show my son how he could fit a whole loaf of bread into his mouth at once. I stayed on the beach to guard the boat, maybe catch some fish.

I heard the crash from there.

Once you learn it, the sound of breaking bones doesn't leave you. Still, I nearly didn't recognise it, because there were so many. Ratatat of creaking and crunching and collapse.

Self-preservation doesn't run in my family.

I sprinted towards the noise.

It was clear enough what had happened. Pyrrhus had been on

the city walls, and now he was on the ground. He hadn't taken the stairs.

His death, I hoped, was quick. There was nothing else to hope for.

It's a glad thing I ran. Poseidon's oceans were doing their best to wash my son away, take him from me forever. Poseidon could have the blood, clean this land of it, but his body was mine. It was the last thing I could do for him.

I laid Pyrrhus where he was safe. I closed his eyes and gave him every coin from my pockets, piled up on his chest like he was some kind of sick prize, and I went running for my brother.

He was sitting on the wall, staring at his hands. Not crying, Hercules doesn't cry – Laonome says it's because his muscles have closed over his tear ducts – but with this *look*. Ask any one of us who are related to him. Ask Mum, or Laonome, or even my oldest, and they'll know it. Other people see the flash and the pomp. But when he stares at his hands like he doesn't understand? That belongs to us.

'I didn't, I don't—' he stuttered. He gets like that, after these things. Shock rattling around inside his head. Because he had to cope with our world and the gods' world, Mum said, and people aren't built to carry all that.

Habit carried me through. I should have gone back to my son, lying on the beach, but I wrapped an arm around my brother's shoulders and I whispered reassurances to him instead. What did it matter to Pyrrhus if I left him? He was dead.

'Come on,' I said. 'Let's get you washed up. We'll talk to the oracle in the morning.'

That was it. When Hercules went bad, you got him cleaned up. You took him to the gods to appeal for forgiveness, and they gave him some arbitrary tasks and that was that. The world would forgive him. He was Hercules, and my son was some illegitimate bastard.

I burned Pyrrhus while his uncle was sleeping.

The oracle was another story. We waited in line with all the other supplicants, and we brought a goat for her, and she tried. I believe she tried. But we sat there for near an hour as she went through all manner of different methods and not once was there any result.

'I'm sorry, but the gods have no message for you,' she said, not lacking in empathy, but she probably had this conversation a dozen times a day. I tried hard to be understanding. It wasn't her son who was dead.

'But they always have a message for him,' I said, gesturing to my brother. He stood staring into space, and occasionally back at his hands.

'Is it him who's asking?' she said, with pity this time. She was right. It wasn't my brother who was seeking forgiveness, it was me – not just for leading Pyrrhus to his death but for leading Pyrrhus to his birth, for hurting my wife and Iolaus. The gods don't care about that kind of problem. Maybe they would for my brother, but not for me.

So I invented a trial, something like what Dad had Herc do up on the mountain, because I had to do something, and I served it right beside my brother. I know what he's capable of and I left him alone with my son, like he should be an exception when Hercules' own progeny weren't.

We served our pitiful excuse for penance, maybe two months of working the fields of a king who was baffled by the request, but happy enough for the free labour. We let the skin burn off our backs, though the king offered us shelter from the sun, and was even more baffled when I refused. No pain I inflicted on the two of us was going to make up for what had happened. Eventually I accepted that and delivered Herc back to our cousin to complete his *other* penance.

He was so sick, so lost for most of that time, I'm not sure he remembers my son any more than he remembers his own.

Theseus I

I didn't really have a dad growing up, even though I actually have two. One wasn't around because he's a god and the other one wasn't because he's a king and he didn't need a son. Not until I was strong enough to be helpful.

So it was just me and Mum and Granddad. That was okay. Lots of people didn't have dads, because they'd died in wars or from disease, or even my best friend Piri, whose dad wasn't there because he was an *outlaw*, though his mum said we weren't old enough to hear why yet.

But I was the only one whose dad chose not to be there.

'Oh, little one,' Mum said when I told her. 'That's not true.'

'It's not?'

'Of course not. *You* are perfect. That's just how it goes for anyone who has a divine father.'

'It is?'

'Like your cousin Hercules,' she said.

That always helped. Mum told good stories all the time, but the ones about my cousin Hercules were the best. In my head,

I wrote myself into them. I pretended I was there on the *Argo*, besieged on an island without men.

His dad still wasn't around for him, after all that, but he only had the god one. I had *two*, and I just knew, if I could be as great as my cousin Hercules, I'd be enough for my dad who was a king.

My king-dad must have known I was going to be a hero. When he found out Mum was pregnant, he left a test for me, hiding some of his shoes under the biggest rock in our garden. He told Mum when I was ready I'd be able to lift that rock up and join him as his son.

Every morning, I woke up, cleaned my face, and ran outside to see if I could do it yet. Only I wasn't born with the special strength my cousin Hercules had. I didn't look like the kid of a god. Granddad called me sinewy once.

I trained harder than everyone else. What I lacked in natural talent I made up for with angry determination to be just like my cousin.

My cousin Hercules. When I was nine, that's how I started every sentence.

When I was ten, he came to visit, and I didn't have to imagine our adventures anymore.

'He's seriously coming here?' I said to Mum.

'No he's coming to visit us in Thebes,' she said lightly, before her laugh cut off abruptly. Back then, I only understood half the joke – Thebes was far away. 'Of course he's coming here, little one.'

I spent years begging her not to call me that. Eventually, I grew a foot taller. She didn't stop, but then it didn't matter so much.

'I have to go train.'

'He'll be here in a couple of days, and he's just coming for dinner.'

'Nothing's *just* dinner, Mum,' I said, already halfway out the door. She could have given me more *time*. I needed to impress him. He was the only other person who knew what it was like.

He was late, which meant more training time for me, and more cleaning time for Mum, who was weirdly worried about everything being tidy for him.

'He's an esteemed guest,' she said. 'Stop tracking mud through the house.'

'Heroes don't care about *dirt*.'

By the time he knocked on the door, I was so tightly wound I could have thrown myself at the walls, but I didn't. That's not how heroes behave. I could still feel it, though, the excitement and the questions all bubbling up inside me, and I knew I wouldn't be able to talk to him without sounding like an idiot child. I hated that. I panicked.

'I have to go wash up,' I said.

'Now?' Mum asked.

'Now.'

I stood in front of the wash basin and took a big breath to calm myself down. I didn't think it was really working, but by then I'd been gone for a weirdly long time so I crept back to the front door. Mum and Cousin Hercules were gone.

There was a lion there instead. A huge lion, sleeping lazily like it belonged, but it didn't. This was our house.

I could hear them talking in the kitchen. How had they not noticed a *lion*? Even adults can't be so boring they think asking about the road conditions is more exciting than a lion.

It didn't matter. This was my chance. I could prove I was a hero, just so long as it didn't eat me first.

I crept as quiet as I could, back out the side door, all the way to the shed where Granddad kept his axe for chopping firewood. I was better with my swords, but they were smaller – made for my height, which wasn't the same as the lion *at all*. With the axe I could sneak up on it and – *boom*. In one blow.

I could feel my heart pumping so hard it made the rest of me shake, apart from my hands. I held on to the axe tighter than I'd ever held anything, just in case I missed and woke the lion. I didn't want to be eaten. I needed to be a hero.

I shut my eyes, lifted the axe above my head and ignored the trembling in my arms. I could do this.

I brought the axe down. It went through *something*. It didn't feel like chopping wood but it didn't feel like cutting meat at dinner either. Maybe because the lion was alive and not cooked?

I opened my eyes.

I'd done it. The lion's head was split clear from its body, eyes still closed. Nothing survives having its head chopped off, apart from the Hydra, and this wasn't that.

Only there wasn't any blood. There was laughing, but not any blood.

Cousin Hercules appeared in the doorway, looking over me.

'My cloak, it's been murdered!' he exclaimed.

He was short. Well, not short, but not that tall either. When I was grown he'd be shorter than I was. He had a chipped tooth and bags under his eyes and he smelled of smoke and blood. His head was shorn. He didn't look like a hero.

And he was laughing at me.

'Thes—' Mum began, but he cut her off.

'I've got this. Thought it was a real lion, eh?' he asked. I nodded, blinking back tears. Heroes don't cry. 'That was very brave of you. I couldn't have killed a lion when I was your age.'

'Really?'

'Really.' He didn't kill a lion when he was that age. He was a month older. 'Shall we go outside, work on that swing of yours? Make sure it's perfect for when you meet a real lion?'

Mum sighed, but we took no heed. She watched for a bit, as he taught me how to swing an axe to kill more than wood, or cloaks, but she said she smelled burning after a while and went to rescue our dinner.

'Cousin Hercules,' I said, once Mum was out of earshot. She didn't approve of cheating. 'Can you show me how to lift things too?'

'Lift with your knees,' he said gruffly.

I went over to the stupid rock where my king-dad left his shoes and squatted next to it, tried to roll it with the tips of my fingers, but it wouldn't give.

'Why this rock in particular?' he asked.

'What do you mean?' I asked innocently.

'You've got shit on your shoes, kid,' he said. I had no idea what that meant, but from the look on his face I knew I was rumbled, so I explained about my dad who's a king and the shoes and the rocks and if he would just help me then I could go now, be someone's son. 'No can do.'

'But you can do everything,' I said.

He smiled, but it wasn't a good kind, more like it hurt him. He rolled his jaw round before saying, 'Sometimes fathers leave us with things to do. Maybe they don't look fair but we have to do them anyway. Otherwise we can never prove ourselves.'

'But—' I started.

'I can show you how to kill a real lion, though,' he said. 'On the cloak.'

He didn't have any normal weapons with him, just his club,

which I could barely lift, so I got out my swords and they looked even smaller in his hands. He laughed it off, saying it was good practice, and we took turns stabbing different bits of it. Then we stayed up late as he showed me how to patch it back together.

'Heroes have to be able to fix things when they break them,' Hercules said. I wished I had somewhere to write that down. This was so much better than my regular lessons.

'Like when Piri broke his arm?' I asked. He looked confused. 'My brother.'

'You have a brother?'

'Blood brothers,' I said. We'd only just done it, with knives across our palms. Piri pretended he wasn't wincing but I saw through him. 'Don't tell Mum.' She didn't like blood, but what did she know? She wasn't a hero. She didn't have to prove herself to anyone.

'You stick by him, then. He might save your life one day.'

'Really? Piri's way worse at fighting than me.'

'Mine did, and he's not much of a fighter either,' Cousin Hercules said.

'Where's he now, then? Aren't you meant to stick together so you can keep saving each other?'

'He had to go back to his family.'

'Why did he leave them to begin with?' I asked.

'He was having some problems but they're fixed now.'

'Cousin Hercules?'

'Yeah?'

'Can you teach me how to *punch*?'

Eurystheus/Augeas Letters

Dear Augeas, of the shittiest horses,

My friend. Ha. But there must be some decorum in these things, otherwise I'll end up like my blasted cousin. It's pointless to enquire whether you've heard of him, I suppose. Everyone has heard of Hercules. Not his given name of course, which he has taken offence to, blaming his inability to control himself on the lovely Hera.

Since his indiscretion, I've been stuck with him, so he may perform his 'labours', to cleanse himself of sin.

Which brings me to the point of this missive. Your stables have reached the point where I can smell their odour from my own palace. Could you do both of us a favour and let my slave clean them when he next has time in his busy schedule? He's currently taken leave of his duties, I'm told, to join some other 'heroes' on a boat trip for frankly unintelligible reasons, though I'm not permitted to punish him for that insolence, a directive from his divine father.

Hera is frustrated too, I know. Were she any less than perfect she might have broken her teeth clenching them so. Regardless, wading through your stables is the most fitting punishment either of us can find for his return.

Politeness dictates I ask about your family. How are your family? Antimache and the children are well. She says when you visit, it would be pleasant for us to take tea. Pleasant for whom, I wonder?

I suppose I await your response with breath. It is not bated.

Sincerely,
King Eurystheus of Tiryns (Should your geography be lacking, as I know people struggle with such things in your particularly unpleasant corner of the country, that's the kingdom that is both bigger and more important than yours.)

Dear Eurystheus, second-most important of Perseus' grandchildren,
My family continues to cope with the loss of my dear wife – do thank Antimache for the lovely note, she forges your signature beautifully. My eldest, Epicaste, in particular, is doing well. Judging by the letters I receive begging for her hand in marriage, she must be quite the beauty, though she'll always be a child to me. She enquires whether your Admete would like to open a line of correspondence between them?

(She claims it's to work on her penmanship. I suspect it's to share the less worthy interests of young ladies.)

I have not heard of your cousin. As a son of Helios, I have better things to do with my time than keep up with the comings and goings of your uninteresting family. I did, however, ask one of my less-educated servants and he prattled on with great enthusiasm. Something about wrestling a lion? I assume this is your lummox.

My horses are thriving – the herd has recently over-taken three thousand. I realise the number may be of some confusion to you, as your fingers do not go that high. Imagine, if you will, all the fingers of every resident in your insignificant kingdom.

I will concede such a magnificent stable creates a not-unnotable amount of leavings. Would your oaf be able to handle such humbling work? Would his esteemed father stand for it?

Awaiting your response, as we must all await the sweet embrace of Thanatos,

King Augeas of Elis (Home of theatre and democracy, though I would not expect one less adept at the art of reading to know such things)

Dear Augeas, king of a region so pointless I've already forgotten its name,

I passed on your compliments to my dear wife, and Admete says she would be delighted to carry on such a correspondence. It will be good for them to have such an outlet. Better, certainly, than idolising so-called heroes, as the youth seemed to be inclined to do these days. There is a gaggle of small boys permanently attached to the oaf, begging him for stories, his own nephew chief among them.

The oaf brings him on his tasks, though the child is scarcely older than our daughters, and looks to him as if it is he who hangs the stars in the sky. I find the mere thought offensive. Most recently, the larger oaf released a wild animal in my house. Do you know his response? Oops.

Humiliation is called for.

Do not even give him a shovel.

I do not need to compare the wait for your letters to Thanatos, for reading them already feels as though I am in Asphodel.

Regards,
Eurystheus

Dear King Eurystheus,
The girls seem to have developed some fondness for each other – Admete must have inherited her personality from her mother. Epicaste would like me to extend the invitation for her to stay with us later in the year. Interactions with my own children have indicated that young ladies like ponies. I have rather a fine stable of them.

After some consideration, I'm inclined to grant your request to send your slave to me. What exactly are the conditions of his tasks? I do not want him staying longer than a week, nor shall he bring whatever travelling bard he has following him to chronicle his adventures.

An unrelated note, but one I thought you might find fascinating, I recently ordered stock to be taken of the servants' supplies. Did you know we're completely lacking in shovels? An unusual circumstance, but as king I have more important things to do than order their replacement, and I certainly cannot trust the stablehands with my money.

Yours with the tolerance I have for flies in the summer,
Augeas

Augeas,

Given the squealing, I would say Admete is very taken by your offer and would love to accept, so I give my reluctant blessing for her to visit. Should any harm come to her, I will use every resource at my not-inconsiderable disposable – including the oaf – to tear both you and your kingdom into pieces so small even the gods would not be able to reassemble them.

I asked Admete, and she does like ponies. She rides well, and would be honoured to have additional tutelage in the art.

The oaf is not permitted aid from another mortal in the tasks, nor is he allowed to demand or accept payment for completing them. His payment is an absolution he does not deserve.

I have received word that he is finally returning to Tiryns. It seems he abandoned the Argonauts and got dreadfully lost on the way back. Regardless, once he shows his face here, I will turn him around and get him sent to you.

Should you wish to make the task additionally unpleasant for him – not that it should need help, for the smell of a thousand horses worth of shit is surely worse than the very depths of Tartarus – he is unnaturally attached to that lion skin of his. Were you to destroy it, or otherwise render it unwearable, I'd be most obliged.

(I had my servants smear it with the urine of wild animals. If anything it made the oaf fonder of the thing.)

The oaf's hands are largely shovel-like anyway. I doubt he'll even notice.

Yours with all the respect you deserve,

Eurystheus

Eurystheus,

It's the shit of three thousand horses. If you must insult me, get it right. Epicaste is already preparing for the visit, as am I, though I have told her we must get through the oaf first. Did you know if you feed mares lucerne, it causes a rapid softening in their droppings?

Fascinating animals, horses.

He is arriving now, so I must away. I may respond further when I am free of the scourge you have laid upon my family and my home.

Keenly awaiting your next missive, if only to pacify my daughter's lack of patience,

Augeas

Eurystheus II

The oaf came back from his *adventure* with the Argonauts alone. He wasn't bedecked with new animal carcasses or, I don't know, a necklace strung with the teeth of his enemies. His hair was short and his eyes hollow. Even with his ridiculous cloak, you could see lines of sunburn crawling across his back.

'You are returned,' I said.

'I am, my lord.' He gazed wistfully in the direction of his rooms, not even sparing a second glance for his usual love – the kitchens. Ha.

'I have a mission for you, with the greatest of haste.'

'Now?' he asked, looking singularly disgruntled.

'Now,' I said. My wife and I had another child, a boy, while the oaf was away. We were not risking his safety. 'It would have been sooner, but you left, unpermitted, for close to two years—'

'But—'

'Do you have something better to be doing, *slave*?'

'What is it you would have me do, my lord?'

When the oaf left for his stupid holiday, I knew in my heart he'd be back. Even he could not avoid commands from the gods

146

forever. I sent missives to my friends, explaining the broad details of the situation, that he had to complete ten tasks to earn his freedom and the gods would prefer it if they were both unpleasant and noteworthy. While plausible ideas didn't exactly flood in – looking in particular at the king with some two-bit cattle thief irritating him – there was one I could work with.

I sent him to an acquaintance of mine, Augeas, and the only place in the world where I could literally bury him in shit.

I cannot communicate the level of my displeasure when he returned in less than a month.

'I have completed your labour, my lord.' He picked up the irritating habit of referring to my tasks as his labours on his sabbatical. I wanted to slap him every time he did it.

'With remarkable speed and alacrity,' I said.

'Huh?' The oaf gawped, mouth slack with the weight of his limited mental faculties bearing upon him.

'That. Was. Very. Fast,' I said slowly.

'Ah, yes,' he said, looking at his shoes. 'There was, um, a—'

'Get on with it.'

'There was a bet involved. That I could get it done in a week.' Oh my. Later, I'd receive a report from Augeas. The oaf *diverted a river* to run through the stables and do the work for him, a never-before-seen commitment to bone-idleness. Augeas refused to honour the terms of their bet – because the oaf hadn't fulfilled his end – and the oaf threw a little oafy tantrum, only cut short by the guards poking him with big sticks and sending him back to me.

Lucky me.

Between the bet and the river doing the real work, I'd later discount the entire thing, but he didn't need to know that yet. I dismissed him.

I next sent the pest to do some pest reduction of his own. Some metal birds of Ares had been disrupting everything from Hades to Stymphalia. Since I didn't cherry-pick his assignments based on his potential glory, I don't care how he eradicated them. I was merely glad when he returned and he wasn't wearing a crown of Stymphalian birds.

He did avoid making an enemy of Ares. In some ways, it would've been helpful to have another god out for his blood but, truly, I was exhausted enough by Hera's demands. As a mortal, I wasn't in a position to say no to her. She gave me the information for his next task, though. I was grateful for that.

There was a bull over in Crete, whose son would come to be known as the Minotaur. The Cretan bull was said to be beautiful – pure white, whiter even than the midday sun. It was a picture of everything wonderful the wild could be. It was so beautiful, I told the oaf not to kill it, that he should return it to me so we could sacrifice it to Hera.

I half-expected him to return riding the bull, but he had it in a headlock instead, thrashing in his arms. I dread to think how he kept it captive on the boat. Maybe they made friends, being intellectual equals.

'The bull of Crete, dear cousin,' he said, bowing and looking unbearably smug. What had he done this time?

'I assumed.' I motioned for my servants to bring it in. 'We'll sacrifice it to Hera this evening.' He blanched, the commoner's tan of his shoulders seeping away.

'Hera?'

'Has the trip deafened you, or is it simply your mind that cannot keep up?' I asked.

'If that is your desire, cousin, then to Hera we shall sacrifice.' Since when had I been demoted from *my lord* back to *cousin*?

We wore the ritual clothes and served the ritual food and held the bull on the altar. The knife was ready to kill it without pain, and we uttered the ministrations to Hera. As the priest readied to deliver the final blow upon the animal, a voice echoed in my head.

'Stop.'

I looked around. Judging by the calm, no one else had heard it. I raised my hand to the priest, bade him wait. He didn't look happy. This sacrifice was quite the boon for him, something to lord over the other priests with their lesser cows.

'I don't want this sacrifice,' the voice said. I knew that voice. Either it was Hera or the oaf had finally succeeded in driving me mad. 'It reflects only the glory of *Hercules*. Don't misuse my name in this manner again.'

Normally, it was warm when I spoke to Hera, like stepping into the sun on a chilly evening. This time, her voice was so cold the shivers shook my spine. It was all I could do to stay standing. I got the message.

She left before I could answer. It must be nice to assume obedience from your servants.

'Free the bull,' I said. The priest looked dumbfounded. 'Did you hear me? Free it or I'll do it myself.'

He didn't move. I took the knife from his hands and cut the bindings on the creature's ankles. It ran far and fast and I never saw it again. I hear it wandered into the desert, made some new life for itself, where its glory was untainted by what was done in Crete.

I relieved the priest of his duties for good measure. I didn't need people questioning me.

Around this time the oaf gained another companion, Abderus, this one especially annoying, since he was in the palace as my guest. His father was of some import, and wanted him to see the world before taking over the management of their land. When he first started to disappear into the oaf's rooms, I considered writing to his father and telling him he'd sired a damned fool.

But I didn't. I stayed both hand and tongue, for reasons that elude me. Maybe it was the gods acting through me, or maybe it was simply that the damned fool finally looked happy, an expression which had thus escaped him in my palace. Abderus didn't like fighting. Nor eating, drinking, and sleeping. According to my wife, who spoke to the servants and worried about the *poor lad* – he was a prince – he continued his unhappy expression even in more intimate circles. The only thing – other than the oaf – that stopped him looking like he had to drink a barrel of seawater, was riding the horses. The confines of the city didn't allow a lot of that.

His father was the protective sort. On allowing his son to leave *his* city, he'd been charged to stay within the gates of ours. We had enough of these strays pass through our hands that I took notes on how not to be a parent, so my well-mannered children should not become impetuous and rude. Never keep them bound in too small a space. That's one.

I summoned the oaf to give him his next task. It went as they usually did, him calling me cousin, calling them labours, smirking when I told him he was to bring back Diomedes' horses. He even snorted, *horses,* hardly worthy of the Great Hercules, he probably thought. They were carnivorous, human-eating horses, but I didn't tell him that.

To be honest, I'd long lost hope the tasks would kill him,

though a light still shone deep within me, reminiscent of Pandora's Elpis, that one of these days a particularly large and foul-smelling rock would fall from the sky and flatten him like the bug he was.

'How many horses, dear cousin?' he asked, without even the pretence of bowing his head to me.

'Does it matter? Are you afraid to tame some simple horses?' For whatever reason, I found his use of the phrase *dear cousin* more grating than when he simply called me *cuz*.

'Only to better serve you.' He smirked. Again. 'If there are many, I was wondering if I may take some men to herd them home.'

'Did your time as a goatherd not teach you enough?'

'If that's your wish, my lord. I'm merely expressing my concerns . . .' I didn't like it. What if this was some directive passed to him by his father that the gods had chosen to hide from me?

'Who do you want to take?' I sighed.

He told me four names, a group of local youths who cared only for drunken tomfoolery. In the years since, they've been wiped clean from my memory. I can tell you only they sprinted well, all the better to escape angry husbands.

On a usual day, I would've denied him. The company of the oaf has an incredible death rate. But I'd been up half the night dealing with the fallout from that drunken foursome's antics. They'd decided it was a good idea to release and then attempt to lasso animals from my royal menagerie. The damage wrought upon my crockery by the cows was unthinkable.

I had been planning on stringing them to the city walls for a few days – separately; together they probably would have found some new way to annoy me – as punishment. It was the heat of summer and it would be easy enough to make sure they never saw the shade. I'd done it before. A week was enough to deflate even the most obnoxious of youths.

But if they wanted to go be mutilated with the oaf, I wasn't going to stop them. I imagine losing a finger would have much the same effect.

If he'd asked me for Abderus I would've denied him. I'm no stranger to protective fathers and I have no desire to strip one of their firstborn. More than that, he was a well-mannered boy. This trip would bear no benefit to him, while significantly risking his death.

Regardless, the oaf didn't ask, so I was denied the opportunity to refuse. I simply woke to the quiet relief of a murderer-free palace. It wasn't until I settled onto my throne, that I met a frantic maid, exclaiming, 'He's gone, he's gone, he's gone.'

'I know,' I sighed happily. 'It's wonderful, is it not?'

'You're glad?' She gasped.

'I'm always glad when he's gone.'

'Of whom do you speak?' she asked, and slowly we unravelled the story. We were speaking of different men – she mourned well-mannered Abderus as I revelled in the loss of the oaf. My house is *still* paying reparations to his father for those comments, but it's not worth sending an army to save myself the fee.

I enjoyed a full year of calm, that time, with almost no word of him. When the oaf returned, nuisances in tow, Abderus was no longer with them. I enquired after him and they said nothing, save significant looks at one of the muzzled horses. An answer, if not the one I was looking for.

Finding the flesh-eating beasts tame, maybe a result of their most recent meal, I allowed them to wander free, under the advice of the gods. Over the years, Diomedes' mares would prove exemplary breeding stock and fathered what seemed to be every horse in Greece.

Do you know what the oaf was doing in that year away from his *god-bidden* work? I spoke to a representative of Diomedes, as I spoke to Augeas, and to Minos, to ensure my slave completed his tasks fairly and faithfully, dedication to the job not shared by the oaf.

He was off founding a city. As you do.

He took Diomedes' city – Diomedes 'disappeared' in another highly suspicious accident involving the horses – and renamed it after his latest lover. One has to wonder how many of these enclaves run along the coasts of Greece, eternal markers to the danger of associating with the man. He never did dedicate one to his wife.

I presented him next with a task: to get me the belt of Hippolyta. It belonged to the fiercest head of the fiercest warriors in Greece, the Amazons. They lived apart from society, so they may better train and live under their own laws. So that they may refuse the company of all men.

My oldest told me once she wanted to be an Amazon when she grew up. I told her no, she'd stay home and safe. I wish I'd said yes, now.

The hope was that he'd go to the Amazons, be an oaf, get his head sliced clean from his neck, and I'd be free. Alas, he returned, months later, belt in hand, bloodstains trailing his clothes. I gave the belt to my second daughter, and hoped it would keep her safe.

(I did not bank on this. My children also had lessons from the best back-alley fighters Tiryns had to offer, criminals usually. I told them I'd mitigate their sentences in exchange, and they believed me. Criminals tend not to be the brightest.)

For his next task, I sent him out of Greece. At this point, I was choosing assignments that were more strictly fictional than anything else, the things bards speak of only when they are very drunk. So I asked for the cattle of Geryon, a giant rumoured to have three bodies and three heads.

He was gone a long time. When he returned, he came bearing cattle, an almost giddy skip in his step. That wouldn't do at all. He wasn't sent to me to be *happy*.

He patted the cow's rump affectionately. I reminded myself to bring up his goatherd days again, and ordered the beasts sacrificed. (Their slaughter was efficient, and the smell of their burning flesh filled the town with warmth and welcome, like coming home.)

The oaf stared at me expectantly. He fidgeted, clumsy as a cow in the crockery.

'Would you like to explain to me why you are grinning?' I asked.

'Dearest and most benevolent cousin—' Suspicious. 'I'd like to respectfully thank you for your aid in helping me atone for my past actions. Now that the labours are done, I will—'

'You will do nothing. You're not finished,' I said. The disappointment laid across him beautifully. 'Did I not mention? Two of your tasks didn't count.'

'What do you mean?'

'Do you remember the terms of your penance?' He did not. He could barely remember the names of the people he'd killed.

'Um—'

'No help from others, no payment, do either of those sound familiar?'

'I suppose.' Gods above, could he sound any more gormless?

'So, when I sent you to kill the Hydra, how did you do it?'

He said nothing. He didn't have to. We both know his young nephew did as much work in killing the Hydra as he did. 'And why do I have a note from Augeas saying you accepted payment for cleaning his stables?'

'He didn't give it to me, though,' the oaf raged. 'He *cheated* me. I'll kill him.'

'Not under my name, you won't,' I said. Augeas might have been a bastard but he deserved better than death by oaf. 'You'll find the gods take a very dim view of it if you do.' I offered a brief prayer to Hera to make it true. I didn't need to. I could feel her anger crackling through me as much as my own. I think the oaf could *see* it, given how he stepped back and made an effort to calm himself.

'Why didn't you tell me about this before?' he said, with a minimum of spittle.

And miss this? But I didn't say that. No doubt, it would trigger one of his rages.

'It is the will of the gods. You will do two more tasks.'

Apples, I sent him for – trying to prick that enormous ego by asking for something I could find on any street at home. Of course I couldn't acquire the magical immortality-granting apples of the Hesperides, but the thought was there.

The oaf came back, wounded, with the apples of the Hesperides. He'd literally carried the sky on his overdeveloped shoulders to get his mitts on it, they said. I would have disregarded it as just another outlandish claim but I saw the scars as he shrugged off his cloak, wicked red lightning marks darting across his back. At least *something* was having an effect.

The apples I left on the altar to Hera.

'For your continued youth and beauty.' I laughed awkwardly.

Another task for the oaf, another failure on my part. 'Not that you need any help.'

What is this? Hera's voice ran clear and cold within me.

One of the apples of the Hesperides, my queen.

These are my *apples to begin with. They were a wedding gift. From* my *husband.*

They were guarded by a dragon. I thought—

You thought wrong. You must do better, my Eurystheus. You only have one more chance.

I've never been afraid of the oaf, never hid from his unsubtle fists or his barely concealed depravity. I'm not too stupid to admit I was scared of Hera then.

She was normally so kind to me. When we lost our eldest, Antimache and I nearly lost each other. The words wouldn't flow between us as they used to, and no amount of trying seemed to fix it, the pain of everything that had happened an insurmountable wall.

I appealed to Hera for help, not to reverse death, but to preserve the rest of my family. And Hera came. She taught us to talk again, brought us a recipe for pomegranate tea. New life, pomegranates. We weren't trying to bring another child into the world in the foolish hope that it would replace our daughter, but to make the pain from where she'd been less ragged.

I had so much to thank Hera for, and she'd only ever asked one thing of me. I'd failed her eleven times so far.

'I will make his last challenge count,' I swore to her, feeling the pain of her disappointment more keenly than all the anger I bore him.

'You had better.' Her voice trailed away, but the fear remained.

I thought long and hard over his last task so I wouldn't fail again. The answer came to me, I'm ashamed to say, through a rumour. Some young want-to-be hero had apparently gone haring down to Hades on a bizarre love-struck mission and got stuck there. If the oaf managed the same trick, he'd save us the cost of the funeral.

Hippolyta I

We were used to men. They came to us, chests puffed up like lions eating their dinner, though the lioness was the one who caught it. They strutted and flaunted and flirted, told us tales of the big, wide world, as if we didn't know.

The Amazons didn't live apart from men because we were stupid, or because we were cursed, like the putrid women of Lemnos. We knew the world where others lived, and we chose our own instead. We chose not to be subjugated, left in homes with squalling children to teach our daughters to be weak. We chose strength, and we were known for it. Men whispered about what we could do to them. Heroes heard, and it offended them.

Hercules had crowned himself with the skin of a lion. He didn't carry weaponry that demanded skill; instead, he had a hunk of wood he'd pulled from a tree. If you were feeling generous, you could call it a club, but Amazons don't lie to pander to the egos of men.

We don't lie to belittle them either, so I'll say, for all his strutting, he travelled well. Many heroes came to us with the barest veneer of bravado hiding how much the journey hurt them.

Hercules sauntered, as if this were a holiday from the rest of his duties. We had others make the journey casually too. But he was different. He hadn't come for us but for a piece of jewellery I was only moderately attached to.

The bards won't admit it, but I swear the belt wasn't so special to me. I cared first for my sister, and then my sisters, the Amazons. True, I cared also for my horses, and my sword, things I could use to strike down anyone tempestuous enough to believe they could take us.

As it was, my belt was a gift from my father, Ares, the god of war, though I didn't like to brag about it. I didn't become Queen of the Amazons because I was his daughter. I was Queen of the Amazons because I fought as strongly and bravely as anyone and better than many.

The belt was beautiful. I don't deny it. It shone even in the darkest of nights. When our opponents saw a flash of metal across the battlefield they couldn't know if it was my body or my sword. It may well have saved my life one day, had it come to that. But it hadn't yet, and that was no sure thing. I wouldn't have wept over its loss.

We welcomed him well. People don't believe we'd allow men into our home without violence and threats, but we did. We had to be *better* than them, don't you see? Meeting friendly visitors with threats wouldn't accomplish that.

I hesitate to call his companions friends, or even comrades, given the glances they threw in his direction, but he came with people.

'What brought you this way?' I asked. As a queen, it was my job to ask, and as a human I couldn't help but wonder.

'It's a long story,' he grunted. Bird meat he'd been eating flew

159

out through the gap between his teeth, all the way across the room, until it stuck on the wall. It hung there for a long time, finally sliding into nothingness with an unglamorous squish.

'We'd love to hear it.'

Once he started, he could scarcely stop himself. He spoke and he spoke of evil goddesses and malicious cousins and a thousand other plagues on his house. When he finally ceased, it still seemed he was skipping parts of the story.

'That is fascinating,' I began gently.

'Uh-huh,' he mumbled, mouth again full of food.

'But what about it brought you here, exactly? We don't often have visitors,' I lied. We always had men trying to save us.

'My cousin—'

'Eurystheus?' I've always had a head for names. It does well to remind visitors we're listening. I'm yet to meet a liar who can keep their story straight.

'Yeah, him. His latest task is that I bring back an item from here.'

'Is that so?'

'Uh-huh.'

'What item is that, exactly?' Our home was full of treasures, some of them not exactly acquired honestly.

'Girdle off some Hippolyte woman?' So eloquent, so charming, how could anyone help but fawn over him?

'Hippolyta,' I said firmly, proffering my hand. 'A pleasure to make your acquaintance.'

'It's you?'

'So it would seem.' His eyes fell from my face to my waist, and stayed there longer than I was happy with, though his appraising look was aimed more at my belt than my figure.

'So?'

'So what?'

'Can I have it?' There's something to be appreciated about a person so completely guileless they ask like that. Of course, I had no particular intention of giving it to him. One doesn't stay queen by giving everyone anything they ask for.

'This was a gift from my father,' I said.

'It's the only way I can earn my freedom,' he implored, his eyes wide, his muscles strained against his chest. I imagine where he's from that would have most everyone swooning after him.

'I would be happy to give it to you—'

'Really?' he interrupted.

'You only have to earn it first.' He was horrified. Work, in exchange for goods or services. Terrifying. 'Don't worry, I won't make you chop logs or scrub floors.' I fished there, for something he'd associate with women's work.

'What then?'

'We'd like to see you fight.' Never before had I seen a person's face light up like his did.

We didn't go easy on him. First, we challenged him with someone good. When he beat her, we challenged him with the best.

Much as he's a puffed-up plump of a man, he could fight. He might have chosen to carry a club – if there ever was a better picture of what men are overcompensating for, I don't know what it is – but he could use a sword too. He had real skill, even if his preference was brute force.

He knew how to perform too. His chest swelled to twice his size and he ripped – *ripped* – the sleeves from his tunic to better exhibit his muscles. I wish I could say none of my sisters cared about his pathetic show and we were immune to this self-aggrandisement that stood contrary to everything we believed, but I cannot, for the moment he stood like that, a swoon rippled across the room.

He dispatched – not killed – his first combatant easily enough. She was strong, but she panicked and allowed herself to be caught off guard. Soon enough she was against a wall, him looming over her, sword to her throat.

The next fight was more interesting. He was pitted against my blood sister, Melanippe. Like me, she'd grown up brandishing a sword more comfortably than a pen. The same seemed true for Hercules, though I can only speculate.

They bowed, chose their weapons and looked to each other, surveying the up and down of their forms. They smiled, as if neither of them could tell what was coming.

Their fight was astonishingly fast. I'd heard complaints of the same when Melanippe and I sparred. *We can't learn the moves if we can't see them.* I told them to pay more attention. I don't believe in coddling. I understand better now.

My sister achieved first blood. A nice little feint to head and cut to flank, but he caught her in a parry, which made it awkward for her to get back to guard. While she was twisting he pushed through for second blood. Any pretence of this being a demonstration of skill went out the door of the training room. I've been at this business a long time, and even I cannot put names to moves they were doing. They coiled around each other, in so many directions it seemed a whirlwind had broken in. At one point she was standing on his head, at another he had her shoulders in a lock – leading to the insertion of her elbow into that unfortunate weak spot between his legs.

When it ended, all too suddenly, from fury to utter stillness, he held the tip of her – *her* – sword to her chest.

They shook hands and congratulated each other on a fight well fought, and he looked at me smugly, eyebrow cocked.

'Well, my queen? Do I fight good?'

I was impressed, though not impressed enough to go to bed with him that night, as he suggested. I know a ruse when I see one. His appetite for all things hedonistic aside, an attempt to enter my chambers would only be to steal my belt, as if I slept in the damned thing.

'You fight adequately,' I said. He mimed an arrow hitting his chest, knocking him back. I was less impressed by this, and he could tell.

'Only adequately? Have I failed to earn my prize?'

'It's a gift from my father, priceless, and incredibly valuable to all of us,' I said gently, motioning behind my back so all my sisters would nod and mumble in agreement.

'Is there truly nothing I can do to earn it?' he asked, his eyes again a picture of sadness. I'm ashamed to say, it tugged at me.

'I will consider it tonight. All should be clear by morning,' I said.

It wasn't clear by morning.

It began at dinner, when I rejected his advances. He propositioned several maidens in order of importance until one swooned and opened her door to him. This sparked an outbreak of jealousy and, worse, gossip.

If there's one thing I aimed for as queen, it was to eradicate petty gossip between my sisters. It can only lead to division when we need to stand together. It would've been nice to be right in a less violent manner.

The rumour was a simple one, almost elegant in its construction: *Hercules is here to kidnap the queen.*

It spread as wildfire through the early hours of the night, until dawn arrived and Hercules crawled out of my sister's bed. He made towards his ship without bidding her goodbye. His men had already made it to their vessel, failing to satisfy a woman being a rather speedier endeavour, so the watchwomen saw only him, clambering onto the ship with what was reported as a 'shit-eating' grin upon his face.

My sisters proceeded to attack him, led by Melanippe. They killed several of his men. This, I was awoken by. A man as large as Hercules, and one so used to sailing home alone, could perform a frankly deafening cry of anguish.

I donned armour on my way to the beach – not my own, that would have taken too long – throwing my belt atop the closest set we'd used for training the day before, making a mental note to scold whoever left it so carelessly scattered across the hall. I didn't know why they were fighting, and it didn't matter. I'd been neglectful of my duties, both in allowing a fight to happen, and sleeping through a dire situation.

Nothing could stop me reaching the man himself. It was my responsibility.

Had I stopped to don my own armour, things may have been different, but I've never had time for *what-ifs*, so let's not dwell on them now. The only person on that battlefield to set eyes upon my belt was Hercules. Between my rush to the front – not my best tactical moment – and his greed, I was lost in the crush. A wound to the belly that didn't kill me immediately, but knocked me down with a cry I'm ashamed of.

Because the rumour claimed he'd abducted me, my sisters

didn't wake me on their way to the fight. Why would they? They thought I'd been stolen by that man. He saw me when no one else did, because he expected to and they did not.

He ripped the belt from me and he was sailing away when my sisters gathered around, clutching my hands. The younger ones sprinted for medical supplies; the older ones knew it was time only for prayers.

I don't resent my death. It was in battle, as it should be, and I was the only one of the Amazons to be lost, *as it should be*. I lied to him. He was attacked. He acted in self-defence. I don't find those events to cast any aspersion on his character, unlike his desperate whining for someone to keep him company at night.

I handed my sword to my sister, so she might lead when I was gone. I asked her to find the malignant girl who'd started the rumour and punish her accordingly. We Amazons do not labour pointlessly over emotional last words. What I needed to say to her, I did in life.

She never did find the rumour-starter, though. Endless conversations, gentle and fierce, couldn't pinpoint a source, as if the words had floated in on air. Ridiculous of course, but not more so than what Hercules would later claim, that Hera pretended to be one of us and started it herself. Our very existence was an insult to everything she stood for. She hated us too much to take our form, even if it meant casting me a mortal blow.

Though I cannot believe any of my women would have done it either, so I suppose the mystery will keep me company in death.

Hylas IV

When H first came to the land of the dead, we crowded behind corners, eavesdropping like children. We clutched tight to the banks of the river Styx as he spoke to Charon, and flattened ourselves against the trees of Asphodel as he walked through, as if the sound of his gait would answer our questions.

We didn't normally have this freedom, those of us who were dead. Most of the time – it's difficult to say how much time, in the absence of sun or moon, waiting only for the waxing and waning in Hades' mood as his wife, Persephone, came and left him again – we were shackled to the ground, waiting for whatever came next, too attached to the memories we once had to be reborn. I'd been here for three Persephones.

I was delayed on my journey to Hades' realm – also named Hades, and I'd thought kings were vain. His ferryman, Charon, is pleasant enough, if you can pay him. You simply pass over your coin and you're loaded onto the boat and taken across the Styx.

If your family is careless enough to bury you without a coin, or you're careless enough to, say, drown in a pool of nymphs, you'll have a problem.

It's a great leveller, being dead. It didn't matter that I was the son of a king, or a companion to the great Hercules. I was passed over in favour of a great many peasants who hadn't drowned in a pool of nymphs and therefore had a coin.

I can still hear H's voice, asking why I didn't simply swim across. *It's only a river, H. You're a great swimmer. Don't be scared.*

To that I have one response: try drowning.

It doesn't matter how cool the water, how lovely the pool, how sweet the voices singing you in, try drowning, then talk to me about swimming. Towards the end, when I was sinking and the last bubbles escaped from my lips, and those voices were the only thing I could hear, the last of H's cries fading away, they seemed only mocking.

So I couldn't swim, and I had no desire to become one of those helpless spirits drifting along the banks, begging Charon for mercy.

I walked backwards down the line. I wonder now what would've happened if I'd kept walking away. No one came after me, no man nor god nor beast, but maybe they knew I was trying to get in, not out. I walked until they couldn't hear Charon, or the boat or the river, until they couldn't know death is a great leveller.

I was no great fan of my father, but on this unlikely occasion that I managed to die alone, in a pool of nymphs, his parentage did come in useful. Dad had a wonderful shouting voice. It took me years of practice, but eventually I could do it too.

'Do you know who I am?' I'd bellow at every new entrant to Hades. The answer, by and large, was no. Do you know how many poor people there are in the world? I didn't, didn't even consider it until I was shouting as loud as I could and nobody cared.

It took me another three cycles of Persephone to find someone it worked on. I shouted so loud that, despite my lack of a truly physical being, spittle flew across his face.

He staggered back, jaw slack.

'Theiodamas' boy?' Seriously. My lover kills my father in a duel, demands I act as his sword bearer, meaning I join the most famous heroic expedition since Perseus, living several years past my father's death, and all I deserved was *Theiodamas' boy*?

Needless to say, when I shouted next, it had some real force behind it.

'I require your coin.'

'But—'

'Now, peasant.'

He handed me the coin. To this moment – do you know how difficult it is to talk in scale of time when you don't have a lifespan to compare it against? – I don't know that man's name. He too will find his way eventually. There are few things worse than being in Hades, but being stuck at the gates is one of them.

I made friends, down in the underworld, different sorts of companions. Megara, yes, *that* Megara, most of all. She was waiting for me when I arrived. She sent her children away, as many as she could beat and bully and cajole into having any life at all. Pyrrha, Deiphile, Therimachus, Creontiades, Deicoon, Deioneus, and Ophitus. Her children, with him – never *theirs*.

She convinced all but two, Pyrrha and Creontiades. They came with us as we snuck behind walls and ducked behind trees. She even covered their ears when we passed the entrance to Tartarus – the land of punishment – as if the screams were anything new to them.

Ixion was at the entrance. He was strapped to a wheel, burning with the force of the sun itself. His crime? He lusted after Hera, and Zeus didn't enjoy the taste of his own medicine. The yells were a horror, but the smell was something else. It made me thankful, briefly. For all I don't recommend drowning in a pool of nymphs, at least it wasn't fire.

A crumpled sob came from Megara. She *had* died in a fire. We crossed quickly towards the Styx, and still she whispered a constant stream of nonsense to her children about the man who burned her. *Look how brave your daddy is, look how strong. He can convince even the gods. You could do that too. There's magic in your veins. He's proving how much he loved us.*

Neither believed it any more than she did.

'Why do you keep trying?' I asked her once.

'They deserve a father. If he's not going to be one I can at least pretend he is,' she said simply. I'm glad our union never produced children.

Meg and I gossiped about how H would make it over the river, when he came on that last of his labours. Only the gods know how he made it that far. Did he walk off the edge of this world?

He had a coin on him. He also had the small disadvantage of not being dead. Apathetic as he is, Charon didn't notice until H was already on the boat, whereby H – taking the most straight-forward course of action – beat him round the head with his own oar, then rowed across himself.

We laughed, where we were standing. How could we not? There's little enough entertainment in Asphodel as it is, and it was so very *him*.

H strode comfortably across the bank and shouted into the air that he wanted an audience with Hades. I never could understand how he did that, how he could always be so sure of getting what he wanted.

He got his audience. We crouched behind the pillars of the palace. I wouldn't have dared do it in my own father's house, but then there is something freeing about being dead. Persephone had just departed for the year, leaving two would-be heroes welded to her throne: Theseus and Pirithous. Far as we could tell, they'd come to 'rescue' Persephone from her husband. Because nothing appeals to an immortal goddess like a man who can't grow a full beard.

They'd come storming into Hades, full of confidence. After all, they'd just kidnapped Helen, said to be the most beautiful mortal woman in the world, though she was still a girl, really. Never mind that they left her with Theseus' mother, and she returned the child as soon as the boys were out of sight.

The confidence was unearned, of course, and there was an . . . incident. I hesitate to call it a fight. That would have required Lord Hades to stop laughing for long enough to kill them. Instead, he cast them both onto his throne to flail for eternity. I think Lady Persephone rather liked having the heroes about. She called them *chickadees*.

When the boys noticed another of the living among us, they redoubled their flailing, and added in some shouting for good measure.

'Mister, save us, please,' Pirithous started.

'Cousin! Cousin!'

'He's not your cousin.'

'Is too, my cousin Hercules,' Theseus said. We weren't usually close enough to hear them bickering. H ignored them as he stomped up to the lord of the underworld.

Hades was almost amused in his anger. 'You want my dog?'

'I was sent by—'

'Some mortal king as some punishment for some mortal act. I get it. So, because you just couldn't wait until you came here the natural way to be punished, you want my dog?'

'It's not—'

'Really, Zeus,' Hades shrieked, looking to the ceiling. 'You stick me down here, arbitrarily demand *my wife* leave me for more than half the year, but that's not enough, not for your dearest brother Hades. You have to send your blasted son to take my damned *dog* too?'

I'd never seen lightning strike through the underworld before.

'Fuck you too, brother,' he shouted, before regulating his volume, just a little bit, and looking back down at H. 'Fine, take the dog, but if you hurt one hair on any of his heads, know, *mortal,* you will die and I'll personally make every moment from then until the end of ages a misery. Do you understand?'

'I—'

'Do. You. Understand?'

'Yes, sir. But, um, the—'

H pointed to the squirming teenagers. Every time they moved another part of them stuck more tightly to the chairs. Still, they didn't stop.

'They tried to kidnap my wife,' Hades said, stonier than the earth itself.

'In fairness, my lord, *you* kidnapped your wife.' What I would have given then to be enough of a person to tackle him and cover his mouth. Who talks to a god like that?

(It doesn't matter that it's true.)

The ground rumbled above us. It was a confusing sensation.

'Whatever. Take the prisoners too. They're not really dead

either. You can just stroll in and out of my realm like you're Hermes—'

H crossed to the throne while Hades was still ranting and grabbed Theseus with an almighty tug. I always knew he was strong – it's hard not to – but no heroic feat of strength emphasises the point quite like tearing a man's thigh off.

He went to the other prisoner, but that was different. Pirithous started to tear, too, but not through his legs. The stretch marks whipped around his chest, his neck. He'd be fully torn in half if H pulled any more, so H left him behind.

Hades was still ranting up at Zeus as H left the room.

'You don't send messages, no *how's work, brother?* Oh no, you pal around with Poseidon in your precious sunlight until it's time to come down here and STEAL MY THINGS.'

I don't know what I was more glad to escape, Hades' shouting or the bits of the kid's thighs still stuck to the throne. It felt like they were staring at us.

We snuck out behind H and his new ally, who was so relieved to be free he noticed neither the loss of his friend nor the missing backs of his legs. They should have been bleeding, I thought, but I guess you can't bleed in the underworld, even if you're still alive. The skin knitted together as best it could, leaving puckered pink lines chasing up the curves of him like veins.

'Cousin,' H said, almost gently, to Theseus. I never did get to grips with H's family tree. It seemed to branch around corners. 'What happened?'

'It is a long story,' Theseus said stiffly. Not a long story then, he was just embarrassed. Happens to all of us. In the underworld, with expired heroes, talk often turns to the

172

dramatic ways you died. You know, captured by cannibals, mauled by fire-breathing horses, drowned in a pool of nymphs. All equally heroic.

Theseus and H walked up to Cerberus. He was, and I don't say this lightly, a Big Dog. Taller than I'd be standing on my own shoulders. More heads too. Cerberus' count sat at three, none of which looked appealing enough for Hades to be so upset. He slobbered. A lot. The dog, not Hades.

(Sometimes Cerberus would wander over to scratch his back on the warmer parts of the underworld. If you get his hair on you it's not coming off until you're reborn.)

Their capture of the dog was simple. Theseus shouted for his attention and H snuck round the other side and grabbed the far-most head in a lock. I wanted to shout then, how stupid it was to put a three-headed animal in a headlock, but I couldn't. It worked. Cerberus gave a happy squeak, H slung him across his shoulders, and started walking away.

He didn't notice us at all. He locked his eyes on his way out and refused to bend from his path. I loved that when we were together. He was so single-minded you felt like the entire world in his gaze. I never truly felt like a spirit until I was in his peripherals, but there I was.

That was H's last labour, and a disappointing end to them. No flames, no great heroics, just the final stage of forgetting who he was before he was *Hercules*. Forgetting us.

We didn't speak so much after that, me and Megara. We'd lost our reason to.

We were good friends down there in Hades. I can only see that irritating H, but we knew each other first, and, as it went, we knew each other last.

Don't get me wrong. I'm no innocent. I loved him, so very much. I loved him whether or not Hera caused his madness, and I loved him despite him killing my father.

(Down here, Dad and I don't speak. It's a reassuring beat of normalcy.)

It's impossible to explain to anyone who hasn't loved him, what it's like to be there in the eye of the storm. To be looked at as though you are more important than any of the gods, to be given adventure on a plate, and to feel safe every minute of it, because you are safe, until you're not.

Lest I become too maudlin, I'll say only this on his last labour. I was jealous of Meg. It was the end of his punishment for killing her, for killing her children, and he didn't look back. She had a line to draw. I'd spend years waiting for mine.

Doodles on a Throne

|||||||||||||
||||||||||||
Bored. Bored bored bored.
What do you call a smart Kymean? Nobody.
A Kymean goes shopping for windows, asks, do you have any
that point south?
|||||||||||||||||
There was a young woman from Thebes—
Who couldn't rhyme anything with Thebes—
~~We are~~ I am so thick
Stuck in the pit
When ~~we~~ I could be with young ladies from Thebes
|||||||||||||

Eurystheus III

Not only did he fail to die, yet again, but he brought a friend with him, as if one murderous 'hero' were not enough to pollute my palace. I whispered a quick prayer to Hera. *Forgive me.*

'Cousin,' the oaf boomed. He never did learn to whisper. 'I have returned.'

'Yes, I can hear that,' I said, resisting the urge to block my ears against the onslaught, or wrap his face in blankets to muffle him. His inability to breathe would be a bonus. 'Did you fail then? Because you kn—'

'I have the dog. It's being guarded outside.' Maybe the years had taught him a lick of common sense, then. 'There's someone I'd like you to meet. Cousin,' the oaf cried.

'Yes, I'm already here, suffering your conversation.'

'Not you,' the oaf derided, though he had no right to, still officially my slave. 'Theseus, this is our cousin Eurystheus. My lord Eurystheus, this is Theseus, son of Poseidon. I met with him and his mother during my labours.'

'Did he help you in your latest task?' I asked, ignoring his outstretched hand.

'No, *he* helped *me*,' Theseus said. If it was task two or five or even nine I might have fought it, insisted the oaf stay, but I was tired. I love Hera with everything within me, but I didn't want to be master of the oaf anymore. I wanted my home to feel safe for my wife and children.

Once he left, if he *ever* came back I would no longer be bound by the rules of being a good host, or the arbitrary restrictions laid down by his father to protect him. If he came near me, or my family, I could have him strung up in every way I fantasised about. I only needed him to leave first.

So, instead of complaining, I shook the hand of the man who revolts me. 'Congratulations, cousin, your trials are over.'

'Really?'

'Truly.'

'This calls for a feast.' He grinned. I hated that, hated how quickly he'd forgotten what he'd done. Maybe he saved lives doing what I directed, but his hands would always reek of blood.

I inspected the dog, of course, but there's only so close one needs to get to ascertain that a three-headed dog has three heads. It was angry, as if the very sight of life offended it. I waved a hand for it to be freed and it took three great bounds before disappearing into the air, returning to its true master.

We did have a feast, to celebrate our freedom from each other. I've never loved my wife more than then; she handled him, asked him banal questions, about what he would do now his life was his own, and he gave banal responses about settling down and starting again. If I learned anything about the oaf, apart from his infinite capacity for murder, it was that he'd never settle. Not with me, not with his companions, and certainly not with a wife and cherubic children.

We ate our finest food and drank our finest wine – he didn't notice that my servants had instructions to prevent him from overindulging. The oaf even wore something untorn beneath that ridiculous cloak of his. Admete sang beautifully, her voice clearer than the first birds in the morning, the belt of Hippolyta hanging gracefully around her waist. She was a shining star in the gloom the oaf had drawn upon our lives.

He flinched as she began to sing. But he got over it fast enough. Between bragging about his exploits – as if I, the person who set his tasks, were not aware of them – and grinning at Theseus – settling down indeed – he sat beside me and poured me more wine.

'Wanting a return to servitude so soon?' I said. 'I'm sure the gods will oblige, if you ask them nicely.'

'How did your daughter like the belt?' he asked abruptly. He never learned tact. Gods forbid one have capacity for thought when that space could be used for additional musculature. But, given what that belt meant to me, I couldn't give him anything but an honest answer.

'She loves it, sleeps with it on, sometimes. She's even learning to fight.' If I smiled as I said it, it wasn't for him.

'I'm sorry, truly, that it couldn't be your eldest.'

If I could've slapped him without incurring the wrath of the gods, I would have. If I could use every skill I learned from the back-alley criminals, I would have. How dare he speak of her. How dare he speak of lost children when he made a choice to lose his, when I would have taken my own life a thousand times over to save her. I would've undertaken all his labours without blinking for even a chance of saving mine, when he did them to forget his.

'I believe your cousin would like to talk to you,' I said. It was a brazen lie. Theseus was deep in conversation with another of our guests – my children having been strictly warned to keep a wide berth of both men – his cheeks getting rosier and growing more pleased with himself by the minute.

'*Our* cousin, Eurystheus,' he stressed. What I would have done to scrub at my family tree, to remove the branches of pumped-up men with murderous instincts. Glory would've been nice, the oaf pretending he was doing any of these tasks in my name, but I'd trade it all to sit at dinner with my cousin without bile rising inside my throat.

He left the next morning, taking his little friend with him. He said, sounding both ominous and vague, that he had *things to do*. I found I didn't care what these were. He took his stupid lion skin and his club and his bow and his collection of animal tusks and teeth and what seemed to be a whole human ear, dried with age, with him.

I could let my daughters walk free in their own home. I could stand in the hallways of my house and breathe. For the first time in twelve years, the air felt clean. He might have thought finishing his tasks earned his freedom. Truth is, he was earning mine too.

Iolaus II

My uncle Herc is a weird guy. I know that, but I forget sometimes, 'cause I'm so used to him and his special circumstances and whatever. It's different for Dad and Gran and Aunty Lao and everyone – they knew him before. For me he was always like this.

Don't get me wrong, he's my favourite relative by a long way – apart from maybe my cousin Theseus, though he's been a bit weird too, since he got stuck to that chair down in Hades – but Uncle Herc gets sad sometimes. Okay, he gets sad a lot. Not like, teary, but quiet. Then he drinks to be loud and then he's too loud and it's all fake and uncomfortable, like when you borrow someone's shoes without telling them.

After his labours were over, Eurystheus kicked him out with nothing, which Uncle Herc wasn't too mad about. He said it was easy to break stuff in Eurystheus' place and it had him on edge. So he walked over to the next village and sent a messenger to come find me – saying *I'd* cover the payment, the cheeky git – but I headed out anyway and here we were. Walking.

We're always walking, when I'm with him. Twelve years of adventures together, and the only constant was *walking*. Apart from when we were sailing and that's no more fun. I used to get seasick, you know. He had us circle the islands three times so I'd get used to it. I was so ill I wanted Hades to swallow me up, but I never got sick again.

So we're walking, and he's like, let's do something fun.

And I stand there, like an idiot with my mouth open. *Huh. What?*

'Something fun, Iolaus. What do the young people do for fun these days?' Gods above, Dad's always telling me not to call Uncle Herc old, even though he totally is, and then he goes and says something like that.

'Why don't we do something you think's fun?' I suggested, all casual like, because I don't really want to be dragging my weird uncle out with my friends.

'I haven't had fun in twelve years, nephew,' he said. Which is, one, a weird thing to say, and two, rude. We spent a bunch of that time together. 'Course I know about his wife and his dead kids and stuff. It's difficult to be a human in Greece and not know, but I'm a kid. What does he want me to say? Hey, sorry your family's dead?

And it's not like I could just say, let's get fucked-up drunk. Because Dad told me not to. He loves his brother but he shouldn't be trusted around alcohol. Which *to be fair* is an instruction I've ignored a bunch of times, but talking about his dead wife isn't an alcoholic pigeonhole I wanted to fall into.

I thought on it, which was harder than it should have been. The question made me forget everything I'd ever enjoyed and for like two whole minutes all I could think about was the taste of celery, which I hate. Eventually I gave up, spat the ghost of the celery out, and said the first thing that came to mind.

'Chariots?' I love chariots. When I'm driving one, I don't have to think about the future, I have to be there, in the moment. Maybe Uncle Herc needed that too.

Plus, girls love chariots.

(I needed to do something girls love after that rumour about me marrying Uncle Herc's dead wife which one, gross; two, gross; and three, she's *dead*, so gross.)

'Young people think chariot racing is the height of fun?' Herc asked suspiciously, like I was trying to trick him into being a lame old man or something, which I'd be too late for *anyway* 'cause he keeps using the phrase *young people*.

'Do old people not think chariot racing is fun?'

'Are you calling me old, young man?' He grabbed my shirt and his eyes did that thing, the kind of green flashy thing that unsubtly reminds you, yo my dad is Zeus, wanna be smited?

'Are you calling me young?' I said without thinking. He laughed and put me down. I never learned to guard my tongue. I just say random shit and hope it works, which doesn't go so well with most people but Uncle Herc liked it. Mum says it's 'cause he has no patience for careful thought but then Dad tells her to shut up, he's family, and them Mum says no family of hers would— But then they see me listening and shut whatever door they're next to or talk more quietly or kick me out of the house to 'find a job' or whatever.

Not long after I came back from my first adventure with Uncle Herc, Dad started sleeping in a different bed from her. Though that might've had something to do with my brother, the one who died. The one who wasn't Mum's.

'I guess not.' He laughed. '*Old man*. Show me a chariot race.'

So we wandered to the closest town and I found some guys

who looked like they'd rather die than spend another day in their middle-of-fucking-nowhere town and offered them a race. The chariots were shit and the horses were worse, but hey, at least it put everyone level.

I drove and Uncle Herc did the fighting. I liked that, thought it was funny I was in charge, and he had to look after me. But he acted like I was just some mobile fighting machine, like a stupid horse. We didn't use swords or bows or anything too dangerous, just big pointy sticks, but Uncle Herc got it wedged right into one of their wheels and they flipped up and over and we cruised to victory.

'That,' one of the kids panted, 'was awesome. We've never seen anyone so good at fighting before.' They crowded round Uncle Herc, which ratted me up. I love my uncle, but no way he did all the work there. Fact is, they got their stick in our wheels first and I managed to manoeuvre out of it without even slowing pace.

When I was a kid, I wanted to be Uncle Herc's chariot driver. I mean, I didn't want to be that, specifically. I wanted to travel with him and be a hero like him, only bigger and better and without the dead wife. But Mum didn't want me to and Dad wasn't convinced, so I had to get good at something so he'd have no choice but to take me. So I got real good at the chariot. Maybe the best in the world.

But all these people saw was his fighting, only Uncle Herc noticed and shrugged it off like an itchy cloak.

'Nah, it was just good driving, right, Iolaus?' See, I know he was being nice because he didn't call me Twerp or Gangly – just 'cause I'm taller than him now – or his personal favourite, Little Shit.

'Better than the turds we were up against,' I retorted, not

really to piss them off, but 'cause it's not cool to say you're the greatest and the best – unless you're Zeus – Optimus Maximus, right? – but I wasn't going to say I was straight-up shit either.

Only the locals got all offended and there was a bit of a scrap and we ended up punching the kids in the face and being invited to leave town at dawn. It wasn't the first time.

'Hey,' Uncle Herc asked as we were leaving, flanked by their best and strongest men, the both of them sporting black eyes. 'Where's the closest real city to this?'

'Olympia,' one of them grunted, but it came out all weird, until I looked close and realised his front tooth had cracked in half. I wonder if one of us did that or if it was some old olive pip wound. Who knows in the sticks?

'Olympia,' Uncle Herc said to me with a grin. 'Has a good ring to it, don't you think?'

'What do you mean?' I asked, with no small amount of suspicion. His schemes are exciting and all, but they come with no small chance of death.

'Like we did yesterday, right, but we get all the best in the world together, for a bunch of different things, and they can drink and compete and have a big old party. What could be better?' That did sound great.

'How do we get people to buy into it?' I asked. There were other festivals of games, though people had been leery of them since the whole thing with Perseus. You know, where he was prophesied to kill his grandfather but his grandfather didn't want to die so he threw baby Perseus into the sea in a box and then grown-up Perseus went to his kingdom to compete in some contest and accidentally hit his grandfather in the face with a discus and he died? I know the moral is to not ignore prophecy or whatever, but the games thing is still a reasonable concern.

I mentioned this to my uncle.

'Simple, innit?' he said.

'Is it?'

'Yeah, we don't have the discus.'

Can't argue with that. So we sat down and drew up ideas for sports: running and wrestling and sword fighting and *chariots*. It was going to be awesome. 'Just running first,' Uncle Herc said, 'don't want to get ahead of ourselves.' Lame, but it was his idea, so . . .

When people talk about the Olympic games now, they say it with all this reverence and stuff – we did get them dedicated to the gods – but it's really just some bullshit I cooked up with my uncle on the side of the road. Good times.

So we got all our ideas together and headed for Olympia. I don't know if Uncle Herc had a real plan for when we got there, 'cause I sure didn't. In the end, we walked straight into the city and stopped at the first temple we saw. Apollo, which felt appropriate.

We found animals to sacrifice to him. Do I remember what they were? No. Was I quite drunk? Yes.

Look, Uncle Herc said it helped him think up ideas and when someone else is buying the wine it's hard not to say yeah.

The sacrifice must have been good enough, though, 'cause Apollo himself appeared to us. I thought the priest was going to shit himself.

'Your mightiness, Apollo,' my uncle said, kneeling. I scrambled to follow him. My uncle said later it wasn't his true form because that would have set me on fire, which would have been more impressive. Apollo looked like us, just better and cleaner. Gods, that sounds lame. But like, in retrospect it was lame. When you think of gods and everything they can do, wouldn't you appear as, like, a dragon with flames pouring out of your eyes or something? They're all just people. Super-hot, super-tall people. Boring.

'S'up, brother,' Apollo said. I wonder if all the Olympians talk to my uncle like that. They mostly called me mortal sprat, and not like, cousin, or whatever it is being Perseus' great-great-grandson (so Zeus' great-great-great-grandson) makes me to his actual godly kids.

'I have a proposal for you,' Uncle Herc said.

'Now, you know I don't want to get married, whatever Hera says,' Apollo muttered. It must be so cool to be a god and say that shit without the immediate fear of someone disembowelling you with crows.

'Games,' Uncle Herc said. 'Sports. In the names of the gods. The strongest young men around, fighting for their favour.'

'Hmm,' Apollo said. He looked like an athlete. All muscle and oil and that shit, though his beard was a little tame for me. 'Fighting? I like it. Do the appropriate blessings and you have my approval.'

That was easier than expected. I imagine people who aren't in my family have a tougher time getting things approved by the gods.

'Thank you, Lord Apollo,' Uncle Herc said.

'Oh, and Hercules?' Apollo said, form already dissipating like the morning mist. 'Make them naked.'

The Olympic Games were born. Look, we were low on wine – my dad's advice about not drinking with my uncle was never going to last for long – and our heads hurt when we came to choosing a name. At least it was accurate. We'd spent ages thinking about, like, the prizes for the victors and the events and the food we'd provide and what we'd have to bribe various people to come and what we'd do if Apollo had said no.

(The answer is nothing. Uncle Herc had this great big idea about storming off to Olympus and demanding a blessing in exchange for something involving giants and literal Mother Earth, but the answer is nothing. My dad's not Zeus. If the gods say no, the answer's no.)

The first Olympic Games was kind of scrappy. We had enough people, just about. We tried to convince Dad to join in but we got a letter back that said, between the lines, *I've lost enough contests to my brother.* A fair point.

I told Uncle Herc he could only compete in one event. That was a joke. We only had one event. It was the footrace.

People came from across the city and cheered, for free food, as much as anything else – I wonder how Uncle Herc came by money. I never saw him get any, especially not when he was, you know, a slave, but he was never short of it.

Laonome's husband, Euphemus, came. He didn't win, but he was real fun to have around and he cheered louder than anyone. Especially when I won the unofficial chariot race we did on the last night. We couldn't have a real one, my uncle said, because the organiser winning the contest is a bad look. Euphemus shouted so loud I didn't know if he'd ever talk again.

We got our inaugural winner and had a party and praised Apollo who praised us right back 'cause, as he demanded, every contestant was buck-arse naked.

I can only imagine what Apollo'd do if they tried to host an Olympic Games where the athletes wore clothes.

Two weeks of revelry later, Uncle Herc and I stumbled into our rooms.

'Why something fun?' I asked. Like I said, I don't think before I speak. It's part of my charm. And it was the first time I'd stopped long enough to question why we were doing this.

'Huh?'

'You said you want to do something fun.'

'Oh. That. The youngest. Would have been an adult. Officially.'

Oh.

See, my Uncle Herc is a weird guy. He's all sweet and lovely and spends weeks organising the most amazing games in Greece technically in the name of the gods, but really to honour every-thing his youngest son could have been, or whatever. But he's also the guy whose hands ripped said child into tiny pieces – at least, that's how Mum describes it. Dad says it was a painless way to die and 'we really shouldn't talk about this, Iolaus' – and I know it was Hera's fault and all, but sometimes he looks at those hands and he looks so disgusted it's hard to put those ideas together.

I remember him holding his son. Maybe his youngest? I don't know. He and Meg had, like, a lot of kids, and all of them real close together. Whichever one of them it was, he proper loved them, you know? His eyes did the starstruck thing.

'You don't have a family,' he said.

'I have you. And Dad.'

'Don't you want more?' he asked.

I didn't know. I'd never thought about it. Whatever it was, I took the most straightforward next step and threw up. It was splashy. As I was going to sleep, I thought I heard him again.

'I want more. I don't want them getting hurt, but I want more.'

Maybe I imagined it. I was very drunk, and it was late. I get weird dreams when I've been drinking.

We didn't talk about the reason for the games again. What could we gain from it? So we talked about the games themselves, how well they'd gone. We talked about the city and how they were going to keep running them. We'd created a legacy.

We split up after that, for a bit. Uncle Herc had heard some rumour about some contest for some princess's hand in marriage, thought he could win it. I didn't want to get married.

I went back to Olympia a couple of times. I never lost the chariot race, but it was never so much fun again.

Race Report, Olympics

Date: Day 6 of 11
Time: Immediately after the slaying of 100 oxen to Zeus
Event: Stade
Winner: Siotades

Race Notes: All contestants – both Cretan and Ephebian – lined up to begin the sprint. There were some complaints over the ground, and the smell attracting flies, but these were quickly quashed by asking whether they intended to snub the sacrifice to Zeus. Our founder, Hercules, chose not to compete, instead judging the final line. He insisted he would have no conflict with the attendance of his nephew, for he would win by such a margin. This was not the case; his nephew seemed to sway as he ran, but Iolaus took it well. He was the first to buy a drink for the winner, and spoke fondly of introducing chariot races in future cycles.

Iole I

My life was improbably still before I met him. When men looked at me, I reflected their mothers and sisters and wives. I was no great beauty then, nor now, but I didn't offend the eyes that looked upon me. I could play the lyre well enough, without writing a song to make the heart race. I could get my point across, without being cunning or clever.

It made me the perfect wife for a hero, my father thought. When it came time for me to be married he brought in a woman to do my hair, and spread the news far and wide.

People came. It helped that I was a princess.

Our island is a beautiful one still, though it's harder to see after all that happened there. The water strokes the shore gentler than any place I've ever been. It promises good harvests and happy lives. Between the backdrop and my new hair, I understand how I came to be called beautiful, but if anyone looked too closely it would dissipate.

I think that's why Father organised the competition. Even if someone realised my plainness, they'd be honour-bound to continue.

'What would you like them to compete in?' my father asked, and I startled.

'You'd have me choose?'

'It's your husband,' he said. I spent a long time considering. I'd never thought about who I wanted before.

I didn't have some friend from childhood I'd convinced myself I was in love with, some flame I wanted to rig the contest for. My closest friends were my brothers. I chose the contest based on what I thought would make me happy.

Wrestling was impressive to watch, but I wasn't of great stature and I didn't want to disappear in the shadow of my husband. The same was true of sword fighting, but with the added concern I'd see them cut meat for dinner and wonder what else they used a knife for.

I might have chosen footracing, which accomplished itself as both a show of virility and not being particularly violent, were it not for that nasty business with Atalanta's suitors. I had no desire to kill mine, nor have any god intercede and force me into marriage with one I abhor.

I thought long and hard over what the challenge was to be, for I wanted to know the winner was someone I had at least a chance of falling in love with.

My parents were in love, before it all. Father brought Mother flowers from the garden and they'd twine their fingers under the table when they thought no one was looking, as if love was some shameful thing. But then she died, and the soft looks and in-jokes were gone, and Father dedicated himself to making sure we were safe.

I had the worst of it, his only daughter. He had three sons and none of them bore the resemblance to our mother that I did. At first, after Mother died, it was difficult to persuade him to allow me outside without guards. It got better, but it was important to Father that my husband be a protector, and it was important to me that my husband didn't die, as Mother did, too young.

I chose archery. I don't believe fighting at a distance is shameful if it keeps you coming home.

'That was smart.' Iphitus, my middle brother, grinned, elbowing me.

'What do you mean?'

'Well, don't you want a husband who can control his arrows?' he asked, his face sweet as butter. I glared at him until he broke, and he wriggled his eyebrows salaciously.

Iph might be my favourite brother, but he's also an idiot with a dirty mind.

'I want my husband to be a man who stays alive,' I said stiffly. I thought then that to be a wife meant being an adult, stiff and serious all the time. I'm thankful I had the chance to learn otherwise.

'Thinking of Mum?' Iphitus asked.

'Yeah.'

'I miss her.'

'Me too,' I said. He wrapped an arm around me. We sat together watching the ships of my suitors come in, commenting on their suitability, against the arbitrary rules he'd invented.

'Oh, his hair, sis, you must marry him. Your children would look like demons,' he exclaimed. It was red as shock and anger, and mine tended towards wild curls.

'Gods forbid, they'd never survive the teasing. How about that one?' I suggested. He looked nice. Broad shoulders, but not too broad. A good head of normal-looking hair. A stride that gave him time to look around our beautiful island. Maybe I could fall in love with that man.

'Terrible breath,' Iphitus sneered.

'How can you possibly tell that from this distance?' I asked, feigning suspicion. Iph never hid his preference for the coarser sex. Maybe he was only there to pick the best for himself.

'Even his dogs recoil from it,' he said. Now, I didn't see them recoil, but at that moment the hunting dog tipped its head back and gave a magnificent howl. We couldn't help but laugh.

The suitors stayed for two weeks while the contest was organised and executed. In that time, whenever we heard a dog howling, my brother needed only lean over and mutter *someone's been eating garlic* for me to collapse in stitches.

'Now, that,' Iph said, breaking himself out of the giggles far before I could, 'is a strong contender.'

He wasn't particularly tall, but gods above was he broad. You could have stacked three of me shoulder to shoulder and barely reached across him. His skin was golden, by the light of the setting sun – Father would be angry if we didn't return home soon – and his gait so strong I could see the imprints of his feet on the sand.

'He'd snap me like a twig,' I said, but my eyes never left his figure. 'Holy cow, Iph, do you know who that is?'

Mum told us the Io story when we were kids. She was beautiful and beloved by Zeus, and she had a similar name to me, so I fell over myself to make comparisons between us. Until the end of the tale when Hera turned Io into a cow. Then it became the funniest thing in the world to my brothers, who teased me relentlessly.

I wasn't sure how *I'd* started using the phrase *holy cow*, but I blamed Iph for it as a matter of course.

'Hercules,' he said softly. 'Gods above, sister, you can never say you're not beautiful again when you have *Hercules* bidding for your hand.'

I didn't believe it, even then. I didn't believe it as we trailed back into the palace, earlier laughter forgotten. I didn't believe it as we sat and he ate, and he ate and he ate. I didn't believe it all the way to the opening ceremonies where all twenty men lined up, waiting for my approval.

My brother didn't suffer the same hang-ups. He introduced himself to my suitors, shaking hands and looking seriously down his nose, asking how they intended to treat his favourite sister. Another old joke, that. I'm his only sister. It was a nice question, though, for how it confused them, these men who could speak so long about their own achievements. When asked what they'd do to make me happy, they largely stood silent, or mumbled something about providing me sons.

I wanted children, a big family. I don't think it takes a particularly outstanding man to provide that. They promised me food on my table, protection against those who'd steal me – the world had been rocked five years before, when Helen was kidnapped by some spotty teens. My favourite of the responses was the man who promised he'd help with my hair, as long as I wanted, and he'd hold my counsel as long as I cared to give it.

Hercules, though, promised me little. He had the gall to smirk at Iphitus, who smirked back, in on some joke of my marriage I didn't get to be a part of.

'I won't trouble you by always being underfoot, and I'll endeavour never to bore you, my princess,' he said. I don't know about you, but to me that sounded like he had no intention of being a husband at all, just a hero and a father. I did dearly want a husband.

I'm ashamed to say now, but I remember only three of the suitors' names. The man with the breath was Thaddaeus. He was rather pleasant to look at, and to speak to, if you stood a safe distance from him. Next to him sat Leander, the second youngest of the bunch, and my did he look it. He was pale where the others were tanned, and he was open where they were proud. He was the one who offered to braid my hair, used to doing so for his sisters.

'Do not tell them, but yours is far lovelier.' He smiled carefully. All he did was careful. The other suitors would eat him up if he gave them reason.

'Scared of offending their delicate sensibilities?' I asked of his sisters.

'Scared of their retribution, more like.' We spoke more of small things, of family. I'd speak to all my suitors about family – I had a lot of second sons, see, come for a title of their own.

And, of course, I remember Hercules. For all his pride, his unbending confidence, I struggled to speak to him. He wouldn't have his jaw bent or his arm twisted into uttering even one syllable about family. I didn't push. We all knew what happened with his first wife. One of many disadvantages of becoming the wife of someone so famous as Hercules.

When my mother died, people were watching us, expecting us to act a certain way, when all *I* wanted to do was curl up in my room and cry. I know we were lucky, I do, to have all the nice things we did, but I didn't want to be watched like that again.

While I had no luck getting Hercules to speak, Iph did. Conversation flowed fast and smooth between them and I could scarcely understand a word that passed either of their lips. They spoke of friends loved, of monsters defeated, of drinks drunk. They spoke of things even I didn't know about my brother. I heard them speak for half a night about the discomfort of being forced to wear shoes.

Meanwhile, my interactions with him went as follows:

'How was your journey here? It must have been some journey from where you were?' I asked. I found it a fair question for all my suitors.

'The weather was adequate and the gods kind.'

'That is good news.'

'Yes.'

In many ways, I was as constrained as Iphitus was not, and in others it didn't matter. If it had been my brother, not me, being competed over, he would have found a way to bestow upon Hercules a blessing to ensure he won the contest. He would have stolen Father's bow – a gift from his father, and from his father before him, the god Apollo – and passed it over, pride be damned.

I didn't do that. It wasn't needed.

The morning of the contest, the men lined up and were presented with bows from our own stores. This was to be a fair test, Father insisted. I think he wanted to prevent accidents.

It quickly became clear half these men could use a bow in a ceremony and that was it. Father respectfully dismissed them and the contest became more difficult. All three of those I remember survived that cut, with various levels of flashiness and charm. I liked Thaddeus' response the best, saying he should be competent, otherwise when he hunts the dogs would be doing all the work. Leander said nothing in particular, merely shrugging and offering that he had good tutors and a steady hand. He didn't fear delicate work.

Hercules grunted that bows were better than swords.

'He finds swords too violent, designed only for killing men,' Iph whispered to me.

'Bit rich from a man who uses a club.'

'A natural thing, pulled from a tree,' Iph insisted. I only had to raise my eyebrows at him for him to drop the pretension of earnestness. 'Swords scare him, I think, for how much damage he could do, and how fast.'

When we broke for lunch, it was inordinately clear Hercules would win. Talented, practised, and steady as my other suitors were, they couldn't hold the smoothness that comes from being the favourite son of Zeus.

'Sister,' Iph said formally. Intriguing. 'Walk with me.'

'You'd drag me away from these men who travelled so far for my hand?' I asked, enjoying winding him up.

'The flowers are beautiful this time of year,' he said. I stood immediately. It was an old signal, when Mother was sick and Father was upset and we needed to escape whatever room we were trapped in.

'Are you okay?' I said once we were out of earshot. 'What's wrong? Is Father okay?'

'Everyone's fine.'

'Then why did you summon me out here, Iph? It wasn't good form to—'

'Hercules is going to win the contest.'

'Anyone with eyes could have told you that.'

'You can't let him win, sis; please, don't marry him,' Iph said. I don't think he'd said *please* to me since infancy.

'Explain.'

You've probably already guessed what my brother said to me

that day. It's easy, when you're a safe distance away, and your life isn't a farce.

'There's little I can do,' I said after he told me. 'Why not ask him to throw the contest?'

'I have. He won't. His pride.' Pride. The bane of every man I met, it seemed. I'd have chosen any of a dozen traits before I chose glory, yet glory they offered.

'Then?'

'Tell Father to exclude him; tell him you cannot marry him.'

'We can't pull him out of the contest, Iph – he's a dangerous man. Imagine how he'll react if we throw him out for no reason—'

'He's not dangerous. Hera cursed him; it wasn't him doing any of those things,' Iph said. My brother. In love with my suitor. But I loved him. My brother, not my suitor.

'You trust him? Completely?'

'I do, sis. I really do.'

'Holy cow, so I'm to go to Father and beg him to exclude a man from this contest for being violent in the past, though we're sure he is perfectly safe now?'

'That is a true fact,' he affirmed.

The whole idea of him murdering his family didn't seem *real*, in the same way him killing the Hydra didn't feel real. They were fairy tales, stories to help small children sleep. Okay, Hercules was a bit short with his words, but he still acted like a *person*. People don't just kill their families.

I don't know if it was the ridiculousness of the situation or the panic it entailed, but we both laughed, hysterically, until my dress was muddy and Iph's hair was as dishevelled as if he'd spent a month's worth of nights outside.

It helped, when I went to Father. The tears of happiness had dried on my cheeks, implying something different when I knelt before him. I begged him to remove the most famous man in Greece, and the rightful winner, from the competition.

'Iole, it would not be politic to remove him.'

'He's dangerous, Father. I wouldn't be able to sleep even a night in his arms for fear of the things he'd do to me. He killed Megara. Who knows what lies in store for his second wife—' I wished I didn't have to lie to my father, but my brother deserved to be loved just as much as I did.

'Okay, sweetheart. I'll remove him. You're safe.'

Hercules didn't take the news well. He raged and shouted and threw his bow to the floor with such ferocity that not only the bow, but also the floor snapped. Over the commotion, Father caught my eye and whispered that I had done the right thing, coming to him. My safety was more important than any glory this man might bring our descendants. I suppose with Iphitus that was less of a concern.

He stormed out, making dramatically for the sea, though he had to wait for his boat to be prepared. We worried he'd strop there for the duration of the tournament, and he did for a time, but then he walked away. We sighed in relief. We were safe.

The tournament continued, making its way down to only Thaddeus and Leander. They were good sports. They dared themselves to move further and further from the targets, until I wondered whether Hercules truly would have won had we permitted him to continue.

Their scores were neck and neck, smiles on both of their faces as they prepared to shoot, when Iph came running up to where we were standing.

'Father, it's an emergency. Autolycus has struck,' he spluttered, out of breath from the climb up the cliff's edge. He was too late; the final shots had been loosed. 'Your horses, they're missing.'

Father sprinted after him, to check on his beloved mares. Leander won the contest, we were married, and that was the end of that.

Iphitus I

I didn't feel wonderful about stealing my sister's fiancé, but I loved him. What else could I do?

I didn't tell Hercules my plan. It would've offended his sense of fairness. It's not so shocking really. When you lose the best decade of your life because a goddess felt like using you as a punching bag, fairness becomes very important to you.

It wasn't love at first sight. Sure, he was beautiful, handsome, rugged, whatever word you prefer, but he only had eyes for my sister, as was right and expected. When we spoke first, Iole lay heavy on his mind.

'What is she like to live with?' he asked.

'I can't answer that,' I said.

'Because it's cheating? I assure you, the competition is merely a formality,' he said.

'And the other nineteen suitors will tell me the same.' I smiled. He returned it. 'But I can't tell you because I can't describe it. She's my sister; she's simply there.' I imagine Iole would have humphed if she heard my flattering description of her, then stamped on my foot for good measure.

'What of you, then?' he replied. 'What are you like to live with?' I was so surprised I gave him an answer that was equal parts exaggeration and flat-out lies.

'Me? I'm a nightmare, a veritable monster upon the house.'

'Is that so?' Hercules smirked, a challenge.

Bravery struck me. 'Walk with me – I'll tell you more.'

We walked together, in an easy loop around the palace. He didn't gaze fondly at the flowers, admit that inside he was gentle as a lamb or some other nonsense. He didn't lie. He looked to the horizon and held his gaze there longer than necessary.

'I like the sea. It's clean,' he said, staring frustrated at his hands, as if it was their fault he couldn't get his message through.

'Because it moves, right? Pulls away all the bad stuff and makes it better.'

'Yes.' He looked at me then. His eyes softer than I had ever seen them. 'That's the truth of it.'

If I had to point to when we fell in love, it would be then. Not that the sea thing was particularly profound. I know my sister thinks the same about it, though I doubt her saying it would have elicited the response I got. Few people tried to understand Hercules. It was the surety of something, anything, I hadn't felt since my family was whole.

We spent a lot of time together. We didn't sneak away because we didn't have to. It was perfectly acceptable for the brother of the bride to maintain friendly relationships with her suitors. I won't tell you exactly how friendly we grew. It was enough. The night before the contest started, I whispered in his ear *shoot straight* and he sighed like I'd stabbed him. But he did.

We took breakfast together on the last day of the contest. I sat opposite him, my feet folded under my legs, my hands lying in invitation for him to stretch out and touch them. He didn't, that morning, when it seemed he'd marry my sister within the week.

'You don't have to marry her,' I ventured carefully.

'It's a contest. I will win,' he said. Straightforward, still, I liked that: being apart from the games of court and the tongues that trip over themselves when all I wanted was to laugh.

'But what if you don't?'

'I don't understand.'

'But what if you don't win?' I said again, putting all the right emphasis on all the right words for him to understand what I was suggesting.

'I'm only a guest here because I'm your sister's suitor. Once the contest's over, I'd have to leave you, Iphitus, and I am sick of leaving people I love behind.'

If you've never loved a deeply broken person, it's difficult to explain how I felt. I knew I wasn't going to fix him, not going to cover the loss of his wife, the pain of being forced to do it with his own hands. I was never going to replace Hylas, forever on that island, or close the wounds of Abderus, who died protecting Hercules from the mares of Diomedes. I couldn't give him the chance to really know his nephew, Pyrrhus, before Hera forced him to kill his own blood once more. Nothing I could do would repair the losses piled upon him.

Not even a god could return him from that pain. I was the best chance he had of being whole again, though, and he knew it. When he looked at me, it was hungry, sometimes, eyes gaping with everything he'd lost, and the fear of what was yet to come.

He was so gentle when he held me. It happens when you've never loved someone without them breaking. When I made him promises, I kept them simple.

'I'll come with you.'

'You cannot. Your family—'

'Iole will understand—'

'You still have a family, Iphitus. Cherish it,' he snapped. I didn't mention it again, didn't tell him my family would go on without me, but *he* wouldn't.

I went to my sister, begged her to reject him for the very reasons he'd reject me. Because I have a family left to cherish. She said yes. My love didn't take it well.

He stormed off to his boat, and I prayed he'd wait for me. I'd planned only to grab my things, say quick goodbyes to Iole, my brothers, and the horses. If necessary, I'd have a loud argument with Father over his exclusion. Then I'd follow him, as long as he waited for me.

Best-laid plans have a truly irritating habit of screwing you over.

I'd already packed, so I picked up my things and went down to the stables.

The gates weren't open, technically. They were completely unattached to the fences. I looked at the breaks and reassured myself – you'd need specialist tools for this, the kind only a bandit would have. They were too clean to be made by human hands. No one shy of a god had the strength for that, not even my Hercules.

So I ran to Father, and told him what had happened. A disaster, the horses had escaped.

'That bastard,' he grumbled, and I couldn't help but agree. The thief Autolycus had been terrorising the islands around us recently. While this was more audacious than anything he'd done in recent times, it fit his style: stealing things he couldn't possibly want, because he could. Those horses didn't provide just us with a livelihood, but many of the locals too. They kept the island running, and I worried what would become of us without them.

'This is egregious, even for Autolycus,' I groused.

Father looked at me as if I were simple. 'This is clearly the work of Hercules,' he said.

'Why would he do such a thing? He doesn't need the money.' That statement was partially true. While I didn't doubt Hercules' ability to make a living with his talents, on parchment he was bereft of assets. He had none from his birth family nor his first marriage.

'He's clearly bitter we didn't let him win our Iole. Only proves we were right about him, eh?' Father allowed himself the hint of a smile.

'A totally reasonable thing to be angry about,' I pointed out, doing my best, and failing, to keep my cool. 'If that was an issue you should have presented it *before* allowing him to compete, not ingloriously pulling him out for doing something he was compelled to by the gods.'

'Oh, son, do you really believe that?'

'Yes.' I had longer arguments planned, but I couldn't force them out. Maybe Hercules was rubbing off on me.

'Who else possibly could have stolen them?' Father looked sad now, almost deflated. He knew then that he'd lost me.

'Autolycus, the famous thief who's been plaguing us for seasons?' I suggested.

'This would be unlike him.'

'I'll prove it,' I announced. I didn't want to fight anymore, merely get it over with and move on with Hercules. 'I'll find the horses and return them.'

'You'd put everything on the line for this?' he asked.

'I would.'

'Then best of luck, my son.' He grasped my shoulder, to say all the things he couldn't. Iole didn't bother with such decorum and clasped me in a hug so tight I could scarcely breathe.

'Don't be an idiot, Iph. You come back to me whole or I'll rip you limb from limb.'

'I love you too, Io.'

She hugged me again. 'Holy cow, I love you, idiot. I mean it. Stay safe.'

'I think you mean holy horses,' I said, and she grinned. Whatever happened with Hercules, there'd always be a home waiting for me. I was lucky that way.

My goodbyes with my brothers were shorter, but no less sweet. I'll leave the description there, lest I embarrass them by showing they have feelings.

I sprinted to the beach so fast I thought my lungs would escape from my body.

'Hercules,' I shouted, over and over again. 'Hercules, I'm coming with you.'

He turned as I caught up with him, face not exactly wrapped with joy. 'Your family,' he grunted.

'It's okay. They understand. Someone stole our horses – Autolycus, I think – so officially I'm going to return them. Restore our family to good standing. Your name too.'

His face screwed up unreadably. 'We sail?'

'We sail.'

We tried tracking the prints of the horses, but we failed. Whoever stole them had tied bark to their feet, so they couldn't be followed. Further evidence it wasn't my Hercules. However many wonderful talents he had, guile worthy of Hermes wasn't one of them.

Our boat was a small one, so we moved quickly. I offered to row, to steer, to help, but Hercules said no. When he lifted the oars, I understood why. We skimmed across the water, as much bird as we were fish.

Our first night on the boat may have been the best of my life. We lay side by side, back to back, on the deck, and looked up to the stars.

'Do you know of the constellations?' I asked. When I was younger and Mother's memory was fading she'd invent new stories as the truth lost its way in her head.

'I prefer not to speak of them.' I'd never known him so stiff. I looked up and saw his constellation. Hercules, forever begging his father to help.

'Then let me tell you what they were in my house.' I told him of the elephant, the lion. I told him of stars cast into the sky for the little girl Eole who was well mannered and better behaved, who was sometimes a little boy called Ephitus. He laughed, smiled, sighed.

We spent months together on that ship. They can more or less be reduced to those three words. Laughed, smiled, sighed.

'My mother told me to look to the sky if I was scared, because that's where my father lives and he's watching over me,' he said. He never called his father Zeus, never made that connection. Scars are always visible, if you bother to look.

'Yeah? What did you say to that?'

He laughed, a good solid rumble of thunder. 'I told her I was too brave to be scared.'

I caught him stealing glances to the sky often, when things were scary, eyes snatching away just as fast. He was lying, of course, about being too brave. I knew of at least one thing that scared him so much he may as well be a child. That came from the sky too.

'How do you remember so much, Iphitus?' he said.

'What do you mean?'

'You remember everything. Names and dates and details. I can hardly hold on to the names of the beasts I have killed.'

'Well, you have killed a lot of beasts,' I said, uncomfortable. If he'd been my sister I would have teased, of course, about her being thick as two short thick things, but we weren't there yet. I hoped we would be.

'I don't remember killing them,' he said, his voice completely flat, then all that emotion coming out at once, in this great breaking tornado that threatened to capsize the boat. 'I don't remember.'

For all I'm meant to be good with these things, there'll never be anything to say to that, so I held him tight.

'I'll stick around then,' I said eventually, when the thickness in the air had lapsed enough to take a joke. 'Do the remembering for you.'

'I'd like that.'

We landed on islands. We spoke to nobles. I challenged one of them, some young man in Ithaca, to an archery contest and lost my grandfather's bow to him. Hercules didn't tell me he'd win it back, or that I should've let him compete. He let me stand on my own and, when I lost, he clapped a hand across my back and bought me a drink.

I met his sister. She was sure of herself, and grown up in a way Iole wasn't. She was also married and, I'm told, happily so, despite the uncomfortable flirting.

Hercules rolled his eyes. 'She's like that.'

She's a dozen years younger than him, more my age than his,

so she fluttered her eyes and pulled the youngest-child card. Then she reminded me of Iole, and my heart hurt so much I thought it'd bleed from how much I missed her.

It became obvious the 'search for the horses' was an excuse for our travels, though neither of us could voice it. Yet after a while, I'd have given up anything to find them, prove it wasn't Hercules, and go home. After those blissful months in the boat together, I began to nag him.

'Have we had any new leads on the horses?' I'd begin gently. It'd be easiest if Hercules thought returning to the search had been his idea.

'Not really. I heard about this beast, though—' Sometimes I would've sworn Hercules had a direct connection to Tartarus, given how much he knew about the animals promenading around Greece.

'We did come for the mares.'

'And we're still looking for them, but what's the glory in only looking for some horses? Live a little, Iph.'

Normally that worked on me. I'd loved our adventures.

Earlier that day, we'd jumped off a waterfall together. I screamed as we went down, then raced him back up to go again. I wore a cape myself, of a wildcat we'd killed together. But that night, adventure wasn't enough.

'We could redouble our efforts,' I said.

'What more is there to do?' I always loved his frankness, the straight lines of him, but when you're trying to subtly introduce an idea, it does rather make you want to slap him.

'I want to go home, Hercules.'

He stiffened and pulled away from me. 'As you wish, young prince.'

We didn't properly speak for three days. It wasn't always silence – simple instructions and requests about the boat were answered, but nothing more.

'I don't mean to leave you,' I said on the second night, a desperate attempt for forgiveness.

'They never do.' I didn't start a conversation again until we hit dry land.

'This isn't Oechalia,' I said stupidly as we brought the boat to shore. The days without speaking had stoppered my brain, made it fuzzy and idiotic.

Hercules smirked unhappily. 'This is Tiryns,' he said. 'Highest point around. To look for the mares.'

'I love you,' I breathed. He probably didn't hear. He'd started running through the city, headfirst into the wind.

'*You're it*,' he shouted, and I thought *not for long*. I was always faster than he was.

I was breathless as we ran across town to the highest hill and the tallest tower on the city walls. We raced each other up the stairs, two at a time. I tagged him on the shoulder as I overtook him, and he laughed deep and sweet, like molasses, swirling around him and filling the air. Deep like I hadn't heard in days.

We kept running until the very top.

Only one of us stopped at the window.

Theseus II

How do you become a hero?

That's not rhetorical. And it's not a moral thing. I wasn't stuck on what traits to embody or what the most righteous path was. I had enough examples of heroes to know what I was aiming for.

My issue was in the practical sense. How do you get into being a hero? It's not like being a king where you're born to it, or being a soldier where you join an army. All the times I imagined it when I was a kid, I could see the before and I could see the after, but I never thought about the bridge you take to get there.

I thought I was on track when I went to Hades with Piri. Like, I never really believed we'd manage to save Persephone and make her Piri's wife, but I thought it would set us up as heroes. A return trip to the land of the dead with a still-beating heart should do that.

All it did was teach me how irrelevant I am, in the scheme of things. Persephone didn't even talk to us. She looked over at her husband, the one who kidnapped her in the first place.

'They've come to rescue me.'

And she *smirked*, like we were so cute and darling and pathetic for caring. Maybe that pity was what saved us. We spent two years stuck to Hades' throne before my cousin Hercules came down and rescued me and together we left my blood brother to die.

After the Hades thing, I spent a lot of time in between. I went back to meet my father who's a king and I learned how to walk again. I'd spent so long working for people to see me as a fighter, and now I was right back to people using words like *whippy* and asking if I was a runner. I didn't want to be fast, I wanted to be strong. But whatever I did, it wasn't going to make a difference to how people saw me.

At least I could walk, I told myself, so I spent a lot of time wandering around Greece, hoping something vaguely heroic would leap out at me. This brought me to Tiryns, with the logic that it was where my cousin Hercules had made his name.

(Though I didn't ask Eurystheus. The first time we met he told me all heroes should be summarily killed. Twice.)

The whispers spun around Tiryns. Someone had fallen off the city walls – no, someone was pushed. Everyone else went to the bottom to rubberneck – it was a slow day, before that – but I ran to the top. I was right. There he was.

'Cousin?' I said. I should have been sure, but he looked so fucking different and he smelled weirdly of perfume. He was sitting with his head between his legs, bowed almost all the way down to the floor, making noises so guttural I couldn't work out if he was choking or crying. 'I didn't know you were in town.'

He flinched, and I saw him take a deep breath before he looked up.

'You're not Eurystheus,' he said.

'I should bloody hope not.'

'Why are you here?' he asked, a question that should have been

213

easy but felt altogether unanswerable. I kind of shrugged and waved my arms like *you know how it is, this hero life, it takes you all kinds of places.* A good enough answer for my cousin at least. He didn't wait for more of a response. 'Why am I here?'

I knew that voice, that particular shade of misery. My brother is still in Hades.

'I know,' I said, though I had no idea who it was at the bottom of those walls. Not Iolaus, I hoped. I liked Iolaus.

'I didn't do it,' he said, not the petulant cry of a child trying to get away with something. This was softer, more confused.

'Did he fall?' I asked, though that was stupid. People don't just fall around my cousin.

'Hera. She took my mind. We were – we were racing to the top and I was going to grab him and pull him back so I'd win and we'd— But she took my mind and everything turned to wine and my arms went the wrong way and then—'

And then he was falling, and my cousin was alone again.

I didn't know what to say, so I tried hugging him. That always worked for me. But Hercules didn't react. I wasn't even sure he could see me. His world was his hands or his hands were his world or maybe it had all been that man, dead at the bottom of the city walls.

'Why did it have to be me who hurt him?' he said, definitely not thinking of me this time as he raised his eyes, just barely towards the sky. 'I loved him.'

Loving people. That's a fucking flaw if you want to be a hero. Being willing to give your life for someone is all well and good but it means sooner or later you'll give your life for someone and that'll be the end of the story. Heroes can't afford for that to happen.

'I don't know where I'm meant to go from here,' he said. Nor did I. It was all I could do not to burst into tears right alongside him. But the both of us sobbing our hearts out up there wouldn't do either of us any good. Someone had to be practical.

'Let's get out of here.' Off the wall, sure, but out of Tiryns too, because killing a man outside of battle is technically illegal. We needed a king to go wipe that off and it wasn't going to be Eurystheus, was it?

I hustled him down and out of the city with minimal fuss. I travelled pretty light and Hercules seemed to travel with nothing at all and it wasn't the first time leaving in a hurry for either of us.

'We had a boat,' Herc said.

'Do you want to use it?'

'It's a boat, isn't it?' he said, more used to the practicalities of being a hero than I was. I still avoided mine and Piri's old haunts, which meant I was rather bereft of places to drink.

We stopped at the first island we came to. We would have had to even without the legal issues because Herc . . . He wasn't doing so well. He was running a fever, he squinted in the sunlight, and his skin was beginning to pucker into pox. He needed to stop, to rest and heal but he wasn't going to do that. He had a mission.

Single-mindedness, I told myself. Something that heroes have.

We managed to get ourselves an audience with the king there. Some Hippo-something. He was already pretty sneery when we got to him – 'reminds me of our other cousin,' I whispered to Herc, but he didn't let me distract him – and then Herc accidentally called him Tyndareus, which was his brother's name and he cast us out on our arses.

'I've never been any good with names,' he croaked. 'Better luck on the next one.'

'Cousin, you need to stop.'

'No, we need to do this. And I know the next guy. He owes me a favour.'

As it transpired, Augeas, king of the next island in the chain, absolutely did not owe Hercules a favour. What they had was an old argument. Hercules was convinced the best way to fix it was by smashing his door down.

'He's hardly going to pardon you if you do that,' I said.

'He besmirched my honour,' Hercules said, like it was the most natural thing in the world. Single-mindedness, I reminded myself. He was the best hero. He knew what he was doing. And so I, the man with roughly two-thirds of a standard set of legs, and Hercules, the man who was mostly pox, came to have an argument through a door with a king who wouldn't give us the time of day.

And, when he wouldn't give us the time of day, it turned into a fight.

'Just like old times,' Herc said. This was beyond me. He could barely stand. I had no idea how I could even begin to help him, so I sent a message to Iolaus.

Something's brewing with your uncle. Because there's a limit to how explicit you can be when you have no idea what's happening.

'Who're you sending that to?' Herc asked.

'I thought I was being sneaky,' I said.

'I got a sense for when people are speaking about me behind my back.'

'And your head doesn't explode?' People were always talking about him behind his back.

'People I like, then,' he said, which nearly made my head explode like I was ten again. *He liked me.* 'The letter's not for my brother?'

His voice was . . . not weak exactly, because it's hard to call my cousin that, no matter how sick he is, but it was weaker than usual, drifting in and out of focus.

'Not your brother,' I confirmed and tried to choke out every single bit of me that was screaming: *he's your brother. You have to stick by him. He'll save your life.* 'But—'

'Iph doesn't want to see me.'

And that was a problem. It was so big and pointy I was too scared to do anything about it. I went back to hammering the door, though there wasn't going to be any movement. We fought the local guards a bit, and we managed to hold them off, but Hercules was flagging and also still kind of wanted for murder.

'Why don't we come back to this when you're not sick?'

'Might not be able to,' he grunted, holding what looked like the entire wall of the castle up with his shoulder. Fuck, even in moments like this, he was still cool. 'Gotta do it now.'

'It'll be fine, just go to the doctor and we'll be back this afternoon.'

'Not that kinda plague. We'll just do this and I'll go.'

'But—'

'No,' he shouted, and for a moment the world listened. And then the world remembered he was a sick man holding a big stick and went back to doing its own thing. 'We're finishing this.'

We weren't. Between us we couldn't take down Augeas' entire guard. We'd need reinforcements or a plan or for at least one of us to be whole and well and we didn't have any of that. But I did get two letters that night. One, from Iolaus: *On my way.* It was actively smudged and the messenger looked like he was going to pass out.

'Iolaus said you'd pay me on arrival.'

'How much?' I asked. He answered, and I'm sure I turned a sicklier pallor than Herc.

'He said you were the son of a king, sir.'

I was the son of a king. I grinned without meaning to and paid up. I took the other letter, the one I hadn't been expecting. It was from my father, the one who was a king. He wanted my help.

'*Seven boys . . . Seven girls . . . Eaten . . . Monster in the labyrinth* – Cousin, this is hero stuff! My—' I read out loud. I looked up. My cousin had left. 'My dad wants me to be a hero.'

I went looking for Herc; I didn't want to leave without telling him. When I found him he was walking through the middle of town with a whole, disgruntled cow slung over his shoulder. He looked like he'd be crushed by the weight of it, which I know normal people would, but he wouldn't. Normally.

'What are you doing with that cow?'

'Negotiating,' he said. The ground rumbled beneath me. Herc looked down and growled. 'Don't you get involved too. I just need a day.'

'Look, I got this message from my king-dad and he wants me to go and—'

'Yeah, all right. I got this.'

'But, Iol—'

'I don't need a childminder. We got this, don't we, Bessie?' he said, patting the cow on the rump. 'I quite like her really. Shame I have to sacrifice her. But I need the favour.'

Another spot appeared on his hand, but I didn't have time to worry about that. I had a monster to kill. Single-mindedness is important to being a hero.

Augeas I

I never thought I'd see the overgrown turd again. I told his erstwhile master I'd kill him if he set foot anywhere near my land or my horses. But then, Eurystheus never had any control over Hercules.

The next time I wasted a thought on him was years later. Eurystheus came across positively euphoric in our usual correspondence. Apparently the labours were complete, and Eurystheus too would be free of *the oaf's* antics. The last letter I ever wrote was the reply.

I believe it arrived after my death.

It offered a curt but honest congratulations to a man who had not enjoyed the last twelve years. It offered astonishment at the atrocities Hercules was capable of, and wonder at the depths of Eury's imagination. *You were right to discount my stables from the list, as they clearly weren't adequately taxing for the man.* I knew, as I wrote it, what Eury's response would be.

Au contraire, *my dearest Augeas, your stables were perhaps the most taxing of any challenge set for the oaf. Stealing Cerberus from Hades may sound dangerous and terrifying, but it held not a candle to the mountains of shit that plagued you.*

As I wrote that last letter, the oaf was hightailing his way to me, foaming at the mouth with animalistic rage. I sent the letter with a courier and he thumped on my door four times, hard enough to dent the wood.

'Augeas, I am here for you,' he bellowed. I didn't respond kindly to the shouted threats of a madman. So no, I didn't let him in, and I didn't go to the door. I sent for my nephews, both strong, strapping young men, to fight him off.

He didn't start by fighting, which was a surprise, if not an altogether pleasant one. Because then at least if we attacked him, we'd be in the clear for skewering him as he deserved. Unfortunately, his first move was *yelling*.

'Augeas, fuckface, I know you're in there. I see that twattish robe of yours.' I wondered if our door would rot as a result of all the spittle he was hurling at the wood.

'This is a very fine robe,' I said, with all the dignity he lacked.

'You cheated me.'

'Oh, would you like a robe?'

'No. Not with— Not like that,' he spluttered. Delicious. 'You promised me payment. You cheated me. I want—'

'What, an apology?' I asked, the most genuinely curious I had ever been with this turd. Would we both sit in our fine purple robes and drink tea as I told him I was sorry with perfect insincerity? Would that really make the man spitting at my door feel better? 'That was seven years ago.'

'I don't care. Give me retribution, or I'll take it.'

'You can try,' I said, and walked away. It was a sturdy door, and I don't know who people mean when they describe Hercules' legendary fighting skills, but it's not the man I spoke to that first day. That conversation robbed all the energy from him. He was weak and flushed, barely able to lift his own club. It was pathetic. There was no way we could lose to this failure of a man.

Even as we faced his 'attack' we could see the pox colonising his face, the spots popping eagerly over his skin so the world could finally see on the outside the putridity that lay beneath. He'd brought help, a weedy-looking youth with the legs of a chicken, but he did naught to help, the two of them alternating between ineffectually slapping at the door and bickering like the overgrown children they are. We retired in the knowledge we couldn't lose.

We woke to the upsetting realisation that we could. His pox had halted overnight. The pustules were still revolting, but no worse than they had been the day before. Someone must have fed him some witch's brew to get him standing and swinging his club with all the vigour of the shit-shoveller I'd met so many years before. For the first time, I felt sympathy for Eury. He'd had to deal with this for over a decade.

He battered towards us, wielding his club with brutal efficiency. 'You denied me payment.'

'You didn't meet my terms. Of course I wasn't going to pay you.'

'You denied me payment.'

He clubbed his way through my door and buried it deeply into my skull. There was pain, blinding, but only for a fleeting moment before my spirit departed for Hades. The oaf left on his merry way, and I worried for Eury.

Deiphobus I

My usual patients were sick of body, but I'd occasionally get those who were sick of mind. People who'd lost too much, endured more than anyone should. It was harder to help, but more interesting too. There are only so many ways one can break a leg.

I'd never had a patient before who was suffering so much from both. I didn't think to ask for a name, not when they first arrived and we were laying the patient across the bed I reserved for the very sick. I knew abstractly he must be a big man, and he must spend much of his time outside, for his skin had a golden sheen to it. But if you asked when I met him, I would've told you he was small in stature and he spent little time in the sun. He'd practically collapsed in on himself.

I'm no battlefield medic. (I was lucky enough, then, not to have suffered through any wars. Give it some years, and the screams of Troy would haunt me. It's significantly more difficult to fix the ills of one's own mind.) I wasn't used to strong men being pulled in on stretchers or in the arms of those they call *brother*. I didn't know what to do with the man on whose shoulder my patient rested.

'Iolaus,' he said gruffly, holding a hand out to me but pulling it away before I could reach for it – dashing back to prevent his companion from falling. I wasn't offended. Given the state of his compatriot, I may have declined if the hand had remained.

We laid the patient down, and I fetched water. Regardless of ailment or affliction, the safest first course of action is to offer water.

I scarcely had to examine the man to have a diagnosis. In many ways, that's the worst kind of patient – I couldn't offer the answer like a prize in itself. Both he and his companion had surely worked it out for themselves.

'He has a plague,' I said definitively, in case they were simpletons. I'd never seen a person so strongly affected by the pestilence before, not without dying. Yet his companion seemed not to be suffering at all. Curious.

The man was covered in pox. Huge, gaping sores marched across his body as ants colonising a new land. There was no green to them at least, no infection come to take the kill.

His breathing could barely be described as such. The muscles that bound him seemed then to weigh too heavily upon his chest for him to operate it. He was trying, pushing, but rarely carrying through. When he did catch a breath, he gulped – a man drowning in his own bed – and hiccupped, made sick from the excess of it. His skin too, was clammy. Sweat rolled up and over his forehead and into his eyes.

My first steps were simple, then, to relieve his suffering so I could better examine him. We wetted strips of fabric, tied them around his head and wrists to cool him and let the doors open so the swift air may carry away the heat, though as we did, the wind seemed to die around us. We dripped water into his mouth and forced mashed food into him like a child.

I ended up slathering him with half a dozen poultices, just in case something helped. Not one even took the edge off what he was going through. Through it all, Iolaus sat by his side, hand atop his, though it must have been unpleasantly warm. Terrifying too. The pox could easily jump from one hand to another.

Finally, our patient dropped into feverish sleep, muttering to himself, and coughing away the lining of his throat. Then, I could examine him.

His reflexes were fine. Even asleep, they were better than most healthy men I saw. I suppose this could've been taken as a good sign that some part of him was functioning correctly, but it felt like more than that. As I checked his eyes, his ears, his nose, I noticed the most horrifying thing of all. The sores were everywhere.

They ran across his face, marring him beyond recognition, and into his scalp. Once I noticed it was impossible not to see, barely hidden by his now-limp hair. I would've shaved his head, were it not for the sores, to reduce the heat again.

I checked places I usually wouldn't, dread settling within me. They'd moved to his inner eyelids, they coated his tongue and his mouth, clearly irritated by what he had eaten before he arrived with us, and by his unfailing attempts to talk. I turned to Iolaus.

'Tell me what has happened.' This was no ordinary plague.

Iolaus sighed. 'It started three days ago.'

'Only three days?'

'Maybe four.' He shrugged. 'Uncle Herc never liked admitting weakness.'

'Why didn't you bring him in sooner?' I asked. Anyone with

half a lick of sense would take one look at this man and rush him to a healer.

'We saw another doctor before,' he said apologetically, as if my concern was that they hadn't chosen me first. I saw red. People's idiocy around their own health has never failed to surprise me, but this was another level. How had he not informed me, told me what the other doctor thought? It could have saved hours.

'And?' I prompted.

'He said it was the plague.' I'm a patient man. Apollo knows, to make it in this business one must be patient, but there's only so much a person can take.

'Anyone would,' I said, aiming to sound reassuring, but I'm sure the young man sensed my irritation, for he loosened his tongue.

'He had sons; they were doctors too, I think? None of them could agree. They gave him herbs like you did, though different ones. They used something red? One of them, this guy Nestor, he thought we should undergo some ritual?'

If the boy finished one more sentence as a question I'd be forced to slap him.

Fortuitously for Iolaus, his uncle chose that moment to roll over and mutter his clearest sound yet. *Iphitus*, followed by uncontrollable sobbing. Not a pleasant sound at the best of times, but worse when it comes from lungs filled with fluid.

'Who is Iphitus?' I said sternly, leaving no room for shrugs and vapid *I don't knows*. There wasn't time.

'He is, I mean, he was a friend of my uncle's?' My hand twitched, ready to slap.

'There's not time for me to draw every answer out of you like blood from a rock,' I snapped. 'Your uncle's dying. What did you mean by *friend*?'

'Wait, you think what happened with Iphitus could be related to what's wrong with him now?' Blessed Apollo, I didn't have the time to explain mental maladies for morons.

'Yes,' I said. 'So? Who was he to your uncle, how did he die, and why is my patient crying?'

'Are you an oracle or something?' he said stupidly. I'd thought well of him before this. He'd clearly dragged his uncle for several days across difficult landscape, and never complained of his own suffering. Suffice to say, I no longer harboured such respect. I merely glared. 'I mean, how did you know he was dead?'

'You said *was*. Now. Answer my question so we have some hope of eventually treating him.' His uncle, at least, seemed to understand the severity of the situation, as he loudly and messily vomited blood onto my floor. I'd lose nights of sleep after the episode, trying to scrub out the stains. It doesn't breed confidence in patients to lie in the blood of their predecessors.

'They were companions. Close companions. I think they were having sex, if it could be from that?' Well, at least he was speaking.

'This is unlikely to be a result of your uncle's sexual exploits.'

'Okay, well, the whole thing was complicated, but essentially they were travelling together looking for Iphitus' family's cows or horses or something because the thief Autolycus had stolen them—' Of course. Gods forbid he answer a medically relevant question, but he could talk for hours of *adventure*. 'So they went to Tiryns to look from the top of the tower on the walls there – you know the really big one, on the hill, with the river down by the bottom? Well, when they were up there the goddess Hera possessed Uncle Herc and he pushed Iphitus off and he died.'

Huh?

'Could you repeat that last part please?' I said slowly.

'The tower? Yeah, it's the one on the big hill next to the athletics—'

'Not the tower. The—'

'Oh, Hera possessing Uncle Herc? Yeah, I mean, this can't be from that, though; she's done it before, with Auntie Meg, and he was okay after that. He was sad and all, but then he went to the oracle and—'

I tuned out to what I'm now sure was a less than riveting description of the labours of Hercules. This interaction led to the sign above my door: *Please inform the healer on arrival if you are a demigod or otherwise have a fractious relationship with any of the divine.*

'*The* Hera, Queen of Olympus, possessed him?' I checked.

'That's what I said?'

'And this has happened before?'

'At least once.'

'Who is your uncle, exactly?' I should have asked the question sooner, though one's eyes tend to gloss over the lion-skin cloak when there's quite literally a man dying on your doorstep.

'Didn't you know? He's Hercules.'

Now, I'm not one to become starstruck. In my profession there's quite literally never the time for it, but I couldn't help asking.

'*The* Hercules?'

'Haven't met any other,' Iolaus said simply. I, to this day, don't understand how someone who grew in the shadow of one so famous managed to have the manner of an insolent bumpkin. Especially since, as I later learned, he was the most successful charioteer in all Greece.

'What I'm about to ask,' I said, slowly again, considering each word carefully, 'is medically relevant, so I don't need the big stories, okay? Just the answers.'

'Got it.'

'The plague, did it start immediately after your uncle pushed his companion from the tower?'

'Just about, yeah. I'm not really sure on the exact time. He was lucky I was so close, and all: when Theseus sent for me I didn't think I'd make it in time.' He looked so genuinely devastated, I almost felt bad for how much he irritated me.

'And the stories about him having the ear of the gods – those are true?'

'Not, like, all of them,' Iolaus said lazily. That would be ridiculous. 'But I know he's spoken to Hades, and probably Persephone, and Artemis and maybe, like Poseidon? He might have spoken to Poseidon about the whole bull thing. Oooh, and Apollo. I was there for Apollo.'

'Not Zeus?' He was the man's father, after all.

'Not that I know of. Normally just lets him get on with his own stuff. Herc's pretty good at that, you know. Not a big *talker* as a whole. What, does he need Zeus' help?'

I nearly laughed at the earnestness he said it with. None of us can help the worlds we grew up in. I suppose his included referring to the gods by only their names, as if they might drop round for a meal and a chat. I was jealous, I'll admit. I'd never met Apollo, the god I'd dedicated my life to, yet I was about to recommend it as a course of treatment.

'Not Zeus, I doubt he'd move against his wife like that. I suspect this plague is a punishment set upon him for what happened in the tower.'

'But that's not fair,' Iolaus shouted. It's a good thing his uncle

228

was so ill, for he was snoring heavily through these outbursts. 'Hera made him do it.'

'It's not my place to comment on the actions of the gods. Given who he is, I think he may have success if he appeals to Apollo for a solution.'

'Do you really think that will work?'

I had no idea, not when I told Iolaus, and not when we'd set up an offering and poured enough herbal mixtures down Hercules' throat he could just about speak.

'Iatrus Apollo,' Hercules rumbled.

'Isn't he Phoebus Apollo?' Iolaus asked, right on cue. 'You called him Phoebus Apollo last time.' *Last time.*

'If you want him for *light* reasons, you may call him that. As your uncle would like to address him in his capacity as the god of *medicine*, this is more appropriate,' I hissed. He opened his mouth to ask another question. I stamped on his foot.

'Iatrus Apollo,' Hercules started again. 'I humbly beg to talk to you as a servant, and as a brother, for we're bound together through our father.'

'I would've come anyway, bro. You don't have to go name-dropping Dad like that,' the voice erupted from nowhere. From the fire, or the trees, or from the light reflecting off the moon, I don't know. Maybe all of them. Moments later, light seemed to pull off the shine of every surface, coalescing into a body. The shape of a person emerged, with arms and legs and even a nose, if you squinted. I could hardly bear it. It shone so brightly it pierced my mind and made my ears ring with pain.

'That was a quick trip,' Hercules said.

'Arty gave me a lift. Couldn't have asked for an audience during the day, could you?'

'My apologies, sire,' Hercules said, with an over-the-top bow. Apollo saw Iolaus and I, whereupon he grew a foot into the sky and rippled into a rather more stately and less shiny bearing.

'My dedicated servant,' he said, bowing to me. I thought my heart would cease then and there. 'Thank you, for the tireless work you've done for me. You're second only to my Asclepius on this earth.'

It was the single most affirming moment of my life, yet tarred because I didn't have the easy friendship he struck up with Hercules. It's enough to make you want to be a hero.

'You honour me,' I said, kneeling.

'As you honour me.'

'We have called you about my patient,' I said, pointing back to Hercules. Much as I would have loved to spend time with Apollo, it was neither the time nor within my duty.

'Truly the best of doctors.' Apollo smiled. That was the most wonderful thing of all. 'What's the problem, brother?' he said, turning back to Hercules.

Hercules merely levelled a look at him. I suspect this was to preserve his throat, but it was a glare to be proud of.

'Just kidding: the plague's got you good, huh?'

'What must I do to free myself of it?'

'Ugh, I hate it when mortals go and get all worried about your mortality, you know. It ruins the fun. Whatever, since it's *you*, brother, I'll tell.' Hercules looked expectant. 'No sense of dramatic timing, you. Fine. I'll do it properly. You have been cast upon by the worst of plagues for the murder of Iphitus, who loved and trusted you as deeply as any mortal. Your only redemption lies in making amends with his family.'

Hercules made a choking noise, akin to a snake with prey too ambitious for its mouth. 'How?' he said finally.

'Fucked if I know, gimme a sec.' The great god Apollo rolled his eyes back into his skull and let the whites cloud across his face, blinding as the sun. 'The prophecy indicates you should sell yourself as a slave. By sending the money to his family and working hard you will atone for what you have done.'

'A slave?' he asked dumbly.

'So it would seem.'

'Where?'

'Can't give you all the answers.' Apollo shrugged. 'Go see my oracle if you don't want to work it out for yourself.'

'No one will buy me looking like this.' He gestured at himself. The exertion of standing had set his spots to oozing.

'Fine, do you promise you'll go and do it?' Apollo asked. Hercules nodded solemnly. 'Ta da. You're cured. Don't make me come back. The punishments for killing your friends and family only get worse.'

The sores disappeared within a minute. They seemed to close around themselves, drawing in at the edges and sinking down inside him until only the ooze remained. A bath and you'd never know what he went through. It was true magic, beyond anything I could aspire to.

But for Apollo, it was everyday. He did a backflip and, with that, disappeared from my garden. I'd certainly chosen a characterful god to dedicate my life to.

'How did you forget his name?' Hercules hissed to his nephew. He must have thought it was a whisper. It was not a whisper.

'I dunno. You know I'm bad with names.' Iolaus shrugged.

'You've *met* him.'

231

'In fairness, Uncle, I was *very* drunk at the time,' he said. This family, honestly.

Hercules and Iolaus were packed up and ready to leave by morning. Iolaus caught me in the kitchen, no sight of any belongings, though I know he arrived with some.

'Your uncle said you were leaving at the break of dawn?' I said, no longer so crabby, for the end was in sight, and the patient was alive. What more could I want?

'He is. I'm staying here.' Iolaus beamed, proud as a cat.

'Why?'

'To become a doctor, like you. Apollo said you were the best, apart from lame old Asclepius. Who better to learn from? I'll be your apprentice.'

My skin fell into a sickly pallor. My heart struggled harder than his uncle's had the day before. This couldn't be happening to me. It was both cruel and unusual punishment, though I had no idea what I'd done to deserve it.

'Just kidding, doc, your face – you wouldn't believe it.' Iolaus laughed, slapping me on the back. 'You're a solid doctor, even if you are a grumpy git, but I don't want to be one. See you next time, yeah?'

He was off before I could respond, the two of them awfully cheerful given the fate awaiting Hercules.

I was left to ponder my final question. *What kind of life do you have to lead where you look at these events and think* 'next time'?

Xenoclea I

When I'm not channelling the spirit of a long-dead serpent, I get to choose exactly who I help. 'No,' I told him. I was the oracle at Delphi, chosen by Apollo to speak prophecies of the future, a process that involved letting the ghost of his python fill my mind. Gods and kings came to me and they listened. There was no reason I should serve Hercules.

'You can't say no to me,' he said, the words as easy as mine had been. I caught a flash then of moments past that led to this man being covered in blood, that led to him demanding a distant sister of mine give him the same help he came for now. I saw power and strength and a club coming down on a lion bigger than any I'd ever seen, not even in the mists of prophecy.

'You murdered your friend; I have no oracle for one such as you.'

He may have been strong, his hands easily large enough to wrap around my neck, but this was my domain. He couldn't hurt me here. Apollo would ruin him for it more surely than any petty act of revenge from Hera had ever done.

And he knew it. When he lunged, he did not lunge for me.

My neck stayed white and milky, clean of the violence that had seeped so deeply below his skin. He grabbed my seat, my tripod, from beneath me, and yanked it, hard.

He's the strongest mortal Greece has ever known; he didn't need to *yank*. He sent me tumbling to the ground. They don't choose the Pythia for her grace, so my limbs flailed in the dust. Awfully dusty place, Delphi.

I huffed as I stood, patting down my robes.

'Didn't see that coming, did you?' he said, not mocking, truly, but with a swagger, a grin. He was *flirting* with me, sworn virgin priestess of Apollo. While he was distracted I stuck my foot out and caught the weak bits behind his ankle – he was rather top heavy – and I knocked him down too. He didn't look so pleased with himself after that. I stood to my full height – tall, for a woman, and taller still for all the privileges bestowed upon me.

'I see *you*, Heracles,' I hissed, the venom as natural as the pride. I'm a princess of snakes, am I not? 'I see all you have done and all you fail to do. You think yourself a hero? I see a coward, a boy too weak to control himself – a slave to . . .'

Before I could continue, before Hercules could finish the retaliation he was obviously planning, my stool lifted high in his hand, the sky began to fight itself. The sun glowed bright into his eyes, so bright it hurt. Lightning flashed across it.

Then I was choking. A prophecy was being spoken through me, whether I liked it or not. Being inhabited by the spirit of a dead snake can be so inconvenient.

I held my teeth and ground my jaw together. I wouldn't be forced to give this arsehole what he wanted, I refused.

'Not for you,' I said fiercely. Not for the man who threw his lover off the city walls. Why should he get his answers so easily?

'C'mon, Xeny, don't be like that,' he wheedled. 'I'll give your tripod back.' He held it out gently, patronisingly. I grabbed it with still-dusty hands and whapped him round the side of the head.

'Ow,' he said, not altogether joking. I'm only *mostly* mortal. I can hit hard, if someone annoys me sufficiently. I was ready to tell him to leave, but the *other* annoying spirit that occasionally borrows my mouth decided to pop in.

My priestess, a disembodied voice announced in my head. Apollo, not sounding thrilled himself. *Help him.*

I snorted. I could get away with the impudence in my own mind. If he wanted politeness he could speak to me on neutral ground.

Be a friend. Help the poor sucker out.

This is unlike you.

He is kind of my brother.

Hasn't stopped you before, I thought flippantly, and I think I felt a smirk back. Outside my mind, though, I looked to the poor sucker.

'Since you returned my seat so nicely,' I said, layering the sarcasm so thick even an idiot couldn't miss it, 'I will do you this favour. But first I must bathe. This dust! I swear. Marina, come.' One of the younger priestesses hurried after me. She helped me scrub the worst of the dirt from myself and coiled my hair elaborately for what it was I would do next.

Everyone acts like speaking prophecy is easy. Open your mouth and let it come. But that's not the case. It's not you and it's not of you. It comes from a place deeper than the ground beneath your feet, a place so deep even the gods are afraid to go there. It must be forced out, with vapours and belief and the spirit of the most stubborn heart.

Which is all to say, it *hurts*.

And what do I get as thanks? Complaints that my hard-dredged prophecies could have been clearer, more helpful. Pah.

I breathed in the air, brought to me through careful rivulets of rocks coiling straight from the very source of my power. It clouded my eyes first, and then my mind, fog descending so deep I never knew if I'd find my way out again.

When I came to, the sucker was looking altogether miserable. Honestly, I don't know what he expected, pissing off the oracle like that. The python might hurt me, but it still *likes* me. It does live in my head.

'I'm going to die,' he said. I hadn't asked.

'Everyone dies.' That couldn't have been the whole prophecy; that would be like if someone came to me and I told them they have hands.

'Not at the hands of someone who's already *dead*.' I raised an eyebrow. He still looked miserable, though anyone could have told him this was *good* news. All he had to do was avoid any adventures down to Hades and he'd be set for as long as he wanted to live. 'I'm not meant to *die*.'

'Apparently you are,' I said. Forgive me. My head was pounding, my eyes unsure at the edges. I couldn't deal with him anymore. 'We're done here.'

'But I have more questions,' he said. 'What of—'

'Go,' I intoned firmly. 'Or you'll regret it.'

I needed to lie down.

Iolaus III

I tried to get the cloak off him but he said no, even though uncles are meant to spoil their nephews with gifts. That's the whole point of relatives.

'It's not like your new master will let you keep it anyway,' I tried. 'And you owe me twelve years of birthday presents.'

'I took you to the Hydra.'

'Some would argue using a child to help complete your penance is something you should pay them for, rather than insist it was a gift,' I sniped.

'That's a good point,' he said.

'Really?' He was normally much less reasonable about the Hydra thing.

'It is. Apart from the bit where I wasn't allowed to count it as a labour because you kept bragging about how much you helped. *And* you said taking you would count as your presents *forever.*'

'Did not.'

'Did too.'

'Did not.'

'I can prove it,' Uncle Herc said with a dramatic flourish, pulling something out of the pocket of his cloak. When did he add pockets?

'What's that?'

'Proof.' It was a small scrap of animal hide – the gods only know which animal, given my uncle's life; it could have been anything from Olympus to Hades – with the line *I promise not to bug my uncle about gifts forever in exchange for being allowed to watch as he slays the Hydra,* followed by my tiny, childish signature.

'Why would you possibly make this?' I asked.

'Because my nephew is a lying, cheating bastard,' he said, deadpan.

'Yeah? Well, it takes one to know one.' We laughed, and we clapped each other on the back and went to get good and drunk before we went through the auction.

I was taking it worse than Uncle Herc – he whistled some old drinking tune. Something about goats?

'You're oddly cheerful,' I remarked. 'Finally realising your true standing then?'

'Oi, remember who the hero is here, kid. And it can't be worse than working for old Eurystheus, can it? It's not like it's going to kill me.' Must be nice, to know you're not going to die.

We enjoyed the night for the freedom it was, and blinded ourselves to the trials ahead.

Do you know how difficult it is to voluntarily register yourself as a slave? It's a proper mess of confused bureaucrats. First we had to travel all the way to Asia. It was another long, long journey, this time by boat. But it went smooth and fast. Suspiciously smooth, my uncle said.

'Almost like we're carrying out the will of a god.' He smirked.

Anyways, since the sailing was so smooth, there's not much to say. We made it without even one monster to slay. Would have been nice, one last hurrah, but never mind, huh? There'd always be the Hydra.

The first bureaucrat we found refused to help us, said our story was clearly false, and bade us *have a good day, sirs*, though he didn't care whether we had a good day or not. That rubbed Uncle Herc the wrong way, so I aimed a swift kick at his shin to get him moving out of there.

'What was that for?' he grumbled.

'I could see you thinking about it.'

'Thinking about what?' he asked innocently, a move that would work better if Dad didn't have exactly the same expression, and if Mum didn't tell him off for trying it. It was invariably concealing the biggest of shit-eating grins, she said.

'Starting a fight with him,' I said flatly, and he laughed. I was glad he was taking it so well, but I worried too, about what would happen when it hit him. This wasn't one year, or five, or even twelve, and it wasn't to be with his cousin, only a handful of days from home. I didn't think he'd ever come back.

'Well, if I were . . .' he chuckled, 'it is clearly because he is both nasty and vicious in his business, conning innocent travellers out of—'

'Uncle—' I warned.

'Fine, fine, I won't. It's not like it would kill me.'

'Yeah but it might kill *me*,' I protested. 'And you know what I would do then? Come back from Hades and kill you right back.'

'You're getting boring now you're grown up, you know that?'

'Am not!' I insisted.

'No,' he said, surprising the shit out of me. Every sibling knows there's only one response to *am not* and it's *are too*. 'You're the spitting image of your mother, though.'

I didn't like it. It was a nice thing to say – my mother more attractive than my father by several leagues – but it felt an awful lot like a run-up to goodbye. I kicked him in the shin again.

'What was that in aid of, dear nephew?' he said, wincing. I might not be blessed with the unknowable strength of the gods, but I kick like a mule, only pointier.

'Out of the goodness of my heart. Let's find another bureaucrat.'

We did find one, late in the afternoon, as Apollo's chariot started to dip out of sight. The last rays of the sun peaked and twinkled over the horizon, as if the god himself was winking at us. Or laughing at us. Hard to tell with Apollo.

We found our bureaucrat not in the streets or at his house, but in a tavern, with a bored posture that practically begged for someone to tell him a story he couldn't believe. With an invitation like that, who were we to decline?

We told him the story. He didn't believe it. We told him more. We bought him drinks – as my uncle mentioned sardonically, 'money hardly matters to me now' – interspersing them with tales. Eventually he'd have to take our word for it.

Uncle Herc's name carried less weight here than it did in Greece. That's not to say he was some unknown peasant, but he didn't have people bowing or praising him in the street like he did at home, apart from, you know, around Thebes. His ego had got so big I worried he wouldn't fit through doorways.

It took until the fifth or sixth story for light to arrive on the bureaucrat's face.

'Oh, I know, don't tell me – you're that Heracles fellow, aren't you?' the man said, looking particularly pleased with himself. I don't know whether it was the drink or the exertion that made him stupid, but I'm glad he missed the stiffening of my uncle, the pause as his hackles rose across his body and his teeth glinted with the light of the moon.

'Hercules, sire,' I interrupted. We were getting through this unpleasant business without any fights, whether Uncle Herc liked it or not. It's not the man's fault he didn't know how much my uncle hated his given name.

'So it is,' he said easily. 'My most sincere apologies.'

I don't know what combination of gods willed it, but my uncle relaxed in his seat, and I thanked all of them.

'So?' I asked.

'Well, if you're *the* Hercules, I guess I'd better help you, huh? You should fetch a decent price,' he mused. 'Polish up those muscles, work on a meek look on your face, could be okay.'

'You think I'll merely sell *okay*?' Uncle Herc shouted, startling half the tavern. They quickly turned back to their own business. I appreciated that about Asia, but it reminded me how far from home we were. I didn't want to leave him here. My uncle smiled – it was a joke. The man realised too, and they began a contest of how badly he would sell. I was the only one not laughing. My wine promised answers, but my stomach turned and my throat wouldn't allow it in. I cursed as the bureaucrat prepared the papers.

'Most unusual, yes, but fully legal, yes, yes,' he said, rubbing his hands together in well-organised glee. 'The next major sale is three days from now. I suggest you enjoy your time in the city before then.'

Enjoy your final days of freedom, he meant, but he'd sense enough to avoid such statements. Uncle Herc did enjoy them. He had strict orders not to appear at the market with a hangover – which he didn't. He arrived there early, in his best clothes, only to be stripped and rubbed in oil – but he did more or less everything else he could sneak in.

He hiked out of town, determined to find something he could kill, to leave the indelible mark of his fame here as well as in Greece. I can't remember what he slayed. I can hardly remember half the stuff I was actually there for, let alone the rest.

He found willing women. Knowing him, there's now a cluster of boys with H names around the area. I let him go when he needed to, and drank with him when he needed that. Upset as I was, I wasn't the one watching my life washing away, like blood in a wine-dark sea.

I came with him to the market, laughed as he scowled through the oil being lathered on. I made faces from the crowd as he was led out like cattle. I imagined his commentary of the others, and of what they had done, to distract me, but it didn't work. My uncle was the only healthy specimen up there, the only one who looked as though they had ever smiled.

I travelled too much to have a slave, anyway, but I vowed then and there I'd never have one, not like this.

Eventually, it was his turn. He didn't look nervous or meek – as our bureaucrat had so valiantly tried for – merely bored. When he found my eyes in his lazy surveillance of the room, he winked. That helped.

Bidding started. It got high, I think. I didn't really understand the currency. People seemed competitive, until jewels were slammed onto a table and an authoritative, female voice announced: 'I believe I win.'

'And . . . sold! To the Lady Omphale.'

I hoped she'd be kind to him. I ran away before I could see.

Sale Note

Receipt of authentication for the sale of goods.

This note officially declares the purchase of goods by Queen Omphale of Lydia. Price of the item equalling current market value of a flock of goats. It may have been higher, but condition is poor. Recent contact with the plague has left a pallor and pockmarks. However, strength is evident should recovery take place. No returns.

Terms & Conditions apply.

Wedding Invitation

You are cordially invited to the wedding of Queen Omphale of Lydia. It is of vital importance you arrive on time. Gifts will be accepted in the form of precious gems and gold, or other beautiful things to match the wonders of the bride, so she may adorn herself as a married woman. She eagerly awaits your arrival, and that of your gifts.

Omphale I

Of course he'd want to marry me. Not only was I sharp of mind *and* uncommonly beautiful, but I was also a queen. A queen in my own right, mind you, after my father and brother failed to hold on to the crown – part of their failure to hold on to this life – none of this queen-by-association nonsense.

I married him on a whim, really. My father was sick, though not with the illness that would eventually kill him. He desperately wanted me married, wanted a man to guide my hand when he was gone. I loved my father dearly, and I wanted to make him happy, but I had no need for a man to make my choices, so I took Tmolus.

I found him on the streets, sniffing around in a rather suspicious manner.

'If you have come to rob us, it will not work,' I told him, back straighter than a board. It took me years to learn to have fun with this life.

'You a bear?'

'No,' I said, mightily offended. Didn't he know hours had gone into the shape and smell of my hair? 'Are you?'

He laughed and muttered something along the lines of *if only*. The impudence of it. He, the smelly mountain man, was laughing at me. 'Not yet. You're safe from my ravages.'

'You ravage bears?' I asked, nose wrinkled and eyebrow raised, though they cause awful wrinkles.

'Only when the situation calls for it,' he said. 'I should find the track. See you, Princess.'

'I have a name, you know,' I shouted after him. Something came over me, and I followed the whim. 'Mountain man!'

I heard his chuckle ring through the streets for what felt like hours, and I went home, fully prepared to forget him, just one more stranger walking the streets of Lydia. He was ugly and he smelled bad. He wouldn't fit in at court.

He came back with a bear for me. We married within the week.

For some years, we ruled together. By that, I mean I ruled, and Tmolus occasionally slept in my palace. He never went away without bringing back a gift. A bear, or a lion, or some strange creature I'd never heard of before. Sometimes they smelled even worse than he, but I learned to cure them, filled a room with our trophies. He laughed himself silly.

'That's one way to make me court-appropriate.' He grinned. He grabbed me and we did something wholly inappropriate on the skin of that first bear he brought.

My husband. My King of Lydia. My mountain man.

Then he went and got himself gored by a boar so I filled my lunches with appointments and closed off the room so I wouldn't have to see it. I lived alone for years. I was happy, truly, just differently so.

It goes without saying that this Hercules would want to marry me too.

I wasn't intending to go to the auction at all. I find the whole thing distasteful. All that potential lost by draping the poor wretches in torn and dirty cloths. I'd offer to reclothe them myself – the gods have blessed me with the money for it – if the auction masters weren't so desperately crooked themselves.

The week before, I'd been taking lunch with my friend Neileia – one of those unfortunate *rich-by-marriage* types – and she mentioned some great hero from the west going up for auction.

'Going *to* the auction, surely?' I corrected.

'No, he is being sold.'

'He can't be that great then.'

'He's said to be the strongest man in all of Greece, and the bravest,' she said dreamily. 'They say he must sell himself to atone for something. It's terribly romantic.'

With my friend, my *married* friend, fawning like this, what choice did I have but to inspect the specimen? I sent a message to ensure there was space for the Queen of Lydia and any companions she should bring. Though in the end, all those with the means to attend had organised their own seating beforehand. I sat again with Neileia, and tried as I might to blank out her endless drones about her equally dull husband.

'—so he apologised to me for—'

The hero was brought onto the stage. He wasn't beautiful, unlike myself, but he had the touch of wild that makes a man exciting enough to bother with. His skin was pocked and marked; his nose had clearly been broken in the past. He strutted. It didn't read as confidence, but insolence. Strong as he was, he didn't look *safe*.

'—but he just didn't listen—'

When I saw Hercules, I thought, *oh my, this could be fun*. He looked a lot like Tmolus – same breadth of shoulders, same beard, same straggles from not particularly caring what civilisation thought of you.

'—and I said—'

Of course, Tmolus could have done with a little more caring about civilisation and a little less being gored by a boar.

'Do be quiet,' I snapped. How much can one woman be expected to endure? Honestly. 'The auction is on.'

Needless to say, I bought him. It's not as if I didn't have the money. Despite my many wonderful qualities, the first time Hercules asked to marry me, it wasn't for any of them.

'I hear if a master marries their slave, they become free again. Is that true?'

'Something like that, I suppose. They're bound by their own kind will,' I said carelessly. I didn't assume his very first sentence would be an attempt to manipulate me.

'You seem like the kindest-willed woman in this whole strange land,' he said, holding a hand out for mine. I waved him off.

'You flatter. I could have your tongue cut out if it displeases me.' I didn't mean to carry through with any such threat. He was too impressive for that, and he knew it.

'Then I shall ensure it pleases you, my lady,' he said, all charm and manners. 'Do me the honour of becoming my wife.'

'Please. I have no intention of saddling myself with a husband.'

It became a joke between us: that he'd ask and I'd reject. Got him out of trouble a good number of times.

I put him in one of the servant's rooms. As a queen without a king, my rooms were simply made up for women. It was a matter of convenience, not an attempt to demean him by casting him as a girl. That's what started it all.

Next was his cloak. It was given to me after the sale – part of his effects – and I nearly threw it away for rags. My hand was stayed by the locked room in my house, the animals still waiting for me.

Instead I did something instead that my late husband never would have considered. I asked Hercules about it.

'This . . . garment? Of yours?'

'A cloak.'

'It scarcely looks like a cloak.'

'It is from the skin of the Nemean lion,' he said, as though those words should bear special meaning. Seeing my expression, he softened. 'I've been through a lot with it. I'd be much obliged for you to safeguard it.'

'Will you not beg me for its return?' I asked, eyebrow raised again. I found him endlessly entertaining to tease.

'Men do not beg,' he said stiffly. I wonder what caused that particular scar within him. 'Apart from for your hand.' He grinned again. It took a dozen years from his age, turning him into a young man again.

'I'm rather attached to my hand,' I said, but he looked afraid, so I allowed him his comfort. 'I will keep it safe.'

'Thank you, my lady.'

That cloak wasn't in any condition to be worn by someone in my service. It had been poorly patched up and strung together so many times it was nigh impossible to recognise whatever beast it had come from. If he cared so much about its safety, he could learn to fix it properly.

I had no need for a man around the place, manning about,

waving his club as a pathetic substitute for another part of his anatomy. I needed something to do with him, so I sent him to learn to embroider, and to sew. Then he could fix that damned cloak, and add some flair while he was at it. It was lowering the tone. He didn't take this well.

'You want me to do *what*?'

'You are to learn to sew,' I said, all the words sweet and simple so he couldn't pretend to misunderstand. It was a great trick of Hercules', to feign idiocy when he didn't want to deal with something. Not that he'd admit to such cunning. It'd destroy his pride to be known for anything other than his formidable muscles.

'Why?'

'Is it your place to question why?' I snapped. The gods above know I found patience exhausting. 'You're so worried about whether your tongue pleases me, you've neglected your fingers.'

'My fingers?'

'Your fingers.'

'It would please you if my fingers learn to sew?' he asked, grin forming. 'Would it be so pleasing you'd take a husband?'

'Well, there's that attractive gardener,' I mused. 'If I must pick from one of my staff.'

Hercules scowled, sticking his tongue out a bit. I laughed. I really had no intention of marrying him. Why would I? He was a gilded-tongued servant in my household. I was happy alone.

It was after he learned embroidery that things got out of hand. Once it was fixed up, the way the lion skin rippled in the light of a fire was the first challenge I felt to my own beauty in years. I had to have it, so I did. I am not, nor have I ever made claim to be, a man. I'm a queen, and I like it that way, but the cloak lay easily across my shoulders. My maidservant, a fresh little thing, giggled.

I rounded on her with the fury of a lioness. That stopped the giggling.

'Am I funny to you?' I roared.

'No?' she said. 'I was thinking that you could pass for Mister Hercules like this, if you had the club too.'

I looked closer into the glass. She was right. He'd been wearing both for so many years I imagine even his family – he did have some; I asked at the auction – wouldn't recognise him without them. His lovers, who presumably knew him without the things on, couldn't be sure without glancing across the room and seeing the skin slung across some chair or dresser.

When people speak of the evil I did to him, *oh nasty Omphale took his manhood away*, they're wrong. That evil was done by taking his cloak at the auction. That was where his manhood lay, not the floor of my embroidery room.

I summoned him from his sewing so he could see how I looked. I summoned his club too, from the mostly empty box of his effects. How sad to be his age and only have two things you care about enough to carry with you. Should something horrible happen, I couldn't be pressed to rid myself of any of the treasures Tmolus gave me.

He gasped when he saw me.

'My lady,' he said when he had regained some semblance of composure.

'What do you think?' I spun for him, the cloak getting a good swish behind me. I doubt it had ever been spun before.

'You look fierce, and beautiful, my lady, but you were hardly lacking in those qualities before.'

'Hold your tongue with this *my lady* business. I was thinking of taking a new name, to go along with this new look,' I said coyly.

'Oh, and what particular name has caught your fancy? Cadmus perhaps? Or Perseus, for the strength of my grand-father?'

'What about Hercules?' I asked, barely paying attention as I noticed the sparkle as my eyes caught the light in the sun. Beautiful.

'Absolutely not,' he said, back to that old stiffness. I'd have to train him out of that. No one likes a stiff man. 'That's the name of an ugly brute. And you, most lovely, are too beautiful to bear such a name.'

In the end, I stuck with Omphale, the most beautiful name in Lydia. Anything else would be a trade-down, and I feared my father would rise from Hades to curse me if I made such an unsound exchange. It was only as I reclined that evening with some wine, that I thought through what Herc had said.

He'd claimed he was an ugly brute, a wild man, but not the way my Tmolus used to, with the lightness of air on the mountains and the rumble of cleansing thunder in his belly. Herc said it with genuine sorrow. I summoned him back to me.

I still had no intention of marrying him. If I had, I wouldn't have been so gauche as to summon him to my chambers unaccompanied. I'm beautiful, not an idiot.

(I was living proof that you could be both, which made a nice comparison to Helen, who seemed on a mission to show there was nothing in that pretty little head of hers, though her husband seemed happy enough with that state of affairs. She wasn't so beautiful anyway. I heard her nose was crooked.)

'You summoned, my lady?' he asked politely. He was only

polite when he was nervous. It was cute, the result of training in his youth. He reached for it in a panic.

'What you said earlier, about the brutishness? Would you like to change it?' I asked.

'I cannot change my name, my lady. The goddess may be offended, which is dangerous for those I love.'

'And the rest of it?'

'I don't understand.'

'I'll show you.'

I led him by the hand to the bathing room, where he was set upon by my servants. The water was hot, almost painfully so, and the potions were cold. I knew that much from experience. My soon-to-be-lovely Hercules did not. He knew not the pain of tangles being snagged out of hair, or of that still-aching scalp being pulled as they teased his golden tresses into elaborate styles. He knew not of the pins to keep it in place. He yelped and wriggled relentlessly through his treatment.

'What are you doing?' he asked, clear effort going into keeping his voice level.

'Showing you that you're not an ugly brute.'

We bestowed him with every treatment we could think of, even those too expensive for *me* to undergo on a regular basis. We bathed him in milk to soften his skin – a lost cause, I think, after all those years fighting – and gently *coaxed* what was left of his nails into a more pleasing shape. At least his hair was long, and could be manipulated into a plait that was truly beautiful. It looked gold, where it had been brown before. Apt, as we were shining him up.

We could hardly follow such lavish treatment with the dirty sacks he wore previously. He would tarnish all over again. Tmolus disdained fine things, so we dressed Hercules as me. They were the only clothes available. I had him washed and shined until he wouldn't think of himself as a monster. I don't understand how that makes me one.

'How do you feel?' I asked.

'Different, my lady.'

'Good different?'

'If it pleases you,' he said finally, 'then it pleases me.'

I set him more of the same work, sewing and embroidering and holding our wool. I couldn't send him into the wilds where he'd further drive himself to believe he was some violent beast. I let him believe those hands could fix things.

Want to know the dirty secret about Hercules? In that time when I kept him inside and tame, when I wore his cloak and he my dress, I saw him smile more than I did before. There was a lightness to his voice that wasn't there when he spoke of his exploits.

I don't think he ever came to love my dresses, but that's his loss. I imagine he disliked anything that obscured my body from him. He was that kind of man.

He'd been with me for about a year, and was developing some competence with a loom and a needle. I took him on a walk in the gardens to celebrate.

'You've been doing well, Hercules.'

'Oh? Do my fingers finally please you? Will you take me as a husband—'

He didn't have the opportunity to finish that thought. He was knocked down by the falling corpse of a bird-man. He stepped back with an *oomf*, dropped the man to the floor, and looked to me in horror as the pins in his hair came loose and it tumbled down his face. I could almost imagine his upset was over the collapse of his hairstyle.

I suppose that's when I decided to marry him.

Of course, he ruined it shortly after.

'Theseus,' he whispered.

'Is that the bird-man's name?'

'No. This must be—' He closed his eyes and moved his finger along as if counting beads on an abacus. 'Icarus. His father's the only mortal who could make something like these.'

'A *man* made these wings? I must have him,' I said. They were a marvel, the joins so fine and clean you couldn't see them without inspection. I'd bet those feathers felt divine against bare skin too.

'If this is what's happened to his son—' Herc waved. The bird-man was very dead, yet still he smouldered. 'I cannot imagine him performing the genius you deserve, my queen.'

'Who is Theseus then? The bird-man's father?' I wanted that genius once he was done mourning.

'No, he's my cousin. He's gone to the island where the bird-man lived, to slay a monster. I hope he hasn't suffered like this.'

'This Theseus, he is of your blood?'

'Yeah,' Herc confirmed.

'Then he will be fine.'

We buried the smoking remains of the bird-man. Well, Hercules did. I called the gardener over to help him. I had a wedding to plan.

I sent my betrothed on a trip first, to let him burn the worst of the feelings that'd been building up out of him. It's not an emotion I feel. I am an adult woman, but I knew Tmolus long enough to recognise it in a heartbeat. I couldn't marry the man in that state, so I sent him away. A simple thing, if I remember correctly; some king was gathering heroes for it. He was having trouble with a wild boar.

I was sure, given the simplicity of the matter, he'd be back within weeks.

I didn't see my betrothed for over a year.

Icarus

Not too high!
   —my father lies
   Not too high, what bull
   (What bull indeed)
We leave, we run, we flee—
   So, one day, we can be free
   Of such things: too high, too low, too slow
   I catch the light
   I fly
I shine, I turn
I fall
I burn
My father turns, he sees
He flees.

A Request

Dear HERO,

I am mightily impressed by your past deeds – particularly noble and wondrous are they! You may be the mightiest hero of this age. As such, I have a task befitting you. There is a monstrous boar that has taken to terrorising Aetolia. Simply kill the beast. The honour will sustain your mighty reputation, though you scarcely need it. I have called upon other heroes, nearly as noble as yourself, to join you in the hunt. The prize goes to he who draws first blood.

    King Oeneus

Atalanta I

I didn't like him on the *Argo* and I didn't like him on the hunt. It's not that I found him more – forgive the pun – boorish than the other men. It's that Hercules was wasteful.

He had something truly special, talents never before bestowed upon mortals, and he acted unconscious of them. Some people found this charming. I know Jason – who had no magical powers of his own – did; enjoyed that he tried to be a hero in his own right rather than in his father's shadow. I found it stupid.

I was blessed by Artemis. That's not so hard, is it? I was blessed by Artemis to be the best of her hunters. I'm the fastest sprinter on this earth. That's not an exaggeration, nor vain: being suckled by a goddess has these advantages, *which you should be honest about*. I've heard maidens ask him how he's so strong and he smiled and said he trains often. If you tried to train enough to reach that strength, you would die.

Maybe his divine father was more lax than Artemis. He lacked discipline, but he was better than half the Argonauts, and he knew to respect me on the boar hunt, which put him ahead of the idiot king there. Maybe he honestly didn't recognise what was a blessing and what he carved out himself. Maybe he really didn't know he almost glowed in the sun, or that objects falling on him in his sleep would simply bounce off his thick skin.

(That became a game on the *Argo*. Entertainment on a ship is hard to come by and, when Hercules has been drinking as only he can, he sleeps *deeply*. For their safety, I won't speak of who holds the record, but it's for dropping an anchor on his stomach. Hercules did not wake.)

I won't pretend any of us went on the hunt to help King Oeneus. I went to hunt the Calydonian boar because I wanted to see my friends. Sure, Jason wasn't there – he was extracting himself from Greece's worst marriage, including mine; don't marry a witch, kids – but a handful of the Argonauts were, and for that, it felt a lot like home.

People took immense offence to my being a woman – gasp, shudder – and my daring to leave home unaccompanied, as though I was *equal* to any man. That felt like home too. Old Oeneus certainly thought I was weak, but thinking such things was what got him in trouble in the first place.

As a man, you're free to choose which god you follow. When kings make their yearly sacrifices, they must sacrifice to all. No idiot would forget that. There are only twelve major Olympians to remember, if you must be pragmatic about your prayers.

Artemis, Zeus, Hera, Poseidon, Hades, Ares, Aphrodite, Athena, Apollo, Hephaestus, Demeter, Dionysus. It's not so hard to mutter their names as you scrape some food into a fire. Is it any wonder my lady Artemis was offended to be forgotten?

It wasn't a harsh punishment, all be told. She sent the boar, not to punish him for forgetting her, but to remind him of her importance. A hunt brings people together.

Oeneus was surprised when I showed up – I'm known for my affinity to the goddess – so he stuttered, choked on his beer like the fat, lazy little man he was.

'No women on the hunt.'

Not even a *hello, Atalanta. I heard of your amazing work on the Argo, Atalanta. How are you, Atalanta?*

'My lady sent me.'

'Tell her no.'

'Are you in a position to tell the Lady Artemis no?' I asked, innocent and wide-eyed. Is acceptance worth having if you don't have to fight for it?

'Artemis sent you? Why?'

Can anyone know the whims of the gods? Do you think Hercules knew whatever the fuck Zeus wanted on any given day, apart from getting into the undergarments of the closest nymph without his wife finding out?

'Would you refuse me?'

'If the men accept you, you may run,' he said, smiling beatifi-cally, like I needed his approval. He could've told me to fuck off and I still would've gone. Saying *maybe* just denied me that opportunity to slap him. No matter, there would be more.

'They will,' I said, instead of bestowing his much-deserved slapping. They would, or they'd suffer the consequences. I didn't bother asking what they thought. I simply appeared in the pile of shirtless men and smiled menacingly at them.

'Who are you?' one asked.

'Atalanta.'

'Of course.' I liked that, liked the easy acceptance of who I was and why I was there, how my name carried weight beyond many of them.

When I saw Hercules, I walked over, and – with a smile – gave him a good, solid clap on the back, like Jason would have done.

'Hercules,' I boomed.

'Atalanta?' In his confusion he forgot to boom. 'I thought you were married now?'

'Ha,' I said. There had been suitors; why does a woman announcing she has no desire to be a wife encourage suitors? But they had failed, and would continue to do so. One suitor might have been brazen enough to claim victory, and I might have been forced to undergo the marriage rites with him, but I wouldn't dignify him with my presence. He could have a wife in name only.

'It will be my pleasure to hunt with you.'

Yeah, it better fucking be. You might be stronger than I, but the gods know I understand hunting better.

'I take the flank, you follow,' I said instead. He'll follow direct orders, if he trusts you. He's a good fighter, and an okay man, only horrible at making his own decisions, so I took them away from him and it was fine. We killed the boar. There was never any question about that. There were nigh on fifty of us, all qualified to take it on alone.

The issue came when first blood was drawn, by me. By right, the beast was mine. It wasn't a surprise. While I was unlikely to deliver the killing blow, I was the swiftest in the bunch by a margin, so I landed the hit, and drew the blood. This caused some consternation. *How could she, a woman, disrespect us by being competent?*

I didn't even care to have the body, before they made a fuss of it. I didn't want to wear the skin of merely one beast, as Hercules did. I fought for the prize because they didn't think I should have it, and Hercules stood up for me.

'It was a good hunt – should we ruin it with this? The spoil is rightfully hers.'

I appreciated his failure to reference the politics. It was a good hunt. That much is true. People shrank down in his shadow and handed it to me. They should have done it unprompted.

I left shortly after.

'Where are you heading next?' I asked Hercules. We were leaving the same way; it seemed polite.

'I'm getting married.'

'Again?'

He'd never said or done anything that suggested he might be suited to marriage, but what did I know? I'd moved out of my own house to avoid my husband. Maybe they made each other very happy.

Omphale II

He came back placid, and without gifts. If I hadn't already committed to marrying the idiot, I would've called the whole thing off. Who leaves their fiancée, the most beautiful woman in Lydia, and comes back without presents?

He was restful, stretching across my couch, allowing me to play with his hair, a spoiled cat pretending to prefer the outside. I didn't ask how his trip had gone, though he tried bragging about it regardless.

'But 'Phale, there was this evil magician—'

'I was thinking we'd have the young wine for dinner. Better with the heat.'

'—And he was making the merchants work his vineyard—'

'Of course it would have been nice to throw a party to celebrate your return, but at such short notice, no one is available.'

'—And he had a daughter.'

I turned to my betrothed, my face as still and beautiful as a statue. 'Did he now?'

He wilted. 'The young wine sounds perfect.'

He bragged often. I don't doubt he did a lot with his life, my second husband, but not nearly as much as he pretended he had. No man nor god could possibly do what he claimed in his span of years. Especially since he lied about his age.

He said he was thirty-five.

If you could only see his face, from some distance, he could pass for that. The spring of youth lived beneath his skin, but the scars of his life danced atop it. His eyes were tired, his hands shook when he did anything delicate. His shoulders bore angry red scars spider-webbing out of them, as if he'd been struck by lightning in tandem. He was beautiful, but he looked like what he was: a man who'd created more stories than he had left to tell.

He managed six – seven? – children with his first wife. Only one set of twins. He spent no less than fourteen years with his cousin. Then the years after, taking revenge. I saw his nephew too. He was no sapling teenager, but a man running straight into thirty with all the grace of a bull in a china shop.

My husband-to-be was forty-five if he was a day.

Even the honesty of his years wouldn't have been enough for all he claimed he'd done. He freed Prometheus, he said, though I heard it was his own grandfather who did that, turning him into stone. I never saw my husband look so constipated as when he had to choose between pride in himself and the pride in his lineage.

Never mind, he claimed more outlandish things regularly. He held up the sky with his bare hands. He bested Apollo in an archery contest.

If I claimed any one of these, I'd have a god wreaking revenge before I finished the sentence. However impressive and beautiful I am, that's the natural order of things. You don't claim to best the gods. If Hercules had known that, perhaps our marriage would have lasted a little longer.

'I've been thinking of our wedding, dear Heracles,' I said, needling him. I wouldn't be forgotten without consequence.

'Yes, dear,' he grunted, all clenched jaws and gritted teeth. 'I assume it'll be a beautiful thing, flowers and jewels and the like?'

'You mustn't do that – it gives you wrinkles. Gods above, people might start believing you're *forty-five.*'

'What of the wedding?' he asked. Boring. He was usually so reliably baited into a fight. Both of us firebrands. But he was still technically my slave, so he feigned tolerance.

'I thought we would attend the Bacchanalia,' I said. That got him sitting straight. Just mention the god of wine and suddenly someone's all aflutter. I didn't want the wedding he first described. I'd done it with Tmolus. He hated it of course, bristled at every moment of manners, every passive-aggressive compliment.

I hoped with this I could repair some of that wrong. In my mind it would always be Tmolus who was giving me away, sneering at the pale imitation I'd found.

So tanned, 'Phale, what fighter gets such an even tan, apart from the one who does it for show? I bet he calls for buckets of hot water when he bathes, too, and sends his meat back to the kitchen when it's not cooked enough.

I imagined Tmolus' voice the first time I invited Hercules into my bed. Sure enough, he bathed with warm water and preferred his meat overcooked. He might have been rough and ready, but my first husband was completely honest about what he was.

'When are the rites?' he asked, interrupting my musing. He generally allowed me to muse uninterrupted, recognising my thoughts for the jewels they are.

'Two weeks – we will begin our travels soon.'

'They're only three days away.' Hercules frowned. Of course

he knew where they were. Always could find the closest way to the bottom of a jug, my Hercules.

'Maybe the way you travel, dear,' I said warningly. 'But I prefer something finer.'

If I was being catty – not that I hold a particular inclination to do such a thing, you understand – I would've pointed out he never had to get anywhere on time, and while he may have travelled faster, one never knew when he'd take a detour and, I don't know, wrestle a son of Poseidon or overthrow a dictator or something. My way, we'd arrive reliably slowly, without a trace of blood or dirt on us.

My husband frequently crawled into palaces covered in both of the above, holding only cloak and club. He wouldn't do so at our wedding. I didn't care about the rest of our lives. But the day he officially became mine, he'd bloody well be clean.

To this end, I brought servants with us to ensure we were looking our best. For me, the work was minimal, for I choose not to live like an animal. They laboured for hours on Hercules, brushing him down and shaping his hair and arranging layers and layers of splendid cloaks, which he'd ruin by throwing his ruddy lion skin atop it.

In the end, I said good enough and married him. We did it at sunset with the priest of Dionysus present. The sun turned his skin to bronze and mine to gold, so we shone against the sky. A sign, I thought, for the value we represented in the world against other people.

As far as I can tell, my new husband had one thought and one thought only.

Get these clothes off get these clothes off get these clothes off.

Soon enough we were lying, toes curled, on his cloak with my finery draped atop us. In true romantic style, my new husband began snoring as if he were Poseidon himself.

I liked the snoring. Tmolus did it too, but I was restless, so I took a walk.

I returned to one very confused husband and an even more confused satyr. Both were naked, and my clothes were all over the floor.

'I thought you were Omphale,' the goat-man said, pointing his finger at Hercules. 'The beautiful Omphale was meant to be here. I am the god Pan!' he shrieked, and sped away with more haste, less speed, tripping over his hooves as he did.

I told you I was beautiful. What could demonstrate that more than a god being so overtaken with lust that he courted me on my wedding night?

'Bastard,' Hercules muttered. I straightened my hair. Beautiful.

With that small business of our marriage over with – I don't think either of us thought of it as more than that – we could get on with the real business of the celebrations. What? Do you think I chose the Bacchanalia because it was *unusual*?

I chose it because it was fun, and the gods know my husband had enough difficulty loosening up. Yes, drinking had gone badly for him before. Yes, he'd lost control and lost his wife and lost his lover and lost his children, but does that mean he had to be a miserable old buzzard all the time? No, it didn't. I was on a mission to show him that.

I knew the stories, of course, of back before everything went wrong for Hercules, when he was fun and interesting and challenged people to eat fire or throw goats or jump off high buildings. I planned to bring him back to that.

There was wine, as is only proper at such an event, and

there was theatre. When people speak disparagingly of the Bacchanalia, they think only of the revelry. They forget the cultural aspects. We saw a play written by an up-and-coming writer called Herodotus. Personally, I didn't think he'd make it much further, a dour little man, but still. Playing for the famous and beautiful Queen of Lydia is certainly a star in the crown of any aspiring artist.

As the wine flowed and we moved through the remains of the play, the evening grew exciting, the moon hanging in the sky as though Artemis held it there only for us, though I can't imagine the tight-laced Artemis approving of our activities.

This isn't to say there were orgies. If people were partaking in them, I never heard of one. But I won't pretend modesty. I lay with my husband under those beautiful stars and I soaked in the beauty as if it could enrich mine. He might have had a tendency towards misery, but gods above, my husband took to sex like one of his labours. It was never so sweet and close as it was with Tmolus, nor as exciting as other travellers had made it, bringing their strange ideas from the west, but it was powerful.

(Even if he did cost me rather a lot in beds. Were I anyone else I would have started buying cheap ones. Instead, I created a booming industry for master-crafted bed frames.)

All was well. We lay together and we drank.

'You are beautiful,' he said roughly, wrapping one arm around me, pulling me closer into him. I didn't need a man to make me feel safe, but he did, anyway.

'Beautiful enough for the god Pan.' I giggled.

'You sound pleased?' he said.

'It's the closest I've come to having one of your adventures.'

'Oh, you wish to be stolen?' He smirked, and before I could

say anything more he had hoisted me atop his shoulders in a most inelegant manner and he was running around the campsite, and he was shouting: 'Come see, come see, the beautiful Omphale. My wife!'

He sounded so proud to have me. It might not have been dignified, but it was *fun*.

There was just one small burr in the ointment.

At this festival of theatre and song, my husband would still not suffer to hear music. Seriously, who has such a huge problem with music they cannot get over themselves to spend time with their beautiful new wife?

Miseryguts.

So I left him to his own business; he probably needed a break after running around like that. That's where the problem began. I should have known I couldn't leave him unaccompanied.

So intently was I listening to the music that I missed the guest of honour's arrival. I was informed by the whispers of his appearance around me, and – for a moment – I was offended. Who was this guest and what did they have that I didn't? Who is a more honourable guest than I?

In retrospect, that question probably answers itself.

He's so slim. He's taller than I expected. His hair's so sleek; I wish mine could be more like that. His cloak is beautiful. His smile glistens. Have you tasted the wine he brought? I'm amazed my eyes can bear to look at him.

Were it not for that first comment, I might have thought they spoke of my husband. But no one in the heavens or the earth or down in the underworld could, by any stretch of the imagination, describe Hercules as *slim*.

I didn't want to look desperate in my pursuit of this guest,

I bowed to no one, so I calmly waited until the musician finished to inspect the interloper.

He had a tent set up already. I was impressed by that, both the fineness of it and the speed. It rose in purple, deep, beautiful purple. Tyrian purple, if I'm correct. I have a dress made in that colour. While stunning, the stuff is magnificently expensive, all the way from Phoenicia. The entire thing screamed of luxury: pillows strewn across the floor in the eastern style, jugs of wine and spittoons placed in easy distance of all of them. My heart ached. This was the kind of accommodation I deserved but couldn't have with Hercules. He tracked dust across every beautiful thing I owned. I once found he'd left his handprints in dust across my back. Is it so surprising I forced him to bathe and perfume himself when he acted like a dog, desperate to cover himself in any interesting scents he found?

There was a man reclining across the pillows, grapes in front of him. He was attractive; I will allow that much to the shrieking girls. The opposite of Hercules. He was pale of skin and dark of hair, his eyes twinkling. He lay on a leopard skin, oddly feminine in his beauty.

'Hello, dearest visitor, we have not met yet. Best wishes to you. I am—' I began.

'Omphale, the beautiful Queen of Lydia,' he said, smiling. 'I have heard of you.'

'You have me at a disadvantage, sir, for you are unknown to me,' I responded, equally polite. I was used to these situations. Everyone has heard of me.

'Well, your lovely husband has spoken volumes of you,' he said, those eyes twinkling with such intensity I thought they'd burn through me. My heart raced. *What has he done now?* 'I am Dionysus.'

'Oh my,' I said. A god. A real, proper, human god. 'I am sorry for my failure, I—'

'No worries. I'm glad you're enjoying the festival.' He grinned. A friendly open grin of someone ready to have the time of their life. I liked him. 'Wine?'

'Well, when the god of wine himself asks, how could I possibly say no?' I said.

He roared with laughter. 'A good response. Come, sit,' he said. I sat. 'Ariadne, bring more wine, will you? We have another guest. She can watch the contest.'

'The contest?' I asked, heart sinking.

'Well, as I mentioned, I met your husband, and he was rather bragging about his exploits.'

'His exploits?'

'He said he could best even the god of wine in a drinking contest, so we are competing.'

Out stepped my husband, shit-eating grin on his face.

He'd challenged the god of wine to a drinking contest. I'd married an idiot.

Ariadne I

Heroes are arseholes. All of them. Especially those related to the particular arsehole who goes by the name of Theseus.

But, Ariadne, I hear you cry, what do you have to complain about? You're immortal and eternally young – you don't want to see the people who were only given the first of those blessings – you're married to the best Olympian, and he happens to think you're the fucking bee's knees. What's wrong with your life?

Heroes.

Jumped up with ideas about their own importance. *And* they're all sons of gods so they're preternaturally beautiful. Even Jason, who couldn't scrape together *one* immortal parent, managed to get two wives in his bed at once. But look how he whined when his wife – who gave up her whole family so he could get his stupid fleece – told him he couldn't keep *her* crown and *her* children but trade *her* out for a younger, less magical model.

Arseholes, the lot of them.

Jason isn't even the worst. At least he followed through and *married* Medea. I give up everything to help Theseus and what does he do? He abandons me on an island. Because he didn't want me telling people he didn't slay the Minotaur all on his lonesome.

I saved his life so he left me to die.

That Dionysus fell in love with me and made me his immortal wife is irrelevant. Theseus didn't know that. Theseus is an arsehole, and his cousin Hercules is too.

Fine. I have a *little* hang-up about that family. My husband thinks it's funny, offers to turn them into dolphins.

(The gods all have their own animals they like to turn people into. It's unfortunate my husband's is the kindest of the bunch. Turning Theseus into a deer and letting him get eaten by his own hounds would be better, but that's Artemis' thing and she was hardly going to scoop me off some deserted island and marry me, was she? Virgin goddess and all.)

For the uninitiated, the whole Minotaur situation is something of an embarrassment for my family. Dad pissed off Poseidon. Poseidon – in an odd yet effective retaliation – sent a beautiful white bull to Crete. With me so far?

I was pretty young when it happened, maybe four or five? But I remember the bull. It was so beautiful, its skin shining in the sun. It wasn't vicious, either. I remember stroking a hand down its flank, marvelling at how velvet-soft it was.

Clearly, I didn't like the bull as much as my mother, who had our resident genius – every good kingdom has one, but Daedalus was especially brilliant. I had it in my head I was going to marry his son for a bit, but that plan, for lack of a better phrase, crashed and burned. Anyway, Mother made Daedalus build a special contraption so she could get closer to the bull. Now, I hear you thinking, that's not so bad. That's kind of sweet.

It's not. Mum fucked the bull.

She said Poseidon made her do it. Fuck, even *Dad* said Poseidon made her do it, but it doesn't matter. She shouldn't have done it. She should have resisted, stayed my *mum* as well as my *mother*.

Our family was never the same, after. The bull pissed off, having completed its disgusting duty. The resulting infant was half bull, half human, and absolutely a hundred per cent insane. They named it after Dad, the Minotaur, even though Mum carried it to term. Tells you all you need to know about heroes, really.

So Daedalus – you remember Daedalus, of the bull-fucking machine? – with suitable guilt builds us a nice little maze. Sorry, Dad still cares about the fame of the thing; Daedalus builds *the labyrinth* to hide the baby. As it gets bigger the creature wants meat. In meetings I wasn't invited to, it's decided it has to be human meat. I'm glad I wasn't privy to that insanity.

Seven boys and seven girls. Every year. We'd stick 'em in the maze – sorry, *labyrinth* – and let my half-brother chase 'em to their deaths. I was seventeen by the time Prince Theseus – twenty-four, exotic, nice legs – came to Crete and took one of their places.

I decided within, maybe, four heartbeats of his arrival I was going to marry him. I needed a way out, away from the screams I still haven't outrun. He just had to kill the Minotaur and I'd be free. I gave him my string and taught him how to find the way out of the maze. Explained where little bro's weak points were. It was a deal.

It worked. Minotaur dead, Father pissed, betrothal promised. I sailed away with him. Go Ariadne!

I got off the boat at the first island, to find food to celebrate our upcoming marriage. And he left. Without me. So I'd die.

Fucking arseholes, the lot of them.

Dio picked me up; we were married; I was immortalised. It was all sweet and pretty and it doesn't change a *fucking* thing about what Theseus did.

Skip forwards and Dio hears Theseus' favourite cousin – can confirm, he didn't stop talking about his cousin Hercules the entire time we were on the boat – was getting married at a Bacchanalia, and did I want to ruin his life?

I love my husband.

We didn't even have to force an opportunity. Hercules openly volunteered to Dionysus that he thought he could outdrink the god of wine. He was already drunk enough to not recognise Dionysus, his own half-brother, as said god.

'Is that so?' Dio asked, smirking. 'How about a wager?'

'What wager?'

'If you lose . . .' Dio stopped, as if fishing for something, though we knew exactly what to demand. 'You put aside your mortal life for a year and join the Thiasus.' That's my husband's troop of followers. Mostly female, all mad. It's a good time.

'And if I win?' he asked, his eyes hungry for power he couldn't possibly earn. Theseus had the same look. I wondered if he learned from his cousin or if it's a prerequisite of herodom.

'I go to bed with you,' I said. Dio looked at me, all wide eyes and sad innocence though we both knew the other took lovers. If you watched the continuing daily disaster of the Aphrodite/Ares/Hephaestus situation, you'd understand. 'What? Are you planning to lose?' I asked, all sweetness and light and that shit boys eat up. Make yourself a prize and they'll do anything you want.

Tell them you're theirs and they'll abandon you on an island to die.

'If you win, you get—' here Dio spoke through gritted teeth; sweetheart '—my wife, Ariadne. As you can see, she is very beautiful.'

I paused, afraid he'd recognise my name, though of course he wouldn't. Boys don't speak of girls they leave behind, just as girls don't speak of boys they crush under their dainty immortal feet.

'Deal,' he said, finally looking from my tits to my face. 'You're married to Dionysus?'

'Proudly.'

'Didn't my cousin—?' I so wanted to hear him finish that thought, that stupid broken half-formed crack of an idea that would let me kill him myself. Alas, his wife arrived, and she had first claim to anger.

'Heracles,' she shrieked. He flinched with his whole body. Interesting way to control him. 'What in Hades' name were you thinking? What have you done?'

'I didn't know?' he tried.

'Didn't you think to ask who you were challenging to a drinking contest before you did it?' She had a shout I recognised from my mother. It's a very courtly shout. Full of rage and fire, but volume never rising enough for eavesdropping servants to hear it. 'Of course you didn't. Did you never learn not to tell gods you're better than them?'

'I did beat—'

'This isn't the time for your bullshit. You're fucked, Heracles.' She sighed. 'There's nothing for it now. Drink.'

I'm glad my father never had to go against her as queen.

If she had the wiles of my mother and the steel of my father, Omphale would've ripped Crete apart with a finger. Vain, yes. Beautiful, maybe. But strong.

I liked her, though I don't know how much of that's because she hated Hercules.

As if by magic – that's a joke; it was magic, my husband's a god – mugs appeared in front of them, for Omphale and me too.

I bent over towards my husband and whispered in his ear, in that tone he liked. *'Destroy him.'*

I've never seen him drink a mug of wine so fast. I don't believe his lips moved. I was ready to look across to our guests, ready to gloat at their failures, when I saw Hercules' mug already empty, him licking his lips, desperately searching for more.

I worried, but Dio just laughed, bright and bold, filling the room. I needed that, needed the reassurance we would be okay.

'This might be a real contest then.' He laughed, bringing his hand across to shake. 'Let's see what else you can do.'

When he next waved his hand, the mugs were bigger, the wine sweeter, stronger. This would be a contest without water, without breaks for food, without even music. Those details were saved for meetings of fun. Whatever happened, Dio would rather walk to Hades and present his soul for weighing than force me into bed with *Hercules*.

The room was intense. I was lost in the fumes of their wine. I tried a sip of it once, and found my eyes spinning into a pit and my stomach following after. Omphale grabbed one of the more attractive servants so she could enjoy the rest of the festivities.

'I see no reason both of us should waste our evening as such. A pleasure, Dionysus,' she said, all flattery and polite smiles.

'I do like you, Omphale,' my husband said, not breaking eye contact across the table. They were onto their twelfth mugs, no signs of stopping.

'Everyone does.'

She was gone with a whirl of perfume and a clearing of air. I was left alone to bite my nails and watch the match. A stupid errant memory from my stupid errant childhood drifted to me, my mother saying: *don't bite your nails, Ariadne; it is not ladylike*. But being ladylike never got me anywhere, so I bit them anyway.

The rules were simple and disgusting. Drink until you pass out, or until someone vomits. Vulgarity aside, I rooted for the second, rooted for Hercules to feel the shame of his own body rejecting his claims of grandeur. I wanted him to lie in a puddle of his own failure.

What? I told you I have a thing about heroes.

The contest lasted eleven hours. By the end, Omphale had returned and napped beside me. She muttered another man's name when she slept. I hoped that ripped Hercules apart.

He stood, claiming he needed the bathroom – a claim he'd been making with increasing frequency – and took one step. Two. Three, and—

He fell hard enough to bring the tent down around us. Omphale emerged looking thoroughly disgruntled. She waved it off fast enough, though.

'Dissolve the marriage,' she ordered. 'I will not be attached to a braggart and a failure.'

And I thought *I* hated the bastard.

My husband was fabulous. He woke Hercules up, leaned over to where he'd collapsed on the floor and whispered in his ear, making sure his tongue flicked out just enough to catch the rim of it, just to see him squirm. Gods, I love that man.

'We win.'

Marina I

I was born to be a virgin, can you imagine? I can't, and I lived it. Mum was out on the hills when her pains struck and she didn't have time to get home. When the sun came up and she looked round, she realised she'd given birth outside Delphi, famous for its oracles.

She thought it was a sign. Plus, it doesn't hurt to have a Delphic virgin in the family and, at the time, there *was* a very public story about how much it could hurt to be someone's wife. What happened with Hercules, you know? Obviously my brothers would be fine, being boys and all, but what he did to Megara hung round like a bad smell. People didn't want that for their daughters.

So I was to be a virgin and a priestess. I was . . . okay at it. I liked the wild, for sure, but I hated shoes, and having my body bound in cloth and leather so tight I couldn't feel the earth beneath me. Apparently a preference for nakedness isn't ideal in your future virgin priestess. I did fine in lessons, clever enough but not so clever my tongue got away from me. I would have been okay. But then Dionysus came along, and I realised my life could be *more*.

He brought wine and music and dancing to the mountain. My first religious order was a sombre one – people are never happy when you tell them the future. But Dionysus, he'd come to the oracle because we shared the spot with his own mortal grave, and he said visiting it was as good an excuse for a party as any. He got us drunk, insisted it was okay, though none of us believed him, and he danced us down the mountain, grinning all the way.

We sang and we smiled and I didn't care if the high priestess was mad. She was shrouded in Apollo's protection; she wasn't scared of speaking her mind to Dionysus. Her words whipped against his chest and bounced right off, so lost was he in his stupor of ecstasy.

But it must have done *something*, 'cause I was the only one to go with him when he left. Maybe that's because he didn't invite us, but honestly whenever has something so pointless as an invitation stopped anyone?

'Long walk without shoes,' he said, the first night, when I tried to sneak in behind him. Growing up in an order of virgin priestesses doesn't give you a lot of opportunities for sneaking. He didn't look back from his fire, jumping and dancing in greens and purples.

'I don't feel the pain,' I said, brazen, tied up with pride I hadn't earned.

'Liar. Come here and I'll sort it.' I crept up, still afraid of him, though he never said a harsh word, not to me. He fixed my feet with a wave. Magic. 'So you want to be a Maenad?'

'More than anything.'

'I'm not going to ask you why.'

'You're not?' I asked, gormless.

'Saw it in your eyes, didn't I? Like you were coming home.

Have some wine.' So I did, and I fell into that same joy, though less manic this time round. He fed me the meat of a goat and the next day we caught up to the rest of the Thiasus. They welcomed me warmly, with eyes that didn't quite focus on the world around them.

'I see you've been having a party without me,' Dionysus boomed. 'We can do better.'

It was brilliant. The most beautiful night of my life. More of that enchanting fire surrounded us as we danced. We drank. We felt the earth beneath our feet. I shed that pesky virgin title, once and for all. I was never going back.

I was there when he brought Ariadne in, not as one of us, but as a wife. It would've been easy to hate her, because he loved her as he didn't love us, but I grew up being told I'd never have any love at all.

Anyway it was obvious why he chose her. Ariadne is brilliant, and fiery, and mad. She didn't hide her story, nor did we hide our nosiness. She shouted it loud and the sky burned with her anger, the flames a colour I couldn't name. She shouted, and we shouted with her. 'We hate heroes,' she said, and we called it back, a mockery of the songs we teach kids. They loved each other, not despite their madness but because of it.

She wanted to trick Hercules into joining – some revenge thing. I didn't really get it, but then I'm only a bit mad. She said otherwise, but I caught her rubbing her hands and cackling in the days running up to it. She won, as we knew she would, and Hercules was bound to us.

I'd seen him before, Hercules. Most of us had, some way or another. Dude gets around. Spending my life at Delphi, I saw so many famous, important people, the excitement wore off. I was kind of alone in that, though.

'You don't stare so much,' he said to me, his first night. Our god was in a state of pure ecstasy with his wife in their tent, which was rapidly banging itself into the ground around them.

'We've met before.'

'I'm sorry,' he said, his voice croaky. 'I don't remember you.'

'I didn't remember you either,' I said, grinning, to make him feel better. He didn't look any less lost than he did when he came to us at Delphi years ago, the blood of someone he loved on his hands. Not even a ghost of a smile crossed his face. 'Do you want to talk about it?'

'What?'

'Whatever's making you so freaking miserable,' I said. I didn't leave Delphi to be stuck with sulking heroes all the time. 'I'm not going to tell on you, if you don't like it here.'

'It's not that. Dionysus is . . . he's nice. One of the better ones.' There are loads of ways to describe the god we followed, none of them *nice*. But then, I met Apollo too, and he wasn't really *nice* either.

'So? I don't have all night.' I had all night. By the sounds coming from Dionysus' tent we had all day again too.

'I've been a slave before. I wasn't ready to be one again so soon,' he said, slowly turning his hands over, staring into them as if he could read the future from his palms.

'Oh, shut up.'

'What?'

'Shut your stupid face. Have some wine.'

'I don't trust wine.'

'Then learn, and dance. Stop hiding from the music or you'll go mad.'

'My head hurts.'

His head probably did hurt. I don't think they exaggerated how much he drank in the contest. But he was lying too. His nose scrunched when he did, like he didn't like the taste.

'The dancing will help,' I promised. Though it wasn't the dancing that helped, really. It was the distraction. It's not like you stopped being in pain, you just kind of got lost in it. Still, I wanted to help him.

The first night I was a Maenad, I woke up covered in ash. We'd set the *world* on fire. We were scattered among animal bones and blood and all the other things that you kind of want to stay inside the animal most of the time. I think we ate the rest of them with our bare hands.

I knew what it was to be afraid of what your hands could do.

I went to bed, and stuck my fingers in my ears. Dionysus and Ariadne detached themselves by morning – bless small miracles – and gathered us to do the rites together. I could do them almost with my eyes closed, so I went to help the new recruit. He was struggling a lot, even though we did a lot of our rites drunk, so they weren't fiddly or difficult.

'I dislike this,' he muttered.

'We're nearly done, then there'll be dancing and music.'

'I don't dance.'

'You will.'

He held out for ages, then when he finally did dance he blocked his ears. Took forever to convince him otherwise. Dionysus was basically ignoring him and Lady Ariadne went out of her way to piss him off, dropping snide comments and laughing every time he winced.

She said we had to call him Heracles. She snuck music onto him, played it into his tent. Lyres, especially. The sight of a lyre sent him into a panic like a lady surprised by a spider.

'Don't tell me to get over it,' he muttered. 'I don't like lyres.'

'And Ariadne doesn't like you. Are you gonna let her win or are you gonna pick up the lyre?'

He picked up the lyre.

He dragged his fingers so hard across the strings they snapped with a *ping*. When the other Maenads – I'm tone deaf, to tell you the truth – tried to help him, he growled and snarled until they ran away. That one got him a cuff from Dionysus.

'Do not upset my girls.'

'Or what?' Hercules growled. 'You'll make me become your follower?'

'Children,' Dionysus sighed. He snapped his fingers and a vine grew around Hercules, yanking him by the neck and holding him there. He could breathe, probably, but it didn't look much fun. 'While I have you here, a question,' Dionysus said casually, like they were having a nice chat in the taverna.

'Hgh?' Hercules said.

'I wish to make my own trip to Hades. Say hello to my uncle, y'know. I want to know if you have any shortcuts or the like.'

'That's easy,' Hercules snorted. A rivulet of blood rolled down his neck. He didn't seem to notice. 'Just go the quick way.'

'How do I access this quick way?' Dionysus asked.

'Poison? Or, ooh, piss off Uncle Poseidon then go swimming. Play fetch with the Hydra? Knife to the chest, but that's boring—'

Dionysus walked away. He left Hercules hanging there a whole day.

Dionysus and Ariadne went away on some godly business. We kept going, it wasn't the first time. After the vine thing, Hercules whined less, not meek or anything, but better. He didn't learn to be happy, really, and he never did like music, but without Ariadne looming over him – I don't know how she managed; she's not tall – he could raise a drink with us and smile.

When Dionysus came back, he looked him up and down appraisingly.

'That scarred, huh? Strong vines,' he remarked, all grins. Immortals are weird. I can't even blame the madness; Apollo would have said it too. The both of them were obsessed with scars, like they don't get how our skin can be so weak. I doubt Hercules was a big fan of the pinpricks circling his neck any more than he was of the burns covering his shoulders. He would take his shirt off and dance with us, but only when it was dark.

In all these little ways, the time ticked down, and a year got a whole lot sooner than it had been before.

'How long's it been now?' Dionysus asked. 'I can never keep up.'

'Three hundred and fifty-four days,' Hercules said stiffly.

'Oh, you are loving being my follower,' Dionysus said, stretching out each and every one of the words. He relished being happy at dour people, thought it was funny when they exploded in rage. 'Tell you what; Ari's been enjoying her time up top – a rest, you know – and she said we can have another drinking contest.'

'Another drinking contest?' Hercules said suspiciously.

'Awesome idea, right? Drinking, contests: what's not to like? Stakes are, you win, you can go right now. You lose, you're with us for another year.'

'I am a terrible follower,' Hercules said.

'Oh, the worst. If you were here by choice I would have kicked you out a long time ago. But look, you don't seem convinced, so I'll sweeten the deal. It's not against me.'

His ears perked up. 'Who?'

'My wife.' Dionysus grinned. 'What do you say? I'll throw in a night in her bed, sweeten the deal.'

'Your wife hates me.'

'Which would make it all the better when you win, no?' Dionysus grinned, bouncing on his toes a bit.

'I think my answer is no.'

'Really? Don't want to get out of here right now?'

'I will wait.'

'Do you mind saying why, nice and loud, so everyone can hear you up top?'

Hercules sighed. I thought Dionysus had broken him then, and he'd take the deal just to avoid saying it. But he didn't. He leaned back and gave a good old yell. 'I won't take the deal for, I think, Ariadne, wife of Dionysus, would best me.'

'Wonderful.' Dionysus beamed. 'You may leave.'

'What? Now?'

'Just needed to teach you some humility, bro. Enjoy your freedom.'

Hercules managed a quick grin and that was about it. Admitting weakness broke him more than anything else Ariadne did, though. He slunk out of camp with only his cloak and his club, without even a goodbye.

'Lord Dionysus,' I asked, once Hercules was out of earshot. I don't like hurting people. 'Lady Ariadne isn't famed for her ability to drink.'

'Can't hold a drop of it,' he confirmed, grinning ever wider. 'That's what makes it so sweet.'

His smile only grew when Ariadne appeared in front of him. If I thought the sounds from their tent were bad when we got Hercules, it had nothing on when we got rid of him.

For all that, something of us must have stuck with Hercules. He might not have enjoyed hedonism alongside the Maenads, but the first thing he did when he left was find a king and sleep with all fifty of his daughters in a single night. If that's not ecstasy then I don't know what is.

Fifty

1. Our father wanted heroic grandsons. He thought the only way to do that was to have a hero father them. Father's a king, so it couldn't be any old hero. He told the world he had a lion that needed killing and waited for Hercules to come crawling in. I knew the minute he walked through the door.

2. Dad took a liking to him, to Hercules, a sweaty, tired, *old* man with a hangover, and invited him to dinner with all us girls. He went all out with the food, saying *Hercules will need his strength later*. I giggled because I didn't understand – strength for what?

3. He told me to fetch clean linens for the bed while the others were giggling and twirling their curls.

4. We're not all sisters. Common mistake. We're a motley combination of sisters and cousins, with varying levels of legitimacy. There are fifty of us though, all girls. That's why our father did it.

5. There's no way the great Hercules could produce more girls.

Not him. Dad fawned so much you'd think *he* wanted to bear his child. But obviously he doesn't have the capacity, so he cast a bit further out.

6. Daddy drew up a little schedule. Fifty was a lot in one night, he said, trying to placate *Hercules*. But I was scared too. We all were.

7. He told Hercules five per hour, sunset to sunrise. Then he had to leave. For all his lack of sense in suggesting the damn thing, my uncle understood we'd run this man out of our home the moment the sun was upon us.

8. I prayed to Artemis, when he was with my sisters. Artemis and Athena and Hestia. Anyone who might help. Anyone whose father tried making their decisions for them.

9. It was scary when he was eating, ripping flesh from bones like he was born for it.

10. The whole thing made me sick.

11. He took my oldest sister first. It wasn't on his little rota who would go when, but she assumed it was her right. Bullshit is it. If any of us could have done something about it, it was her. She'd made the choice not to marry yet. Most of us were too young to.

12. I went on a walk, took the younger set with me. The babies, we called them. We couldn't do that anymore.

13. We could hear the sounds coming from the bedroom. Wait, were we all going to have to use the same bedroom? The same bed? The same sheets and pillows as well as the same man?

14. Walking was good, the scent of autumn heavy in the air. It was fresh, a reminder of change, death and rebirth. That was the way of things. Who was I to change that?

15. I was excited. Hercules! And me! Me and Hercules. I didn't get why my sisters were so mad about going to bed with the famous, sexy Hercules.

16. He's old. Nearly as old as our father, who's old enough to have sired an unreasonable number of daughters, all on different nights.

17. And he's scarred, all gnarly like some tree branch growing every which way. He's too golden to be unused to light, but the darkness suited him, covered the worst of his flaws.

18. Worst of all, he was bored. Clearly, and utterly bored with me. I could hear the counter in his head. *Eighteen down, twenty-two to go.* I didn't tell him that only makes forty.

19. We played games in the corridors, those of us who hadn't gone in yet. Silly, quick, simple things with dice. They couldn't be any longer or—

20. The call to come in. The loom of an open door and heavier breathing than could belong to one of us. I imagined some strange animal the merchants told us about. An elephant, maybe.

21. I didn't go back to finish the game. It didn't feel right to demand entry with the children, when my father had so adamantly decided I wasn't one of them anymore.

22. We sat together, those of us on the far side. We didn't speak. We knew, then, we'd never speak of it, never tell our sons how they came to be brothers.

23. It wasn't so bad, but I was used to it. The press of sheets cool against my back, then that coolness enveloped in fire. I liked it.

24. He was intense. I kept looking into my sisters' eyes afterwards, seeing if the seeds of fire were behind them too. It seemed impossible to spend a night with him without it.
25. Father had food sent up from the kitchens.
26. I suppose that was kind of him.
27. Nothing fancy. Sweet, simple things from our childhoods, things that tasted like a home. A plea for forgiveness, then?
28. Drinks too. Wine. For us and not for him, he kept saying that. For us and not for him. Good blood for sons, bad for a husband.
29. That explained my uncle's actions a bit. He didn't trust him with his girls. If he did, he would've only had to sacrifice one of us, not all fifty.
30. The games stopped around the middle of the night. The real middle, where Apollo was off duty, partying his night away.
31. The games stopped because our sister walked the wrong way out of the door.
32. She wasn't broken exactly. She wasn't broken at all. She looked like she'd had a solid night in bed.
33. But we could see the marks of fingerprints across her waist where he held on to her. The servants didn't think it was worth worrying about, ushered her into the unofficial area for those who'd done their duty, away from us.
34. My turn. The door opening. The door closing around me.
35. Not bad. Could be worse, all wonderful words for those who are losing something they'd planned to share with their husbands. Especially the younger end of us, the ones with so many older sisters we could believe in marrying for love. We thought we'd be allowed.

36. This was a weird power play from Father. My uncles are dead. Gods above know what they would have thought of it. Maybe it's to spite their memories.
37. I wonder what they did to him.
38. I wonder what we did to him.
39. He's speeding up now. If I didn't find the word so distasteful, so unfair to attach to my sisters, I'd say he's almost churning through us. Maybe it's better that way. No broken hearts, not over *him*.
40. There are still noises coming from the room. Changing in tempo and beat. Sometimes screams, but not in a bad way. I'm not sure I'd like to scream.
41. The servants are awake. They're putting breakfast together. I've never been awake this time of night before. I didn't know it took them that long to cook. I envy them.
42. He's chanting with every thrust. Eight. Eight. Eight more to go. I don't appreciate that.
43. At least I am seven. At least I'm enough that he thinks of me as a number and not part of some haze in the middle of the night where all accounts indicate he was a damp fish with a penis.
44. To hear the thirties talk, he's always a damp fish with a penis. Much of the room after is occupied with telling unflattering Hercules stories.
45. Gods above, is that fucker a prick.
46. The first rays of sun are peeking over the hills now. It's so warm, so clean. We can afford to be kind now.
47. We're sisters. Sure, we're cousins as well. But we're sisters. Our father doesn't know yet. He's done a dangerous thing.
48. No one questions whether we're pregnant. We're all

pregnant. All boys. A change in tradition for our family. None of us has a brother.

49.   I go in and he looks right through me. I'm not a girl, not a person to him. I'm one more number in a line he regrets signing up for. I'm grateful to not be the last.

50.   It takes a long time. Savouring the last bite when you're already too full. He tires himself out, poor dear, and he's snoring by the time I make my escape, stealing out like a thief, closing the door softly behind me. He belches in his sleep. My sisters wrap me in hugs and kisses and blankets. Whatever happens next, we are fifty.

Graffiti

H is an arsehole

An arsehole with a little cock

You're just jealous because he didn't want to spend more time with you

      whereas you had an incredibly meaningful twelve minutes together?

      with him and his tiny cock!

I didn't think he had a tiny cock

Sister! How do you even know that word? You're too young for such coarse language

From the graffiti, obviously

      Tick here if you hate Hercules:

Tick here if you think graffiti polls are stupid:

Tick here if you don't want to destroy our father's home further:

Maybe our father deserves his home to be destroyed

The bed's already gone!

And someone vomited in the hall urn

There are fifty pregnant women in the house – I think everyone vomited in the hall urn

That's revolting. I certainly didn't

No, you vomited in the kitchen!

You said you wouldn't tell anyone about that

Yeah, well, Father said we'd be pure until marriage. People say a lot of crap

Like when you said H had a tiny cock

She said little. You're the one who added tiny

Don't be so mean to him, just because he didn't like you

Oh, shut up, sister.

Laonome II

My brother's getting tattered in his dotage, but I can't tell him that. Herc doesn't know what dotage means.

'Lao, darling,' my husband pleaded. 'That's unfair. He's your brother. Family's important.'

He's my brother and I do love him, despite the things we don't talk about, despite the fact I was on my way to Thebes when it happened. I love him. Fact.

So when Herc showed up at our door, I couldn't refuse him, could I?

'Sister.'

'Brother.'

Our love had nothing to do with the strings of family hanging limply between us and everything to do with being the only members of our clan who're remotely *fun*. So we said the magic words and we embraced, and my husband grinned smugly.

'I have a small favour to ask of you,' Herc said.

'Oh, I see how it is, only comes round when he has favours to ask, not to see his lovely sister Laonome. Doesn't even bother when her *children* are born—'

'I—' he stuttered. I always loved putting him in awkward emotional situations and watching him flail.

'Just kidding, brother. I don't care.'

'Shall I speak with your husband, then?'

'Ah,' I said. 'One of those favours. No, I think it can wait until tomorrow, thank you.'

'It's—' he began.

'It's not urgent,' I informed him. 'Come on, I haven't seen you for years. Catch up first, *then* man business.'

He scowled. People get so caught up with his prodigious strength and his goldish skin and all that balls they forget my brother's literally all eyebrows. Like an angry little bird.

As it turned out, Herc had slain some monster or another – what? You think I can keep track of what monsters my brother's killed? – for this guy Laomedon – great name, if I do say so myself – and he'd offered payment and then refused to give it to him. Only Herc couldn't chase up on it then on account of being a slave and all, so he was doing it now, fifteen years later. Boys.

'But why?' I asked.

'I didn't have anywhere else to go.' Right. My brother, technically homeless.

'Mum misses you.'

'I don't want to deal with Amphitryon,' he said. I frowned. 'What?'

'No one told you?'

'What?'

'Dad *died*.' It wasn't tactful, I know, but I was in shock. 'How has no one told you?'

'Mostly people want to talk about me,' he said. He blinked, twice, straightening everything out in a head that didn't have space for *maybe*. 'It doesn't matter. People can't see me scuttling back to my mother. Defending my reputation, you know.'

'Dad died and you're worried about your reputation?'

'I can hardly bring him back, can I?' That hung heavy and difficult. I don't like difficult. Fortunately, Herc didn't either. 'We can call for wine?' he asked. He must have seen something change in my face when he said it. I hate that. 'I am . . . Things are better now, sis. She is less angry.'

I've never really known if I believe him about the Hera thing. It was his hands, his eyes, his shouts, Mum said, when she was drunker than strictly advisable. But I have to believe him too. He taught me how to swing a sword when it was still taller than me, and Meg gave me tea, after. I could do what I did with the Argonauts because he taught me to protect myself, so no one could do to me what he did to *her*. He's my brother.

I miss Meg.

'Wine,' I called. 'Let's get good and drunk, shit-talk your brother.'

'Your brother,' he said.

'Your *twin*,' I emphasised.

'Your full, two-shared-parents brother.'

'Amphitryon gave you the sex talk, Herc. He was your dad, and Iph's your twin.'

'You seen Iph recently, then?'

'Yeah, the funeral. And he came round a few months ago. Another pilgrimage over you-know-what,' I said.

Iph was always on some pilgrimage or another because his son died. Not Iolaus but the younger one, who wasn't his wife's. Iph's a sucker for family – when he calls me sister, he means it – and he loved the little shit. Then he died in some adventure involving Hercules. That's all I wanted to know on the matter.

Herc didn't react. I'm not sure he did *know what*, but I didn't want to talk about it, so I left it at that.

'Bah, and what of you, sister? Holding up the family name for fun?'

'Something like that.' I smiled. I liked my life, and lived it more dangerously than most in my position, but there was no denying the excitement rose when heroes showed up. 'How about you? I heard something about a drinking contest . . . ?'

He blanched, always a wonderful sign.

'I will need more wine for that, Lao. A lot more wine.'

'And here I thought you'd never want wine again, after,' I joked, but I called for it anyway. 'We could have our own drinking contest.'

'Sister—'

'*Brother*—'

'Fine,' he grumbled, eyebrows front and centre.

I'm never going to beat him in a straight drinking contest. I'm a third of his size. Happily, what I lack in being wider than I am tall, I make up for in cunning. When I called for wine, I had my brother's at full strength, and mine well watered, with pigment to hide the fact.

I cheated.

It's the only way of getting anything out of Herc when he gets in those moods. You know, the *I'm a hero and everything's so hard and I'm so dark and enigmatic* moods? The ones that are wildly inappropriate because minstrels literally write tales of his escapades, and his entire body, eyebrows included, sometimes seems to be carved out of gold. Dark and enigmatic, my arse.

'You *married* her?' I spluttered. 'She literally *bought* you, then made you dress up in her clothes, and you *married* her?'

'It got me my freedom, didn't it?' He shrugged. 'And they weren't her clothes. She got me my own clothes.'

'Like when I used to dress you up.'

'You didn't.'

'I did.'

'You didn't.'

'I can write to Mum and ask her,' I suggested. It was a little mean. I can win any argument by bringing Mum into it. But the wine was hitting me and I couldn't be bothered to fight properly. 'Do you not remember? I did your hair in those wonky plaits, and tried to hide the wonkiness with flowers?'

He glowered. I continued.

'And your feet wouldn't fit in any of the shoes—' His feet truly are enormous. You don't notice, until you do, and then it's unsettling. They're just there, being bigger than the average child. 'So we used . . . what did we use again?'

'Ribbons,' he grumbled. He knows I can drag that kind of thought out for hours.

'You do remember!'

'I hate you.'

'Uh-huh. Shall I remember that for tomorrow when you're asking me for favours?'

'Technically, I'm going to ask your husband. And you won't say anything, or I'll tell him about the time you got drunk on Bear Island and fell into the sea.' He smirked.

'You wouldn't.'

'What was it your beloved husband thought you were again, when you were caught in those fishing nets? It wasn't a nymph, or a dolphin, was it, sister?'

'I hate you.'

'What was that?' he asked again, cocking his head like he didn't fully well remember. He'd definitely learned some tricks.

'He thought I was a rotted sack of corn. Happy?'

'You have no idea.' He grinned. 'How are your sons doing?'

Mother stopped him, when Hera took his mind. She stood in front of his fists and hoped. I was too young, then, not to have a mother. I'm still too young to be without a mother, and I'll never be old enough to lose a son.

'No.'

'They're doing *no*?' he said facetiously.

'No. As in, they're not old enough to follow you on one of your hare-brained schemes around who knows where.'

'I wasn't going to—'

'Yes you were.'

'Okay.' He grinned again, sheepishly. 'I was. They're older than Iolaus was when I took him to see the Hydra, and he was fine, if you recall.' Yes, and Iolaus begged for years to go with his Uncle Hercules on an adventure. My kids think their father's the greatest hero and I'll fight to keep it that way. I love my brother but he has a less-than-stellar success rate with his travelling companions, and he knows that.

'You stay away from them, you hear me?'

'Loud and clear, Lao, loud and clear.' He thinks he's funny. Lao-d. Please.

'How's your multitude of sons? I hear you have another fifty of them,' I said, expecting a denial, expecting an outright refusal of this clearly exaggerated story, but he shrugged uncomfortably.

'Their father insisted.'

'Oh. Gods. Fifty, really?'

He explained. I called for more wine. He told me of his newest

304

batch, mumbling, 'I can never keep the names straight,' which is less than surprising when you have clear of a hundred children running round the country. I told him my adventures in court, being a bad influence on the well-brought-up princesses, sneaking sword-fighting lessons to my eldest – I don't much rate their tutor – and my happy little life.

Then things got to that stage, the three-carafe stage, where it can only get very loud or very quiet. We started so loud, the only way we could go was down.

'I heard a rumour about you,' I said.

'There are always rumours.'

'They said you went to Hades.' I looked over to him. He sat, impassive. Yes, then. 'I was scared. I don't want to lose you.'

'You didn't need to do that, sis. You know I'll come back.'

'People don't come back from Hades.' There was another rumour about him, a stupider one, that he could only be killed by someone who was already dead. If that was true, Hades was just about the only place I *could* lose him.

'I had a plan. I went to the mysteries.'

'At Eleusis?' I asked. He nodded. 'What do they actually do there?'

'Can't say. It's a mystery.' I punched his shoulder, which I'm fairly sure caused me more pain than it did him. 'Really, I can't. The guy running it, Musaeus, I owe him.'

'What could you possibly owe someone for?' My brother was an itinerant hero. I don't think he even carried money. People threw things at him through a mixture of fear and awe.

'Do you remember Linus?'

No. The whole incident happened before I was born, but I'd heard his name whispered often enough.

'Your music teacher,' I said. *The one you killed.*

'He was Musaeus' uncle.' He started staring off into space. I couldn't have that.

'Did I tell you about the first time Euphemus took the boys hunting?' I didn't wait for a response, just launched back into the story and pulled us out of the slump.

I woke with a pained head and a clear mind, as nights with Herc often leave me. He'd already been in to see my husband, who'd granted his request without asking me. I suspect the subsequent shouting match could be heard from several miles.

'What do you mean, you just granted it?' I asked, calmly, at first.

'He is your brother, dear.'

'Right. And do you think for a second I would have granted him eighteen boats to wage war against some country I've never heard of, over some slight from twenty years ago?'

'When you put it like that,' he said, shrugging. 'I'm sorry, dear, but we can't exactly rescind the offer now.'

We could have, if it was Iph my husband had made the promise to. But taking it from Herc could have ended with him waging war against us. He has a real thing about his honour, and people besmirching it. Which is weird, really. When we were kids you could call him a no-good son of a bitch as much as you wanted and he didn't give a shit.

They were bound for a place called Ilium. Pretty name is all I really knew about it. My husband gives me shit for my geography, but our world is made of a series of thousands of tiny islands, each with its own tiny kingdom, and I remember the kings' names, which is more than I can say for him.

He stayed with us for two months, while we prepared the

ships. I thought it was my husband giving us time to bond – he can have those ships ready to sail in two days if he wants – but it turned out to be something else entirely.

My husband was stalling, waiting for a second visitor.

'Sister,' Iphicles boomed, as he strode into our hall, not a trace of irony in his voice. 'How I have missed you.' Uh-huh.

'This is a surprise, dear brother.'

'Your husband sent for me.' I glared at the aforementioned husband. I meddle; I am not meddled with. 'I brought my son.'

If he was Herc, I would have smirked and asked which one, but with Iph that would be cruel. He'd never get over Pyrrhus. Iolaus looked good, though. Happy. I'm not used to seeing men in my family look happy when they come off boats. They're normally buried so deep in shit they can't see the sun.

We embraced. Herc walked in and chest-bumped our nephew.

'You're not a slave,' Iolaus said.

'You're not dead,' Herc beamed. Boys.

'Shall I call for some wine?' I asked. 'We can all catch up?' Herc and I were more or less caught up. I'd even forced him to go to some fancy events, just to watch him squirm. In return, he'd taken me hunting and we'd failed to engage anything larger than a rabbit, just how I like it.

'I don't like to drink after a long journey,' Iph said slowly.

'Da-ad,' Iolaus whined. Iolaus is close to my age. Too old to be whining, but hilarious for how well it worked on his father.

'One glass.'

It was not one glass.

Iphicles III

I've never been able to say no to my brother. Not when we were kids and he wanted to go hunting for monsters when we were meant to be in lessons, and not when we were adults and I received missives saying: *come quick, we're going on an adventure.*

I'm not an interesting person when I'm away from him. Even my son thinks so.

Herc's just so *alive* all the time, I can't say no.

Lao greeted me kindly. It's an act. My sister's many wonderful things, but kind isn't among them. I appreciated it anyway.

We sat down to eat together, and my eyes widened when I was reminded what damage my brother could do to a pig. When you spend that long away from him, you forget what he's like. You brush off all those stories and insist to yourself, he's only a man. He couldn't possibly do that. But oh, he does. The eating is just the leaves on the tree.

Lao leaned across to me, as we watched the boar disappear down his gullet.

'We have him hunting now, for food. We'd be paupers if

we didn't.' She grinned. She got his vividness too. It sneaked a smile out of me.

'Am I to assume we're partaking in the Hydra later, then?'

'If only,' she exclaimed dramatically. 'We could cut off a new head for every meal, have an endless supply. I bet you boys never thought about that when you were killing it, huh, Iolaus?'

'Feeding your family wasn't my first thought when the bugger tried to kill me,' he admitted, all grins too. 'Next time though, I'll grab it for you, m'lady.'

'You better.'

'It'll be my honour,' he said.

'Here, have more wine. I won't have those sad faces at my table,' she said, summoning a servant before I could object. I don't like to drink after a long journey, or ever, really. To be honest with you, I'm afraid of what could happen. That blood runs through my veins too.

Yet I drank. Conversation moved between my siblings, and my son, too fast for me to keep up. Jokes about society and power and taking over the world one dinner party at a time. Even Euphemus could join in, used to my brother. When I couldn't hold my own, I allowed more wine to be poured for me.

Gods above, that was stupid. I'd only drunk once since I was twenty-six and my brother showed the world all the damage being drunk can do.

Lao's sons came in from wherever it is they spent their time – Lao took a rather backseat attitude to parenting – and they joined in with this *thing* my family does, where they talk too much and drink too much and everything moves over you too fast to keep up with the tide. It wasn't so bad at Amphitryon's funeral, when it was just Lao. She was still herself, still fiery, but she was hurting. I understood her better like that.

The five of them started playing some stupid game that involved getting as close as you could to cutting your fingers off without actually doing so. I can understand this being a specialist subject of my brother's, but I have no idea how my sister and my son came to be so good at it. I don't think I want to know.

I tried to sit there, be quiet and be a part of it, but they just kept *talking*, dragging me in when I needed to be alone in my own mind.

'Have a go, Iph,' Lao said, gesturing at me with a knife. It would have felt threatening if she weren't slurring her words.

'I shouldn't, I've been drinking,' I said.

Herc snorted. 'Haven't seen you drunk since I got married.'

Our sister opened her mouth, but he beat her to it. 'The *first* time, Lao.'

That's not true. When we found him on that island, when he was broken and hurting and I went to get him because he's my *brother*, we drank together. Because *he* needed it. He snuck my son the strong wine so he could feel like a real man, and three days later he pushed him off the city walls. But that wasn't worth remembering. Not when we could forget and play the happy family now.

The wine was clouding my mind. I went on a walk.

Lao has a lovely home. Their whole island, really, is a beautiful one. Their house sits atop the biggest hill – I've never understood this particular insistence on building palaces on top of hills, like the rich want to spend that much time walking up and down – with the cliff dropping dramatically behind it, a break behind the city walls. I sat on the edge, letting my legs dangle over the sea.

They have a clear sea, crystal. It's deep – I sailed in it only hours before – but it looks as if you could reach down and touch the bottom. Good sea, that. You'll be warned if something comes.

It must be weird for Lao, being the only person in our family to have warning when something's coming.

I tried not to think about Pyrrhus when I was with my family; I really did. I tried to just *be*. That's all they wanted. All they ever asked for was that I have fun with them, and I couldn't. I couldn't forget all the hurt like my brother could.

I still couldn't trust myself to keep my mouth shut about any of that, so I left dinner at Lao's, left the wine behind.

The next morning, I was the only one of us to board the ship without a hangover. It's the little victories. Far as I could tell, I was the only one who wasn't along for the sheer heck of the thing. If I heard another person say *this one time, on the* Argo, I would've happily jumped off the ship myself.

Our destination was Ilium, or what everyone calls Troy, since that fits the metre better for poets. We took it by surprise. We had, after all, come to avenge a long-lost ill against a man struggling against the tides of age. Laomedon was grey and withered. His eyes were fading. When we pulled onto the coast we weren't met with enemies, but with an offer to talk. Quite unlike his usual self, my brother said yes.

I don't know what was said in that meeting, only that Hercules returned determined to tear Troy to the ground.

Priam I

My father's a stubborn man at the best of times and I didn't doubt the claims they made against him. He collects *things* and there are few circumstances where he'll happily part with them.

In the original accord, the crusaders promised to slay a sea monster troubling Ilium. We were away visiting my wife's family when it happened, so I can't speak to scale, but to hear Father describe it, it was a mere trifle: a worm spitting at passing ships. To hear the crusaders, it was larger and more fearsome than Zeus himself.

In exchange for slaying it, Father offered his prize horses. I don't know who'd make such a deal without extracting a binding oath, but the crusaders did. I also don't know why Father would promise them such a prize if the monster was unconcerning, as he claimed, and I find the idea that he was toying with them dubious. Regardless, it happened, and here we are.

Though, on a connected note, I can't possibly say why they wanted the horses when they were travelling on a *boat* propelled by their *arms*.

They completed the task. Father refused payment. They came

back many, *many* years later. Those seem to be the facts of the matter.

I loved those horses, grew up with them, brushed the hair on their flanks and, one day, gods forbid, should I be forced to go to war, they're the only beasts I'd want to carry me.

But I would have given them away in a heartbeat.

I value my life and the lives of my people more than any horse, and when angry, scary men appear on your shore demanding something that rightfully belongs to them, it seems wisest to give it.

They responded well to our request to parlay. Gods know we would've been screwed if they didn't, so we sat down with Hercules for a chat. We invited him to bring more of his men. I have five brothers and all of us were there, but he came alone.

'You have besmirched my honour,' he said grumpily, slouching in his chair. Furniture was unnatural on him. None of it fit like the club in his hand.

'Have we?' Father asked facetiously.

'Father,' I muttered under my breath. My brothers distracted him. 'You know you did it, just give him the mares and we can get on with our lives.'

'They're worth more than this.'

'It needn't be all of them,' I stressed.

'It's a matter of pride, son,' he hissed, like I was some child he could shut up with a word, when my own sons were sprouting like weeds. Even our youngest was approaching adolescence.

'It's his pride too,' I said. This fell on deaf ears.

My father ordered Hercules and his brother imprisoned. Maybe forever. I snuck down to see them, because I'm stupid. I thought I was saving lives when I passed them swords through the bars. They killed their guards and escaped.

So we briefly went to war. Over horses. I'd always thought wars were huge, grand things where people fought for the gods, or for themselves and for the land they grew up in, not for the sake of one man's pride. I would've given them both the horses and Father if I had to.

I shouldn't have said that.

Father died ignominiously in that battle, slain by a shipmate whose name we never learned. They took one of my brothers, too, but they left the bodies with us, so we could perform the correct rites. I was glad for that; it was important to Mother that she could lay their souls to rest. Knowing Father, his soul may never be at rest, but I can hope.

They fought us all the way back, and they took the city. In the climax of the battle, Hercules stood upon my father's throne, waving his club, and his brother looked over to him, eyebrow raised, *now what?*

'I don't want your land,' he bellowed, like that cleared everything up.

'What is it you want, then?' Mother asked from where she stood in the kitchen. We'd tried to make her hide but she refused. Strong woman, my mother.

'Where is he?' Hercules said, spinning dangerously, still on that stupid chair. 'You.'

He pointed at me. I stood strong against his pointing finger.

'What of me?'

'I wish to make the land yours.'

It took everything I had not to gape at this odd proclamation.

'For what reason?' It didn't sound smart or regal, but at least I didn't sound like a drunk peasant dressed in someone else's rags.

'You told him to return the horses. Wise counsel. You'll be

a good king.' With that ominous statement, he hopped from the chair to the floor – not lightly; I'd spend the rest of my life rearranging the furniture so the marks of his giant feet were covered – and left. He didn't even take the horses, the victory apparently enough to pay for the snub years ago, or maybe just finally realising the impracticality of *horses* on a *boat*.

I took my youngest riding after the intruders had gone. He stroked their necks gently, fascinated even then by beautiful things. I didn't have to tell him what they'd cost to keep.

My whole family walked to the beach to see them off, the peaceful end to this weird, bloody revolution. The crusaders smiled as they waved, lifting anchor on all eighteen of their ships. It seemed a lot for horses.

Something came upon me then, something I'd never felt before, but my son could describe it fluently. He called it the whim of the gods. Not force, but enough of a push to take you out of your right mind. I took my knife from my belt and swept it across my palm, letting the blood drop into the sand.

'I'll make this place safe. I'll build walls and fortresses to protect us, so Ilium can never be taken by surprise again,' I whispered, more fiercely than I ever yelled. I knew the prophecy, of course – our city was bound to turn to rubble – but I thought I could beat it.

My son had stepped onto the beach behind me, to watch the ships sail away. He waved them out too, and my resolve grew stronger.

I'd do it all for him, for Paris.

Laonome III

My brother – the one I like, rather than the one I love – always looks smug when he returns from journeys. His shoulders puff up until they're nearly level with the tops of his ears. He looks like a bird who only recently figured out he has wings.

My other brother wasn't happy, the two of them bickering about it as they stepped off the boat. Iolaus was rolling his eyes. I laughed at the picture of it.

'Is that any kind of welcome for the conquering heroes?' Hercules boomed. 'My sister!'

'Dearest brother,' I responded, with equal aplomb. 'I didn't realise you'd gone to conquer, merely to retrieve some errant livestock.'

'I was under that impression also,' grumbled Iphicles. Whoops, I wanted to annoy Herc, not get in the middle of their argument.

'Well, I won't be having any of that war talk at my table,' I said brightly. I learned that tone from our mother. You don't mess with forced cheer.

'I love hearing Daddy's war stories,' my youngest said, tugging at my hem. 'Why can't we hear them anymore?'

'It's a new rule, dear. Now go play with your swords, okay?'

I gathered my brothers and corralled them for dinner, my husband sitting between them as a buffer. Neither could complain, then, that I'd favoured the other by placing them closer to the head of the table. I put Iolaus on one side of me and my eldest on the other.

(You know nothing about politics until you organise tea for a crowd of women who can barely pretend they don't hate each other. Semi-estranged brothers are nothing.)

The semi-estranged brothers had worn themselves out butting heads over whether they should have started a war, and were butting heads over who'd be allowed to leave first. The whole thing was ridiculous.

'I have taken enough of your hospitality already, sister.'

'I must get back to my wife, sister – you know how she misses me.'

'There have been attacks in the city where I lived, sister.'

And on and on and on, until both of them were mewling, wide-eyed, 'prepare me a ship, sister,' and I was telling them in no uncertain terms to shut the fuck up. At least my husband had the grace to pretend he was horrified by my language. Neither of my brothers even looked ashamed by their attempts to manipulate me.

'It's simply not possible for us to organise ships right now, for either one of you. We must prepare for the wedding.' I smiled beatifically. They shrank back from the light against my teeth. Forced cheer. Works every time.

It wasn't the wedding I wanted my brothers to see, it was my *life*, everything I was doing while they were off being heroes. It's stupid, but I wanted them to be proud.

Hercules recovered first; he normally does. His eyebrows

pushed all the way up to his hair, which doesn't make him look any less like a grumpy bird. It was worse on the *Argo* when he shaved his head. He could only save one of them, and he'd preferred Hylas look beautiful. An old romantic, my brother.

'A wedding?' Herc asked, all innocence. Bullshit.

'A wedding.'

'The bride?' Herein lies the evidence of the bullshit. Had he really cared, he would've asked about both parties in the marriage.

'Of average beauty, if ravaged by an unfortunate case of the pox,' I answered smoothly, prepared for this eventuality. I wasn't prepared, however, for my husband betraying me and gesturing something rude about her form.

'What of the groom?' Iphicles asked, and to him I spoke the honest truth. The groom was a nice young man, though maybe too young for such a bride, and not particularly brave. They would, I thought, be happy enough together.

'And their dogs are fire-breathing hellhounds whose gaze can turn a man to stone,' I finished, once it became clear that neither of my brothers were listening. Herc had stopped as soon as he decided he wasn't interested in the bride, and Iph only ever asked his question out of politeness. Iolaus burst out laughing, though, and he took me down with him. The boys looked confused, and more alike than they had in years.

The rest of the evening passed pleasantly enough. When we went to bed, my husband very seriously said to me, 'I don't understand your family.'

'Honey, you're not supposed to.' For all that it's messed up and it's broken and my brothers don't like each other, and even though the only nieces I ever properly knew are dead, it's *my* family.

It's not for you, or my husband, or anyone else to understand. I know what it is to be my brother's sister. Don't pretend you can claim the same.

I tricked the boys into dressing up for the wedding. I suggested to Herc he might be more comfortable in a dress and he was ready faster than I've ever seen him. Iph, on the other hand . . .

'You know,' I said slowly. 'Lots of important people will be there.'

'We're us, Lao – there are always lots of important people there. Why should I do anything different?'

'Oh, I'm not saying you should. Hercie's not; looks like a right slob.'

And that was Iph dressed and ready. I don't love playing them against each other, honestly, but it's embarrassingly easy to get them to behave that way.

The bride looked beautiful. Brides tend to, filled to the brim with blessings from whichever god they favour, or whichever favours them, but this bride had more than that. Under the blessings and the joy, she was tough. So, as a well-brought-up lady of court, I muttered *shit* under my breath and left my husband to embarrass himself in front of our guests.

(I love the man but he's never remembered a name in his life. At dinner with my family, he mustn't drink more than a glass of wine or he'll get inextricably tangled in the old Iphitus, Iphicles, Iolaus, Iole mess.)

'Lovely Deianira,' I exclaimed. 'How happy I am to see you on such a blessed day, where you look so wonderful and—'

'What do you want?' she said. It was technically a question, though it didn't come out as one. Again, I muttered *shit* under my breath. Herc was going to love her.

As anyone knows – including me, in more detail than I ever wanted or needed to – my brother's a demon in bed, and will bring any willing person into it. As fewer people know, my brother's got a soft streak a mile wide, if anyone can worm their way in.

He was young when he married Meg, and there was a lot going on there, but I think he'd only ever fallen in love with two people, the both of them men. Iphitus and Hylas.

He loved the beauty of them. The softness trying and failing to cover up the strength. He's not a man of contrasts, Herc. He's all the way muscled, all the way strong, all the way hard, and it fascinated him when he saw people be both. He's half mortal, half god, and he never worked out how to be either.

And here was someone, someone beautiful and strong, who could bear him children and who spoke in the same straight, angry lines as he did. It would, without doubt, end badly if he was allowed to see her before she was bound to her husband. I didn't say any of this to the girl.

'There's a tear in your robes,' I pointed out delicately.

'Probably from riding my chariot earlier. Last-minute hunting,' she said. *Shit.*

'Walk with me,' I said. 'Humour me, in telling you the secrets for a happy marriage.' I smiled that impossibly bright smile at her and she caved.

We walked, I blathered.

'So it's important to let him think he's the head of the household when in reality—'

'You make all the decisions. I figured,' she finished. I blathered more, about what flowers meant, and how to please a husband without making them think they have the right to demand anything. A balancing act, I said, full of cunning and stealth.

'I was just going to stab him with a fork if he got out of hand,' she said.

I kept her walking so long she was nearly late to her own ceremony. This created as many problems as it solved, for we were followed back. By a centaur.

(Fun story, I wasn't allowed to say the word *centaur* when I was a child, because some big mean one refused to teach Herc how to fight.)

Azan – the groom – was a good kid, but entirely unprepared for what happened at the altar. Picture the scene. The beautiful couple were standing, hands joined, as they made the various dedications to the various gods that mattered to them. All was going well. Herc was even distracted by their semi-continuous mention of Hera's name – she is the goddess of marriage, when she's not trying to ruin our family. It was all very cute; they were all very in love.

The centaur burst in.

'I want her,' he demanded. Not eloquent beasts, centaurs.

'Well you can't fucking have her,' Deianira said, sounding more bored than anything. I'm glad the wedding captured her attention so.

The centaur, equally upset about the reaction, snatched her from where she stood. A number of things happened very quickly.

One, Herc dived onto the centaur. Two, Deianira pulled a sword from somewhere I assume I don't want to know and stabbed it in the shoulder. Three, it released her. Four, I sprang into action, propping the girl in front of the altar so she could marry Azan quickly, while Herc wrestled the beast. I feared if I delayed the marriage until the fight's conclusion the two would bond over their mutual love of killing things.

Why was I so against their union, you ask? Well, she was promised to marry someone who certainly did love her, even if he didn't react with panache to the threat against her life.

And two, while I could claim it was a moral decision, do you know how much it would damage my reputation if people heard I couldn't throw a simple wedding for a small-town princess without my brother running away with her?

Regardless, Herc was offended by my interference. He barely drank that night and he woke in the morning growling like a bear. The only reason he didn't immediately take a ship and leave the island was because he bumped into a messenger on the way down.

He returned, sullen and hungover. He tapped our brother on the shoulder. 'Iph?'

'What do you want?' He wasn't hungover either. Just tired and done with us.

'Can you come with me?'

'What? No. I told Automedusa I was on my way back.'

'Iph, our cousin just declared war on me.'

Neither of them had to ask me to prepare a ship that time. It was clear they were going together, and I wanted to keep them safe. I gave them the best we had.

Our last night together, everyone was in good form. Me and my husband, the boys, and Iolaus. Everyone was sure they would win the war and return in glorious victory. Iolaus was chattering like a happy child, having discovered from the bride some new chariot race he'd never heard of and he wanted to check it out.

The wine got flowing and one thing led to another and the four of them ended up drunkenly racing on poorly cobbled-together carts around the palace and the cliffs. Cheating abounded, with Iolaus in the lead for much of the race, until Herc shot him off – blunt arrow – and Euphemus knocked Herc out, leaving Iphicles the winner.

He ran and cheered and drank wine out of an old cup we had lying around.

That's the last memory I have of my family together. Still broken, but holding. Soon enough, the final piece would fall out, and we'd be too broken to fix.

Wedding Notice

In lieu of a more personal message from the couple, this shall serve as official notice of the wedding of Azan and Deianira. While their wedding was not without problems — a wild centaur intruding — Azan assures us that they are happy together. Deianira dismisses all things of the sort as 'hippy bullshit'. Azan would like to reiterate that they are very happy together.

Eurystheus IV

I wasn't naive enough to believe I'd ever live an oaf-free life, but I didn't think it would be how people addressed me when they arrived at *my* court. Not, King Eurystheus the wise, or King Eurystheus the rich, or even King Eurystheus the devoted. No. Any of those reasonable titles were forsworn for the child's answer, fresh from the songs of trumped-up minstrels.

'Oh, Eurystheus, you helped with the labours, right?'

You helped with the labours, right? Those words, in that order, were uttered to me by more than one visitor over the years. More than a dozen, to be truthful. It's frankly astounding I didn't develop a more vicious punishment for the upstarts who asked. Having the servants put sand in their shoes may have been petty, but I couldn't let the insult pass freely.

It would have been better, if only barely, had they called me his cousin, *even though* I am a king and for a reasonable time the oaf was *my* bound slave. Yet still they cast *me* as some sad sidekick, scurrying after the oaf with his quiver.

I know one young visitor thought exactly that, for he followed his stupid opener with an even stupider idea: 'Aren't you too fat to keep up with him?' Had I lions at my disposal I would've gladly fed him to them. As it was, snakes make wonderful playmates. I learned that from the oaf.

His stain followed me like an unpleasant smell. Unfortunately, the only emitter of such a strong odour is the oaf himself, so either you know him, and know both meaning and metaphor, or you don't and must take my word.

On completion of his labours, he decided his next step was to murder Augeas, a man I held in the highest esteem. Did the gods care even one whit?

They did not.

Unabashed favouritism, we can all agree. Had I not had unfortunate cause to see the offending body parts – the oaf wore his chiton short and sat with his legs spread as wide as he could manage – I'd say you have to admire the balls of the man who follows up his penance for murder with more murder.

Thanks to the aforementioned favouritism, we were left with the oaf killing someone else, becoming a slave, marrying his owner, becoming a slave *again*, becoming free *again*, and going on a little secondary revenge spree. And *I* know all this, despite an active ban on discussion of the oaf within my halls.

The latest blow against Laomedon was the final straw. The irony is, if the oaf hadn't gallivanted off on his little side quest, I would've sent him after Laomedon's sea monster as a task, so he wouldn't have been able to take payment for it anyway.

Laomedon was a good man. I traded with him on occasion, though his wares were generally too useless for my liking. In my experience, he stuck to his deals to the letter. The fun was finding the extra letters he'd slipped in. Doubtless the oaf didn't find it in their agreement but it will have been there.

(What is it heroes do for fun anyway? Cheat on their wives, I suppose.)

Action had to be taken, and I was the only one with the bravery or sway to take it. I was in a unique position regarding the oaf, and the complicated mess I reluctantly call *our* family.

I didn't gather troops. Gathering troops is for idiots. I gathered men and precedent, so we could prove to both gods and kings that the oaf had gone too far.

We sailed to him, our ship kitted out for any eventuality. I brought my sons with me – the middle ones; the oldest and the youngest stayed at home with the girls. My oldest daughter would've been the most use in a fight, for she'd taken bearing Hippolyta's belt more seriously than I expected, and I've no complaints on that front. A woman must be able to defend herself.

We called him to court, presided over by the relevant priests and officials, and we put forward our argument.

'It's clear, now, that he's been left too long with his behaviour unchecked. He knows no law, mortal or otherwise. With this latest blow, the problem was not pride lost or a deal reneged on, but a greedy lust for power he thinks he's earned.'

The oaf looked dumbfounded. I'm sure he doesn't know the meaning of the word *reneged*, or *earn*. He probably thinks *oaf* is a term of endearment, crafted from the mouths of the muses solely to bless him.

'Laomedon promised those horses,' he said, no attempt at any real defence, no nod to the beauty of a trial, of rhetoric. He used words as subtly as he knocked his club against a tree, too lazy to fetch an axe to cut it down. 'Eurystheus. Cousin, why are you doing this to me?'

His eyes filled with tears. Clearly someone had undertaken the painstaking task of teaching him the basics of mortal emotions. He hadn't mastered the art of lying, though. I saw a smirk in the corner of his face. He knew he was going to get away with this, like always.

What should I say? That we were never truly cousins?

I paused too long. He barrelled through before my riposte. Terribly uncouth, that.

'After all we've been through together,' he said mournfully, a single tear splashing against the surface of the table.

'What is it, exactly, we've been through together?' I spat, emotion finally getting the better of me.

I shouldn't have bothered with the farce of the trial. We all knew there'd be no ending but Hercules being blessed and allowed to roam free, murdering any king he wanted. At least, when he was *eventually* struck down, the circumstances were *perfect*. I couldn't have chosen them better if I had penned them myself.

When he was let free, he tried to shake my hand, invite me for wine or whatever the hell it is oafs do when they want to pretend they love each other really. I could only lean across his stupid chest and whisper what it is I had to say.

'This means war.'

It was, I concede, melodramatic, but I didn't want to complicate matters for his tiny little brain. Who knows how many more of us he'd take down, and claim justice or vengeance or whatever he wanted? It didn't *matter*. His daddy would forgive him. I had to work for everything I ever had. Why should he be different?

'What do you mean?' he asked stupidly. My plan foiled by his ever-more-impressive inability to understand.

'If the courts won't stop you, I will.'

As I said, it's only stupid men who go to another land with war in mind. But it's also a stupid man who fails to prepare for war.

'But we're cousins. Family.'

328

I stared at this, maybe the stupidest thing he'd ever uttered in my presence – and he once asked if my children liked to play with snakes. Should he get them some while he was away?

'And when has that ever mattered to you before? Family?'

'So be it.'

We gathered in an organised manner along the battlefield. I'm sure the oaf was used to running in, waving weapons and screaming like a heathen, but in my battle we would conduct ourselves like adults. We didn't bring a lot of men, either one of us. I hoped to keep the bloodshed limited to him, and the sons stupid enough to follow him.

I didn't think his twin could be such an idiot, either.

Despite my endless disdain for his brother, I got on fairly well with Iphicles. He visited the palace a couple of times and paid all respect due to me as a host. I found him not lacking in manners or eloquence and, were it not for his miserable excuse for a twin, I would've been content to call Iphicles *cousin*.

As it was, we lined up facing each other, the oaf cowering at the back. When we were children he'd do the same behind his mother's skirts, and at the oddest things. Anything that could kill a child, he was okay, happily strangling it with his mighty fists, but anything fragile frightened him. I've seen him scream when asked to hold a china vase.

Now that's a song worthy of bards singing.

Battle is hard to describe. Let me say there's no countdown, that even the most civilised of affairs cannot leave your hands truly clean. Let me say a black bird flew over us and crowed three times: a signal, it seemed, from the gods themselves.

I half-expected the sky itself to split in two, the Queen and King of Olympus fighting alongside us. Hera, as always, had been my guide, warning me of the coming danger from the oaf and his little oafy sons.

They were of all ages, and they seemed to number in the hundreds. Many claimed the oaf as father when they were simply the bastard of the village drunk, and he was so animalistically virile it was impossible to know which was which.

They're my cousins too, and I should name them, but I'll spare both of us the trouble and call them only the oaflets.

Hera told me they were after my crown, my throne. But not only that.

Since the day he killed Megara, the oaf had been looking for a wife who could run a household as well as she, and his beady, roving eyes had landed on my lovely wife and stayed there. He was after my family. My beautiful, perfect family, when he'd destroyed his own.

Did I have any choice but to kill him?

I stood across from him, ready to tear him into pieces too small to possibly be put back together. I charged at the oaf, but he disappeared to the back of the crowd, hiding again. Behind his myriad offspring this time, not his mother.

No matter. I was a king, a son of Zeus. I had trained in sword-fighting since my infancy. I would dispatch whomever I needed to reach the oaf himself.

I engaged the closest oaflet. His sword clashed against mine. I twisted it free. My blade slid into his stomach, his eyes widening like the child he was. Something churned within me.

When the kid's sword slid back into me, I didn't fight.

I'd lost. Hercules had turned me into an animal too.

Last Will and Testament of Eurystheus

Upon his death, Eurystheus makes the following requests:

- To my wife, Antimache, I leave the home we were so happy in. Tear down the rooms where naught but misery lies. You know the ones I mean. Be happy, wife. Wear your jewellery, and stand beautiful, as we both know you are. Don't marry an oaf.
- To my sons, I leave the kingdom. I know you'll rule in a manner to make me proud.
- To my daughters, I leave my blessing to marry whom you choose, and to protect yourselves from those who would hurt you. I've left money for you to be tutored in defence. Carry knives to your wedding beds.
- For Epicaste, daughter of Augeas, I leave the same provisions as my own daughters.
- Should anyone hurt them, I have left aside money for a mercenary to be hired and revenge borne. Let it be in my name, and wear upon my soul and no others.

Iphicles IV

My brother got a taste for death. When he wanted to fight, he could find any slight in the way someone had treated him.

Such was the case with Hippocoon, and everyone knew it. Especially so soon after the attack from Eurystheus. He said it was about respect, reputation, that if people would just treat him how he deserved, he wouldn't have to fight anymore.

He only slept well the night after a battle though. Or when he was in the arms of someone young and willing, but lately he'd been looking at the young and willing morosely, like he could already see their epitaphs.

Herc didn't even need to put out the call for fighters. They'd appear at his side, sons in tow, ready to put their entire line in my brother's hands. People trusted him.

The whole time we travelled, he was the same grumpy version of himself, scowling at the bow of the ship. I've never seen a vase of him where they didn't make him taller. He wasn't short really – I skated above him, though I think that's just posture – it was mostly a function of his bloody enormous shoulders.

When people think of his strength, they think of the lion – he was still wearing the cloak and it smelled *bad* – or they think of Atlas, how he held up the world. They don't think of how he can pull a ship out of a sandbar in shallow water.

He seemed almost embarrassed after he did that, like he didn't want us to see this side of him. I nearly took him aside to remind him I've known him all our lives; I know most sides of him. But I knew he wouldn't appreciate it, so I took to distracting him.

'Why are we waging war against Tyndareus, exactly?' I said. It wasn't subtle. Herc doesn't call for subtle. He likes obvious, and he likes war. Thus a question of both.

'Not Tyndareus. Good man, Tyndareus. War against Hippocoon.'

'The question is the same, brother.'

'He has slighted me,' Herc snorted, and turned back to the sea like that would possibly be enough explanation. When my continued staring proved it wasn't, he sighed. 'After Iphitus died, he refused to help. Life would have been a lot simpler had he agreed.'

Brother rarely talks of his lovers, living or dead. He's afraid the living ones hold some unknown power over him. The dead ones, well, I feel that's obvious. I travelled with him often enough to know he'd never step foot in Thebes, not for anyone's bidding, not even with a pardon from Zeus himself.

I never told him what became of Thebes. I entered only if no other route presented itself. I have the look of him, in my face and in my stride. I'd never pass as my brother, but I brought back memories of him. In Thebes, that was too much, I could feel their dislike bristle against my skin. They never said it, but we all knew I wasn't welcome.

There's no statue to Meg, nor anything to their children. The latter I imagine, would be particularly tasteless. Their youngest didn't yet speak. How do you carve that, knowing how he died? But she has gardens in her name – I think she would've liked that. She liked to be outside, where the kids could have fun and she could watch over them.

'It's silly,' she said to me once with a laugh. 'Their father could be a hero if he wanted; he'll keep them safe. But I can't stop watching.' They were both so young back then, practically kids themselves.

But we weren't going to Thebes. We were going to wage a war I couldn't fully understand.

'Do you miss him?' I asked Herc, of Iphitus. I don't know why. That's the kind of question our sister would ask. Intrusive. Unkind. My brother sighed again and sat heavily on the deck.

'I miss all of them.'

'Me too.' It's so easy, when you live like we did – on an endless series of boats to see an endless series of kings – to get used to loss. But I missed my friends and my wife and my sons, and some of those weren't even dead. They were waiting for me to come home. At least I had one to go back to.

'I asked for kindness, after Iphitus. I was a mess. Plague and sorrow, altogether. I asked for a place to sleep and an ear to listen, and he said no, I'd bring the plague to his city. That's why we go to war.'

'That was a long time ago.'

'And does it hurt less? Have the people you've lost come back to you? Is the pain gone?'

I had little to say to that. I was unused to him speaking so much, and about his feelings, no less. We joked he could never access that part of himself. Truth is, I lack a talent for it too.

'I'd go back for all of them, if I could,' he said. 'I'd go down to Hades and carry every one of them back up to Earth.'

Can't you? I thought.

'But I can't.' He smiled sadly. 'Hades is . . . he's not a nice man. He doesn't like his things being taken from him.'

'You brought Theseus back,' I said. Forgive me. I rarely saw my brother in such a talkative mood. Theseus spoke of that as fact. His legs bore the same scars Herc's shoulders did.

'With shit on his shoes and all.' Herc grinned, briefly. I laughed, and for a moment everything was easy, light. Of course it couldn't last. 'The muppet thought he could kidnap Persephone. He was alive, just trapped. If I tried for one of the dead? Hades would have me before I could think it. He still hasn't forgiven me for his dog.' He smiled wryly at this.

'Tell me about it.'

'Our cousin Eurystheus, he was trying to keep the labours interesting, worthy? You know?' I was amazed he could speak so easily about Eurystheus. He'd only been dead a couple of weeks. And dead trying to kill my brother too. But then, Herc was used to death; he'd had practice. 'Once you've killed the Hydra you can hardly go back and fight any old snake. Well, anyway, he said I was to go down to Hades and fetch Cerberus—'

The men didn't appreciate our conversation. They knew as well as I did Herc could man the oars alone and give everyone a break to sleep, but we spoke to each other rarely enough they could go suck it. I wanted my brother to myself.

Hippocoon I

I'm a big enough man to admit I started it. Though really, Father started when he died without leaving clear rules for who he wanted the new King of Sparta to be. I said we should have a contest of wits and strength – I had a plan that may or may not have involved cheating – and Tyndareus said that was stupid, it should go to the oldest who – oh look at that – just happened to be him. How surprising. Our other brothers had their own suggestions, but Tyndareus and I teamed up and crushed them.

In the midst of my plans to cheat, I didn't notice Tyndie enacting his own plot. While we were bickering, he went ahead and got himself coronated on the quiet. Rude, right? Do you know how big my coronation was going to be?

Well, I imagine you do, because I became king and had it anyway. But that's not the point. Becoming king while we were still debating was very unsporting. I was just going to put glass in his shoes and/or food, depending on the test.

He was very patronising about the whole business, after.

'Oh, brother, as your benevolent king, I'll allow you the choice of any house in Sparta to be your palace.' Dick, lording it over me. He even waved me off, saying, 'Since we're brothers, you don't have to call me king,' just because he knew I wasn't going to anyway. Following his orders rankled just as much as calling him king would have.

He can't have been surprised when I overthrew him. I had all these sons, you see. I didn't want them fighting when I died, over who'd become king – such things can ruin fraternity, don't you think? – and I figured such a rebellion would help thin the pack, as it were.

It was almost embarrassingly easy to steal the crown. When Tyndie made his original plot to steal it from me, he didn't have a back-up. That's the kind of short-term thinking that gets your throne immediately stolen in an almost-bloodless midnight coup.

We poisoned the food. Not very much – we didn't want to kill anyone. That would ruin the fun. While they were passed out we tied them up and stuck them on a boat heading west.

Tyndie had the best constitution, a good trait in a king. He woke up first and waved from the deck, screaming bloody murder. Rudely, I thought, since there was no blood or murder involved. Only poison and maniacal cackling.

'You bastard,' he yelled, pumping his fist like his life depended on it. 'You wine-poisoning bastard. What did the good wine ever do to you?'

'Should you return, you won't have to call me king, since we're brothers and all.' I smiled benevolently. Even from distance, I was sure his testicles retreated into his body in pure impotent fury.

'I won't be calling you king. No one will. You know why? Because you'll be dead, and I'll have killed you. How do you like that, *little brother?*'

'Oh, is that rain I feel?' I asked innocently. 'I must be away. Do enjoy the provisions I packed for you. I know how you love olives.'

Tyndie gave a cry of pure anguish. He hates olives more than anything else in the world including me, even after I'd cursed him to weeks of the olive-only diet. I grinned. It was going to be so good, me and Tyndie exchanging kingship and Sparta growing ever more powerful as we strove to beat each other.

Until that prick Hercules showed up.

It was maybe a year after I banished my brother. Everything was settled. People barely even spat at me on the streets, though that *might* have something to do with that time I had someone's tongue burned, so they could do no more spitting.

Hercules showed up. He was red and splotchy, like both face and body had been sobbing.

'I need to see the king,' he panted, collapsing on my floor. When we got him moved he left a yellow pus stain on the floor.

'I am he.'

'I seek absolution.'

Urgh. I hate these stupid holy travellers who think any old king will absolve them of whatever crime they've committed, for they've always done something horrifying, even if they're just getting comfortable with the idea. They expect me to set them nice little tasks to cleanse their souls, forgetting the important fact that I don't give a shit.

'Leave.'

'Please, King Tyn—'

Ooooh, no. He *might* have stood a chance before that, but after? No. No one mixes up my kingship with my stupid older brother.

'Leave. I don't want this plague ravaging my city.' I had the guards carry him to suffer on my doorstep. Plagues wreak havoc in walled cities and whatever he had was most unattractive. He even had spots on his tongue.

I thought that was the end of it. Another peasant supplicant rejected. Alas, half a decade later, he showed up on my shore again, not only with ships, but with my brother. Prick.

This was only ever supposed to be between Tyndie and I. Even our brothers barely got a look-in. It didn't affect them. We barely enacted new laws or new taxes and neither of us went on peasant-murdering rampages. It was our fight, and I don't believe Tyndareus thought of bringing in help on his own.

I don't know what Hercules' problem was, but he didn't need to do it in my house. He didn't need to barge in with his swords and his shouting.

Then he looked oh so surprised when we came back at him with swords – *how could this woe have possibly befallen him?* How dare we defend our homes and families and wives and – more importantly – my kingdom, hard-won from my little shit of a brother.

I led the charge against them. This was, in retrospect, a mistake. I could have used the smaller, more poorly trained soldiers as some form of meat shield, and it would have been cleaner. But I'm no coward; if I was to die defending the traditions of my family, then so be it.

(My sons are little bastards anyway. I suspected the next ruler would sit in a puddle of my blood. It wouldn't be that surprising if it were my brother instead.)

I fought a good fight, my men taking courage from my wonderful leadership. We slashed and we stabbed and we all looked very dramatic and dashing. I even got a good slice into the interloper's right-hand man – his brother, I think; they had the same colours to them. He had the gall to grin back at me.

Little did he know, he was done for. I edge my blade with poison – a holdover from when I was seizing power.

Of course, we never stood a chance. My men knew, when they helped me seize power, if I ever lost it they'd be killed. It makes for wonderfully loyal men, that. So they battered me back until I was fighting the interloper himself on the very crest of my throne – a wholly unnecessary place to have a battle if you ask me, but it seemed important to him.

I'm sure I would've killed him dozens of times over, were it not for his cloak. Whenever I lunged at him, my sword, poisoned as it was, would slide away pointlessly. It must have been enchanted, for I am an excellent swordsman. No trainer of mine has ever beaten me in a fight.

He grinned a grin I knew well, toothy and vicious. The sign of a plan coming together.

He prepared to take the killing blow, but he was knocked out of the way. Instead, my brother stood before me, sword raised.

'Tyndareus,' I said. 'I was wondering when you'd show your ugly face.'

'Perhaps you've merely been bereft of a mirror, brother.' An easy comeback. I would've done better.

'Relying on the help now, are you?' I sneered, and something fell away in Tyndie's eyes, like he didn't quite understand how he got here.

'He was insistent,' he said, this time as a whisper. 'You know I wouldn't have planned it this way.'

'We could take him instead. Together,' I suggested.

'No, we couldn't,' he said. He drew his blade across my throat, fast, as if he might turn back if he dawdled. Coward. 'I am sorry, brother.'

The interloper took his men and left. They joked of drinks to be drunk and food to be eaten and women to be fucked. And my brother stayed.

He knew, until he performed the rites he owed to me, my spirit would be stuck there listening, unable to respond. Bastard always wanted to get the last word. So he told me some stupid story of his exile and the interloper approaching him so full of anger he was afraid to say no. I hated him for that. Hated that our story would end with someone else. He told me his own plan to dethrone me, a much more elegant thing, involving a woman dressed as a man, an uncommonly intelligent dog, and a poison that would only render you speechless. So neat, so *us*.

I would have told him so, if I still had a throat. My body shuddered in the memory of what it had been like to laugh. It was a relief to be free of it.

Tyndie crouched over the body formerly known as me and began to sob. Not elegant. Not cunning or clever at all. I appreciated it nonetheless, that I could be lying throatless in a pool of my own blood and still he'd be the uglier.

Eventually our brothers came and pulled him off me. They didn't reproach him. What would be the point? I was dead. They pulled him gently by his shoulders so they could wash my blood from him. They took him to eat and my sisters came to wash my body clean of blood.

They buried me in the proper way, and I had as easy a journey to Hades as anyone. Even then, whenever Tyndie needed to think up plans to take down newer, stupider interlopers, he'd sit at the spot where I died and he'd tell me them. I would've given a full year of my life to appear, just once, and tell him: *you're going mad, brother.*

As it was, he got the last words, a great many years later, when the Fates took him in the same spot. *Our* spot.

'It was never meant to end like this.'

No, brother, it wasn't. It was meant to end with *us.*

Iolaus IV

My dad's dead. He's not all the way gone, yet, but we all know it's coming. Is that better? I can't tell if it's better that I know or if it's worse cause I'm just fucking sitting here, dick in my hands, waiting for him to die.

We won. Does that make it better? We killed Tyndareus and replaced him with Hippocoon or we killed Hippocoon and replaced him with Tyndareus – I can't remember half their names. I just learn what colour their standards are and aim. I don't even know why we were there in the first place, what whichever one of them we killed did to piss off my uncle so badly, or if it mattered. I never questioned him because we were *safe*.

Blah blah blah. Hylas, and Hercules' wife and his children, and those other companions of his. They all died and whatever and that's really shitty for them and their families, but mine? Mine was safe. Gods above, look at the shit Auntie Laonome tagged along with and she was fine and she's not even, like, a fighter or anything. She's a *girl*. But she's one of ours and Uncle Herc was there and he'd make sure we were okay. Whatever you want to say about him, he has some big old scars from taking hits for me.

It was a sword that did it. Big shock, right? It wasn't heroic or anything. It barely grazed my dad, across the shoulder. He looked back to me when he was hit, as he took down some other guy, and grinned – *look, son, I can do it too* – even as the blood dripped down his back. Never been a big fan of blood, tell you the truth.

My dad was a bit of a badass, when he wanted to be. Not even 'cause you can't be Uncle Herc's brother without being a badass, 'cause, true as that is, he never needed his twin to be cool. Not cool. Cool's a stupid thing to say. He's my dad and he doesn't really have a sense of humour and he's always using pointlessly long words and he cheated on Mum, but none of that meant we wanted him to die.

He was kind, my dad, in a way big heroes aren't. He'd sit with me when things were hurting and he'd distract me and he'd let me talk about girls even though he thought I should marry and settle down already. You might have wanted Uncle Herc when you were a big winner, but you wanted my dad when everything went to shit. He'd be all calm and patient and there. So he wasn't cool. Not at all.

But, for all that, he was a better fighter than I could hope to be. If you were scared of a monster, he'd never tell you otherwise, not even if it was the size of your hand.

It festered. The wound. This tiny glancing sword wound from some fop of a king. Of course it did. Of-fucking-course, because my dad couldn't be taken down by something that could be bandaged up. It festered colours I'd never seen before, never wanted to see again. It smelled worse than the shirts of a dozen sailors.

'Poison. On the sword,' my uncle murmured.

'I never thought of that.'

'Me neither.'

344

That was when we thought there was a chance, but knowing there's poison on the thing doesn't mean knowing what kind of poison and even if we did there was probably shit-all we could do about it. And then it was too late.

I tried sitting with him, right? 'Cause that's what you're supposed to do when your dad's dying and there's fuck-all you can do about it. You're meant to sit there and pat his hand and tell him reassuring lies he doesn't believe. You're meant to be all patient and pious and the rest of that fucking bullshit, because it's all that's left to you. Well, you know what I say?

Balls to that.

Balls to all of it. So I patted my dad's hand only once and told him I'm going out. He looked at me with a tired expression. He's given it to me every day of my entire fucking life, hasn't he?

'Don't get yourself in too much trouble.'

Ha. If I stayed out of trouble I'd hardly be worthy of our family, would I? Even Auntie Lao's some kind of badass, and Cousin Theseus killed the *Minotaur*. My plan was tame in comparison.

'Uncle,' I demanded. I couldn't see him, but you can never fucking see him and somehow he's always there. When he sits still you wouldn't know him from a rock.

'Nephew?' he asked, suspicious. Over recent years I've made a real effort not to call him uncle to his face. He looks like he needs a shit when I do; think it makes him feel old, which is a stupid thing for him to be upset about because he is old.

'I need your help.' There. Simple. Straightforward. Step one, done.

'Oh? What with? Has something infiltrated the camp?' Camp was a kind description of where we were staying. Shack. Hut. Forest. Closest place with a flat surface to lay Dad down.

'Only the plague,' I said.

'Nephew—' Uncle Herc said warningly. 'I don't know that I like where this is going.'

Right, so you know he's fucking cut up about this too, if he's resorting to all the stupid bollocks fancy language my dad uses.

'I'm not planning anything stupid.'

'Well, that's good news, at least,' he said, visibly deflating. I don't know what those fucking shoulders are full of. Wine? Gristle?

'Yeah, it's fine; we've done it before,' I said, with some speed, before my uncle could point out that us having done something before doesn't mean it's not stupid. 'We just need to summon Apollo. He can save Dad, right? He's a god, isn't he?'

'Nephew—'

'So what, we need some fancy sacrifice and whatever and we can make a fire and you must remember how we summoned him last time, what that uptight doctor said and all?'

'Iolaus,' he said this time, like it was any better than *nephew*, like anything we called each other mattered. 'That's not how the gods work. I'm sorry.'

'It *is* how they work because it worked when you were sick. I was there. Remember.' It was a command. A threat.

'I was sick because the gods caused me to be,' he said gently. I hated that. Come on, big guy, get angry. We should be angry because it's my dad and your brother who's dying, and if any of us should be dying, it's not him. 'Your father was struck by a mortal.'

He was talking about it so calmly, like he was the fucking expert on dying when he was so bloody extra-special he got to know he wouldn't die, not really. I would and Dad would and he would just sit there looking fake sad and wringing his hands and pretending there was nothing he could do.

'You could at least say his *name*. He's your fucking brother.'

'He is,' my uncle said, doing that bullshit gentle sadness thing again. 'He's *my* fucking brother. I've known him my entire life, and he's known me mine. And I'll miss him. Gods know, I'll miss *Iphicles*. Is that what you want me to say?'

'I want you to fix it,' I shouted now. Nice words. That's all it was. All he was doing, for the first time in his fucking life, was trying to placate me with nice words when he could do something about it instead.

'So do I,' he roared, his lion skin lifting with the force of it. 'I want nothing more in this world than to be the one dying right now. But I'm not, and the gods won't come for him.'

'How can you say that when you haven't even fucking tried?' I screamed right back. Maybe I was weedy next to him, but I matched him, exceeded his volume.

'I haven't tried?' he said. I'd never been afraid of my uncle. Not once. Not when everyone told me he's dangerous and I shouldn't get him drunk and a million and one other slams against his character. Not until that moment. 'Hera, my love, most beautiful of all the Olympian goddesses, take me. Kill me, make me your slave, whatever it is you want; take me instead of him. You can be free of me. He's family. You like family, right?'

'Unc—' I began. His voice was wavering, crackling as he burnt in his own flames. I'd only ever heard him call Hera *that bitch* before. These words could get us all killed.

'Father,' he shouted over me, louder this time. 'Almighty Zeus, to whom my greatness is dedicated. You lay with my mother, pretending to be my father, so save my brother, and I'll dedicate the rest of my life only to your honour.' He took a deep breath, seemingly waiting for a response, but he didn't look to the sky, only me, eyes wide and angry. 'So, Dad? What about it?'

'I—' I tried again.

'Apollo, god of music and sunlight and healing. My wonderful brother who's helped me so. Tell me what I must do for this plague to be lifted. Tell me who I must sell myself to, who I should give the money to, for this to be better. Tell me, so I can save my mortal brother.'

No response.

My uncle shouted the names of every Olympian. He appealed to Hades himself. He worked his way through every god I'd ever heard of, and even those I had not. He shouted his voice raw and my ears cold. And still, he kept going.

'Do you see, nephew? I have fucking *tried*,' he said eventually, slumping again. 'I've tried so hard.'

The gods weren't listening. They'd come for my uncle, one of their own. But they wouldn't come for Dad, and they wouldn't come for me, when my time came.

We were interrupted by a spluttering from the tent.

You spend enough time at war, you come to know these things. My uncle and I didn't even look at each other before we sprinted to Dad's side. We didn't ask about his condition, and he didn't answer. That way none of us had to lie.

'Did you stay out of trouble?' he asked me.

'Always,' I said.

'Liar.' He winked.

And my dad died. Just like that. From some stupid glancing sword wound from some stupid imitation of a war we had no stakes in.

How was I supposed to tell my mother?

I took a walk.

I came back, hours later. I couldn't tell you where or how long I walked, only that my feet moved and my mind didn't. My uncle hadn't either. The dust was settling on his cloak.

His eyes were red, but so were mine. So were Dad's. I closed them. I wanted to shout: *how could you forget? How could you leave him staring?* But he was dead, and my uncle had already taken too many trips to the underworld for a lifetime.

We gave him his coin, and we built his pyre without speaking. We lit it together. The flames took over Dad's body, pulling it to Hades, and something disappeared between us. We were family still, but not so much. The link that bound us was gone.

When my uncle pulled himself together enough to tell me we should go get good and drunk, I told him no. I needed a little time. He should go. So he did.

I didn't realise *a little time* could mean forever.

Iolaus' Speech at Iph's Funeral

My father. Well, he was a man. Before he was anything else, he was a man, but then he did something none of the rest of us managed, and he was a good man. The best. He loved his wife. He loved his kids.

He went on adventures, sometimes. He loved them. Loved that macho wind-in-your-hair, seizing the beast by the horns bullshit, but he loved his family more. Even when he fell, and he slipped up against my mother, he cared for the son of the union.

He did have a sense of humour. Yeah, I see you all there grinning and thinking *as if*, but he did. He kept it quiet when he was out. He was tied to his sense of duty, but when he was at home, he had the stupidest sense of humour. Made the worst jokes, and I wanted to slap him sometimes. He snored quietly, and he sneezed like a fucking monster.

He was mortal. He was so mortal in everything he did. He ate too much, then farted and the room smelled like shit and he blamed it on the dog. Or on Mum, who made him sleep outside so he didn't do that again. By the time he started blaming me I could out-fart him and then no one would believe him when I blamed mine on him. I'm not even sorry, Dad.

Maybe none of that makes him a hero, but it does make him my father. The best.

Deianira I

My husband died, so that's unfortunate. Wait, that's not fair. I don't like words. They twist around you, changing meanings into *meanings* and they're altogether too complicated when you could just *do* things instead.

Let me start again.

My first husband was a nice man, and he loved me dearly. I was attractive, apparently, and a princess. He wasn't so wound up being a Man that he didn't like that I could take care of myself. I was a huntress, and a damn good one. He came to court seeking my hand; my father looked at me. I nodded, so Father said yes, and we were married.

We were married near the court of Laonome and Euphemus. You can tell there was drama because I remember their names. I'm useless at names. Anyways, we were there and not at either of our homes because I wanted to get married outside. I never liked walls.

I didn't realise getting married outside meant a wild centaur could try to kidnap you. Which one did. Neither my father nor my groom stepped in to save me – they both knew I could handle it myself, thank you very much. But someone else did. Someone broad and bronze who looked like he preferred to be outside too. Laonome's brother. That's all I took in of him – it was my wedding day; I had other things on my mind – so I went back and got on with the business of getting married.

We were happy. Neither of us fans of politics, neither of us in line to inherit anything that would make us have to be. We had a nice house, smaller than it could have been, but warm and on the edge of the woods. We didn't have any children. I don't know why, but I wasn't too upset about it. We were young. The gods would bless us sometime, or they wouldn't.

They didn't. My husband died. Azan didn't die from any outrageous stupidity. He was by his nature a careful man. I liked that, sometimes. It felt right.

His death was horrible in ways I don't care to remember. He died from some wasting disease that stole the colour from his complexion. He died with my name on his lips, I am told, probably some romantic nonsense from the servants. He died while I was out hunting. I preferred it that way.

I was given a year to grieve. Generously, my father said, but it didn't feel so. I lived that year to the fullest. Azan's death lay heavy upon me, but I was unlikely to be so lucky again, with a husband who wanted me to go out and fight. I travelled, far and wide, and rode my chariot and fought my wars. Given the choice, I would've stayed that way for the rest of my life. I would have liked children, but I didn't need them.

There's little sense in mulling over these things. Father announced to the world in general – I never understood how these announcements could travel so far, so fast. When I was *ready* to be engaged, it seemed as though suitors were weeds, sprouting from around your feet overnight.

I attract wild things. In my life, I had three centaurs, separately, declare their love for me. The first, of course, was at my wedding. The second made himself known on the occasion of my second courting and the third, well. That's a story for later.

The second centaur's name was Achelous, and he repulsed me. Wild centaurs in general aren't attractive creatures, but he took it further. He had *never* washed. His beard was matted with mud and detritus. He snored, even when he was waking. And he sought to cloister me.

His first words on seeing me?

'That's not very ladylike,' he said. 'I like my ladies to be ladies.'

I was carrying my sword, and there was mud spackled across the backs of my legs. My face was red from the sun. I looked as I did every day I successfully avoided the ministrations of my maid.

'Find a real fucking lady, then,' I said. The words were reflex by that point. My father didn't react well to it, but I've long been able to tune him out. The centaur only leered closer at me, grinning below his foul beard. Specks of grime lined the crevices of his teeth.

'Fire, I do like that,' he said, and he laughed. 'You will please me.'

I'm not stupid. I knew that for the petty, disgusting innuendo that it was.

'You'd have to please me first,' I said with the same leer, a raise of my eyebrow at his surprisingly lacking physique. 'I have my pick of suitors.'

'A word, Deia?' Father said. He pulled me behind a pillar and began to whisper too furiously for his failing voice.

'What?' I hissed.

'You don't have any other suitors.'

'How could I possibly not have any other suitors? There were a dozen of them *yesterday*.' I asked. I was a princess. I could be old and ugly in addition to my failure to be a lady and I'd still have dozens of suitors, all of them more pleasing on the eye and nose than this.

'I think he's chased them all off,' Father said. He was being politic. The wretch may have chased some of them off, but I was the more likely culprit. So it goes.

I shrugged, and we moved to make the arrangements. There was no option for me but to marry Achelous. The wretch was beside himself, sniggering and making comments every which way.

'I like a clean house,' he said, as if it would be my responsibility to clean up after him. Bastard almost definitely lived in a forest, anyway.

'I find that unlikely.'

'Oh, does my appearance not *please* you? I could have you clean me too,' he suggested. He licked his lips as he did so. Only more evidence of his repulsiveness.

Given future events, this seems a damning statement, but I'd begun to formulate a plan for his death. Not to kill him myself, I know what they do to husband killers in Hades, but a death nonetheless.

So I was grateful when another suitor appeared, saving me from committing such an act, but not overly so. I did not *fawn*.

Hercules approached the palace with such enthusiasm it was a wonder he didn't break a door. But we have good guards, so I could spy on him on the approach. He carried a sword and club both. I don't know enough about clubs to evaluate them, but his sword was good. Well worked and worn, not some awkward ceremonial thing screaming wealth over skill.

He looked me up and down. Not like he wanted to fuck me. Like I looked at him, to see if he could handle a sword. 'Are you Deianira?'

'Yes.'

'I heard you were strong. Are you?'

'Yes.'

'Healthy?'

'Yes.'

'Then I have come to court you, Princess Deianira,' he said. Straightforward. Direct. Clean beard. Three traits I cobbled together to come to a conclusion: good enough.

'And you?' I asked. 'Strong? Healthy?' I didn't want to go through what happened with Azan again.

'Yes.'

'Then I will marry you,' I said. Father squirmed in his chair. Nice man, my father, big on upholding oaths. So I knew what he was about to say.

'We have already agreed—'

'Unagree.'

'You are already promised to another?' Hercules asked. I liked that too. Spoke to me first about my marriage.

'No,' I said, as my father, with equal vehemence, promised '*yes*.'

Hercules looked uncomfortable. It did not suit him. 'If that's true, then I of course withdraw my argument. I don't wish to interfere—'

'You are not,' I said. 'You don't look like a man who'd give up so easily.' I raised my eyebrow at him. I do a good eyebrow. Makes men shrink in their seats.

'The agreement is not complete?' he said.

'No.'

'Then my offer stands.'

And my answer remained the same. Father looked unhappy about it. But, he said, on balance, he'd rather I was happy. That he said it under threat is irrelevant. Achelous took the news about as well as one can expect from a beast revelling in his future bride's discomfort.

'We agreed,' he growled. I liked him better like this. Honest anger rather than his show of greasy lechery. 'You're mine.'

'Not officially,' I smiled at him, a nice, ladylike smile. Very co-operative. Like I'd willingly clean for my husband.

'I wasn't aware I had to make my bride swear on the bloody Styx,' he said.

Arguably for the second time, Hercules saved me from a centaur then. He raised his hands placatingly and spoke slowly.

'I've had people steal my bride before,' he said. 'Because they didn't understand agreements. They blamed me for stealing their livestock.'

Achelous growled in agreement. I don't know how the straight-forward, straight-talking Hercules managed to talk his way onto the side of the man whose bride he was stealing.

'How about a contest?' Hercules offered. 'Your choice. We would have done one, had I arrived a day sooner.'

At the time, I thought this was stupid. Who gives their opponent free choice of tournament?

One who knows they'll win, regardless. Thus, my second husband was decided in the most ancient and noble of arts: arm-wrestling.

It wasn't even close. Were Achelous not so distracted, he would've noticed Hercules was barely exerting any effort, trying to save the centaur's pride and damning it in the process. After a minute, he grew bored of the act and quickly slammed Achelous' hand down. Happily, Achelous took this as his sign to leave and stomped grumpily into the forest.

'That was an impressive display,' I said.

'Well, I am the son of Zeus.'

'You went easy on him.' I did not ask it as a question. It was a test, in some ways. Did he respect me? And if he did lie, what were his tells?

'You have a good eye,' he said neutrally. The former, then.

'And?'

'I know a lot about contracts. And pride. This was the safest for everyone involved.'

'Did you say you were the son of Zeus?' I asked, everything that had just happened crashing into me at once.

'I did.'

'You're Laonome's brother,' I said.

'That's not the name people normally go for, but yes.'

'It wasn't a question. You ruined my wedding, you little shit.'

'Ah. Yes. Let me make it up to you, give you another one.'

'Smooth talker, huh?'

That became a joke between us. *Smooth talker.* The irony of it almost painful, both of us talentless with words. When he heard that I did not – could not – sing, he nearly fainted in delight. He actually did when he learned I could keep up with him in a hunt.

Our wedding was a small one. We'd both done it before, with people we really wanted to spend our lives with. Neither of us wanted to besmirch their memories by copying what we'd done. So we kept it small, and Father was happy enough with that state of things.

And nine months later? Well, you can probably guess what happened.

Hylas V

H had a lot of sons. As the minstrels tell it, he only had sons, but really it was by virtue of sheer quantity. He had a lot of daughters too. What he lacked was children he'd spoken to, even just commenting on the names they'd bear.

He barely talked to Meg about it. She listened to him speak, and she hoarded ideas like gems. A favourite aunt, a well-respected neighbour, a hero, an off-hand comment that something rolled well off the tongue. She kept these titbits so when she came to naming their children, he'd love them. All he ever told her directly was, don't name them after me, not Heracleia.

Not after me, he said. We could all see what that meant. Not after Hera. After what happened with Meg and the children, it's a relief she heeded his wishes.

I was happy for him and Deia. Really. My H had a rough time of things. After his brother died, I worried we'd be meeting him down below all too soon, prophecy be damned. All mortals have an hourglass, and his sand was running through. It wasn't even a question whether he'd blame himself.

When I went, he wandered around an island for a year, calling my name into the sky. The only reason he snapped out of it was because Iph and Pyrrhus went to scrape him back together. Now Iph was gone and Iolaus had turned from him. I was worried. I didn't want to see him again, not yet.

(Don't ask me when I would've liked to see him again. It's all irrelevant now, isn't it?)

I'm not sure why he went when Deianira's father called for suitors. Was he like a well-trained dog who goes running when he hears *princess looking for a husband*? Or was he so afraid of what he'd seen in Hades that he was looking for someone to tie him to the earth?

Whatever the reason, they were good together. He didn't move in with her, nor her him. They found their own house on the edge of the woods, with walls that could barely hold their weight. Both of those weirdos liked it. I'm a country boy, more than H ever was, and I never knew how to be comfortable in the wilderness like that.

They slept on the skins of animals they killed together. They didn't talk much. Soon enough, her stomach swelled with life. Congratulations, H. I know you wanted another son.

I am not, nor have I ever been, jealous of the girls who bore his children. I never held any odd fantasy of that; ours was a different partnership. But I know he ached for more children. He didn't need to be a father again – gods know he has enough *kids* – but he wanted to be a dad. How many years had it been? Since Meg? How many years had he been too scared to settle down with someone he could hurt?

I don't think he hunted down Deianira specifically for that purpose. But that's why he relaxed, in a way that he never did with Omphale. It helps Deia wasn't dressing him up as a woman either.

He didn't get all protective and weird over her while she was pregnant. Men do that, and I've never known a woman who didn't hate them for it. Deianira would have, for sure.

He didn't sing to the baby, or to her stomach. He didn't coddle. But he held that child with all the tenderness I remember from him, and he did something he'd never done before. He gave it a name.

Why am I harping on about this? Why could it possibly matter to me, a man so long dead I'm barely a whisper along the wind? Well, that's simple enough.

He called the child Hyllus.

The only child he ever named, and he did it after me. Tell me that doesn't mean something. I've spent years questioning my memories of him, years asking whether there's any truth to the love I attribute to him, or if I was just the start of a long line of pining lovers.

I've been dead over twenty years, and for the first time since the pool of nymphs, I can breathe easy. Because he named his son for me. As I waited for him, as I watched through the bars of Hades for his visits to other people, as I spoke to anyone who might have news of him, he held on to me too.

I can't speak for Meg, or for Abderus, or Iphitus, or any of the other people who died for the love of him. But I can say I needed it, to know he remembered me.

They had another son, and a daughter. H and D. They called the girl Macaria. Pretty, isn't it? She who is blessed. I can imagine H saying it with such force the ground rumbled, and his father had to acknowledge she's not protected by the gods, but by her father, who'll rip anyone who tries to hurt her into pieces. Their other boy was unfortunate enough to be Ctesippus. I don't know the meaning, but I can only imagine it's unpleasant.

Their children grew into people. Not full adults, but people with thoughts and ideas and the words to express them and the ability to get themselves into trouble. Would they be H's kids if they couldn't get themselves into trouble?

For a long time, his life was quiet. Not fully quiet – he was married to a lioness – but she'd never let him stand still, or ask him to. That probably contributed to the longevity of it. They went hunting as a family. They feasted, raised their children on the freshest of meat.

He was happy, and my heart ached. It could have been his ending, the trailing line of joy at the conclusion of his song, but down here, on the wind, I could feel it, the end of the first true happiness he'd had since before I died. I could feel this breaking thing, and I ached.

The end came in an unlikely form.

Were I asked, I would've said his downfall was based on wine. I love him, but I know his weaknesses. If not wine, adventure. Then meat. Then family, his nephew, especially. Then women. And finally, after all that, I would've guessed the gods, his sister, some unclaimed child. I would have been wrong.

I never would have guessed he was trying to make amends.

But I didn't need to follow him anymore. I knew he'd remember. When I knew there lay only pain ahead, I stopped asking about him. Stopped trying to piece together his story. He was mortal – we'd meet again someday.

I stopped watching and waited for him to come back to me.

He promised he would. He meant it.

Deianira II

My husband had interesting friends. I don't know where he got them from, but they showed up at the house often enough. Always young men. My mother once winked at me about that, said it was better than *young women*, like I didn't know my husband had a hundred children before we had ours.

The thought didn't bother my sons, and I can't say it bothered me. It did annoy Macaria, but lots of things annoyed her. She wanted something from her parents that neither me nor Herc were ever going to give her. She and my mother have always bonded over my failure to live up to their expectations in this regard.

The kids didn't stay babies forever. A lot of women cry over that. For us, it was nice. Once they were big enough to stay home without me, Herc and I would go out hunting together. Those periods tended to herald the birth of another child.

I was trying to avoid a repeat of that. I loved the kids, but there's nothing I hated more than being pregnant, being stuck inside with nursemaids fussing over me like one chariot ride was going to be the difference between life and death. My husband tended to agree with me, but what did he know? He never carried a child – that I'd heard of, though I could believe it, with him – and he was practically immune to death.

'Shh, you'll summon it,' he joked one evening when I told him that. The servants had told me the sun on my face would be too risky. I was ranting.

'Is death hiding behind the table or the children?' I said.

Eventually the pregnancy was done and I could freely leave my house. My husband presented me with a list of animals we could hunt.

'Oh, you smooth talker, you,' I said.

We went. We killed a wild bull. Its horns curled nearly all the way around. We snapped off one each, joking about how you'd drink out of them.

As we looked round and realised we had no wine to fill them with anyway, my husband put his hand on his chin and made a *hmmm*, a parody of the thinking man.

'I have some friends around here.'

They weren't expecting him. That's not a surprise – even I didn't know when to expect my husband – but Admetus and Alcestis *really* weren't expecting him. They were having the worst day of their lives. It was meant to be the last day of one of them.

'How do you even know these people?' I asked. He didn't go out, he wasn't active in court, but he never ran out of acquaintances.

'From back on the *Argo*.'

I shouldn't have asked. There were only fifty people on the *Argo* and, somehow, there was one every place we stopped off for dinner.

I was impressed by them, though. A lot of these places we went to, they glared at us. That's not just my husband. Some of them hated him, sure, and some of them feared him. It led to an odd kind of host-hood, lots of scuttling and bowing and not really talking to us.

A lot of them hated me too. Not for anything I'd done, but for what I was like as a person. They invited me to leave the room so the men could talk, or to stable my horses for me because that's *such a pretty dress*. As if I were not perfectly capable of speaking for myself, and my maid weren't perfectly used to getting mud out of my hems.

When I rejected their offers of more feminine pursuits, they'd look to my husband for approval, and he would shrug. 'It's her life.'

We had none of that there. We had a fantastic night with a great deal of food, and even more to drink. All of us spilled wine over ourselves some way or another. They asked about the hunt we'd been on and our plans for the future, but whenever we asked about them, they deflected.

They happily remembered the Argonauts and the Calydonian boar hunt, but a question about even tomorrow was brushed off.

'We live for today,' Alcestis said calmly, laying a hand on her husband's. Tears streaked down his face.

Herc and I looked at each other. Neither of us were equipped for emotional outbursts.

'Are you okay?' I tried.

'Is something hurting you?' Herc asked, the undertone of *I will kill it* there in force.

'It's fine,' Alcestis said.

'It's not fine,' her husband exploded, flipping his plates in front of him. 'My wife is too kind.' It was a strange sentence to shout, but he did it.

'We weren't going to tell them about this,' she whispered.

'Tell us about what?' I asked.

They looked at each other, full of understanding. I had that look with Herc sometimes, when we were hunting and we heard the same noise and I knew enough about Herc's sister to know dinner parties were some people's hunt. I just didn't get it.

Alcestis sighed. 'Do it.'

Admetus sighed even louder. Everyone had been laughing two minutes ago. 'The Fates decreed today would be the last of my life. My wife appealed to Apollo to save me.'

'Which he did,' Alcestis pointed out.

'In exchange for *you*.' He wrapped his arms around her. The cloying kind of touch I never liked, but they seemed to take comfort in it. 'I don't want to live without you.'

I can't imagine loving someone that much.

'And that worked?' Herc said, disbelieving. Admetus and Alcestis looked aghast. Not the point here, and he realised it. 'Sorry. I tried something similar once with Apollo. It didn't work.'

Alcestis laughed. 'Apollo got the Fates drunk. Thanatos is coming tonight.'

'Why did you let us in?' I asked. If it was my last night to live, I wouldn't spend it with Herc's old war buddies.

'You're our friends,' Admetus said, like it was so simple.

'I need to go outside for a moment,' Herc said. I think he was trying to be subtle. 'Pour more wine.'

'What do you think he's doing?' Alcestis asked once Herc had left. She sounded a little scared.

'Fighting the god of death,' I said.

'Really?'

'What else would he do?'

They can't have been that close with Herc. Otherwise they'd

just know this shit happens around him. They poured more wine and we papered over the issue with flimsy conversation, until the fighting and shouting outside got too loud to ignore.

'Aren't you afraid for him?' Admetus asked. They were sitting nearly on top of each other, hands gripped together like they were on a cliff face. Alcestis leaned her head into his shoulder.

It was hard to watch the two of them. Like missing something I never wanted to have.

'I don't know. Do you think the god of death is dead?' I said.

'Yes.'

'No.'

'I'm not worried.' I had other fears with my husband, but not that he'd die on me. Still, the two-headed couple monster was staring at me with incredulity. It itched. 'I'll go check on him.'

Thanatos was tall, and impossibly hard to see. He had a human shape, but he wasn't all the way there. It felt like you could pass a hand through him if you tried hard enough, but that was probably bullshit. My husband had him in a headlock.

He liked headlocks.

'You let them go.'

'I don't make decisions for the Fates,' Thanatos said. It's hard to sound snooty when you're in a headlock, but he tried.

'You can this time,' Herc insisted, squeezing just a bit tighter. He had a black eye. There were wrinkles spreading out of it. 'So do it. Or I ensure all the gods know of this.'

Thanatos' eyes seemed to melt from his sockets. Not fully. Just dripping. 'You think you're so special because you have your daddy watching out for you?'

My husband flinched. This was unfortunate for the god in a headlock.

'I don't need him,' my husband said, his mouth barely opening. He was ready to pop too.

'He'll forget you one day, and then *you're mine.*'

That was all he said before melting out of my husband's arms and back into the shadows. Herc wobbled. I rushed to catch him before he collapsed completely.

'Come on, stand up. I need you to work with me here,' I whispered. I was no weakling, but my husband was built like a mountain.

I looked through the shutters, into the house. The happy couple nodded approvingly. They probably thought this was one of their lovely snuggles.

When Herc announced they were safe and free, everything else fell away. They wanted to celebrate after. They called for their nicest wine and sent someone to find the best sweets in the city, though it was the middle of the night by then. They wanted my husband to be the hero. The centre of it all.

Normally he took to it like a pig in shit. Not that day. He lay on a couch and barely raised his head, even when the servants brought him snacks.

We slept there that night. That was a mistake. My husband woke me, trying to whisper in my ear.

'Deia. *Deia.*'

'What? It's early.' I normally rose early, but normally I didn't stay up half the night to celebrate vanquishing the god of death.

'I can't move.'

'What do you mean?'

'*I can't move.* I've been cursed.'

He hadn't been cursed. He just wasn't twenty anymore. Fighting the god of death had consequences. I tried to convince him he needed a carriage to get home – staying there while he recovered was out of the question; the fawning was starting to chafe – but he insisted on riding.

'It's your life,' I said. I didn't slow down to coddle him, and he didn't ask me to.

We were sent off with tears and waved handkerchiefs and as many sweets as we could carry. Those sweets didn't make it back to my house. When my husband is bored, he snacks. In the two weeks he spent recovering, he visibly changed shape.

It was a stressful time for everyone. We had three children under seven and all of them wanted my attention. My husband did too, but I'm only one person, and I choose to be my own person first. When he reached a hand out, begging for something or other, I snapped.

'I didn't marry you to be your nursemaid.'

'You married me because you didn't have a choice,' he grumbled. I don't think he was the injured party there.

His young men still came round, telling him about whatever beast was marauding this time. He wasn't well enough. He'd be hurt for longer and we'd end up hating each other. So when he tried to struggle up out of bed – there was a lot of grunting involved – I pushed him back and sat on his legs. I'd done it before. Normally he flipped me high in the air. It was fun. This time his legs flopped like a fish out of water.

'You're not going.'

'I have to go.' You may see now why we chose not to communicate in words.

'Why?'

'People are dying.'

'People are always dying,' I pointed out.

'I have to do something. I can't stand living like this.' He gestured around. I don't think he meant being beaten up. He definitely didn't mean the young woman sitting on his lap. I think he meant the *house*. My husband and his itchy feet.

'Why don't you find something else to do then?' I liked my freedom and he liked his. It's why we worked well together.

'What do you mean?'

'I don't know. Go visit old friends or something. Just don't go out fighting.'

'Old friends,' he murmured. 'Yeah. I can do that.'

He spent the rest of his invalidity putting the plans together. It gave him energy. He made *lists*. I didn't really understand the point of it – he tried to explain, something to do with forgiveness and preventing new wars. He claimed it was to make sure our sons would be safe at one point.

'You know I'll beat the shit out of anyone who tries to hurt them, right?' I said.

He smiled. 'Then call this a back-up.'

I would have been happy if he just went for dinner. It definitely would have been simpler.

Iole II

I've lived more than I ever expected, though I can't say for sure that's a good thing. It's been a long time since my brother died and I don't cry for Iphitus so much these days. I wish I was still that girl, but it's not an easy life we live, and it's been stripped away from me.

I suppose you don't care about my marriage, my Leander? I did love him, right up until he died, and I kept loving him after. I'd like that to be on record, thank you.

I ruled alone after he died. That shouldn't shock you. My husband was dead. My father was dead. My brothers were dead. My sons were too young to do much but babble and get lost in the house. So I did it.

I wasn't flashy. I heard about the handful of other queens ruling alone; all of them had some chip on their shoulder or a point to prove and I just . . . didn't. I had my kids. I needed to get them to adulthood safely, to make sure there was still a country for them to rule. I didn't shout about my being a woman, didn't claim to be the most beautiful or the best fighter. I didn't tell people the mighty Hercules once fought for my hand.

I kept up to date with his escapades. People talked about him everywhere, as if he were the weather. Perhaps that's the most apt description of him, some force of nature you could never hope to control. He was wind and wildfire, flood and drought all worked into one. When it was your turn to have him, you could only hope to steer your people to safety.

Needless to say, I could've been happier when he showed up at my home again, bowing and scraping and pretending to be humble.

'My lady, it is with the most sincere of apologies that I find myself in your presence and—'

'Cut the shit, Hercules,' I said. Gods above, he jumped so hard I thought he'd fall over and never stand again. 'What are you doing here?'

He took a moment to compose himself. I respected that. He hadn't known that trick last time he was here.

'Sorry,' he said slowly, 'Iole?' Like it was a question. Was it because he didn't remember my name or because he didn't know how to treat me like a person and not a queen? Last time, he was awkward but honest. That was better. Just ask Iphitus.

'Let's take tea,' I said. I didn't particularly want tea, still don't like the taste of it, but my brother loved him, so I took pity on the wretch, even after all these years. We sat and my servants brought us our food with well-practised ease. 'Are you here for work or for pleasure?' I asked.

That was a hard question to phrase. Difficult to come up with a way of asking *punishment for the murder of someone close to you, or pleasure* that wouldn't offend him. He seemed to appreciate it, at least, nodding away.

'Did you get the money?' he asked, back to awkward.

We did. It was no small sum, and it was wrapped to the heavens as though this were some marvellous gift we should be thankful for. I remember looking at it, horrified. Shouting.

I don't want money; I want my brother back.

I want my brother back. That fact will remain true until my soul meets his in the underworld.

But, instead, we had money from the sale of his murderer. My father had to physically restrain me from throwing it into the ocean. Two weeks later, my husband stopped Father doing the same thing. It sits in the vaults, untouched. It's the last bit of him, but it's so cold, when he burned hot. None of us ever knew how to handle that.

The news of his death was hard. The details were blurred but every passing traveller would fill in more of the story. He fell from great height. He was looking for our mares. He was pushed. He was pushed by Hercules. And they said all of this with a matter-of-fact, *isn't that interesting* tone.

It wasn't interesting, not when you know what I know. He was pushed by the man he loved, the man I lied to my father about so they could run away together.

It's hard, even now, not to let the guilt of it crush me.

So, in response to his question, *did we get the money*, I could only nod.

'Why?' I asked.

'Hera,' he said simply. 'And then Apollo.'

Of course. The gods played a day-to-day role in his world. I'd never heard from any of them and, frankly, I hoped I wouldn't. Almost always, hearing from the gods meant anger.

'Why are you here *now*?' I asked. It had been years since he left with Iphitus.

'Because it's been too long already.'

I wanted to slam my head against a bowl, and hard. The gods may have forgiven him for what he did, but I never would.

'You've done enough. Leave.' I was raised in a certain way, to do certain things, so it was hard to make demands, but I deserved it to be over. I wasn't expecting him to refuse.

'I have not,' he said in that blunt way of his. My brother loved him for it. I wish that memory could have made this easier, but it didn't. I only stood there and thought how unbearably rude this man was being.

'And you never will. So go. Leave me to grieve.'

'The time for grieving has passed,' he said, which only shows I was right and Iph was wrong. The man's not refreshingly straightforward. He's an out-and-out moron.

'I didn't say who I was grieving for,' I said.

Hercules looked around and finally took in the sparseness of the halls. I had the pictures taken down when Father died, and the mirrors when my husband did. I didn't want my face staring back at me, reminding me how alone I was.

'It hurts,' Hercules said finally, like the words had to be drawn from the stone beneath his feet, through his bones and his sinew until finally it crawled without energy from his mouth. 'To keep grieving, one right after the other. I hope you can be free of it.'

And he left. I sat alone in a throne room that would never truly be mine. The seat was built preposterously high, even for a man, so when I sat upon it my legs dangled below me like a child's. I brought them up under me and stared at the walls and I cried.

I didn't throw him off my island. I should have. I know, like a storm, he never brings good things to the rocks. He was persistent, the man my brother loved. I could imagine him laughing down there with Hades, as he watched Hercules, for the second time in his life, try his hardest to woo me.

'All this effort for you, and he never even brought me flowers.' He'd grin. 'Maybe I should be more bovine in my movements.' And I'd hit him for his impudence and both of us would laugh. But, as you know, my brother's dead, so it's harder to see the humour in the thing.

Hercules did bring me flowers, as his first gift. Before, his gifts were trophies; animal hides and tusks and heads to be mounted on the wall so you could say *look at my husband and all the wonderful things he can do.* Harder to brag when he goes hunting for flowers.

He brought me hyacinths. I don't know about that. Hercules doesn't seem like the kind of man who'd know the stories behind the flowers, unless he knew the men behind the stories behind the flowers. For me to be anything but furious at him, that has to be the case, because I do know the story and the whole thing's a little on the nose.

They're named after a man, Hyacinth, shockingly. He was a great friend and companion of the god Apollo. All was jolly and fine until Apollo accidentally threw a horseshoe at his head and he died. Apollo, being a god, didn't let go and barred Hyacinth from Hades, turning him into a flower, crying at what he'd done.

Like I said, on the nose.

But I tell myself that's not what he's going for. Maybe Hercules didn't choose hyacinths for the story, to convince me he would've done the same for my brother if he could – which he shouldn't have anyway; I can imagine nothing Iph would hate more than a life standing still – I tell myself he chose hyacinths because they were, and probably still are, Iph's favourite.

He brought me more gifts. He brought meat and furs. He

brought rare foreign spices. He brought jewellery. And all of it, every last earring and every single animal, was Iph's favourite. His favourite meat, his favourite colour, his favourite flavour, his favourite metal. I half-expected him to summon the muses themselves to sing his favourite song to me.

He's not a man of words, Hercules. He's a man of action. And he was using them to tell me one thing, to shout it nice and loud, until all of Greece could hear.

I loved him too.

I loved him as wholly and deeply as I could love anyone. I'm not trying to appease the gods. I'm here because I knew him, and I want to make this hurt better.

I'd never known if he killed my brother, but as the days went on, the doubt ebbed from my mind. Iph was no idiot; he wouldn't love someone who could hurt him so.

Eventually, when he was leaving his latest offering at my door – vases, with Iph's favourite stories painted upon them – I waved him in.

'Tea,' I said. An order. I could only manage those if I kept them short.

'My lady.' He bowed his head.

'Come in.'

We took tea in my chambers. It didn't occur to me that there'd be whispers about us. Why would there be, when it was so obvious our only connection was Iph? Ditto, I didn't think there'd be whispers from his own wife, who I assumed had been told of this escapade, and at least somewhat approved, even if only for the virtue of her own freedom.

He loved his wife. I knew that. It was impossible not to know. While he was courting my forgiveness with gifts for my dead brother, he was sending her gifts of her own. I cannot pretend I understood much of the reasoning for them, but then circumstance made it clear that she didn't much understand his reasoning for mine either. So while he brought me fine things, serenaded me with someone else's luxury, he sent her twigs and bones, sticks and weapons.

Maybe most baffling of all was when he sent her a single chariot wheel. Not one person in the entirety of my kingdom could bring me an answer for that.

I liked the exploration of it, trying to solve the mystery of this person on the other side of his life by part. All I learned is that he loved her differently to my brother.

There was never anything between me and Hercules. I don't know how there could have been. All any of it was? Whispers.

The end of our reconciliation went like this. We were taking tea. It was maybe the third in a series of terse talks where we didn't discuss pain but stayed on practicalities. After the first meeting we banned all use of the phrase *what he would have wanted*. We were defrosting, working on it. Sooner or later we'd have come to some agreement where he could buy forgiveness for what he'd done.

After he left that day, when I was preparing for some indelibly dull meeting with my advisers, my personal guard came rushing in.

'I'd prefer it if you'd knock,' I said. Normally in response he'd give an exaggerated bow and invent an elaborate secret knock that we'd both immediately forget. I'd had the same guard since I was a child and we had these jokes with each other. His family was dead too.

'It's an emergency.'

'Isn't it always?'

'That man, Hercules, he's coming for you. For the kingdom. But for you first, he's swearing and fighting. You have to get out of here.'

I prepared for my escape. Maybe that's all I need to say about our meetings. When someone told me he was attacking, I fled.

'Where is he?'

'We're not sure. The back-up route is best. We already have a boat prepared—' I later learned they'd had a boat prepared since the day Hercules arrived. No chances, this time. 'Best of luck, my queen.'

One does not get to be the sole queen of a small island nation after the death of significant parts of their family without a healthy dose of paranoia. My sons were too young to rule alone. They always would be.

I prayed for my sons, then I took three short, neat steps to my window, and I jumped.

I thought I'd be afraid, if I ever had to jump. I thought I'd be sweating and squeaking. But this stupid calm washed over me as I looked out of the window, and I thought of my brother. I stood in a room filled with gifts for him, being courted by the man he loved, and I fell as he fell. Only I was lucky enough to land too.

It was an outrageous plan, but not an uninformed one. The fabric of all my skirts had been chosen in such a way that should I lift them and catch the wind, they'd carry me safely to shore, where a boat would be waiting.

The boat took me to sea until the furore calmed down. I returned to confusion, but to peace. The guards had chased Hercules out of town, and no remnant of any plot to attack me or to take over my kingdom could be found. My sons were safe.

It didn't take long to conclude what'd happened. Gossip had gotten out of control and I was never in any danger, apart from being dashed against the rocks.

I never did see Hercules again. There was a time when I would have been glad for that, but I didn't know anymore. Our lives were more tangled than the Gordian knot, and I had no idea what lay at the centre.

Then, it seemed the simplest thing would be to send him a letter. Little was I to know how much trouble a few short words would cause.

Nessus I

Have you ever met a female centaur? They're not a lot to look at, not to mention their temperament. Think about the angriest horse you ever met, frothing and foaming and raging at the mouth. Now take that horse, cut its head off, and stick a human inside the cavity. Think about how angry that horse is, and that's what female centaurs are like.

Us male centaurs were blessed by the gods to keep both our sanity and our wonderful personalities.

We live as we were born to live. This much we can agree with those hellish lady centaurs. We weren't meant to live in houses, to manipulate the elements to do our bidding. This carefree attitude makes us significantly happier, and with notably fewer politicians than the blasted humans. We do not drape ourselves in unnatural fabrics or perfume our beards with the smells of flowers, unless we have a particular desire to eat a horde of bees.

The humans don't understand. Just because we don't live in their silly boxes. Oooh, the centaurs are evil. Oooh, the centaurs smell bad and steal our women.

First off, if you don't want people taking your women, you

should keep better hold of them. You wouldn't be surprised at a dog snatching bones from the floor. Second, we wouldn't have to *steal* them in the first place if they weren't raised to be such uptight prigs.

So, yeah, human women have better personalities than the hellish lady centaurs, but that is, as I mentioned, a low bar. And they do look delicious. Imagine my delight one day when I was walking through the forest and I met one wearing no unnatural scent at all.

'Hello, lady,' I said courteously.

'I have a husband.' Rude. But I'm no brute. I intended to show her that.

'Then you may be exactly the person I need, for I find myself unable to win the love of a certain lady who has enamoured me.' Not a lie. She had enamoured me, and she certainly wasn't in love with me yet. I needed only to win her friendship first. It wasn't as though she'd recoiled at the sight of me. (Human women do that sometimes.)

'That's a lot of words to not say much,' she said. Prickly, spiky, no stupid games. I fell a step more infatuated with her.

'Walk with me,' I said boldly, gesturing back in the direction where she'd come, so she'd feel safe and cared for and all that. 'And I will tell you everything.'

Don't let it be said centaurs lack imagination. I wove her a tale so deep and richly coloured it may well have been true, for all that my heart ached for this imaginary woman who wouldn't have me. For all the good it did it.

'Sounds like a bunch of airy-fairy nonsense to me. Why not just tell her?' Because, dearest Deianira, before I could tell her, she told me she had a husband and brandished the fact like a weapon. 'You're tolerable, romantic bullshit aside. Come again if you want to walk.'

It scarcely needs saying that I returned for her, the beautiful, clever, blunt Deianira. Her sons were but young, too young to be any protection or company – not that she needed the latter and only on rare occasions would she admit to a desire for the former – and her husband, the much-famed husband! Well, he was away on business.

'I get the impression he's away often,' I said carefully. She had a habit of hitting me with the flat of her sword when I spoke like that.

'He has a lot of business.'

'The mighty Hercules, I can imagine,' I said, holding that thought for a long breath. One, two, three, to see if I could trick her into answering a question without me technically asking it.

'Holdover from the labours,' she said. Hardly an answer, but still more than my farce of a question deserved.

'What brought him to do the labours again?' I asked, too sweetly. But then, however I asked it, she was going to know it was bullshit, know I was pushing it too far. I believe she worked out by our second meeting that there was no other woman who captivated me. My original tale was too clever, too beautiful, and I couldn't remember the details of it like she did.

Maybe the reason she spoke so short, so blunt, is because she actually listened when people spoke. An admirable habit, but it'll drive you mad if you're not careful.

'You know as well as I do.'

I didn't ask if his being away worried her. She would slap me. She trusted herself to keep her, and her kids, safe. She'd kill her husband without a moment's thought if he threatened her.

Unfortunately, that was the only situation where she'd leave him. She *loved him.*

'Isn't that more romantic bullshit?' I asked her when she told me that.

'He's very independent. And he's all about action. He doesn't hide what he is.' From Deianira, this was almost a sonnet on his beauty. But I was pretending to be her friend, worming my way into her good books, so I didn't say such a thing. I took the riskier path.

'Do you miss him?'

'More than I like to admit,' she said.

'Do you worry, when he's gone, about, you know, other women?'

The silence in response, and the lack of the slap, told me more than I ever needed to know about that. I had my way in.

I didn't bring it up often, and I certainly didn't bring it up so directly again. The fact is, I hardly needed to bring it up at all. We all knew his reputation, knew about the single night where he begat fifty sons. The longer I spent with Deianira, the more apparent the rest of it became. I learned about his companions, the young men he fell in love with, the years spent searching for them, making penance for them. These companions scared Deianira far more than anything he could do with women.

'Sex is just sex,' she told me once, quite drunk. 'It's fun, but when you're a man it doesn't mean much. Love, though.'

'You're afraid of him finding love?' I asked probingly.

'I try not to be afraid of anything,' she snapped.

Until Iole, Deia wasn't afraid of what her husband would do with other women, because he didn't love women. Deia knew his history with the family, and through her I came to know too. If he was ever going to love another woman, it could be her.

We didn't just talk about our feelings of course; neither of us is built that way. All of this came to me in snags and burrs while she notched an arrow or pressed forward to deliver the final blow to whatever it was we were hunting.

'He sent me a chariot wheel,' she said one day with a grin.

'Just one?' I asked, reluctant to give him any credit.

'From our wedding day,' she explained. 'I rode the chariot to the ceremony, even up the stairs. It popped one of the wheels off, but he fixed it before we were married. Said I shouldn't start this thing on an uneven keel.'

She smiled again, clearly pleased with her gift, and it didn't sit right with me. Someone like her shouldn't be so happy to receive the barest scraps of someone else's affection.

'Isn't that like he's preparing you for life without him?' I asked slowly. Deia didn't respond. She darted through the trees and I had to canter to keep up with her. Next time she didn't tell me about what she'd received.

I only saw the man once. That was enough for him to kill me.

It was a hot day and I was bathing in the river – truly an unforgivable crime – when I heard them talking. I'd never met him, but it didn't matter. His voice carried unlike anything else.

'I must prepare to go again,' he said.

'Does she even want you back so soon?' Deianira asked.

'We're making progress, Deia.'

'Towards what?' she asked. She turned her face away from him, towards me, though she didn't know it. I raised a hand to wave at her, so she'd know I was here; I'd always be there. Even when her husband wasn't.

He didn't answer her question. He'd spotted me.

'Look there. The brute seeks to attack you.'

Brute. If that's what it means to be true to myself, then so be it. Deianira finally saw me, realised who I was.

'It's fine. He's out of range and he's not coming our way,' she said. 'You have somewhere to be, remember?' Her tone was acid, but he didn't hear her.

'You know what centaurs are like around you.'

'We don't have time for this.'

'I've never known you to back down from a fight,' he said. He almost sounded disgusted. He didn't wait for an explanation, but it didn't matter. He would have killed me either way.

I should have turned and charged him, but I didn't want to hurt her, so I waited. I could outpace him if I needed to. I wasn't expecting *the mighty Hercules* to shoot an arrow like a coward. It struck my arse. Painful, but it shouldn't have been life-threatening.

'Come on,' Deianira hissed. 'You'll miss the boat.'

Hercules humphed and let her pull him away. I yanked the arrow out. When Deianira turned, I waved it at her so she'd know I was safe. It was only as they rode out of view that I felt the burning course through me. The arrow was dipped in the blood of the Hydra.

I was going to die. Painfully.

That clarifies things in the mind. Deianira was special. I wouldn't allow him to hurt her anymore. I had maybe two days to enact my plan.

We have our own magic, us centaurs. Nothing as flashy as gods and witches, but there are things we can do. With my last afternoon, I cooked up something special for him. The power of the Hydra in those arrows was going to kill me – I couldn't change that – but with my magic, it could kill him too.

I started with my blood. Then I moved deeper. He didn't deserve to die anonymously from some poison from some monster he killed so long ago he could hardly remember. I wanted him to die at my hand, for what he did to me. For what he did to Deianira.

I poured every part of myself into that potion, and I wove it into a shirt. I stitched it as fast as I could, not caring too much for the craftsmanship, the shoddy edges. The bottom got more ragged as my hands began to shake but I kept going. I had no other choice.

When it was done, I rode to her house and banged on the door.

'Nessus. You're okay?'

'I brought you a gift.' She scowled at me. She only did that to the people she really liked.

'If it's flowers, I will hit you.'

'It's not flowers,' I assured her and handed it over.

'Why in the name of the gods have you brought me a men's shirt?' she said, finally.

'It's a gift.'

'You wish me to dress as a man? I thought my form pleased you.' She smirked, knowing full well how I felt about her form. She was growing bold with me.

'For your husband,' I said, and the grin slid directly from her face. 'It will ensure he stays loyal to you, always.' That was technically correct. Once he wore it he'd never lie with a woman other than his wife, because he'd be dead. Of course, the likelihood of him sleeping with her again was also fairly low, but that's what you get for hurting her.

'Marriage is about trust.' She spat the words out like they

tasted bad upon her tongue. A well-taught line from her mother, most likely.

'Just take it, okay? In case you ever need it,' I said, hands up in front of me.

'Fine.'

'Thank you.' I dipped my head at her. 'Now shall we see about capturing that bull?'

We had a wonderful afternoon on the hunt – I had her take point so she wouldn't notice so easily when I dropped back or stalled in pain – and that evening we ate ourselves silly. Neither of us mentioned the shirt again, but she'd occasionally look over her shoulder to where she'd packed it away. It gave me hope. He didn't deserve half what he had.

At the end of the night, I was the one who left without a goodbye. She wouldn't want one. I galloped to my favourite spot in the forest, where I could hear the river and see the stars. Only there did I lie down to die.

Iole's Note

For Hercules,

While I appreciate your aims in coming to visit my island, now that you have departed I find it would be prudent if you do not soon return. The nature of our relationship, as you are aware, is complicated, and further visits would only serve to confuse my children and subjects. We both know the damage rumours can do to a man, so let's not stoke them any further.

As far as your original aim is concerned, consider it done. Love is a powerful thing.

Yours faithfully,
Iole

Deianira III

How long is it normal for your husband to spend wooing forgiveness from a woman he once tried to marry? I ask rhetorically, of course, because it's a stupid question.

While there are a great many things I understand about my husband that others don't, this trip to see Iole wasn't one of them. I've never killed a person. I've never even killed an animal with my bare hands. I don't see the need for the additional cruelty.

When I told him to go see Iole, it seemed simple. I know now it wasn't. When he left, he looked upon me adoringly, ran a hand gently down my cheek and told me: 'Take care of my swords, will you?'

He loved me.

I heard rumours of the gifts, of course. One can hardly be married to Hercules without taking the rumours of his whereabouts and behaviours largely as fact, otherwise you'll hear nothing until he comes riding to your door on a wave of fire. But in the early days I could brush that off, because he sent me gifts too.

It was only months in – *months* spent wooing the sister of his dead lover – that I thought of the gifts he sent me, and I thought of the gods.

It was Prometheus – Prometheus, who my husband so casually mentioned in sentences as a man he'd freed, *Prometheus* who gave man fire, and my husband mixed up the letters of his name and called him Prothemeus – that made me think of it. Back in the early days of man they were deciding which part of the animal was to be sent to the gods as sacrifice. Prometheus allowed Zeus to choose, but he tricked him. He hid all the worst parts under the best-looking layer, and all the good meat under the gristle.

When my husband was sending Iole flowers and gems and rare spices and embroidery he'd done himself, and I got one more horn snapped from a stampeding animal, the thought drifted into my mind and refused to shake itself. *Which of us is truly getting the meat?*

It was a good trick when Prometheus did it, but imagine if he'd convinced both man and god they were getting the best bits.

It was around this time I met Nessus. He looked bad and he smelled worse. But he was funny, and he hunted well. I found myself friends with him. He was refreshing in many of the same ways my husband was, but wilder still.

We were just friends, despite what Nessus clearly wanted. But no matter how uneasy my husband's behaviour was starting to make me, I wouldn't cheat on him and lie with another. I'd threatened to cut off Hercules' balls if I ever found him out and I didn't want to learn what the female equivalent of that was.

When Nessus gave me the shirt I wanted to vomit. He knew. I couldn't have people knowing I was afraid, couldn't have my husband knowing. If he saw me care for him too much he'd lose any respect he had for me. I packed the shirt in a box in the house and prepared myself for a lifetime of never considering the possibilities it held.

My resolve, I'm sorry to say, lasted less than a week after my husband's return. I was so anxious, I didn't stop to think why Nessus hadn't stopped by.

Hercules came back looking miserable. Common, for him.

'I thought it was going well?' I asked. It was the latest from the rumour mill.

'Blasted rumours,' he spat. 'Don't know if it was Hera again. Word went around saying I planned to abduct Iole. Pure nonsense, still got me run out of town.'

'I'm sorry to hear that,' I said, because I felt I should. 'Would you like to go kill something?'

'More than anything in the world.'

Hercules took to the woods like he'd never been gone, and I rode behind him, thinking. With him, rumours are so rarely anything but true. It's a nuisance. In the early days of our marriage I'd defend him against such accusations. He couldn't have done that, he wouldn't. But they'd inevitably be true and I'd be left with the taste of lead in my mouth.

With him back, the rumours took on a life of their own. I heard of visits to her room, daily, for hours, uninterrupted by anyone, with a guard bidden to knock before entering.

I am a good wife, a trusting wife. I'm not stupid.

It felt like every sentence my dear husband now uttered began with the phrase *Iole said*. I didn't care what Iole said. By all accounts she's a rainbow made of daisies and feminine sunshine. Even the idea of it makes me nauseous.

I was suspicious, but suspicious isn't worth salt. Not until Iole's letter arrived. It was couched in flowery, romantic language, so sweet and feminine it almost disguised the layers of innuendo. For Hercules to tolerate such a thing, he must really have loved her.

Without Nessus' gift I probably wouldn't have done anything – I wouldn't have been able to – but with it I had options. I could keep my husband, and I trusted my friend. For all my attempts not to be the gullible bride, I'm an idiot.

Stubbornness took me through weeks before I actually handed the shirt over. I'd practically talked myself back out of it – on the grounds of being some shrieking harpy – when he made an announcement. He was going back to Iole's.

'To see if she's safe, Deia; so much of their family is gone. I can't be responsible for another one of them dying.'

An admirable sentiment, had he not pushed the brother from a tower. Had he not been missing for some of the biggest months of our children's lives. Still, I was taught to be a dutiful wife, and I can play the part as easy as slipping on a glove made of fire.

I helped him pack. He sat beside me, on the bed, as I folded his clothes, both of us knowing the pointlessness of it. He'd leave in the clothes he was wearing, and he'd return in the same, smelling worse. Yet there was something soothing about packing together. Our tradition.

'New shirt,' he remarked.

'Homemade,' I said. Not wrong. Just not made in our home.

'I like it.'

'Thank you.'

I finished packing for him and walked him to the door. I kissed him on the cheek, sweetly, to remind him of our home together. I brought the kids out to say goodbye. It was wholesome, and in so many ways completely unlike us.

I leaned over to my husband and I told him, 'Put that shirt on tonight, okay? The new one. It will make me happy to think of you in it.' Damning, I know, but I trusted Nessus, my friend. My friend I hadn't seen since the day after my husband shot him, but still my friend.

My friend could have mentioned the screaming. Herc's shouts caught in the wind and carried his voice all the way back to me.

Acid came from the shirt and bit so far into his skin it tore the organs out of him. My beautiful, animal husband always could shout so loud. I loved it about him. It means I knew, as soon as it happened, when something was wrong.

If I was a better mother, I would have stayed home and blocked my children's ears so they couldn't know what was happening. But I am myself, and not suited to such womanly pursuits, so I told them to be good, stay safe, and I tore into the woods after a husband I'd never catch up with alive.

Through this, Herc screamed. From a whole day's travel away, I could hear it. I had a horse prepared, and I rode my chariot straight to him. I wasn't fast enough to catch the end of his life. My husband could travel far in a day.

I didn't cry over his corpse. I didn't appeal to the gods to save him. If they wanted to, they would have done so long before I got there. I didn't even marvel over how he'd had the strength to pull up *trees* for his own pyre. I merely tore the shirt from his body, staring dumbly at my own fingers, for they survived touching it unscathed.

I'll never know what Nessus did to that shirt. I'm okay with that. I know enough things I never wanted to.

For instance, I know my husband was not unfaithful to me. Not with Iole.

It does not make him any less dead.

Iolaus V

I wasn't expecting the message when it came. We weren't supposed to die.

Mum said that was the problem, after Dad went. Said I'd inherited the family foolhardiness and she didn't have any of it in her family, no siree. I don't know. She said it sternly, like when she said I shouldn't go fight the Hydra, but her hand shook so bad as she lit Dad's pyre I had to help her with it.

It was empty, of course, that pyre. The one I lit with Uncle Herc was the real one, with his body, because it was hot and I wasn't in a state to go carting my father's *body* halfway across Greece. But the one with Mum felt more real somehow. Uncle Herc didn't go to that one. Mum turned up her nose about it, said he wasn't bothered, he didn't care.

I don't think that's true.

I know my uncle pretty well, all things considered. He's a grumpy git, for one. The grumpiest of gits. You can hardly blame him, can you? Wife dead, kids dead, brother dead, stepfather dead, abandoned by his favourite nephew, because I did abandon him, in the end. When I got home I was so angry I had a courier take the Hydra's head back to him. I couldn't look at it. I needed to not think about either of them for a while.

That was stupid. *I* would've told him to fuck off with the idea of going to make things up to his dead lover's sister who was kinda sorta his ex-fiancée as well. Horrible idea.

But you can never know with Uncle Herc whether anything would've changed his mind. Stubborn fuck, he is. Was. Mum blames that on both sides in me.

Mum was there when I found out. We'd been spending more time together since Dad died, neither of us used to having the other around. I basically moved out when I was what? Twelve? Something like that. I'd been away for all the major milestones in my life, and all the recent ones in hers. I was there when she found out Dad was having an affair, that he had another son, but I wasn't when she decided to give it another go. I'm glad of that, really. I heard her blame Dad for being too much like his brother as it was.

Anyway, Mum was there when the messenger came panting to our door. He was all sweaty and red and worried-looking.

'The great Hercules—' he began. I breathed a sigh of relief. People were always thinking I'd be surprised or worried about my uncle's most recent adventures, like I didn't know he'd be fine, like I hadn't survived a half of them myself.

'Save your breath.' I waved him off. 'Would you like some wine?' Without Dad there to glare I'd taken to drinking in the day. It helped me sleep.

'I should—'

'Please, sit, sit,' I insisted.

'Fine, I'll sit. But, first, listen—'

'It's fine.'

395

'The great Hercules has died,' the messenger snapped. Silence landed on the house, heavier than the world he'd once held up. No one breathed. No one dared.

'You're wrong,' I said finally. I should have said it sooner. It was so simple. People thought he was dead all the time. 'He's probably gone to the underworld to fetch something.' As if it were so simple, as if it were milk or cheese he could grab from the market.

'This is from his wife,' he said. Smart messenger. If he'd argued more I would have disagreed harder. Or killed him.

He passed me the letter.

Hercules dead. Have body. Magical causes. Come fast.

It was, all in all, a very Deianira message. Were it not I could have believed this wasn't happening. I lifted my wine from the side and swallowed it in one smooth motion. I didn't want it. It was too sweet, cloying and clogging my throat as it went down, but I didn't trust myself, what would come out my mouth if I opened it.

'Thank you for bringing this. We'll act on it appropriately. You may leave,' Mum said, all crisp like. She had the right training to speak like that, like someone had shoved a stick so far up her arse she spoke with it instead of her tongue. That's what Uncle Herc used to say, but in a nice way. He was much nicer to the ones he hated.

The messenger left. I collapsed into my mother's arms. I didn't even do that when Dad died. Dad, who I cared more about than I ever did my uncle, no matter what he thought. I really fucking wish he hadn't died thinking that.

'Shh,' Mum rumbled. 'I'm here.' She didn't tell me it was okay. That was the only thing that held me together right then. No one was pretending it was fine, that the world hadn't just been torn into two, time split into that time where he was there and this great missing blank space now he wasn't.

'I'm still so mad at him,' I said.

'I know, honey, I know.'

'Why does it hurt this much, when I'm so mad at him?' I asked.

'Because you loved him very much too,' Mum said, more sympathetic than I expected. She never liked Uncle Herc. She caught my surprise. 'What? Your father hurt me so much, son. I hate him, and I miss him.'

She wasn't upset, which given Herc's comments about her seemed fair enough. But she understood. She knew he was the reason Dad died, and she knew how much of my life he helped build. She helped me gather my things.

'I'll be here, when you want to come home,' she said as I was leaving. It meant a lot to me. But I was never good with words like she and Dad were, so I didn't say anything back. I had to go go go go go.

I rode through the night.

I didn't think about anything at all when I was riding my way over there. Not how he could have died or what could have caused it or how he was feeling.

You know what I thought about? Riding.

Deianira had dry eyes and hunting clothes on when I arrived.

'He's over here,' she said. 'We were waiting for you.'

What the fuck was I supposed to say to that? So I said nothing, and let her lead me over to the pyre and, sure enough, he was there, dead. Not even a little dead. It looked like someone had left him to bake in the sun for days then pushed him into a pit of poisonous plants and forced him to climb his way out. His skin was red and angry and puckered, the worst of it sneaking out over his arms and across his hands, like he'd tried to rip it off him.

I cut those thoughts short. I didn't want to know how it'd happened.

So I thought about the colour of the puckering, how it was the same as the scar he wore across his shoulders, how they'd covered it up.

There were more gifts of mourning than there were guests. There was me, and Deianira, obviously. Aunty Lao was there, doing her woman-of-court thing. A scattering of local nobles. I desperately looked around for more familiar faces. There had to be someone, right?

But then, who would there be? Dad was dead. So were Meg and the kids, and Iphitus and Hylas. Grampa was gone, and Gran was too old to travel. Even that cousin he didn't much like, dead. Jason gone in a rotting boat accident. Omphale lived too far away. He didn't know his other kids. His relationship with Iole was too long and complicated and messy to have her there.

And then, the whole thing just seemed altogether too *sad* to keep going. I forced myself to make eye contact with Deianira as she passed me the flame and I held it to the pyre.

Having so recently burned my dad, I thought I knew what to expect. The smell. The ash. The crisping. And we got all that, no doubt. But this one was different.

The smoke, for one. It didn't act like smoke. It didn't tendril lazily into the wind; it wasn't clear or white. It burned gold and it shot towards the sky as if Zeus himself were propelling it.

Zeus wasn't there, either.

The wood didn't take time to catch; it didn't cough in starts and fits. The logs took to the flame like they were born to it and erupted so magnificently I could hardly bear to look upon it. It burned like that for many hours.

The smell was the same.

I forced myself to sit by that fire, until it burned all the way out. The truth was, until I saw the last of the ashes peter away, I wouldn't believe he was dead. As I sat, I felt the rumble of a horse being ridden too hard towards me.

'Am I too late?' the voice shouted. A strong, heroic kind of voice.

'Fire's still going,' I called back.

There was a rapid dismounting and even footsteps sprinting towards me. I didn't take my eyes off the flame, not until arms were wrapping themselves around me.

'Iolaus, I am glad to see you.'

'Theseus.'

'It hasn't been that long, cousin.' He smiled. We decided a long time ago that whatever our actual relationship was, it was too confusing, so we stuck with *cousin*. 'It's really true?'

'Lit the fire myself.'

'I brought wine. Tell me of it,' he said.

My cousin sat beside me on my vigil. Three nights, it lasted. Three nights of a fire that refused to burn out. We drank a godly amount of wine and we told tales of him, far kinder than any I'm telling now. We told them, not because they were new, but because we needed to know we weren't the only ones who cared.

We talked until the words didn't matter, and we could say what we were really thinking.

'Do you think he's really dead?' I asked.

My cousin looked at the fire, and looked at me, too far into the wine to hide his true thoughts: *you're an idiot.*

'No, not like mortal dead, he's obviously that,' I explained. 'But he was so great, maybe Zeus'll save him from Hades or something. Make him into a god.'

'Hades doesn't like having his things taken from him,' Theseus said slowly, his face hard against the fire around us. He was the expert, I guess. He did live there, once. 'The gods don't make exceptions for that.'

'They made a lot of exceptions for Uncle Herc.'

'They did,' he said, still not managing to hide what he was thinking, but you don't tell grieving people they're stupid. That's not fair.

'And that smoke is really weird,' I said, like convincing him was what mattered.

'It is.'

Three nights that fire burned. Three days and three nights, all bundled into the space between Artemis rising and falling. Our mortal world needed as long to let go of him as it needed to let him in in the first place. And, like when he came in, I can say one thing for sure.

The world wasn't ready.

Mere weeks after my uncle died, a ripple spread through Greece. *War.*

The Epitaph

Here lies Heracles, Son of Zeus

Dramatis Personae

You can use this list to keep track of who's who in this book, but beware, for it contains many, many spoilers. Enter at your own risk.

THE IMMORTALS

Zeus – King of the gods, Herc's father, and not so great at the marriage thing
  • Heracles/Hercules/Herc/H – His mortal son, a very famous man
  • Io – One of Zeus' (many) lovers. She gets turned into a cow by Zeus' wife
  • The Muses – Zeus' daughters. In charge of music and the arts

Hera – Goddess of marriage. Married to Zeus and not thrilled about his fidelity issues

Apollo – God of the sun and music. He's the patron of the oracle at Delphi and a bit of a lad
  • Hyacinth – One of his lovers. He died in a terrible horseshoe incident

- Xenoclea – The oracle at Delphi. Uncoordinated future-teller
- Deiphobus – A doctor who's perfectly happy with his mundane life, thank you

Artemis – Apollo's older twin. Goddess of the moon, the hunt, and childbirth

The Fates – Goddesses who weave the future together. Everyone's a little scared of them

Chiron – Centaur, half-brother to Zeus and teacher of many famous heroes

Hermes – God of thieves and messengers. He makes frequent trips to the underworld

Aphrodite – Goddess of love. Married to Hephaestus, sleeping with Ares

Helios – Titan of the sun until Apollo nicked his job

Thanatos – God of death

Ares – God of war

Hades – God of the underworld, which he has humbly named after himself
- Cerberus – His dog who happens to have three heads

Persephone – Goddess of springtime, daughter of Demeter, and married to Hades

Charon – Gets you into Hades, for a price. The price is money

Poseidon – God of the sea. Also earthquakes

Atlas – Titan who holds up the sky

Hestia – Goddess of the hearth and home

Asclepius – Son of Apollo and god of medicine

Athena – Goddess of wisdom

Hephaestus – God of the forge

Demeter – Goddess of the harvest. Seems nice until you kidnap her daughter

Pan – God of the wild. Half-goat, claimed to be dead

Dionysus – God of wine, ecstasy, and madness. He will party until you're dead from it
- The Thiasus/The Maenads – His followers, all female

Ariadne – Former princess of Crete, now the immortal wife of Dionysus. She has trust issues

Prometheus – Titan of forethought, he gave man fire. Then he had his liver eaten by eagles

THE FAMILY

Alcmene – Herc's mother. She has knives *everywhere*

Amphitryon – Herc's stepfather, a military man. It shows

Iphicles – Herc's twin and half-brother. The responsible one
- Automedusa – His wife, with the good eyebrows
- Iolaus – Their son, a charioteer and drinking partner to Herc
- Pyrrhus – Iphicles' son. Not Automedusa's

Laonome – Herc's half-sister. Not the responsible one

Megara – Princess of Thebes, she's Herc's first wife
- Creon – Her father, the King of Thebes
- Pyrrha – Her sister

- Pyrrha, Deiphile, Therimachus, Creontiades, Deioneus, Deicoon, Ophitus – Herc and Meg's kids
- Myrina – A young lady in Thebes, jokingly betrothed to Creontiades. Cakes hang in the balance

Perseus – Herc's grandfather, on the mortal side

Eurystheus – Another grandson of Perseus, he has Hera as a patron and he's the King of Tiryns. Had a good life, before he had to oversee Herc's labours
- Antimache – Eurystheus' wife. A jewel
- Philopatho – Their first daughter, who died too young from an illness they couldn't stop
- Admete – Their daughter, just old enough to have her own interests

THE LOVERS

Hylas – Herc's first friend, lover, and everything in between
- Theiodamas – His father, King of the Dryopes

Abderus – A mopey prince staying at the court of Eurystheus during Herc's labours

Iole – Princess of Oechalia. She meets Herc during a competition to see who she'll marry
- Thaddeus – The suitor with the bad breath
- Leander – The suitor with the braiding

Iphitus – Iole's brother. The adventurous one

Omphale – Queen of Lydia. The most beautiful woman alive, she thinks
- Neileia – Her friend. New money
- Tmolus – Her first husband, her mountain man

Deianira – Herc's final wife. A huntress, and a good one

- Azan – Her first husband. A nice boy, if a bit scared of getting his hands dirty
- Hyllus, Macaria and Ctesippus – Deianira's kids with Herc
- Achelous – A centaur who wants to marry her, but loses that battle in an arm wrestle
- Nessus – Another centaur who wants to marry her

THE COMRADES

Mester – Shepherd who doesn't pay for drinks

Jason – Patronised by Hera. He goes on a quest with his Argonauts:
- Atalanta – The best sprinter. She has a mean right hook
- Argus – Built the ship
- Eribotes – The only half-useful physician on board
- Talaus – Got drunk and relieved himself somewhere unfortunate
- Calais – Son of the north wind
- Euphemus – Son of Poseidon, can walk on water, later married to Laonome
- Polyphemus – One-time fighter of centaurs

Theseus – Herc's cousin, via means too complicated for anyone to work out. Spent a couple of years stuck to a chair, and a couple of days stuck in a maze
- Pirithous – His best friend. Spent longer stuck to a chair and less time stuck in a maze

Marina – Former virgin priestess at Delphi, she ran away to join the Thiasus

Admetus and Alcestis – Old friends of Herc's, they're very much in love

THE KINGS & QUEENS

Hypsipyle – Queen of Lemnos, who may or may not have been
involved in all the murder
  • Euneus and Deipylus – Her sons with Jason. They're
    kings now

Cyzicus – King of Bear Island, visited twice by the Argonauts, and
attacked once

Augeas – Owner of the smelliest stables in Greece and also
a kingdom

Epicaste – His daughter

Diomedes – Owner of horses with unusually human tastes

Minos – King of Crete. They used to have a bull there, now one
half-bull

Hippolyta – Queen of the Amazons
  • Melanippe – Her sister

Oeneus – A foolish king who did not make ample sacrifice to
Artemis, so she set a boar on him

Laomedon – King of Troy
  • Priam – His son
  • Paris – Priam's son

Hippocoon – King of Sparta, sometimes

Tyndareus – King of Sparta, the rest of the time

Medea – Princess of Colchis. An accomplished witch

THE OTHERS

Linus – Herc's music teacher. A man with resilient ears
- Orpheus – His brother, with a lot of talent and even more ego
- Eurydice – Marries Orpheus, then dies. He goes to fetch her, unsuccessfully
- Musaeus – Their son. When grown, he runs the Eleusinian mysteries

Rhadamanthus – Orator

Autolycus – Rustler of livestock and son of Hermes

Pandora – Woman who owned a box containing hope, along with other, more depressing things

Geryon – Three-headed giant, and cattle owner

Ixion – Man tied to burning wheel because he has bad taste in women

Siotades – Winner of the footrace at the first Olympics

Nestor – Son of a doctor

Helen – The most beautiful woman in the world, actually. Her marriage woes – well, that's another story

Icarus – A young man who flew too close to the sun
- Daedalus – His father, who built some very impressive wings, alongside some less salubrious things for a bull

Herodotus – A playwright

Author's Note

When I put together the character list for this book – my apologies to everyone who read the drafts before that existed – I kept trying to add more people. To give more context, I told myself, but that's not true. It's because their stories are related and tangled together and I want to tell you *all of them*.

Spoiler alert, dear reader, I haven't told you all of them.

The myths are a big messy web of people, and Hercules is right there in the middle of it. Any story he could be in, he probably is. As a reader, this is the best. Every single thing I read, from novels to web pages, gives me a dozen more leads to go chasing down.

As a writer, it makes for an exercise in logistics. With a thousand years, I couldn't find every person Herc loved, every monster he killed, every town he saved. Even if I could, I wouldn't be able to write them down in an order that makes sense.

I'm not the first person to tell these stories. There have been more versions of Hercules than I can count, let alone everyone else. Even seemingly simple things come with different sources and interpretations. It's one of the wonderful things about myths: reading through accounts to find the version you like the best.

So I had to make some choices. I won't pretend to be unbiased with what I included. The characters act the way they do because it's what makes sense to me, in my world, not because it's objectively the right answer. Apart from Eurystheus pretending he didn't hide in a jar, which is my favourite and I love it.

I don't love it for Hercules. I love it for the attitudes, the image, the petty justification. It's probably the first myth I read that wasn't about fighting and glory. It's about someone trying to get on with his life with all of this improbable, inexplicable *stuff* going on around him.

That's the thing about mythology – the heroes weren't heroes in a vacuum. They walked through the world having all kinds of influence on other people. Maybe if a hero's coming through town, you just have to batten down the hatches and hope things turn out your way.

Maybe you even hide in a jar.

So this book is about those people, and the impact Hercules had on them. I've tried to include a whole range of them: the ones who saw him as a hero, a husband, a brother. By letting them tell their own stories, it feels closer to what I grew up with – a hodgepodge of different accounts from different sources.

I've had so much fun writing this book. I might complain and hit my head against the table when I've mixed up Iphitus and Iphicles again, but I've got to take some of my favourite stories in the world, and obsess about them, translate them so other people can see them the way I do, not as heavy translations to be studied at school, but as stories. Sometimes sad ones, sometimes silly ones, but always so very human.

Even when your dad is Zeus.

Acknowledgements

I like lists. This one, in particular, is very important to me.

To everyone who made *Herc* the book that it is, and who made me the person who wrote it, I appreciate you more than I can say. My eternal gratitude to:

Both Meg Davis and Anne Perry at Ki Agency, an unstoppable force in agenting, and without either of whom *Herc* wouldn't exist. Thank you for your enthusiasm and support, and for making me think more deeply about the things I take for granted.

My editor, Cat Camacho, and the whole team at HQ, for taking an unwieldy Word document and turning it into a book. It's been a delight all the way through.

Kirsty Capes and Becci Mansell for doing such a brilliant job getting *Herc* out into the world.

Andrew Davis for the most beautiful cover I've ever seen.

Peter Joseph, Eden Railsback, and everyone at Hanover Square for their endless patience and attention to detail.

My beta readers – Robert, Patrick, Meghan, Kyle, George, Callum, Bex, and A – who read through various stages of messiness and suffered the slings and arrows of outrageous commas. I'm so glad I got to share it with you first. (I really am sorry about all the names.)

Emily, my number-one gremlin, who read it faster than I ever could have hoped for, and who's always on board when the silly train is departing the station.

My parents, and the house they filled with books.

Hope, who told me half a lifetime ago, *just write a book, then.* Lava choo.

Ross, we're such fancy people now!

Layla and Linda, for luck.

Ed, I acknowledge you.

All the fantastic teachers I've had in my life, but especially Mrs Jones. Not everyone dies at the end!

And Luke, who is *finally* allowed to read it. Thank you for being a better partner than any hero has ever been, for listening to the jokes while they were still a long way from funny, and for helping me unravel Gordian knots. There aren't enough words in this world for you, but that's not going to stop me trying.

ONE PLACE. MANY STORIES

**Bold, innovative and
empowering publishing.**

FOLLOW US ON:

@HQStories